LOUDER
THAN THE
SEA

For Tony and Anna

— And for the stories and songs
you heard from the best liar
in Newfoundland.
Thanks. Wayne

LOUDER THAN THE SEA

WAYNE
BARTLETT

CORMORANT
BOOKS

The publisher gratefully acknowledges the support of the
Canada Council for the Arts and the Ontario Arts Council
for its publishing program. We acknowledge the financial
support of the Government of Canada through the
Book Publishing Industry Development Program (BPIDP)
for our publishing activities.

Printed and bound in Canada.

Canadian Cataloguing in Publication Data
Bartlett, Wayne
Louder than the sea
ISBN 1-896951-28-7
I. Title.
PS8553.A7746L68 2001   C813'.6   C00-901552-3
PR9199.3.B3747L68 2001

CORMORANT BOOKS INC.
Park Centre
895 Don Mills Road, 4th Floor
Toronto, Ontario, Canada M3C 1W3

For Andy, Angie and Bill

CONTENTS

1

WATCHING THE GLASS

The year was 1969 and winter had just begun to release its hold on Newfoundland, at the eastern edge of Canada. To be loosed from the clutches of a killer climate did not mean absolute freedom from it, nor did it mean the winter was over, for temperatures were still below freezing, the land was still covered in a thick layer of ice and snow, and a raging blizzard that had been lashing the northern peninsula for a full week and a half seemed intent on destroying it. The sun's rays, even on good days, hardly fall on this narrow three-hundred-mile promontory jutting into the open Atlantic like some naked emaciated limb. Snow-devils are born here, frigid Arctic whirlwinds feeding on granite-hard snowcaps, tearing them off and gorging themselves on the powdery crystals underneath. Such is the feeding frenzy that most times the winter sky is driven back and replaced by a stinging volley of ice pellets. The sparsely forested valleys and scabrous hills offer no shelter from the open tundra, and the frozen sea pushes and prods at the shore, forcing its icy fingertips into every fissure, trying to hook out what little life still remains after the ravenous winds of January and February. The land would cry for mercy but for this paralysing drug administered by the gods, if in fact there are gods involved in its destiny of obliteration. Only when March begins to wane does it seem the land may endure.

Ambrose Bellman tapped his marine barometer with a nicotine finger that was missing the nail and was severely crooked near the top. The ship's wheel turned to starboard. One tap did not satisfy his hunger for the true value of the glass, so he roughly but cautiously tapped it again. It swung back to port. Every morning and night he would walk across the canvassed floor of his small rotting house and raise his giant hand, callused and swollen from swinging his axe throughout the long northern winters, pause for a brief moment and then — *tap tap*. Tonight the black arrow jumped from 29.6 to 29.9 and stopped.

"Gonna have a change, Ida maid," he said. His high cheekbones gave power to his muddy flashing eyes and, pinned in their shallow sockets flanking a once broken nose that had never been set, they could pierce a young boy's heart without cracking the skin. He was missing three or four bottom teeth directly behind his chapped lips, and his grey hair looked as if it had been cut with scissors that had cut chicken wire.

He rubbed his nose vigorously with his palm, walked briskly past the forty-five-gallon water barrel at the end of the cupboard and instinctively stooped at the door to allow his more than six-foot frame to enter the long porch. He was broad and muscular, with not a hair on his milky chest, and in his fifty-seven years the summer sun had never seen him with his shirt off, although it had baked his face the colour of well-roasted turkey.

A great gush of cold, smoky steam poured into the white-papered kitchen and clung to the ice crystals on the low ceiling. The vengeful rapist mist sent a ghostly chill throughout the bungalow before Ambrose's hulking shape in the mirage was swept away in a sea of moving shadows.

"My God," Ida said, heedless of his observation of the weather glass. "You'll have to shut the door or we'll all perish for sure!" She knew her husband needed light to see the firewood packed against the wall. Feeding the hungry Master Climax stove seemed an everlasting task — one that required tending every half an hour or so.

"Can't see in the dark, maid," he said. "Job to see in the light."

She sat with her knees under a square wooden frame filled with burlap that had been cut to fit and then lashed tightly between the rails. One end of the frame balanced on the back of a chair and the other on the kitchen table. A breath of night air crept across the floor and crawled up her legs making her shiver. She ran both hands up and down her bare arms to flatten the goose pimples, and brushed the short, wormy pieces of cotton and silk off the brin. "Hurry up, Ambrose," she said, "for the love a God. You're gonna have the house froze to death and me 'long with it!"

With the strokes of her mat-hook she slowly brought out the image of an Eskimo sitting on a long sled pulled by eight huskies. Each of these dogs wore a bright red harness and was tied separately to the front of the sled by a different length of black rope. The Grenfell Mission, in its effort to eulogize the northern way of life, encouraged local women to work on commission by paying, this year, fifty cents to four dollars for a mat that took at least two weeks to complete.

Ida had been hooking mats for the Mission for nearly thirty years, and every one she had delivered over the counter to the tall, scrawny, birdlike woman in the Handicrafts building at the medical outpost in St. Anthony had had a flaw. Had she believed in the validity of the appraisal process, she would also have had to believe that she had never once hooked a perfect mat. Her commission sometimes brought her no more than a few cents but she never complained, and out of necessity kept hooking, for as soon as the ice moved offshore in May month Ambrose would take her and her mats to the outpost in his fishing boat. After being paid she would pick up more burlap and choose her patterns: a man on snowshoes, a flock of geese, a polar bear against a setting sun, seals on an ice pan or an Eskimo crawling inside his igloo — always a northern theme.

Ambrose piled the short lengths of wood on one arm, hurried in and closed the door behind him. Eighteen years ago, at his former home on Sacred Island, a chip had struck and blinded his right eye and the pupil had taken on the contours of South America.

"I believe 'tis gettin' colder, Ambrose," his wife said. "Certainly, should be gettin' warmer now. Soon be the last a March."

Ambrose threw his load into the woodbox behind the stove and dropped a junk of the sticky fir into the firebox, onto hot, smoky coals that glowed like pieces of pure Baltic amber. "Well well well," he tittered. "'Tis a good thing I looked at the fire. Sure 'tis almost gone out!" He liked to exaggerate.

"What's wrong again now, Ambrose?" Ida asked. "You're always complainin'."

"I don't know what'd happen to you fellers," he said, "if

it wud'n for me. Martin wud'n put n'ar junk in, that's one thing for sure. He'd rather freeze to death 'longside the stove and let his 'magination put it in. I don't know what's gonna become of 'en, I don't know! He'll never make a man; I knows that much."

Martin had been born on Sacred Island and was their only natural child. After serious complications had forced Ida to make an emergency visit to the outpost two days after his birth, the doctor there had told her that the boy would be her last. Their older son, Garf, had been three and a half when they had got him, and just last August, two days short of his twenty-ninth birthday, he had moved out on his own, into a rat-infested shack, after chastising his father about his fierce threats to Martin. Both Garf's parents had been born in Labrador and had died there of tuberculosis, at the Grenfell hospital in Mary's Harbour, and the nurse in charge had had the young orphan brought to St. Anthony, where for the next three weeks he had stayed with the Mission gardener. From there word had spread of a child in need of a home, and soon the news had struck Ida's ears.

She stopped hooking. A short, rounded woman. "How ya figure Martin can put wood in the stove, Ambrose? That's the heights a foolishness you're gettin' on with now. Ya knows he's not home."

"Not home," Ambrose said aggressively. "He's never home, is he?"

"Don't start," Ida said, a stirring in her stomach. "Not tonight anyway."

Ambrose punched at the wood with the lifter. "Up to the restaurant again, I s'pose — where he always is."

"He's out with the other boys; that's where he's at. He'll be home the once." Ida believed her husband meant no harm to the boy. After all, Martin was fourteen years of age and if he lived to be a man maybe his father would be proud of him. But somewhere deep she wanted him to stay a young boy, and not become a man whose responsibilities would draw him from his father's house.

"Hark, somebody's comin' in!" Ambrose poked another piece of grout in the firebox and put the damper back on, squeezing the wood down onto the other pieces already being licked by the soft orange flames.

The visitor stamped the snow off his boots in the porch and pulled open the door.

"Oh," Ida said with a tinge of excitement. "'Tis Garf." She poked her hook through the brin and pulled a thin strip of cloth to the top. "I kinda figured 'twas you, Garf," she said. "I could tell by the way ya stamped your feet." On the day that Garf had packed his suitcase and moved out she had cried for hours, and for nearly a week she had said only yes and no to Ambrose. Begging Garf to come back had been in vain for he said it was time that he was on his own, but to ease her mind he had promised to still visit and watch over them.

Garf was short, dark and stocky, well suited to the long northern winters. Even as the snow began melting on his clean-shaven face, the darting of his hazel eyes revealed a longing to do something other than talk. Seemed he had a permanent adrenalin drip. He had been a man, according to his father, at fourteen, when he had taken on his first major carpenter job in helping to renovate their old house back on the island.

He took the mop from behind the water barrel, wiped his boots and leaned against the end of the cupboard. "'Tis blowin' some hard, Uncle Am," he said, his nervous eyes darting back and forth between his mother and father, uneasy glances in the quiet relaxing warmth of the only people he called family. Because he was a big boy when they got him, they had accepted "Aunt Ida" and "Uncle Am" instead of "Mother" and "Father".

Ambrose knelt on the daybed between the stove and the table, pulled the window curtains open slightly and pressed his lips to the frosted pane. He blew five or six long breaths making little puffs of steam on both sides of his cheeks, then rubbed the melting lip prints. He peered into the round hole, his left eye gazing into the darkness, and through the drifting snow he faintly made out a small, winking light in the frosty turbulence of the northeast gale. Aunt Nel Peyton, an old Salvation Army soldier, midwife and schoolteacher from the island, lived at the other side of the cove with her retarded nephew and usually went to bed early, but some nights she'd stay up late, reading her Bible while Alfred cut pictures from a catalogue.

"What's Aunt Nel gonna preach about this Sunday?" Ambrose questioned. He looked up at the moonless sky through the tiny ice hole on the window. "Preach on the weather, I daresay." He pulled the curtains shut again and fell lazily back on the daybed, fixed the feather pillow in just the right position between his head and the wall, crossed his legs, put his hands behind his head, shrugged his shoulders, coughed and locked his fingers.

"What's the glass sayin'?" Garf asked.

"Movin' up."

"Southeast wind," his son said with a touch of disappointment. "Figured somethin' like this had to happen. Now if we was back on the island, be a different story. Any seals comin' outta the bight with that kinda wind is guaranteed to bring up on Trimm's Point. Ya don't get 'em there, ya won't get 'em nowhere."

"Don't warry 'bout back on the island," Ambrose said. "'Twas always a sea runnin' with that kinda wind off there anyway, and 'tis not gonna strike us for 'nother couple a days so we got lotsa time to get our seals off Cape Bauld. And I heard on the radio this marnin' there's a big patch on this side a Belle Isle, but never said how big."

Belle Isle, nine miles long and fourteen miles from Cape Bauld, stood in the middle of the entranceway to the strait between Newfoundland and Labrador, and its only visitors were its summer lightkeepers and a handful of nomadic fishermen.

Garf flung his hands downward in a single stroke, as he would do to shake off his mitts. "I can see it now," he said. "'Nother bad spring. That wind veers round to the southeast, there won't be 'nough ice left to piss on."

"By the time daylight breaks," Ambrose said, "them seals is gonna be pretty close to Cape Bauld, so we got a good chance. Time that wind changes, we might have a hundred ashore."

"All right to say that, Uncle Am, yes, but they're a week late so ya knows what that means — no whitecoats again this year."

"Aahhh," the old man said, "black ones is just as good; tastes the same thing and brings the same money."

Ida fixed her eyes on the shiny hook in the wooden handle held firmly between her thumb and forefinger. She felt it press against her palm as she skilfully worked the pointed instrument through the woven cloth. "Perhaps the seals might come right in the bight this year," she said. "Long's we can get enough carcasses to bottle up and enough money to do somethin' with this ol' shack — that'd be good enough for me."

"Long's they comes, Aunt Ida," Garf said. "That's the main thing — long's they comes." He went to the glass and tapped it as he'd tap a child on the nose to awaken him. "'Cause if they don't come you can whistle goodbye to seeing any money." The arrow shivered as if it were afraid of being shaken violently by another *tap tap*. This was his father's glass and only his father, Uncle Am, could tap it that hard. He tapped again and the arrow moved up another tenth.

"Geez, Uncle Am, don't look good."

"I got a feelin' you fellers is goin' down the cape t'marra," Ida said. She poked another ribbon of cloth underneath the mat, hooked and pulled it topside.

Garf took off his red tossel-cap and sat on the chair underneath the barometer, folded the cap over and over on his knee until he could fold it no further. "Well," he said, "we'll go down and have a look I s'pose, yes, but I knows the ice is not gonna be in 'cause the sky still got some black in it off there in the strait. I seen it this evenin'."

Ambrose sat upright on the daybed and brushed his arm against the drapes, revealing the frosted window. Silently the drapes fell back in place, as he swung his feet over the side and reached above Ida's mat for his pack of tobacco beside the square-faced timepiece on the radio shelf. He already knew by the winds and the look of the sky that the pack ice would not reach land before daybreak, and he was glad his son had made the same assumption. Garf had always shown good judgment.

"Pump up the light, Ambrose, I can't hardly see the lines on the mat!" Ida hooked her foot in a rung of the chair and pulled the mat closer. She squinted. "I 'low I'll be blind 'fore I gets 'en finished."

Ambrose rolled a flat cigarette, leaned over the mat again and lit his smoke at the underside of the glass globe covering the Tilley lamp mantle. A couple of deep draws and he sat down, coughed a little and tipped back on the daybed again.

Garf, realizing that the light needed some fast pumping, jumped from the chair, made a quick step forward and reached for the lamp. His hand brushed his father's shaving mug on the radio shelf and he looked into his own eye as the attached mirror reflected a jiggled image. He cupped his hand around the base of the Tilley, where it rested in a double layer of cotton cloth used to soak up the leaking kerosene, and lifted it from the wall hanger.

Ambrose giggled like a child when Ida gave him a stern look. He blew a train of smoke rings at her. "So what time ya figure we should leave, Garf?" He had no reservations about Garf pumping the light, and as far as he was concerned his son was welcome to do as he pleased.

"Well," Garf said, screwing the handle back in, "I gassed up the Ski-Doo this evenin' so we can get up around six o'clock, half past six; that's time enough. Leave around seven."

Ambrose stood up, leaned backwards and stretched his belly muscles. He downed a couple of mouthfuls of smoke, then flicked his cigarette butt into the slop bucket near the porch door. It hissed and went out. "'Nother one gone," he said. He put his hands on his lower back and rubbed until his shirt-tail came above his belt. "What's t'marra anyway?" Tucked his shirt in.

"Thursday, boy," Ida replied with a hint of sarcasm. "I know ya don't know the days a the week now. Sure, Good

Friday is right upon us. The winter'll soon be gone."

"If Martin never had to go to school," Ambrose said with genuine concern, "I'd get 'en up to go to the cape 'long with us. He might stand the chance a gettin' two or three seals for hisself. Good price on pelts again this year. Ol' Tucker is payin' thirty-two dollars for young harps and sixty-five dollars for young hoods. Perhaps I should speak to 'en about it."

"Yes," Garf agreed. "I think he should go over 'long with us, but not t'marra." He wiped the lamp base with its cloth. "Be a full day 'fore that ice tightens up on the land so I figure Friday should be a good day for 'en to go with us — that's if the wind is still in on the land by then. I'm sure he could use a bit a extra money, the poor young bugger — everybody can."

"No trouble for 'en to spend it, that's for sure," Ambrose added with a mean little smile. "His claws'll never maintain his jaws. He got no more regard for money'n I got for that mop stuck up in the corner there."

"Leave the boy alone," Ida blasted, her eyebrows pulled down and narrowed. "He got so much regard for money as you got for him so leave 'en alone." She drove the hook in the brin and reached for another strip of cloth. "Say somethin' a bit nice once in a while, for God's sake do!"

Garf flicked the shut-off valve on the side of the lamp and the light went out; he flicked again and, with the sudden burst of kerosene to the hot mantle, it buzzed like a thousand bees and lit up the whole kitchen. He wrapped the cloth in layers around the base. "I gets a chance I gotta fix that leak," he said. "Next thing you're all gonna be burned to death here in the house. Only for that rag to catch and everything you're the owner of is gone up in a blue blaze. Ya won't have time to put on your boots."

"Can you fix it?" his mother asked.

Garf rooted with his fingernail at the threaded nipple where the generator stem entered the reservoir. "I believe that's where 'tis leaking — right here." He took an edge of the cloth and wiped. "Yep, there's your trouble all right."

"Well, can ya fix it or not?"

"Don't know, Aunt Ida. Can't do it now even if I could. Gotta turn out the light for that and then I won't see what I'm doing. Too dark."

"Well," Ambrose said, digging into his tobacco pack, "the old woman got a flashlight in her room ——"

"No, not tonight," Ida said staunchly. "Mother might fall up against the stove or somethin' in the dark and burn herself. Best thing is to wait for daylight. Lamp is not that bad anyway."

Ida's mother, affectionately known as Aunt Kizzie by her friends, was seventy-nine years old and long-time soldier of the Salvation Army. She loved chewing gum, strong coffee, lemon cream biscuits and a good argument but, of all her loves, chewing gum was probably her favourite. Wrapped or unwrapped, she was happy to see either. Fresh or already chewed and spat out, she was happy to see that too. When Ida entertained company, her mother would eye the room searching for the lady guest doing the most chewing and then casually rise off her chair, walk across the kitchen and strike up a conversation with her. As soon as the lady opened her mouth to speak, she would be shocked to find the old woman's fingers rummaging inside her mouth. Aunt Kizzie would not apologize but just say innocently that she had watched her chewing for quite some time, and had decided that someone else ought to have a go at it. After withdrawing her fingers with the juicy knob clutched firmly in her grasp, she would quickly pop it into her own mouth. If her skilful manoeuvres could not retrieve the prize, the distasteful act would cause the victim to spit the gum across the kitchen, or to turn towards the ashtray or slop bucket and remove the defiled object in a dignified manner. Either way, Aunt Kizzie ended up with the spoils.

In her twenties she had married a widower twice her age, in a small ceremony on Sacred Island, but her parents had not been particularly fond of her choice because of Fred's years and the fact that he had no previous offspring to prove he could impregnate their daughter. That following summer, when the cod stock moved offshore in its annual migration pattern, twenty-nine of the thirty-one Sacred Islanders, including wives and children, chased it as far as Belle Isle and set up camp there. Because they had no family to tie them to one particular place, Fred and Kizzie were picked as caretakers for Sacred Island's six dairy cows, an industrious position requiring cutting the local stiff, saltwater grass, and making a dozen trips to the distant mainland in their small, flat-bottomed sailboat to cut good hay at the base of the Karpoon hills. For this they would be rewarded with an equal share of the summer's catch.

Sacred Island, two miles from the Newfoundland mainland, got its name from English explorers who went ashore there and found two bleached human skulls on the beach. The island was no more than a barren strip of volcanic rock topped with patches of blackberry bushes, surrounded by treacherous reefs and separated from the coast of Labrador by twenty-eight miles of unforgiving ocean. Only one place on the island was safely accessible by small boat, so their hay-cutting trips were geared around the weather; during stormy days they tended the vegetable gardens and combed the shoreline for driftwood. Fred kept a fishing net at the back of the island to help broaden their diet but hauled in only kelp and seashells, and Kizzie worried whenever he went there because she could not see him. But most of the time his hook-and-line exploits kept him off the point and within shouting distance.

The shallow, unpredictable waters, frequently caused a great sea to heave, and in a matter of minutes the sheltered cove would mutate into a cauldron of boulders and sea-weed. Unable to land his fishing boat during such an upris-ing, Fred would wave a temporary farewell to his wife stand-ing on the shore and head for Karpoon, a small fishing town on the other side of the hills from his grasslands. He would have no choice.

The nights she had spent without him on the island were without sleep or rest, for she had seen him disappear in the swirling mist with no assurance of his safety, yet amidst the howling wind and the rain beating on their small cabin win-dow she had felt a sense of oneness with her prison. Sacred Island was a barren rock and she was a barren woman.

That September, Fred was lost during a stormy crossing. When the villagers returned from their fishing expedition at Belle Isle a month later, they found Kizzie hiding in the hayloft. Her parents wanted her to come home with them but she refused and went back to her cabin, where Ida was born the next spring. When she turned sixteen, Ida mar-ried Ambrose and took her mother to live with them in his father's house.

Aunt Kizzie stood now in the doorway leading from the kitchen to the inside part — a living-room in English terms — her round spectacles glistening in the light from the Tilley lamp. A long white apron encased her from the hem of her black dress to a few inches below her chin, making her look like a penguin. She raised her arm in a crude salute that blocked the light from her eyes, her right hand groping for the back of the chair facing the end of the stove in the small walkway. Behind the chair was a storage bin with a hatch under its cushion, used as a bench whenever there were more people than the kitchen seating could accommodate. The old woman considered this chair to be *her* chair and did not like anyone to pass by and disturb her when she sat on it.

"Where's Marty?" she asked, gazing across the kitchen. She called to the man fitting the cloth around the lamp, "Is that you, Marty?"

"That's Garf, Mother. Martin's not home yet."

"Garf? Oh," she said, with a trickle of a smile on her wrinkled face. "How 'bout that bit a gum ya promised me a while back — where's it to?" She reached into her knitting bag hung on the backrest and pulled out half a wool stocking — pinned open by three long knitting needles that held fourteen stitches each — trailing a ball of grey yarn.

"Gum?" Garf looked surprised. "I never promised ya no gum, did I?"

She sat down and inserted a fourth needle into the first stitch. "Told me one day last week," she said. "'Member?"

Garf lifted the lamp up and positioned it above the bracket on the wall. "No, Aunt Kizzie maid," he said, "I can't. You must be mistaken — I don't think I told ya that at all."

"Well my son," she said, "you did tell me and Ida there can go witness." She secured the yarn by wrapping it around her right little finger. "You heard 'en say it, didn't ya, Ida?"

"My God, Mother," Ida said, picking up a short, wormy

piece of black silk and examining it against a strip of black cotton. "Whatever ya does, don't rope me into sayin' I heard somethin' I didn't hear."

Aunt Kizzie guided the yarn under and over the point of her needle. "Well, I heard 'en say it," she said. "And you — a upholder is so bad as a thief."

Garf turned his back to the old woman and lowered the lamp into its bracket, unaware that she was already chewing. Something. He said, "All I got is the bit I got in me mouth, Aunt Kiz, and I can't give ———"

"That's good enough for me, my son," she said, gently but firmly drawing the needle with its loop of yarn back through the top stitch. "I only wants enough to chew."

Ida tossed the black strip to the side of her mat and picked another from a pile at the top. "Leave Garf alone, Mother." She put the short piece against the strip and examined it. "Well," she said. "Still the wrong colour."

"You got plenty a gum in your mouth, Garf," the old woman persisted. "So tear off a piece and give it to me."

Garf wiped his oily hands on his pants.

"Hear me talkin' to ya, Garf; hear what I said?"

He grinned. "Yeah, I heard."

"What'd I say?" She counted the stitches on her needle — "One, two, three, Jesus." The old woman had no education and was unable to count beyond three so every time she'd come to the fourth stitch — the turnstitch — she'd call it *Jesus*.

"Have a cup a tea with us now, Garf," Ida said, trying to cut her mother off.

"What'd I say, Garf — what'd I say?"

"Leave Garf alone, Mother, I told ya! He ain't got no gum to give ya so leave 'en alone! Give it up, for God's sake do!"

"I'll leave 'en alone when he answers me — not before. Now, Garf," she demanded, "what'd I ask ya?"

"Shut up, Mother."

Garf held his gum in front of her face.

The old woman flicked her hand and grabbed it like a frog licking out its tongue and pulling a fly back into its mouth.

"I goes to the shop again I'll see if I can get a pack for ya."

"When's that gonna be?"

"Geez, Aunt Kiz, I don't know — I knows it won't be tonight!"

Ida threw the hooker on the mat and put her foot down hard. "Give it up, Mother! I'm tellin' ya now — give it up for the love a God!"

Garf gave his hands a few extra drags on his coat sleeves. "Y'know," he said, "I think she'd walk to hell and back on rusty razor blades just to get a stick a gum. I never seen a woman love gum so much in me life. 'Tis unbelievable — un-friggin'-believable!" He went to the cupboard and opened the top door.

Ambrose sucked the last of the smoke from his cigarette butt. "Listen," he said, cocking his ear towards the door. "I believe I hears Martin comin'."

Aunt Kizzie took a twig from the woodbox, poked it through the draft hole in the stove and let it fall. Began singing:

Onward Christian Soldiers
Marchin' as to war
With the cross of Jee-suss
Goin' on before. . . .

Ida stuck her hook back in, delighted with her husband's achievement at stopping the argument. Her mother, it seemed, had taken on a whole new personality since leaving the island, and sometimes she believed that the old woman had lost respect for everyone and was afraid of no one — except Martin.

Four yellow packs of Vogue tobacco in the cupboard lay fallen over in their thin, cardboard carton behind the dishes. Garf moved the pink mother-of-pearl cups trimmed in gold to the side and saw that one of them contained two packs of cigarette papers. He reached for a plain cup, for these fancy ones were for special company only. "Kettle boiled, Aunt Ida," he asked. "Or have we gotta wait?"

The hook clicked when she pulled it back through the brin with a cloth worm. "He's boiled," she said. "I s'pose he is — we'll say he is anyway." She looked at her mother hunched over on the chair, asleep with her chin pressed into her bosom.

"What ya got for lunch, maid?" A light shone in the old man's eyes, the soggy butt dead in his fingers.

"Oh, I'll find somethin'," Ida replied. "Just hold onto your wool." She turned and beat her hand against her thigh to rid it of the hook handle sensation. "What ya want, Garf, anything in pa'tic'lar? Or don't ya?"

"No, I don't want n'ar lunch, maid." He coughed and clinked the dishes. "A cup a tea is good enough for me."

Ida knew he was lying.

A gust of wind struck the house as if it wanted to break in the wall. Of the forty-three houses in Karpoon, forty-two would be buried nearly halfway up the windows by the time the storm had blown out, but the grounds around Ambrose's house would be swept clean. Spared at the cost of nearly collapsing under the pressure of the wind, due to its position atop a rocky hill, the house would not be buried.

"I got some fresh bread. Ya likes fresh bread, don't ya, Garf?" Ida teased him. "I know ya used to like it one time."

Garf laughed, his complexion making his long teeth seem whiter than they were. "Oh yes," he said, "likes it, yes."

Ida pushed her chair back and stood up. "Here, Ambrose, put the mat in the inside part for me while I gets a lunch for us."

Garf put four cups on the table. No saucers.

Ambrose threw his cigarette butt in the slop bucket and picked the mat up. Anxious now — a lunch. He studied Aunt Kizzie on the chair, wondered if she was asleep or waiting for him to cross her. He saw one of her eyes open, scowled and turned back. "Here Ida," he said. "You better carry it in, maid; the old woman got everything barred off solid again."

"Haul out the table, Garf! Put the butter on the stove! Take that batch a bread outta the breadbox!" When Ida played captain she could make even the most seasoned infantryman in Russia's cold Siberian army surrender, but not without his reward of hot bread and sweet partridgeberry jam. "Just put it all there on the table," she said. "I'll look after the rest when I gets back." She took the mat frame and faced her mother.

Ambrose and Garf watched like spectators at a cockfight.

"OK Mother, move for God's sake, maid, and lemme get in."

The old woman's eyes were closed again and she was heedless.

"C'mon, Mother! I knows you're not asleep so move outta the way, OK?" She tapped the old woman's shoulder. "You gonna move today or t'marra?"

Aunt Kizzie raised her head, stretched her gum halfway to the loft and let it coil back down in her mouth, pretending not to hear.

Ida crawled over the storage bin with the mat frame in front of her, mumbling something no one understood.

Garf set the table. One plate, two plates, three. Four.

On returning from the dark inside part Ida confronted her mother again. "Ya wud'n move, would ya, Mother?" she said with her lower jaw pushed forward. "Certainly, you wud'n move for the devil hisself!"

The old woman shoved a finger up her nose and muttered something about Ambrose and the devil.

"That's enough now, Mother," Ida said, stepping onto the storage bin again. "You been grumblin' all day; that's long enough. Have your lunch now, when I gets it ready for ya, then go to bed." She had not heard her mother's words but knew exactly what the muttering was about.

A year and a half ago they had become involved in the provincial government's resettlement plan. Simply, the plan had suggested that everyone in the small isolated outports of Newfoundland should jack up and leave. Move to a bigger, more industrialized setting where there was plenty to eat, plenty to drink, warm houses, better schools, new jobs and new friends. Some Newfoundlanders believed that the plan was implemented to save the government millions of dollars. To supply electricity, running water and highways to these outports would have cost the province a fortune.

Distance was not measured by time zones, and a day was defined by its amount of daylight, not by twenty-four hours. This northern tip was where their fathers had lived and died and where they would live and die. Here in their isolated surroundings, contentment was having good grub on the table, a sharp axe, a warm bed and a warm ass to cuddle into. The general store in Karpoon supplied what could not be harvested from the land or sea and the merchant, Azariah Tucker, always took great pleasure in serving anyone with brass in his pockets.

For outport people who had had enough of the old ways and signed in favour of the move, the two-thousand-dollar compensation package offered by the government seemed a godsend, and within a matter of days they had disassembled their outside porches and packed the lumber inside their kitchens. Then they began tearing their houses from the land with blocks and tackles, launching them into the sea for the long tow across the bays to their new homes. After setting the houses up on the other side, they returned in their motorboats and dismantled their twine stores, stages, henhouses and barns, then stowed what they could in the midships and arranged the sawed-out wall sections across the gunwales. Another trip or two brought the cows, the sheep, dogs and cats, and hens with one leg tied to the leg of another to keep them from flittering overboard. Firewood, cod traps, ropes and anchors, anything they could pack aboard or tow. Some families refused to leave, believing they could still make a life for themselves in their isolation, but before the summer passed, most had followed, with the government money leading the way. For those left behind, the decision to stay was not entirely their own. No one could convince their aged parents that destroying everything it took a lifetime to build was in the best interests of the family. The elders retaliated and said that to be torn from the place of their birth was wrong — only a lunatic would do such a thing.

In its determination to rid the small coves and outlying islands of all human life, the government of Newfoundland and Labrador shut down the entire education system in hundreds of outports around the province. For parents wanting proper schooling for their children, this act of brutality forced them to mutiny against their old relatives and pull up roots as well.

Ambrose had been the last to take his family and leave Sacred Island. He wanted no part of resettlement, including the two-thousand-dollar bribe, but he did want an education for Martin, and he readied his house for the tow to Karpoon by tearing off his porch as the others had done. Aunt Kizzie kicked up hell when he told her they were leaving and he had to literally drag her off the island and into his fishing boat. Since that moment she had not spoken to him kindly or given him a moment's peace.

The table was set. Carnation milk can in the centre. Sugar and butter dish on either side. Bread at the end waiting to be sliced. Cups for everyone.

Ida reached into the lower cupboard and pulled out the big jam dish, a beige ceramic bowl adorned with blue imprints of stone farmhouses. Between the houses lay a small, winding road upon which a horse and buggy travelled. Flowers on a blue vine bordered the top and bottom of the mural. A thin line showed a crack that extended from the lip of the bowl straight to the grassy field in the centre. From there it turned sharply and continued through a chimney, broke a window, ran roughshod over the buggy, then turned again and crossed the bottom border.

Ambrose took his usual place, at the end of the table by the stove, and Ida sat next to him, her back to the weather glass. Aunt Kizzie sat adjacent to her and faced Garf across the table, as he sat crouched below the radio shelf like a humpback, smearing jam on his bread. There was another chair beside him — Martin's chair — but there was none at the other end of the table, because a chair there would have interfered with the opening and closing of the cupboard doors.

The stovepipes shook violently and there was a puff of smoke from the damper.

"What's that noise? Certainly God it can't be wind!"

"Wind yes," Ambrose told his wife, waiting for Garf to say something. Anything.

Garf sucked at the bread, the sweet jam squeezing between his teeth and making his mouth red. He licked greedily at his lips. "Tell ya the truth," he said, "I believe it blows harder on this hill'n it did back home."

"I don't think 'tis gonna last much longer," his father said. "Gonna drop out 'fore ya knows it. The glass is still up, I can see that. But I can tell by the way the hand jumps we're gonna have a ca'm pretty soon. Mark my words."

Garf picked a partridgeberry shell from his teeth. "You puts too much faith in that ol' glass, Uncle Am. This wind could be on till late Sad'day evenin'."

"Harder it blows the better I'll like it," Aunt Kizzie said, a devilish grin spreading across her gnarled face. "Time daylight breaks t'marra I'd like for this place to be blowed halfway to hell. Wud'n be one thing left standin' on this knob, only that snowbank out there on the back a the house, and I'd like to see buttercups stickin' up through the middle of that so'n'so so big as dinner plates." She dunked a lemon cream biscuit into her coffee and glared over her spectacles at Ambrose. "You turns my friggin' guts!"

He ate in a silence broken only by his slurping. He could

never drink hot tea without making his face into a caricature. Wide popping eyes. Lips pursed. Shivering. Long inward breaths sucking more air than tea. Steam. Tea was too hot, he'd say, even if he put cold water in it.

After lunch Garf said good night and closed the door behind him. Ida put the dirty dishes in the tin pan on the cabinet, put the bread in the breadbox and undressed for bed. Ambrose checked the fire, turned out the light and pulled back the sheets. His wife slipped in beside him.

Nearly an hour later the porch door swung open. Closed. The kitchen door opened. Martin was home.

2

ISLAND RAT

Ambrose grunted in the half-light of the early morning as he pushed himself up on his elbows. "Time to get up, Ida maid," he said. "Garf is gonna be here the once 'fore ya knows it. I'll light the fire and time ya gets your clothes on, the house'll be all warmed up." He jumped out and grabbed his trousers from the back of the chair by the bed, his combinations drawn up in the crack of his ass. He reached for his socks and pulled them on, first the left and then the right; he always did it this way, for he had his habits and had no intention of changing them.

In the kitchen, he pulled the damper off, hacked and spat in the cold firebox. He tucked the front of his shirt in, grabbed a handful of birch rind from the woodbox and carefully shuffled it about in the stove before putting a dozen splits on top. Bigger wood went on the dry kindling and then he coughed, spat in the stove again and struck the match. "OK, Martin my son," he called. "Time to get up and cut that mattress off your back. Spends more time lyin' down'n ya do on your feet." He checked the barometer. Hard fingers struck the face. *Tap tap.* The arrow jumped clock-wise, shivered and stopped.

"What time is it, Dad?"

"Soon be eight o'clock."

Martin cared not whether it was eight o'clock or twelve. He had longed to leave his old one-room school on Sacred Island, not because he disliked it there but because, on his trips to the Karpoon general store with his father, he had seen a much different schoolhouse, with two red brick chimneys and at least a hundred small windows. While his father picked up his supplies and watched Mr. Tucker write them down in his ledger he would poke around town, sizing up how the mainlanders lived, wondering how it would feel to sit in a proper schoolhouse instead of a church with five grades and eleven students. Ambrose always had to go hunt him down, telling him not to wander around in a strange place, and sometimes told him he believed his words went in one ear and out the other — "like talkin' to the stove," he'd say. Now Martin wished he had stayed on the island, but school would not start until nine anyway so he turned over in his comfortable bed, let off a tiny fart and closed his eyes.

Ida made his breakfast and peeked into his bedroom at the side of the kitchen near the barometer. "C'mon, Martin m'dear, get up now," she said. "The house is all warmed up and I got everything on the table for ya so get up and eat it while 'tis still hot."

He heard his mother's voice through the warm haze and somewhere in his world of dreams he smelled hot porridge and toast. He wished he smelled eggs too, but knew there would be none unless she stopped blaming his father for drowning her hens, which had all battered off of John

Parsons' wharf with their legs tied together while he celebrated his misery in the fish-stage with John and the welcoming committee. She had sworn that she would never raise another chicken.

"OK, Mom, I'm gettin' up. Bring in me socks to me." He threw back the heavy covering of patchwork quilts and shivered momentarily as the coldness struck him. When his feet touched the floor they almost stuck to the freezing canvas.

Ida threw his socks on the foot of the bed.

Martin grabbed his trousers from the steamer trunk in the corner and pulled them up, then shut the door and reached under his bed. His hand gripped the icy handle of the chamber pot and he pulled it across the floor and lifted it into position. He watched in wonderment as the warm jet of water struck the yellow ice. He nipped his penis to give more pressure to the flow as he aimed carefully to carve a face in the flat ice under the piss. He flexed his bladder muscle and drove the jet deeper, happy that he had not used the pot during the night, for it allowed him to carve a simple face with not only two eyes, a nose and a mouth but eyebrows and ears as well.

He put on his white cowboy shirt with black trim on the arms and pockets and buttoned it, pushed open the door and zipped his trousers near the stove. "Where's Dad?"

Two hefty slices of hot buttered toast and a bowl of steaming porridge lay at his father's place at the table. "Gone down the cape with Garf," his mother answered while she poured milk into his tea.

"What time did he call me for school then?"

"Half past six," she chuckled. "Ya knows what Dad is like now. He wants everybody outta bed 'fore they gets asleep."

Martin took a half-rolled tube of Brylcreem from the wash-stand drawer, squeezed a glob of the sweet-smelling white cream into his hand and massaged it lightly into his scalp. He combed his hair back and made a small wave at the front.

At the table he buried his bread in partridgeberry jam, doubled up a slice and dunked it into his mug. He sucked the hot milky tea through the sponge and said, "Lookin' for seals, is they?" Yawned. "Anyone else gone down?"

Ida pulled open the oven door and he felt the hot air strike his back.

"Heard a couple a Ski-Doos go 'long 'fore daylight," she said. "And a few more went 'long just now."

Martin took a big bite and said with his mouth full, "How come they never called me up to go over with 'em, I wonder?" Tea dripped from his chin as he swallowed fast so he could speak again. "I'd like to get me hands on them friggin' seals; I certainly would."

"You'll get your chance, boy. Easter is comin'." Ida encouraged the boy as best she could. She wished that Ambrose had called him to go on the seal hunt with him but as soon as that thought registered it was lost. No! What could she have been thinking? She was glad Ambrose had not called him. Cape Bauld was no place for a youngster, especially on the ice. Although Martin was growing and she knew he would soon be making his own decisions, she dreaded the day when he would take a knife and follow his father to wherever his father led him.

The first month in his new four-room school with sixty-seven students, Martin had missed six days. The second month he had missed nine. By Christmas he had developed a fierce hatred for education because of some harsh name-calling by other students, directed towards his being from the island. He had been in fights to prove he wasn't an *island rat* or a *nuggle-head,* and he had fought for his friends as well, but as the new year wore on the name-calling had stopped.

Just two weeks ago, shortly after mid-terms, trouble had started again, this time with Howard Lewis, a pesty eighth-grader seated directly behind him. Tall and skinny with a mouth that practically stretched from ear to ear, Howard had marked several times with his ballpoint on the back of Martin's shirt.

Martin finished his tea and brushed the breadcrumbs off his shirt, pulled on his jacket and bolted down the road to the schoolhouse across the cove. He swore silently that if Howard lifted his pen against him today he would defend himself.

Jack Burns — slim, wiry and sharply handsome, with an interest in French cuisine — taught French during the first period in the afternoon, and strutted about the classroom calling for translations from his seventh-graders and eighth-graders with quick jabs of his finger in the spiritless faces of his twenty-one inanimate subjects. Sometimes he would bring small pots of familiar-looking meat and vegetables to school for the children to sample, but the smell was generally foreign to them. They knew it was useless to ask how he could make potatoes taste like apples, cabbage taste like turnip greens and beef taste like mutton, because Jack would never tell. Telling, he said, would cast aspersions upon the kitchens of France, for his herbs and spices were a secret between him and a mail-order house in mainland Canada.

Howard held his peace the whole morning but then it happened.

Martin felt the ballpoint dig into his back. He did not look up. Thinking. Feeling. Laughter — somebody was laughing! Who was it — who? The pen dug deeper. Sweat. He could smell it. Then silence.

"OK, *qui a terminé ses devoirs? Est-ce que tout le monde a lu jusqu'à la page 186? Apportez vos feuilles à mon bureau et continuez à conjuguer vos verbes.*"

Martin heard the coarse syllables roll off his teacher's tongue but had no idea of what he said except *OK, est-ce-que* and *tout le monde*. And he had no idea for a solution to the pen and shirt problem. He had warned Howard to keep his hands to himself. Maybe Howard would not bother him again, he thought, if he ignored him, or maybe he should ask to be seated someplace else, like near the window by Evelyn Stone, the pretty seventh-grade brunette who never knew he existed. Perhaps she looked at him as being a weakling. What if he fought back? The pen dug into his back another time. Maybe he should quit school and look for a berth on a sealing schooner. He'd heard Garf say something about the captains of these wooden vessels not really caring about age or size when recruiting sealers for the ice, as long as they had meat on their bones and a knife strapped to their belt. Especially if they showed a lust for blood by lying about their age. Someone laughed again.

Buttons scattered across the classroom as Martin tore off his shirt. He wheeled around and grabbed Howard by the throat, pulling him from his seat despite his feeble cries, despite Jack's threats and pleas for truce. Despite anything.

Everyone laughed when Howard hollered like a stuck pig.

"Holler, you lousy bastard! Now you're gonna get my boot up your arse!" Martin dragged him to the front of the class and stepped on his head to keep him down while he opened the door to the corridor.

"*Arrêtez! Arrêtez! Arrêtez!*" Jack's voice flew by.

"Don't try to stop me, Jack!"

"Come on now, Martin, boy," Jack said weakly. "You can't go at that kinda stuff in here."

"I can't? Just watch me!"

Howard screamed as Martin threw him through the door. Jack sat despondently on the edge of his desk. "*Tu vas rendre Monsieur Shelby fâché.*"

"To hell with Mon Sewer Shelby!"

Howard huddled on the floor in the fetal position under a plywood chart painted with nine school regulations. NO MINISKIRTS, NO CHEWING GUM and NO BLASPHEMY had been scratched out with the tip of the I.X.L. knife that Martin carried in his pocket. The sign was meant mainly for those outsiders not reared in a civilized manner. With the recent materialization of several conflicting religions inside its defences, the school board claimed that the values of modern Christianity would soon be corrupted if laws were not firmly established at the beginning of the school year.

In the corridor, Martin knelt on Howard's chest, held onto the boy's throat with his left hand and drew back the right. Fist clenched.

"Don't hit me," Howard cried, shielding his face with both hands and drawing his knees up farther.

"Why not?"

"'Cause!"

"'Cause what?"

"'Cause you'll kill me if ya do!"

"That's right. I will kill ya, too," Martin said gravely. "Mark on my shirt once more and you'll be sorry."

The whole class formed a ring around the fighters.

He slapped Howard in the side of the head. Once. Twice. He heard someone laugh, heard the jeering, then felt the coldness in a familiar throaty voice directly above him.

"Get up! Get up, you little savage!"

That strong English accent. Calm and steady. Steady as dust falling through the air from the blackboard eraser and covering the floor — settling on anything that might be on the floor. Settling on Martin.

Howard screamed again as his show of strong character came forth with the entrance of the principal. "Lemme up! You're foolish, ain't ya, boy! What's wrong with you at all?"

Martin nipped a little harder.

"Geaagghhh. . . !"

"That's enough now! You're in trouble this time, mistah!"

Mr. Shelby wore a black suit, blue shirt and red tie. He was tall and thin, with sunken eyes and a badly receded flaxen hairline, and Martin looked on him as the devil disguised as a teacher. He never changed his clothes from one day to the next and was always a board in a suit. Now here he was — accuser, prosecutor and judge. Executioner.

Howard wriggled and clawed at his attacker's bare arms.

Martin felt the principal's clammy hands on his shoulders and around his waist. Pawing. "Lemme bide," he said rather crossly over his shoulder. "He's the one who started this, not me!"

"You cheeky monstah; get up right now and go to my office! Both of you!"

As Martin let himself be pulled away, Jack sat on the corner of his oak desk and leafed through his French manual. He crinkled one side of his face into half a smile. A little more than a whisper: *"Tu devrais avoir fait ça il y a longtemps."*

Yeah, Martin thought, whatever that meant.

In the office he stood bare-chested by the door and wondered what his fate might be. Maybe Mr. Shelby would kick Howard out of school; perhaps he would even kick *him* out. Martin didn't care either way.

Howard stood by the principal's desk and rested his hand on a pile of papers.

The verdict came in.

"I'm sorry, Mahtin," Shelby said, tight-lipped. "But we don't have a choice. We have to expel you from our school."

"For how long?"

"One week."

"What 'bout Howard?"

"One week also."

Martin rubbed his chin with a thumb. "I won't be back."

Walking slowly across the cove with his hand on the knife in his pocket, he turned to see Howard coming down the steps. He stopped and thought he should go back and finish the fight right there.

"Ah, forget it," he said aloud. And kept walking.

3

CAPE BAULD

A strip of island rock and tundra three and half miles long forms the eastern perimeter of the harbour at Karpoon. French fishermen from the coast of Brittany fished here for over three hundred years and named this island, as well as the settlement, after their own beloved Isle de Kerpont far away in France. With the signing of the Treaty of Versailles in 1783, the predominantly French-occupied territory in Newfoundland and its French place names gradually fell into English hands and English corruptions.

At the north end of Karpoon Island lies Cape Bauld, where a lightkeeper's summer station clings to the rocky cliffs one hundred and five feet above sea level. Being the closest piece of land to the Strait of Belle Isle entranceway, Cape Bauld has been equipped with the best in marine navigational aids. A whistle house with four powerful diesel generators set on a concrete slab now heralds the presence of fog with an earth-shattering *aaaarrrr-ummpp*, and the lighthouse is capable of casting a revolving beam fifty miles out to sea.

The station closes in late December for the winter months; the lightkeepers move off the island to their homes elsewhere in Newfoundland. Another two months or so would pass before they returned. Since the station had been built in 1865, landsmen sealers had used it as a shield against the piercing wind while they watched and waited for the harp seal migration from Baffin Bay southward.

Farther out on the cliff stands a radio transmission tower one hundred and twenty-feet high. Below there are only the rocks, and certain death if someone fell.

Garf braced himself against the tower and stared watery-eyed into the biting northeaster. Hood tied under his chin, he clutched a gaff in his hand with the hook pointed towards the sky. A long-sheathed hunting knife hung from a cowhide belt around the waist of his khaki jacket. Somewhere off there, he thought, was a part of his past. Two parts, actually: the part he was proud of and the part he wanted to forget.

He had been to the ice in big ships commanded by fearless captains who hovered on the brink of heroism and madness. He had seen blood flow like rivers, seen it melt the ice and form black holes deep enough for a man to stumble in, sometimes deep enough to lie in. Seen the winching aboard of the pelts. Red. Always red. Warm and cold. Greasy. He had smelled the stench of compressed fat in the holds, and the bloody decks. Seen the crimson path rise and fall with the swell; how the serpentine ribbon of blood clung to the contours of the rough ice, weaving an intricate pattern of death.

Garf saw blood flow not only from the bellies of whitecoats but from the eyes of his shipmates as well. Several weeks on board a sealing ship covered in blood and grease made it easy to think of ramming a knife into a sealer for the very least of reasons. During his trips to the ice he had never once drawn his own knife in anger, only in the perpetual need for survival. He knew of times when his drawn knife might have persuaded another sealer to think differently, but he had always managed to avoid such confrontations by doing his job and keeping his mouth shut. He remembered how a serious card game one night on a pile of bloody seal pelts below deck had led to the disappearance of a cheating sealer. The ice had a way of devouring a man, the captain told his crew.

Garf brought himself back to the present. He dug his gaff into the hard crust to keep from falling as he ran around the whistle house to the leeward end, where a group of sealers had gathered. The wind struck him, pressed the jacket onto his back and moulded his shoulder blades into the shape of seaplane pontoons.

All eyes were on Ambrose jumping up and down, swinging his arms wildly back and forth across his chest, looking as though he were trying to wrap them around himself to keep warm. He blew heavy breaths and kicked his heels together to circulate the blood in his cold feet. "Who got the baccy?" he asked excitedly. "I'm just 'bout gone for a smoke. Ain't had n'ar smoke since I left home this marnin' and Garf wouldn't stop that Ski-Doo, no sir, not if I was dyin'."

Max Butler looked at Ambrose. He was a small man with rosy cheeks and a likeable face. He had been the second man on Sacred Island to accept the terms of resettlement and leave with his house tied to the stern of his motorboat. Now he lived in Karpoon and cursed the day he had gone there. "Should a drove the Ski-Doo yourself, Ambrose," he said. "Then ya could a stopped when ya like."

All eyes turned to Garf, who said nothing but moved farther to the windward corner.

The old man pretended to look into the distance, eyes squinted and nose notched like a washboard. He had never bothered to learn how to operate his snowmobile, even though Garf had urged him to try, and there was no reason to learn, he told the men, because as long as Garf could drive then that was all right by him.

Max laughed. He had nice teeth, a gold canine, and irises the colour of Clothes Blue. "Here ya go, Ambrose," he said, pulling his tobacco from inside his sweater. "Roll yourself a nice cigarette. Papers in the pack."

Ambrose turned his back to the choppy wind spiralling down off the building and pinched out enough tobacco to fill his cigarette paper. He twisted it into a log, licked it and popped the roll into his mouth. "Gimme a light, Max," he said and returned the tobacco.

Someone in the crowd shouted, "Time for ya to give up that smokin' racket, Ambrose. Gonna kill ya, boy!"

Still kicking his heels, Ambrose waited for a light with his hand held out. "Can't do it, my son," he said, searching for the voice. "Me mind won't 'low me to do it."

Max pulled a Zippo lighter from his inside pants. "Here ya go, Ambrose," he said. "Try this!"

The old man lit his cigarette, inhaled long and hard and kept the smoke in until he turned almost red in the face, then emptied his lungs into the crowd, purposefully aiming the blue cloud at the men who had ragged him. He held up his cigarette. "Look," he said soberly. "The day I gives this up is the day I closes me two peepers for good."

The sealers laughed and went back to scanning the ice floes.

"I thought 'twas gonna be a solid jam here this marnin'," Max said. "But 'tis runnin'. Not fit to get on, see boy, and most of it's only two-man pans. Gets on that ice it might go right to pieces under your feet." He poked his finger in Ambrose's upper arm to get his attention. "Finished with me lighter or what?"

"Oh," Ambrose replied, with the cigarette clamped between his lips. "Forgot to give 'en back to ya, boy." He took the lighter from the front pocket of his trousers. "Here ya go," he said. "Good shot ya told me 'bout it or I would a keeped 'en."

"Look! There's a old one," someone shouted. Heads turned in the same direction at the same time.

Three or four men ran to the edge of the cliff and stared unblinking into the white open expanse. As they stood there leaning into the wind, one man inched his way behind another to break the wind from his face, and another inched his way behind him, and within a minute or so the man who had been nearest the edge was behind everyone.

John Parsons leaned against the end of the whistle house and explored the loose pack ice with binoculars held firmly to his eyes. He was a bald brute with broad shoulders and arms like the main roots of an old spruce tree. Scabbed knuckles and nicotine fingers. Square jaw and hooked nose. A black-handled hunting knife sheathed in tanned cowhide hung from his waist, black rubber pants shielded his legs from the cold and he wore a royal blue sweater with the pattern of a polar bear standing on its hind legs against a red setting sun. He had married Max's daughter, Audrey, but twelve years ago she had taken off from their home in Karpoon with the history teacher, an American from Boston, and had left him to raise their son, Alec, on his own. She had called almost a year later and wanted to come back but he had told her no.

"I sees 'en," he said with a quick spit to the side, pushing his back against the wall to steady the binoculars. "That lake a water!" He adjusted the focus with the thumb wheel. "There she is right there in the blue drop — ol' bitch harp!"

At the other end of the whistle house Garf saw a black speck on an ice pan about a mile offshore, and thought it might be a seal. To make sure, he crawled up the side of the condemned, rusty steam boiler, now lying on its side and half buried in the snow. Once used to supply power to the facilities at the cape, this chunk of iron piping and rivets made a hardy perch for sealers wanting a better view of the strait. He stuck his toe into a hole and boosted himself up, almost knocking another sealer off.

Paddy Mitchell, short and round as a barrel from the neck down, fought for balance and grabbed ahold of Garf to keep from falling. "Geez boy," he blurted, his apple cheeks aglow with the morning air. "Be careful what you're at, for God's sake!" He had a small bit of fuzz on his chin that refused to grow any longer, and thick prescription glasses on his eyes that kept falling down his nose.

"What's that off there?" Garf asked, pointing at the speck.

"Seen that there just now," Paddy said, "Thought 'twas a seal but didn't see it move." He shielded his eyes to see better, then found surer balance and pointed straight towards the eastern end of Belle Isle, off nearly a mile from the cliffs of Cape Bauld. "Out there, Garf. Just look. I believe that's a seal there." He hesitated, unsure of his judgment.

"Where to, Paddy — where?"

"Off there," he said, still pointing. "I s'pose that's one."

He was puzzled but tried to equivocate. "Well, looks like one anyway."

"Put the glasses on 'en," Garf said, as he searched the area.

Paddy did not particularly want to determine whether it was a seal or not — it was not uncommon to hear sealers suggest that a crow perched on an ice pan was a young seal, or that a black clumper of ice was an old harp — but he felt compelled to pull out his binoculars because of the way Garf had commanded him to.

Garf had that kind of authority about him, and Ambrose had grown accustomed to him shouting orders on what to do and what not to do, but Ambrose was the kind of man who needed guidance. Whatever his oldest son suggested, he always thought it sounded like a brilliant idea. Ida had asked him on several occasions what he would do if Garf jumped off the wharf to drown himself. His answer: he would jump too, but not unless Garf said it was OK.

Paddy yanked off his mitts and glasses and put the binoculars to his eyes. After a few seconds of searching, he said, "there he is all right — right there!"

"I sees 'en," Garf said, his jawbone jumping excitedly. "But he's safe enough for today, and perhaps safe enough for t'marra too. Everything depends on the wind."

Paddy smiled, knowing that Garf was waiting impatiently to look through the binoculars. He pushed his sealskin cap back over his head and raised them a little above his sightline, to see Garf pacing the boiler.

Garf leaned against the side of the whistle house, scrunching the hard, flaky paint scales on the clapboard with his jacket and driving them into the wind.

"Looks like there might be a couple off there," Paddy

said. "Wanna have a look or what?"

"Sure!"

Paddy shifted the binoculars back onto his eyes. "Hold on," he said, "I sees another one! Ol' bitch — right there!"

"I sees her," Garf said, "sees her with the naked eye. Right there behind that pinnacle." He was proud of his eyesight. "'Nother one outside that with just her nose stickin' up over." He walked to the end of the boiler and stopped. "If the old ones is this handy, you can be sure the young ones is not far away. Time t'marra the place is gonna be maggoty with 'em!"

Paddy continued searching the ice floes.

"The main patch is not reached here yet," Garf added. His foot slipped near the snowy edge and he fell to one knee. Without caring to comment on his slight accident, he said, "T'marra is the time. That ice'll press in solid tonight and close up them lakes a water; you just watch and see. See how much I'm out."

"Here," Paddy said, giving Garf the binoculars, "have a look and see what you can see."

Garf clutched them in his hands like a hymn book and said, "your father's."

Paddy nodded and put his spectacles back on. "Yes," he said, a headful of nightmarish visions springing to life. "Father's glasses."

Fourteen years ago his father had gone seal hunting from this very place and, thinking the loose slob ice could bear his weight under his worn-out snowshoes, he had walked until the webbing — sealers called it *babiche*, narrow strips of dried sealskin interlaced across the frame — gave out and he began sinking. He tried clinging onto a small pan but he sank in the polar quicksand in less than a minute. A group of sealers waiting on Cape Bauld for the ice to press in heard him screeching, saw it swallow him alive.

Garf stared wide-eyed into the binoculars, afraid to breathe lest he jiggle his hand and lose sight of the bitch harp he was focused on. He had heard stories of how Paddy's father had died and did not care to talk about the old man's stupidity.

"See anything, Garf?"

No answer. Garf pushed the binoculars up and spied the far line of the eastern sky. There was a cry from the other end of the whistle house and he dropped them to his chest. "Who's that singin' out?" He pulled on the half-bow around his chin, pushed his hood back and listened. "Somebody must a seen a seal over on the other side a the cape."

"Crow, I daresay," Paddy replied. "Still for all it might be a seal."

"Well, whatever they seen is gonna have to stay there. No one is gettin' on that ice today." Garf kicked at a short piece of rusted pipe sticking up through the boiler as he passed the time while expecting another cry. He put the binoculars back up and heard the shout again. A cry like that could mean that a herd of seals had been spotted, or that someone had fallen off the cliff.

"What's goin' on?" Paddy asked.

"C'mon," Garf said. "Let's go over on the other end and see what they're doin'." He gave the binoculars back, jumped off the boiler and sank knee deep into powdery snow that had been softened by the many feet clambering up in the last few days. He plucked his gaff from the hard crust near the building and ran around the corner, his hood plastered against the back of his head. Paddy followed.

One restless sealer, tired of standing around in the cold

and doing nothing, tore a strip of clapboard off the south side of the whistle house. Another, wearied by images of an empty hauling rope, broke the strip into short lengths across his knee, and Ambrose was helping out by laying the pieces criss-cross on the snow, where they apparently intended to start a fire. When he saw Garf, the old man wiped his mouth and went to the cliff, where a dozen men huddled together at the precipice.

Two gaffs and a 30-30 Winchester rifle stood jammed in the snowbank, and a black rubber coat, crinkled and folded indiscriminately, lay near the gun, kept in place on the snow by a bulging green packsack.

"What's the trouble, boys?" Garf asked.

Without looking around, the one man tore another clapboard off the building. "Gonna get a warm," he said. "Try to stop from perishin'."

Garf smiled at the answer. "No, I'm not talkin' 'bout you fellers lightin' a fire; I meaned what was all the shoutin' 'bout." He turned to a man pouring gasoline from a red plastic jar onto the pile of kindling. "Didn't ya hear it?"

"Crowd out there on the bank, I s'pose. Must a seen some seals." He lit a match and threw it on the wood. There was an audible *poof* and then the soothing crackle of a smokeless fire.

Garf and Paddy warmed their hands over the flames.

"Like to have a little nip?" asked the fire-keeper. He pulled along the packsack and opened it up. Inside was bread soaked with molasses, a bottle of nearly frozen black tea, rifle bullets, matches, worsted socks, worsted mitts, and a flask of moonshine that he pulled out and passed to Garf. "Here ya go," he said. "Have a glutch."

Moonshine was considered a drunkard's feast if taken

within the confines of four walls with a hot stove, but in an open environment of ice and snow it was considered medicine — in the event that someone fell ill due to frostbite or a near drowning. Most times such medicine was taken here on Cape Bauld, in small doses, and prescribed by one happy sealer for another.

"Just a taste," Garf said, twisting the cap off and tipping the bottle carefully to his lips. He let a stream of alcohol with no bubbles run down his throat then put the cap on and handed it back. Without breathing.

"No no. Give your buddy a glutch!"

Paddy tipped the bottle up and downed a river of bubbles.

"Beejaysuss," the fire-keeper said sharply. "Don't eat the bottle, ol' man, whatever ya does!"

Garf tore the flask from Paddy's mouth and found breath enough to scold him. "Shouldn't a done that, look! More people here 'sides you!"

Paddy wiped his chin and went into a fit of coughing.

"Pity ya don't choke," quipped the infuriated sealer, tossing another few pieces of clapboard onto the fire. "You'll get no more drinks from me."

"My birthday," Paddy wheezed. "Twenty-one years old today."

"Well, now you've had your birthday present, so fly to hell's flames!" The fireman accepted the medicine back from Garf, with a nod of his head and a depressed look at the bottle. Garf thanked him for his good-heartedness and went to the cliff to find Ambrose.

After stepping into the crowd and finding his father, Garf tapped him on the shoulder. "Just as well to go home, ain't it, Uncle Am?" he said. He answered his own question be-

fore Ambrose had a chance to speak. "Yeah, let's leave. Be
no seals hauled ashore here today, like I said for." He looked
through the crowd at the open water near the shore.
"Whaddaya see here, boys — anything or nothin'?"

"Ol' dog hood off the point," came a voice from the side.
"But now he's gone."

Garf stretched his neck and squinted hard into the howling wind around the craggy headland, wanting to convince
himself before heading up the hill to his Ski-Doo that his
decision to return home and wait another day had been the
right one.

4

FISH FOR SUPPER

Martin stamped his feet on the bridge — a small wooden platform leading to the door of his home — reached down and brushed the rest of the snow from his boots. Wondered if his father had returned from the hunt. Wondered if he should tell him he had been kicked out of school. His mother and grandmother were sifting through a carton of rags when he went inside, searching for a bright red piece of nylon to put the finishing touches on the top of the Eskimo's seal-skin boots. He asked if his father and Garf had returned yet.

"They're home," his mother answered. "And they're goin' down the cape again t'marra. Said if ya wants to go 'long with 'em you'd better go to bed early tonight and get your rest."

He took a sweet biscuit from the bottom cupboard and bit it in half. "Good!" He swallowed and put the other half in his mouth. "Look out seals 'cause I'm a-comin' to get ya!"

"Got any gum, Marty?" his grandmother asked. "I wants a chew some bad."

"No," he said. "I don't. But I'll get ya some when I goes to the restaurant again."

"When I gets me cheque," she said, "I'll give ya the money."

"Good," the boy said. "Good!"

"Don't lose your rope when ya goes sealin'," she instructed him. "And stay away from them ol' dog hoods. They're the savagiest thing on the face a the earth. Gets in tangle with one of them 'tis the same thing as facin' the devil."

"Oh my God, Mother," Ida said, bringing more worry to herself. "Don't say that, maid, whatever ya does. And Martin, for God's sake, listen for once in your life, do. Don't go handy to them ol' hoods like your grandmother said, 'cause if they gets fast to ya they'll eat your legs right down to the stumps!"

"G'wan," he said, thinking his mother was only joking. "They're not savage like that, is they?"

Ida wiped her forehead with a scrap of black cotton. "I heard it said that after ya kills a ol' dog hood and hauls the pelt off 'en, he'll still make a snap at ya. And I heard people say they'll even crawl 'cross the ice after they're killed, and jump in the water with n'ar pelt on their back!"

The boy grinned and looked to see if she'd crack a smile. She didn't. "Well now, that's a bit too much to take in, that is," he said. "How can he still be alive if he's dead?"

"Got a piece," his grandmother said, proudly stretching the red scrap in front of her face.

"Mightn't be true," Ida said. "But that's the way I heard it. And I believes it!"

"And don't eat no blue ice," the old woman warned. "Takes all your strength away."

Ida pulled a red scrap of cotton from the box. "Outta school a bit early this evenin', ain't ya?"

He was quick to reply. "Comin' 'wards Easter, the teacher said we could leave early."

"Strange I didn't hear no youngsters go 'long by the house."

"No," he lied expertly. "They all walked home on the harbour."

"So whaddaya gonna do?"

"Me?" he asked. "'Bout what?"

"Sealin'," Ida said. "Ya goin' with your father or not?"

"Ya knows I am," he said, thinking she had somehow sensed his dishonesty. "What time's he leavin' anyway?"

"Never said."

He went to his room, stretched out on the bed with a bunch of old comic books that he had read over and over. He heard his father's axe biting into the chopping block outside his frosted window, but imagined the sound as coming from the tomahawks of renegade Indians as they overpowered a wagon train and butchered a group of white settlers.

Ida pulled down the oven door and felt the rush of scorching heat. Five thick, steaming chunks of salt codfish sizzled on an aluminum pan, bubbles of hot juices trickling down the sides of each piece before evaporating and leaving a brownish salt residue. She reached into the hot cavern and hooked the edge of the sheet with a fork, hauled it across the rack, then dug the tines underneath the chunks and pried them loose, the crispy grey skins sticking to the pan as they broke free. She slipped a stray flake into her mouth, dropped the fish onto a platter and carried it to the table. The smell wafted through the kitchen and invaded every room in the house. She sniffed deeply. "That's good fish we got there," she said to her mother. "But perhaps I should a keeped it in a little longer to brown up more.

Ambrose likes it that way."

"Am likes it any way," her mother replied. "Tell 'en 'tis fish and he'll eat it."

Ida had felt a little apprehensive about cramming the stove because of the wind, and her grumbling at Ambrose to replace the fragile stovepipes had been a waste of breath, but she would hold him to his promise of buying new ones after the hunt.

A white cloth trimmed in red lace hung kitty-corner over the edges of the decked-out table. A small wicker basket frilled on one side held the sliced bread, and the jam dish lay next to the lemon cream biscuits piled high on a small plate. The cutlery was mismatched. Some spoons and forks had wooden handles, some had plastic; others were stainless steel in their entirety.

The spoon and fork at Martin's setting had black plastic handles. Salada Tea had a promotion scheme under way, with the company offering instant prizes to anyone who bought its product, and inside every package of tea bags there was a piece of cutlery. His mother had four or five pieces of each except for the knives; her knives were all stainless and part of the set she had brought with her. Very seldom did anyone get a knife, but she was proud to display her new set along with its stainless counterparts every time she had company over.

"OK, Mother," Ida said. "Go and let Ambrose know 'tis suppertime."

The old woman went to the porch and opened the outside door barely enough for a cat to squeeze through, then shut it again. "There," she said. "When that smell strikes his nose he'll be on the bridge like a buck on a she."

"Come on, Martin, supper is ready!"

Martin tossed the comics on his bed.

Feet stamped on the bridge and the door opened. Ambrose brushed the snow and wood chips from his red and black lumberjack coat, took off his matching cap and beat it against the doorpost, then picked the ice from his eyebrows as though it were knobs of dried glue. The smell had drawn him as Aunt Kizzie had said it would.

"Oh, you're up," he said as Martin came from his bedroom. "Who cut the mattress off your back?"

Martin eyed his father with contempt. "Cut it off meself," he said, and sat in at the table.

"Look," Ambrose roared. "You see how brazen that youngster is? For God's sake, Ida, put 'en in his place!"

His wife said nothing. She had grown tired of the words that now stuck in her throat, for she knew that Ambrose simply wanted her to say something just to torment the boy.

Even on weekends, when Martin slept in until nine or ten o'clock Ambrose never let up on the boy. He could accept that his son was lazy and didn't have to work for a living but he could not accept that Martin had no interest in doing anything, because he believed everyone was interested in "something". Perhaps, if he had forced him into the fishing boat when he was a young gaffer and kept him there, he wouldn't be like this today. The boy might have become interested in being a fisherman — like him.

But Martin remembered the day he had decided not to be like his father: On a cod-jigging trip one morning at the back of Sacred Island, when he was only ten, a small swell had caused a gentle rocking of the motorboat and an uneasy feeling in the pit of his stomach. Seagulls had circled, dipped low on the water and waited for someone to throw out a piece of fish liver. With the changing of the tides the fish had disappeared as quickly as they had come, so Ambrose pulled in his jigger and began smoking. Garf went to the grub box and began eating. The fish would pick up again when the tides reversed, but the next hour would be a time of leisure for anyone not seasick, and Martin used it by trying to sleep with his back against the planking. He wanted to leave the fishing grounds and go home, but then he felt a bitter taste on his tongue as the seasickness hooked him, driving him to stick his head over the gunwales and vomit his heart into the sea. For the rest of that day he did nothing but cringe there in a ball with his eyes closed, determined not to be a fisherman. His father said it didn't matter because he would never amount to anything anyway.

"We're goin' down the cape in the marnin'," Ambrose said, looking across the table at his son. "If ya wants to go with us ya better be ready when Garf gets here 'cause I'm tellin' ya now — he's not gonna wait for ya."

Aunt Kizzie dunked a biscuit into her coffee and gnawed it down to her fingertips, ready to pounce any minute.

Martin dug into a piece of the gluey fish and lifted two pieces off the plate. Shook his fork and one fell back. "Garf won't have to wait!"

His father took a slice of bread and buttered it. "You knows what you're like tryin' to get outta bed, Martin."

"Oh don't you warry sir, I can get up!"

"Not if someone don't call ya, ya can't!"

"Oh yes I can!"

"OK, we'll see t'marra." Ambrose broke off a piece of crust and shoved it in his mouth.

Ida brushed her hair back and spooned sugar into her tea. "I'll call 'em meself if I got to."

"Well, ya knows how hard he is to get up for school, Ida. Ya don't want no one to tell ya that, do ya?" He seemed a bit confused, sweetening his tea a second time, maybe because he had just seen his wife sweeten hers.

Ida stirred with her spoon. "Ah, stop it, Ambrose my son, for the love a God. Stop it, do! Drink your tea and be quiet!"

"My God, maid," he said, "I only said he had to get outta bed if he wanted to go sealin' with us."

"*Only* said! That's all ya ever says, ain't it? *Only* said!" Ida wrung her hands and drove them into her forehead. "I must be cursed!" she cried. "Cursed and double-cursed!"

"OK," Ambrose said, shaking a fork at his son. "I'll call ya but if ya don't get up the first time — like I told ya — Garf is not gonna wait for ya!"

Aunt Kizzie poked a finger in her mouth and rooted an irritating strip of biscuit mash from the side of her gums.

Martin pushed a forkful of hot fish into his mouth and threw his head back to keep it from falling out. Swallowed. "Anyhow, if he do have to wait for me 'tis no more'n he oughtta do."

"And why's that?" Ambrose asked. "Is that 'cause you're special or somethin'?"

A spoon clinked against a cup, as if signalling a boxing match.

"Ya wud'n mind waitin' for someone else though, would ya?" Aunt Kizzie informed.

Ambrose shifted uneasily in his chair.

"Y'oughtta be ashamed a yourself talkin' to the boy like that," she chided. "You're always on his back for God's sake! Why don't ya leave 'en alone once in a while? If I was the boy I'd drive your head up your arse and make a jug outta ya!"

Ida leaped from her chair, grabbed her mother by the shoulders from behind and started shaking her. She drew back her arm. "You little jeezler!" she fumed. "Only for the sin of it I'd drive ya down through the friggin' floorboards! Now shut your so'n'so mouth or I'll shut it for ya! Ambrose tries to do his best for Martin ever since he was barn and he tries to do his best for you too. 'Tis a wonder he don't drive ya the hell outdoors somewhere! Where ya gonna go then, eh? Hear me talkin' to ya; where ya gonna go then — hear me?"

The old woman's head recoiled into her body. "Home," she said, with an air of easiness about her.

Her daughter responded with rage. "Where — where'd ya say you was goin'?"

Aunt Kizzie poked her head out a bit and blinked. "Home, I said — I said I'd go back home!"

"Back home," Ida drawled, as much interested in talking about Sacred Island as in having her leg cut off. "There *is* no 'back home'," she said. "This is our home now so get used to it!"

"I can't," the old woman argued. "And this'll never be my home, not so long as Fred's memory is still on that island!"

"Dad is dead, Mother — drownded."

"I can't even visit his grave," Aunt Kizzie cried. She turned her anger on Ambrose. "If that bastard never hauled me off like a dog, I'd still be out there!"

"You'd still be out there, yes, Mother, but you'd be under the sod."

"Look at Marty, Ida — just look at 'en. He'll never know nothin' 'bout his roots. Won't even know where he 'longs to. Give 'en 'nother ten year and he'll be goin' back searchin' for somethin' he'll never find."

Martin slammed his fist on the table, tipping over his glass of cold water. "Shut up, ol' woman! One more word outta you and *you'll* be the one they'll never find!"

Ida had expected this reaction. "Now Martin, m'dear," she pleaded. "Lemme eat me supper in peace this evenin'. Yes'day it went down in me in lumps." She pulled the bra strap up onto her shoulder, sat down and picked at her meal.

Aunt Kizzie slipped out her dentures and dunked them into her coffee.

"Put your teeth back in your head, Mother!" Ida's tone had hardened with reinforced vigour. "No one gives me a break round here," she said. "No one!"

Martin jumped from the table and stood up, his chair banging against the wall. "I'll put 'em back in her head for her, Mom, if that's what ya wants me to do! And they won't come out no more either!"

The old woman flicked her teeth back into her mouth. Coffee stained her apron.

The boy grabbed her by the throat. Her glasses fell down her nose and she let out a loud cry of anguish. Her teeth slipped and blocked her mouth as she tried to scream again.

"One more peep, ol' woman, and that'll be your last. Now I means it!"

"Sit down, Martin," his mother said. "Sit down, for God's sake! I'm tired a talkin' to ya! I don't know where you're gonna bring up, I don't know!"

"I knows then," Ambrose said easily. "He's gonna bring up on the broad of his back if he don't watch his mouth."

Ida threw her slice of bread back in the basket. It missed and fell against the sugar dish. "I think 'tis all right for someone to put *you* on the broad of *your* back," she said.

"Leave the boy alone — for once, just leave 'en alone! Whaddaya think he's gonna say when he gets a man and looks back on the way you're always puttin' 'en down — tellin' 'en he's no good for this and no good for that? Whaddaya think he's gonna say?"

"*Man?* He'll never make a man, m'dear! Ain't got sense enough to bring in a yaffle a wood, let alone be a man. He don't know what 'tis like to clave up a split, too lazy to beat the ice off the water-barrel komatik. That's all he minds, look — that kinda stuff!" Ambrose nodded his head in the old woman's direction. "I s'pose he's gonna strangle your mother, is he?"

"No Martin, let her go!"

Aunt Kizzie began to turn pale. Her eyes rolled back in their sockets and thick, warm saliva dripped off her chin onto Martin's hand.

"Let her go, Martin," Ida yelled again, grabbing his arm. "Let her go, I said!" Tears welled up in her eyes as she tugged on his arm, trying to free her mother. "I don't know what I'm gonna do with ya, I don't know. You're gettin' worse, I believe!"

"I knows what to do with 'en," Ambrose remarked, his eyes flicking from Martin to Aunt Kizzie. "He wants to be transported; that's what wants to be done with 'en. He wants to be put off on a island somewhere on the other side a the world where nobody can't see 'en — and the ol' woman 'long with 'en."

Martin latched onto his grandmother's dress above her apron and yanked her halfway across the table, tipping over her coffee, the milk can and the bread basket.

"Go over for Garf, Ida," Ambrose said. "Tell 'en Martin's gone off his head. Tell 'en he's gone loony!"

The boy glared wild-eyed at the old woman and pushed her backward into her chair. "I 'low one of those days I'll make away with that," he said in a mouthful of anger. "Be the best thing that ever happened!"

Ida said, "I can't see no redemption for ya, my son, only put ya in refarm school." Her voice shook as she sobbed into her hand.

Martin had not eaten since breakfast but he pushed his plate back and left the table. "You can eat your supper by yourselves now," he declared. "'Cause I'm finished."

5

GOING BACK

Since he'd come to Karpoon, Martin had spent as much time as he could with John Parsons' fifteen-year-old boy, Alec. They had been friends for as long as he could remember but the distance had only allowed them to see each other for a few weeks during the summer months, when John would bring the boy to visit his grandfather's house. There had been times when Martin had met Alec at the general store for ten or fifteen minutes, but Ambrose had always been in a rush, and had not always taken him along.

The first two months of living here, Alec had come each morning to walk with him to school, but Ambrose had mouthed off. "Look, Alec," he'd say, and push open the boy's bedroom door. "Just look at 'en in the bed, covered up head and ears. Where ya think he's gonna bring up, eh? Where ya think he's gonna bring up?"

Alec had never commented on Martin's sleeping habits, but he did tell Ambrose during his first visit that he himself did not require his father to call him out of bed, and that he had made his own breakfast since he was ten. After getting to know the family, Alec never mentioned his early rises again.

Ambrose had been intoxicated by the boy's innocent words, and every time Alec came around and waited for his son to get up he'd prance around the house chanting, *Oh what a man — Oh what a difference.*

Before Alec gave up his visits, Martin often heard his father goading him into talking more about himself, and when the boy refused to carry the conversations further Ambrose would go into a rage and beat his fists on the wall. Under the bed covers and looking at the darkness, Martin had often wondered if his father cared for him at all.

Martin slapped his palms to his ears and pressed them tight to relieve the burning cold. He wore his green parka with the orange fur lining and his woollen mitts but his head was bare. As he approached the restaurant he heard pool balls clink like the choppy xylophone in the old-fashioned waltz emanating from the jukebox, and smelled the stale holes of frozen urine in the snowbank near the bridge. He stamped his feet and opened the door and felt the warm rush of air welcome him.

Weeknights would never draw a big crowd but tomorrow was Good Friday, so he was not surprised to see ten or twelve youngsters by the jukebox and another dozen or so hanging around the open wicket at the snack bar. Four pool players and another bunch were looking on.

The red lettering on the small wooden sign above the outside entrance said RESTAURANT but this was not a dining restaurant. It was a place where young people could hang out, an old fish store that Lewis Moores had bought off the merchant and renovated, then stocked with consignment goods and coin-operated amusement equipment from a dealer in St. Anthony. There were six or seven round wooden tables standing in no orderly fashion around the room, their dark laminated tops cluttered with soda bottles and paper, some with four chairs and some with two. A few stray plank benches littered the walls and there were two pinball machines at the far end with OUT OF ORDER signs taped on their score columns.

A snack bar directly across from the jukebox sold candy bars, potato chips, gum, soft drinks and a few candies but no hot foods — only what came in a bottle or wrapped in paper. A small diesel generator out back supplied enough electricity to the hangout to run the machines, including a freezer chest of ice cream and three bare light bulbs. There was one bulb in the snack bar, one above the dance floor and one on the wall near the pool table, with a cardboard sign nailed directly underneath, NO BEER ALLOWED.

Martin loved it here because the regulars at the restaurant were so friendly and easygoing, and Lewis and his wife were as young at heart as their fourteen-year-old daughter, Louise, who sometimes helped them run the place. There was a pleasant feeling here. Relaxing. Warm. And the songs on the jukebox made him feel good.

The jukebox stopped playing and a small voice called to him from a table in the corner.

"Oh, hello, Judy," he said, turning to the good-looking seventh-grader whose father had been drowned on a duck-hunting trip at Sacred Island just two months before they left there. Her mother, Dulcie, originally from Karpoon, had married her old high school chum, Jack Burns, here a week before Christmas of that same year, and now they lived with his parents in a three-bedroom bungalow at the far end of town.

"Hello," she giggled, her dark hair skinned tight in a ponytail. "What's ya doin'?"

"Not much," he said. "Passin' time. How 'bout you?"

"Oh," she said, patting her forehead with the tips of her fingers. "Just had a fast-dance and I'm beat." She nodded towards a group of teenagers chugalugging root beer by the jukebox. "With that bunch up there." She stuck her eyes in him. "Heard ya got kicked out today. Is that true?"

He was not surprised that she knew. Everyone in the town probably knew by now, he thought. "Too bad you wud'n there to see it," he said.

"Stayed home to look after my baby sister," she said, her smile showing her perfect teeth. "Be a year old this August comin'." She drove her two arms into her coat hanging on the back of her chair, and hunched it on. "Mom and Mrs. Burns" — she cupped her hand around one side of her mouth and chuckled — "still calls her Mrs. Burns; ain't got the nerve to call her Nan yet. Well, they're havin' a little Easter service t'marra after dinner down at the Army, and that's where they're to now, gettin' ready for it. You goin'?"

"Well no," he said rather sharply. "Barred in school all day long is enough for me, and I got better things to do."

"When's ya goin' back?"

"Never."

"Never?"

"No," he said with conviction. "Never!" He remembered her obsession with him when she was ten, and how he had said the same words to her when she wanted to kiss him on his eleventh birthday. "'Nough 'bout me," he said. "How 'bout you? How ya makin' out with your French?"

"*Très bien, monsieur*," she said confidently. "*Merci beaucoup! Et tu?*"

"Oohhh," he mocked, craning his neck in and out. "Madame Mademoiselle!"

She reached over the table and pinched his side. "Stop makin' fun!"

"Oohhh!" Martin rubbed her touch away. "Geez maid, that's a dirty fashion ya got there!" He weaved from side to side, putting on a show as if waiting for the pain to go away.

Judy smiled impishly, her eyes filled with delight. "That's called a pinch *à la* French," she said.

"Pinch *à la* French my arse!" He leaned over the table. "Got any money?"

"Yes. Why?"

"How much ya got?"

She pulled two quarters, one dime and seven coppers from her coat pocket. "Got none, have ya?"

"Could I have the two quarters? Pay ya back later."

"OK," she said without hesitation. "Here ya go," and held them out for him.

"Nah," he said. "Just jokin' with ya. Wanted to see if ya changed since we moved off the island — see what the big city done to ya." He pulled a chair from another table and sat down. "You like it here, Judy?" he asked. "I mean do you ever think about goin' back home?"

"Well," she said, shuffling the coins around on the table. "Thinks 'bout it sometimes, yes, 'specially when I goes to bed."

"I'm goin' back," he said.

Judy jerked her head up. "But you can't! There's nothin' back there."

Martin moved closer. "Your house is still there. Dad's house is still there."

"That's 'cause Mom didn't want no one to tow it 'cross for her. Dad wud'n've left anyway if he'd a been alive, I knows he wud'n've. I think that's why Mom left it there."

"Well, Dad didn't want to leave either. I heard 'en say that his father — my grandfather — built our house a long time ago and he was too old to move — the house, I mean. But Dad and Garf tore the porch off to get 'en ready and then they changed their mind. Perhaps they 'xpects to go back to live, I don't know. Dad's wharf is still there. Max Butler's twine store is still there in the cove. So is some a the boats. There's lotsa stuff back there — just the way they left it."

"I don't know," she said, shaking her head in disbelief. "Goin' back don't sound like a good idea to me." She put the money in her pocket. "What'd your father and mother say 'bout all this?"

"Sshhh," he cautioned her. "No one knows 'bout this only me and you." He was almost in her ear now. "You wud'n tell on me, would ya?"

"Well," Judy began. "Shouldn't ya let 'em know? I mean what's they gonna say if ya goes off there and they don't know where you're gone? Ya knows they're gonna be warried 'bout ya."

Martin looked around to see if anyone was listening. "Warried? They wud'n even miss me."

"I don't know, Martin. You're not thinkin' right."

He went back to his original position on the chair. "Would ya tell on me?"

"I don't know. You goes off there and gets in trouble, I'll never forgive ya."

"I'll be all right," he said. "So would ya tell everyone or wud'n ya?"

Judy stared at him without speaking, then struggled with her thoughts. "When?"

"Soon."

"Oh Martin," she said with a heavy sigh. "Why'd ya have to get on like this tonight?"

"I asked you a question," he said. "Would you tell on me or wud'n ya — yes or no?"

"But ya might be drownded goin' off there. And what's ya gonna do when ya gets there? Ya won't have no one to talk to and ya won't see nobody 'cause no one lives there no more. The island is dead, Martin!"

"Would ya tell on me?" He got in her ear again. "I'd do it for you, Judy. Do ya know that?"

She bit on her little fingernail and watched the yellow pool ball sink in the side pocket, heard it bang against the wooden chute inside and saw it roll into the string of balls in their rack at the end. "No, Martin — I won't tell on ya."

"Good," he said with a true smile. "You're a islander."

Judy picked a perfectly good straw from the paper and dirt on the floor and looked through it at Martin. "And you're one," she said.

He took a dollar bill from his jeans pocket and tucked it inside her sweater.

"What's that for?" she asked, pulling it back out. Unfolded it.

"A keepsake," he said.

"No, I can't take your money, Martin," she said, pushing it at him.

"You're not takin' it, Judy — I'm givin' it to ya."

The jukebox started playing again.

She held the bill out to him. "You'll want that 'fore the night is gone. Take it."

He reached into his pocket and pulled out two more dollars. "Look — see! I got more'n I needs."

"But where'd ya get all the money?"

"Nan. Gets a cheque from the gov'ment every month for gum."

"Gum?"

"Yeah, whenever she gets her cheque come she gives me enough money to buy her some gum and gives me a few dollars for meself."

"So 'tis her money then."

"No, this is what I've been savin'. And she won't get her cheque till — I don't know — sometime next month."

"You sure?"

"I'm sure," he said. "You put that in a safe place now and don't warry 'bout it. When we sees each other again we'll spend it right here in this restaurant, on chips and drinks and bars. And," he added, "we'll sit at this same table. Just the two of us. OK?"

Judy nodded and zipped her jacket. "All right," she said, showing him the dollar. "Soon's I gets home I'll put this in my room drawer. Just don't get yourself in trouble."

Martin told her he'd be seeing her and went off to the snack bar.

Dot Moores — short, petite, about fifty and wearing a long mauve pleated skirt and a white blouse with baggy sleeves and tight wrists — busied herself with two gallon-bottles of barrel-shaped candies on a shelf behind the wicket. A small yellow tin cross dangled from a flat-linked chain around her neck and she wore clip-on earrings cut from the same alloy. Her high cheeks gave way to tantalizing eyes and richly painted red lips, and in a poorly tuned voice she sang along with the jukebox as she added the few remaining candies in one bottle to the contents of the fuller one. *Clickety-clack.* Pretty colours. One candy fell to the floor and disappeared under a pile of cartons but she got on her knees and pushed her arm in under, her long chestnut hair brushing the floor, fastened to her scalp by three inches of the lightest grey.

Louise had her head in the freezer, and from where he stood outside the counter all Martin saw was her shapely thighs and tight ass through her faded Levi's. She pulled out a small cardboard box with round holes in the sides and withdrew four Long Treats — ice-cream sandwiches with a bar of vanilla ice cream between two shorter chocolate wafers, which gave them a circumcised look — then put them in the freezer basket and tossed the box through the door of the back room. With the mauve blouse she was wearing, the ballpoint in the breast pocket and her light hair chopped off in a bob she could have passed for twenty. Then she saw Martin. "Please," she said, closing the lid and extending her hand as if to ward off anything coming her way, "don't take off your shirt in here."

"A fine way to say hello," he said, with a faked look of hopelessness about him. "And no, I won't take off me shirt in here. I promise."

Louise shot a glance at herself in a small mirror around the corner from the shiny bottle opener nailed onto the side of the wicket, and then propped her elbows on the counter, her palms flat against her round face. "A full week off from school, Martin," she said, beaming. "How lucky can ya get! Listen, t'marra is the beginning of Easter holidays and we got a full week off, so do that count, I wonder? Or do it mean you'll still be kicked out after school starts again?"

He hadn't thought about it that way. "Howard's kicked out for a week too," he said.

Louise rubbed her hair back with her hand. "Should a kicked that brute out for the rest of the year." She popped a Dubble Bubble into her mouth. "I seen what he was doin' there with his pen. He used to look around and laugh every time he marked on your shirt. And that Evelyn — that Miss Snob-Nose — well, she just takes the cake!"

Martin let his mind go back to the classroom. Saw them all in their seats, felt the pen dig deep into his back. . . . "What'd she do?" he asked.

"Laugh."

"Laugh?"

"Yeah, that's all she done was laugh! She thinks herself so prissy. Two years in grade six and last year they put her on. Ooohhhh," Louise said, with a grimace, "I hates that girl — I honestly do!"

He pictured Evelyn relishing his discomfort, putting her hand to her mouth to stop from laughing too loud, then taking it away again to snicker. How could she, he thought. He hadn't given her any reason to laugh at him or taunt him. He hadn't even had a conversation with her other than to ask her the time. He wouldn't have asked her then except some of his classmates had dared him. Maybe she just didn't like him.

"Well," he said, embarrassed and demoralized by the unpleasant news. "She must've thought it was funny."

Louise laughed to enliven him and slid a quarter across the counter. "Here, play me a song on the jukebox. And make sure 'tis a good one."

"Gimme a Pepsi first," he said. "And two a them bars right there on the top shelf."

"Which ones?" she asked, swinging her arm back like a hoisting boom on a ship and tapping the boxes of Five Star and Crispy Crunch. "These or those?"

"Ah, gimme one of each."

She tossed the bars onto the counter and then collared the cap of his Pepsi bottle in the opener and pushed down. The cap went *pop*, white smoke clinging to the neck. "Twenty-two cents," she said.

"And a pack a Juicy Fruit gum too."

She tossed him the bright yellow pack and he caught it and put it in his pocket. "Twenty-seven cents," she said.

He flicked the folded bill on the counter, tore the wrapper off the Crispy Crunch and stowed the bar in his mouth.

Louise gave him back his change, then burst her bubble and inhaled the sweet air before it escaped. "You couldn't've had much for your supper," she said. "What'd ya have?"

He drank half the Pepsi and put the bottle down. The soda stung his throat. "Had enough," he said. "Had more'n I could handle."

She could not have known what he meant. "OK, play my song now."

"Whaddaya wanna hear?"

"I don't know. Play whatever ya wants to play. J9 is a good one."

"J9 — what one is that?"

"Play it and see."

On weekends the boys and girls would dance here every night with the light off above the dance floor, their arms locked around each other, hoping to sneak a small kiss from their partner providing Dot was not looking in their direction. She mostly minded her own business, but she had the eyes of a hawk and no one dared to cross her.

Martin pushed the button at the side of the jukebox and the index bar rolled. "Let's see. . . ."

"Play a slow one."

He recognized the voice before Hazel Caine put her arm around his neck.

"Play a nice, slow song now," she said softly. "And me and you'll have a nice, sexy dance." She was slender and fragile, with long, flaming red hair twisted and curled like wood shavings halfway down her back. Ashen skin spattered with freckles. The way she rolled her scarlet-rimmed eyes and the way she whispered instead of talking out loud were torture to any boy she spoke to. And she was sixteen.

Martin felt her breath on his neck as she closed in. "Nah," he said, shying away from the fantasy. "I might tramp on your toes."

"No ya won't."

"Yes I will."

"You can be careful, can't ya?" She touched her cold nose on his face.

"Ah, here it is — J9." He pushed the J button, held it and pushed the 9.

"*Don't be angry with me, darlin'*" — that's a nice song to dance to," Hazel purred as she read the label on the index bar. She nudged his leg with her knee. "No one can ever be angry with you, Martin, can they? Just one small, teensy-weensy dance. Pleeasssse."

He could smell her breath. Sweet and hot.

"Can't find the right song, can ya, Martin?" Louise's voice ripped the shroud and permeated the sultry air inside.

The wheel stopped. A shiny arm reached out from its sleep, latched onto J9 and dropped the record onto the turntable.

"Well, maybe some other time," Hazel whispered as the music began. Her arm slid down and a finger dug into his lower back.

How could he dance with her, he thought. The lights were still on. And it was Louise's quarter.

6

THE LOST GAFF

Martin heard his father tap the glass and take the damper off the stove. He felt restless in the semi-darkness while he waited for his wake-up call, wondering if he should tell his parents of his expulsion from school and his decision not to go back. Awake now, he could no longer lie there so he threw back the bed covering and jumped out, dressed and pulled the empty pot from under the bed. His mother had emptied it yesterday but with the three bottles of Pepsi he had drunk last night at the restaurant he soon had it half filled again. He peeked through the doorway in time to see his father force another handful of dry splits onto the fire, and the cloud of wispy blue smoke that rose from the damper hole and struck the ceiling. Then he saw him put the butter dish in the oven and shut the door.

Ida came from the bedroom, brushed her hair back with her hand and stood by the stove buttoning her blouse. "Is the kettle warm yet, Ambrose?" she asked, watching him light his second cigarette of the day. "Me eyes feels like they're scabbed right over. Must be from them bloody mats."

"Warm? Ya knows he's warm, maid — what a silly thing for a woman to say. I been up and had the fire lighted for a hour or more."

A thick, tangy smell of woodsmoke hung in the kitchen.

She lifted the tin kettle off the stove and took it to the washstand. "I heard ya when ya got outta bed, my son. You've only been up 'bout half an hour yet." She tipped the spout into the washpan but there was only a dribble. "Ambrose, the kettle is full a ice!"

"Put 'en back on the stove then."

"Well, no water. Very good, boy." She flattened her palms in the pan, soaking up enough water to daub on her face. After wiping off the dampness she hung the towel on a nail above the stand, then knelt on one knee and combed her hair while looking in the bottom cupboard. "How 'bout a couple a eggs for breakfast?" she asked.

He was busy with his knife and file, rubbing his thumb over the edge of the blade every so often to test its sharpness. Said with the cigarette on his lip, "Eggs — where'd the eggs come from?"

Ida grinned. "I'm too much of a lady to tell ya that, Ambrose, but I will tell ya that Aunt Nel brought me a dozen yes'day. Said her hens is layin' more'n she and Alfred can eat and if I wants any more just to let her know."

He rasped the knife on his knee some more and cut a notch in the chair. "Ain't had a egg that long now I wud'n know what to do with 'en."

"Betcha you'd know what to do with the hens though."

Ambrose grunted. "Go and get Martin up and put on two apiece for us."

"Don't warry — I'm up, my son," Martin said, yawning, going to the table and taking a sweet biscuit from the plate.

"Got me knife sharpened yet or what?"

His father pushed the file harder, the minute filings dropping in a grey powder onto his knee. "Your knife — who's gonna trust you with a knife?" he laughed banefully. "Not me for sure."

The old man knew nothing about the I.X.L. and Martin had never trusted him enough to show it to him. "How 'bout me rope then?" he said. "Ya got a rope ready for me, I s'pose."

"Oh yes, I got your rope ready. Seein' ya got n'ar knife you'll have to use the gaff. I'll do the stickin'. Perhaps I'll even let ya use *my* knife if ya behaves yourself." He muttered to himself, "Don't know what that means, he don't."

"Where's the butter, Ambrose?" his wife asked. "I thought I put it on the table last night 'fore I went to bed." She moved a dishcloth on the cupboard and checked inside the breadbox.

"Butter's in the oven, maid." He sheathed his knife, put it on the end of the cupboard and brushed the filings off his knee.

"In the oven? Sure that's all gone to oil now!" She pulled down the hot door. "Look! Instead of using a knife to put it on your bread, now you'll have to use a spoon!"

Ambrose pulled back the damper and spat his butt in. Hacked a few times and spat again. Sat at the table and waited to be fed.

Good Friday was considered a religious holiday everywhere in Newfoundland — a day without work. A day to dress up, attend church, eat salt herring and potatoes for dinner, eat canned fruit and jelly for supper and keep the water in the washpan until Saturday morning. To eat red meat on Good Friday meant disaster befalling the family, and to throw water outdoors was believed to be the same as throwing it in the Saviour's face.

Seal hunting, however, was not considered regular work, because the seals had no choice but to come south when they did. These fat balls of white fur crawling helplessly on the ice like cats with broken backs were prime targets for landsmen sealers with sticks and knives, but they had begun their moulting a week ago and in another week or two they would mature enough to escape into the water, forcing the sealers to launch their small boats and give chase. This was considered a last resort because the seals by then would be wild, and most times farther out to sea than the men could travel.

Ida asked Martin if he had enough clothes on. "For God's sake, boy," she said, "put enough on so ya don't get cold. Once ya gets on that ice, all ya got with ya is what ya got on your back."

"That's OK, Mom," he said after finishing his tea and toast. "I got enough on now. Can't put on too much or I won't be able to move."

She took one of his boots from the warmer above the stove and put her hand inside. "Your logans is a little wet," she said. "Should a come home earlier last night — at least they'd a been dry by now. When your feet is cold, everything is cold."

Martin had heard stories about sealers getting lost on the ice, some freezing to death and others losing their limbs to frostbite, talking crazy talk and walking deliriously into the open sea after being adrift on an ice pan for days on end. He was wearing his thick worsted stockings that his grandmother had knitted, but took another pair off the nail in the wall behind the stove and pulled them on too — just in case.

"Hurry up, my son," Ambrose said, taking his black nylon ski jacket from another nail below that one. "Don't be all day puttin' on your boots now! Hurry up — c'mon!"

Martin sat on the edge of the daybed and leaned forward. His two shirts and lined windbreaker inside his nylon parka nipped him across the gut and he spoke in a strained voice. "Soon be ready, Dad. Soon's I gets 'em laced up."

"Well, hurry up then, 'cause Garf is gonna be over the once 'fore ya knows it! I can guarantee you he won't be waitin' for ya!"

"I know, Dad. You already told me."

Ambrose put his cap on, pulled the ears down and left the house.

Ida ran behind him. "Hold on, Ambrose! I got some salt herrin' took out. Think ya might be home for dinner?"

He stopped by the corner of the house. Smoke from the stovepipes blew to the ground and buried him. "Don't know," he said through the cloud. "'Tis not likely, but if we're not, well, put another water on 'em and we'll have 'em for supper. That's if we gets back time enough. If we don't, well, I s'pose we can have 'em for lunch 'fore we goes to bed."

"Want a few greens to go with 'em or don't ya?"

"None left. Eat the last of 'em couple a weeks ago."

Ida went back in and cut off ten slices of white bread, topped them with molasses and shoved them in a wrinkled brown paper bag.

"Martin boy, don't use your father's knife today," she said. "'Cause if ya cuts yourself out there on the ice off Cape Bauld, 'tis not the same as here in the house, y'know. Ya might bleed to death before ya gets halfway in. Now promise me ya won't use his knife!"

The boy stretched his black tossel-cap on his head and

kissed her. "Don't warry, m'dear, I won't use Dad's knife. I promise."

Ida poured black tea from the teapot into a white porcelain jug, spooned in four teaspoons of sugar and stirred with the knife, then took a flat fifteen-ounce bottle with a bull's head on its white label from the bottom cupboard.

A month or so ago Ambrose, having run out of homebrewed beer, had invited a few of his friends over for a store-bought drink, a game of cards and a scoff. He didn't play — he didn't know how — yet the party had been a success, with his wife keeping score. The men were contented to play without him; the low alcoholic Beef, Iron and Wine — a real non-prescription medicine — tasted sweet, the mutton tasted salty and Ambrose was glad he had someone to talk to. Ida saved the bottle.

Now she filled it with tea from the jug and tucked it inside two worsted stockings. "There," she said. "Should still be warm when they drinks it." She brought Ambrose's green packsack from the porch and put the lunch inside, along with a box of matches, a blue checkered shirt, a pair of stockings and a handful of raisins wrapped in brown paper.

Ambrose, with a full cigarette in his mouth, left the outhouse on the edge of the hill, coughed loudly and shut the door. He tugged on his overalls from behind and kicked his leg out several times to adjust his underwear. A carpet of snow ridges that the wind had drifted into hard waves lay from here to his snowmobile garage a little over fifty feet away. He kicked one and broke its crest.

Low drifting on the harbour indicated that the storm had passed, and Karpoon Island, half a mile in the distance, was clearly visible, its whitened hills glistening in the early morning sunlight. The high headland in the east rose above the barren tundra and cast an ominous shadow across the snowy foothills and onto the harbour ice. Sunburst orange trapped like cooling lava between phantom silhouettes on the snowy slopes reflected an infinite beauty, and shrubbed evergreens clinging to their walled fortress on the side of the headland basked in the freezing warmth of colour. Always first to see the crimson rays of a rising sun, the big hill shimmered and sparkled while the quiet town soaked in a strange, subdued light.

Garf tipped the Ski-Doo on its side in the garage and knelt on his mitts. He checked the bogie wheels and spun them around at the end of their shafts, then drove a squirt of grease into each one with the grease gun.

Ambrose saw his son working on the snow machine. "What's wrong with her, Garf — broke, is she?"

"No, she's not broke, Uncle Am. The middle set of bogie wheels was tipped over, that's all. I just shoved a bit a grease in her there 'fore we leaves, but I daresay 'fore the spring is gone I'm gonna have to put a new wheel on her. I think one of the bearings is wore out."

Ambrose dragged on his cigarette. "Wore out?" His eyes fell on Martin near the workbench. "How come he's wore out?"

"Don't look at me," the boy said, "I didn't do it!"

"No, you wud'n do nothin' like that, would ya, you little angel!"

Garf let the Ski-Doo fall upright. "Nobody didn't do it, Uncle Am," he snapped. "I s'pose everything gotta wear out sometime, boy! 'Tis only a bloody old wheel anyway. Mr. Tucker got plenty of 'em down there."

"Wants plenty a money for 'em too," his father replied.

"A little wheel like that shouldn't be too dear — two or

three dollars I daresay. No more'n that for sure."

Ambrose drew down a gutful of tobacco smoke and blew it across the garage. "You don't know Mr. Tucker so well as I do, Garf. Long's he's makin' money off a ya he's number one — you can have anything ya wants, but his two or three dollars for somethin' can change into five or six dollars pretty fast."

Garf grasped the two skis and pulled the snowmobile around. "Wheel's good for the rest of the spring anyhow," he said. "Gets round to it we'll put a new one on her next fall."

The cold morning air on Ida's naked arms did not daunt her as she walked down the narrow footpath to the garage. She kept one hand — the one holding Ambrose's knife — on her behind to prevent the wind from blowing her dress up and held his packsack in the other. "Here's your lunch, Ambrose," she said. "You'd forget your head if he wud'n on your shoulders."

"Give it here, Mom," Martin offered. "I'll stick it in the head a the Ski-Doo."

"Now Martin, you behave yourself today," she warned. "Here Ambrose, take your knife." She placed it in his hand and peeked through the frost on the windshield. "My my," she said. "You fellers won't see where you're goin' through that sure. Be off the path in no time! Why don't ya get a rag and wipe it over?"

"Behave?" Ambrose had obviously missed the knife and windshield part of what she had said and was more concerned with what the day might bring. He wrinkled his brow and made a firm jaw. "I can see the trouble we're gonna have now," he said. "'Fore we starts. See it just like a open book!"

Martin looked at his father and grinned. "But you can't read!"

"Boyohboyohboy! We got it comin' to us today, no mistake no mistake! Same thing as facin' a firin' squad!"

Ida gripped her husband's arm. "Look after 'en Ambrose, for God's sake, and don't let 'en outta your sight!"

He took the last draw from his cigarette and flicked it into the air. Made a low guttural sound, blowing smoke from his nose. "I can try, Ida, but he's not gonna listen to me anyway. If he was only a bit sensible ———"

"Don't warry 'bout it," Martin said nastily. "I can look after meself!"

Ambrose pushed a finger up his nose and rooted. Laughed mockingly. "How ya figure that, my son? You ain't got sense enough to carry guts to a pig, let alone look after yourself!"

"If I kills more seals'n you, what would ya do?"

Ambrose fiddled with his privates through his clothes and shook his leg again. "I guess that'd be the day I give up smokin'."

"Look, Dad," the boy said with sincerity. "If someday I didn't come back to this house, what would ya say?"

Ida gave her husband a dirty look. "Stop rootin' yourself, Ambrose, for the love a God!" She turned on Martin. "And you," she admonished, "you better watch what you're sayin'! Anything can happen off there on that friggin' ice so be careful what ya says! Anyhow, be better if ya stayed the hell in out of it!" She spun on her heel and went to the house.

"What would I say?" his father asked, looking directly into his eyes. "I don't know what I'd say." Now he seemed to be thinking. "What would I say — I'd say you wud'n hungry."

"Come on, boys," Garf said. "Give it up." He pulled out

the choke lever at the side of the carburettor, hauled on the cord twice, and the eight-horsepower Rotax burst into life. The engine sputtered with too much fuel and died. He clicked the choke off, squeezed the trigger to the handle and hauled again, a blue cloud rising underneath the snowmobile when it started. The gassy smoke filled the garage as he accelerated and moved forward.

Ambrose strapped his knife to his waist and stared across the harbour into the wind, talking to himself. "I don't know I don't know. I just don't know!"

Garf turned the key and stopped the Ski-Doo near the sled at the corner of the bunkhouse.

"Can I drive her down to the cape this marnin'?" Martin asked with his hand on the throttle. He licked his lips and waited for the likely answer.

"Not this marnin' no," his father said as politely as he could. "We're in a rush so Garf is gonna drive her."

With more confidence than knowledge, Martin said, "I can drive her just as good as Garf, y'know. All ya gotta do is nip the trigger and hold on!" He saw a wild look come on his father's face.

"Nip the trigger and hold on," Ambrose said with indignation. "Simple as that, is it — nip the trigger and hold on? Well, that's why the wheel is broke on her. That's why Garf gotta be fixin' her all the time — 'cause *you* got her smashed up!"

"Smashed up? Go 'way with ya, boy! I know I got her smashed up, mind now!" His voice rose. "I bet John Parsons lets Alec drive *his* Ski-Doo! So why can't I drive yours?"

Ambrose said wearily, "'Cause Alec got more sense'n you got, that's why!"

Garf sat on the snowmobile seat and listened.

"Well, can I have her some other time for a few hours or so — y'know, take her for a ride round the harbour or somethin'?"

"No my son!"

"Why can't I have her, Dad?"

"'Cause ya can't and that's that!"

"I'll steal her!"

"That'd be the only way you'll get her."

"Come on, Dad boy," Martin begged. "Don't be so foolish. I can handle the Ski-Doo. I'll be careful!"

"Foolish?" Ambrose boomed. "You're calling *me* foolish? You're the one who's foolish, my son! And take your hand off that trigger! Next thing you'll have her flooded!"

Garf brushed the frost crystals off the windshield. "You can drive, Martin," he said. "If that's what ya wants to do, just take your time and watch where you're goin'. Nothin' to it."

Martin grinned at his father almost mockingly.

Ambrose looked at Garf as though he had ten heads. He was lost for words.

"If ya wants to get on the Ski-Doo with Martin, Uncle Am ____"

"Well no, my son," he jumped in. "I'm not gettin' on no Ski-Doo with Martin! I don't wanna be killed — not yet anyway! The few miserable days I got left in this world now, I wants to live 'em in one piece." He turned around to walk down the hill to the ice.

"Well, you can get on the sled then," Garf suggested. "That's no problem. And I'll get on with Martin."

Ambrose stopped. "The sled?" He blew his nose, then sniffed hard several times, the cords at the side of his neck bulging through the skin. "A very good place to put me," he said. "Be killed 'fore I gets halfway 'cross the harbour."

"Whaddaya mean?" Garf said, the whites of his eyes setting off his dark features.

Ambrose shook his head. "Won't be on the sled two minutes 'fore Martin has me brains beat out."

"Don't ya talk so silly, Uncle Am." Garf took the plastic T-handle of the pull cord in his hand. "Look," he said. "If it'd make ya feel any better, I'll get on the sled and you get on the Ski-Doo. Be more comfortable for ya that way."

"No, I'll get on the sled, I s'pose. Don't look like I got much choice, do it?" Ambrose blinked a few times and said angrily and dejectedly, "Tell Martin to stop for me down under the hill!" He disappeared around the corner and Garf started the engine.

"Here ya go, Martin," he said. "When I gets the sled hooked on, you can give it to her."

Martin slithered up the red leather seat and gripped the handlebars. Garf hooked the sled onto the hitch and got on with him. Martin nipped the trigger slowly until the engine revved enough to engage the spinning clutch, moved to the top of the hill and let the snowmobile coast to the bottom, where his father's overturned fishing boats lay buried near his stage with just their keels sticking through the snow.

As he drove the Ski-Doo across the frozen wasteland to the other side of the harbour his head spun with the excitement. What a feeling! He was in control now and Garf was only a passenger. He glanced back at his father kneeling on the sled and holding onto the two wooden horns at the front — used as supports for carrying firewood — as though his life depended on them. Watching Martin looking back at him and laughing, the old man believed his life did depend on them.

At the other side of the harbour the Ski-Doo path connected to Karpoon Island by an up-and-over approach to the ice-covered rocks on the shoreline.

"Watch out ya don't hook one of the skis," Garf yelled.

"What?" Martin yelled back through the sound of the snowmobile engine.

"Them ballycaters there in front a ya — be careful ya don't tip us over!"

Martin gunned the throttle. The extra speed helped get them over the clumpers with less chance of a mishap but bounced the Ski-Doo and the sled around a little more heavily.

After they had driven for ten minutes, the snowmobile path ahead of them lay diagonally along a steep grade instead of up and over. This meant everyone would have to lean into the slope to keep the Ski-Doo on a straight course, or at least prevent it from sliding off the path. Martin stood on the running boards and quickly shifted his weight to one leg and pulled the handlebars into the hill. He brought his other leg around and almost struck Garf in the mouth with his boot. Snow flew from the skis. He dropped one knee onto the seat and hauled harder.

Iron shoes on the sled runners cut and shaved the snow, rolled it and turned it to powder. Martin adjusted his weight again, his head spinning with the thought of the sled slipping off the path and dragging the snowmobile off the hill, maybe even tipping it over.

Near the top he saw a long stick in the middle of the path. Six feet long, with an iron hook and a spike jutting from one end. He shouted to Garf, "Someone lost their gaff!"

With the engine racing, Garf shouted, "What?"

"Right there ahead," Martin yelled. "Gaff in the path!"

He was worried that he might not have enough room to pass it, but if he did he could stop at the top of the hill and walk back for it. He knew that without a gaff a sealer would have to depend on someone else to kill seals for him, so it was the right thing to do, he thought — walk back and pick it up.

Garf suspected that Martin had seen something ahead so he leaned farther off the snow machine and into the hill. "Don't run over it for God's sake," he yelled at the top of his lungs when he saw the gaff. "Or you'll tear the track off her! Go to the one side!"

Martin hauled the skis to the left, missing the gaff by a mere inch.

Garf leaned inwards as far as he could, one hand trailing the snow and the other keeping him on the lopsided snowmobile. "Keep against her, Martin," he bawled. "Keep against her!"

Ambrose saw what was happening and jumped off the sled and ran alongside. He pulled on the horns to help keep it on the path, but the Ski-Doo seemed to have a mind of its own and preferred to go down the hill.

Martin had the choice of either turning sharply for a direct run to the bottom, or keeping the skis as they were and flipping the snowmobile. He turned.

Ambrose realized the boy's decision and jumped back on the sled again, fully aware that his help would be needed to get the Ski-Doo back to the top. Nearly halfway down, the snowmobile picked up enough speed to make the vertical shale rocks, projecting through the snow and now zooming by, look life-threatening as his son steered through the network of havoc and possible mutilation.

"Hold on to her boy, for God's sake!" Garf shouted,

grabbing onto the backrest and digging his toes in the running-board straps.

Martin looked behind at his father holding tightly onto the horns, with his foot over the side scooping a channel in the snow and sending a barrage of powder above the sled as he tried to slow the runaway snowmobile. Their eyes did not meet. Instead, Ambrose was focused on the six-inch nail used in place of the proper hitching pin that Garf had misplaced during a sled disconnection. Nails had a tendency to work loose so Ambrose gripped the horns tighter. If it came out —

Almost to the clearing, the old man's eyes widened in terror. The nail had worked to the top and now balanced there like a matador's sword in a dying bull. Then it popped out. The drawbar slipped from its socket, dug deep into the snow and, with the momentum, drove the sled high in the air and held it impaled like some wild beast atop an iron spear. Ambrose sailed through the morning air like a cat tossed out a two-storey window, taking both horns with him. When he landed, one horn hooked in his coat and tore it from the waist to the elbow. His cap flew off as he rolled onto the snow, twisted and bent, trying to bring himself to a halt while he tumbled over and over like a drunken acrobat, finally skidding to a stop face down in a snowbank thirty yards from the snowmobile.

Martin swung the Ski-Doo around in the clearing at the base, jumped off and ran back to his father. "Dad, is ya hurted?"

Garf stumbled to the scene and screeched a string of words only a Newfoundlander would understand. "MyGodUncle-Amisyakilledboyor'enya?" He brushed lightly at the snow on his father's back as if he was afraid to touch him.

Ambrose stirred, groaned and rolled onto his side.

"Uncle Am, Uncle Am," Garf said, full of pity for his father. "You killed, boy? Not killed, is ya?"

Ambrose wiped the snow off his face and said in a stupor, "Killed? Yes I'm killed!" He stood up, his legs wobbling like those of a newborn calf.

"What happened, Dad?" Martin asked with half a smile.

"Happened? What *happened*? What ya *think* happened?"

Martin looked his father squarely in the face and hoped he could keep himself from laughing. "Nail come out, did it, Dad?"

Ambrose whisked the snow from his coat and held his torn sleeve open. "I don't think I'll ever be the same," he said. "I got meself shook right to pieces."

Garf brushed more snow from the old man's back. "Well, long's you're not hurt, Uncle Am — that's the main thing."

Ambrose straightened and cleared his head. "Whaddaya mean — not hurt? My son, I believe I got every bone in me body smashed off!" He brushed his overalls with one of his mitts. The other one lay on the snow fifteen yards up the hill. "Look," he said, examining his condition. "Ya wud'n know but a team a dogs got fast to me!" He glared at the wide-eyed youngster. "What's *you* lookin' at?" he said. "I s'pose you thinks this is funny, do ya?" He pointed to his torn jacket. "Don't look very funny to me!"

"Not funny at all, Dad," Martin replied gravely. "Nothin' funny 'bout it."

Ambrose continued brushing his clothes. "Boyohboy-ohboyohboy! I don't know what's gonna become a ya — I don't know I don't know I don't know! Your name'll go farther'n you'll ever go yourself, my son!" He rubbed his head and groaned. "Oohhh, I believe I got me head split

abroad." He looked at his hand. "What? No blood," he said.
"That's a funny queer thing. Got me brains beat out and
n'ar stain a blood to show for it!"

Martin skinned the cap back on his father's head. "You're
gonna be all right, Dad. Next time, hold onto the harns
tighter. And don't fall off!"

Garf turned his back to the old man, smiled and walked
up the hill.

"Next time?" Ambrose's voice took on a high pitch.
"There's not gonna be a next time, brudder — you can count
on that!" He fixed his cap. "You're crazy, my son! Gone
right clean and clever off your block altogether! Young man
got hisself throwed away! A proper lunatic! A proper
meaniac!"

Martin tried not to laugh. "Just put it out of your mind,
Dad; just think like 'twas a bad dream. Forget it ever happened."

"A dream?" Ambrose squealed. "A dream? My son, this
is no dream! I'll never forget this — not so long as I lives!"
He looked around the snow and patted his pockets. "God,"
he said in a fit of anguish. "Hope I didn't lose me baccy."

Garf rooted in the snow and found the nail, pulled the
drawbar from under the sled and let it fall to earth. He guided
it down the hill and secured it to the snowmobile again.

"C'mon Dad, jump on." Martin pulled the starter cord.

"Jump on," he said. "Is you foolish or gonna be?" Ambrose
saw the smirk on the boy's face and figured that, if he got
on the sled again, Martin would have him right where he
wanted him. "No," he said firmly, "I'm not gettin' on her if
you drives. Let Garf drive and I'll get on — not before!"

"I'll be careful this time, Dad — honest!" He pulled the
starter cord.

Ambrose stuck a horn back in and tapped it down with the other one. His torn coat flapped in the breeze. "No, I'm not gettin' on."

"Get on, Dad — c'mon now. That gaff was in the middle of the path, boy. 'Twas a accident. I had to haul her clear. I made a mistake."

"You're the mistake," he said. "If your mother'd listened to me when you was barn she'd a went the work and drowned ya in the slop pail."

"Come on, Martin, set her goin'!" Garf's eyes went uneasy. "All the seals'll be killed by the time we gets there!"

"Gettin' on, Dad?"

"Nope."

"Come on, boy!"

"No, Martin, I said! I'm not gettin' on that sled if you drives. Now, how many times have I gotta tell ya? Only a few minutes to the cape so you fellers can go on — I'll walk."

This was turning into a problem, Martin thought. He hauled on the cord again. The engine caught then died. He hauled twice more. "What's wrong with her?" he asked Garf. "Flooded or what?"

"Perhaps she's not gettin' her gas," Garf said, flicking his mitt at the plastic hose to the carburettor. "Choke her. We been here now long enough for her to get cold. Choke her!"

Ambrose stuck the other horn in the junk, hammered it down with the heel of his hand and drove it deeper into the hole. "He's good at that, Garf — chokin'."

Martin flicked the choke on and hauled continuously until his breath came in short gasps. He let the greasy, plaited cord snap back into its metal housing. "I can't haul no more, Garf," he panted. "You have a spell at it."

"The spark plug is dirty," Garf said. "That's what's wrong with her. I'll take 'en out and have a look at 'en."

Ambrose sat on the sled and pulled out his tobacco. "Sure he got it tore to pieces. I told ya what he had done with it just now and ya wud'n listen to me! Anyway, I'm havin' a smoke for meself and then I'm gonna walk on down the cape. You fellers can do as ya please."

Garf raised the small flap underneath the windshield and pulled out a hammer helved with seven inches of hockey stick handle, and a screwdriver, its flat tip looking like a chipped tooth. Also inside this built-in toolbox were several old spark plugs, a piece of sandpaper and two small open-end wrenches. He placed the tip of the screwdriver at the base of the spark plug and tapped it lightly with the hammer to unseat it. The notched corners on the plug showed that he had used these tools for this reason before, and after a few twists with his thumb and finger he had the plug out.

Ambrose lit his cigarette and threw down the burning match. A small streak of soot appeared on the snow — a sure sign of neighbouring mild weather.

"Look," Garf said, holding the spark plug for all to see. "I told ya what the trouble was — hair 'tween the points."

Long draws shortened the cigarette in Ambrose's mouth. "What's a hair doin' 'tween the points?" He knew nothing about engines and never wanted to learn.

Garf scraped the sandpaper over the plug and slipped it back and forth under the ignition point. He blew several hard breaths on it to loosen any dirt accumulated near the coned porcelain, then stuck it back in and turned it hand-tight. He used the same implements to seat it. "Now boys," he said. "We're ready again."

The smoke from Ambrose's nostrils trailed behind him like the breath of a snorting bull. "Just as well for me to walk on," he said. "Take me time and dodge away."

"Hold on now till we sees if she's gonna go," Martin said. "We might have to walk 'long with ya."

Ambrose turned his back, tucked his mitts under his arm and groped for his penis, stooped slightly with it between his finger and thumb and moaned with relief as the steam from his urine disappeared into the wind. He felt the heat from the cigarette butt on his lip and spat it out. "'Nother one gone to hell," he said. "And lots more to chase 'en."

Garf hauled on the cord and the engine started. "Here, Martin, take her 'fore she cuts off again. And give it to her goin' up the hill this time and don't slow down for nothin' — not even the devil hisself!"

"What 'bout Dad?"

"No, not even for him!"

"No, I didn't mean it like that," the boy said. "I meaned, y'know — is he gonna get on the sled or what?"

Garf walked back to the sled. "OK, Uncle Am my son, get on her if you're goin'!"

"No," Ambrose said. "I'm not gettin' on." He bent his knees, looked down, shook his penis and tucked it away. "I'm not crazy, y'know!"

"No, I knows you're not crazy, Uncle Am. Geez, I s'pose none of us is crazy for that matter!"

Ambrose pointed at Martin. "*He* is!"

"I only told ya ——"

"I knows what ya told me, Garf — I knows what ya said! I might be half blind but I'm not deaf!"

"Well, what's ya gonna do then — gettin' on the sled or ain't ya? We're gonna want some help gettin' up over that hill again, and if ya leaves to walk, me and Martin'll never get down the cape today!"

"Look at 'en," Ambrose said. "I gets on that sled, this time he'll kill me for sure. That's what he wants to do, y'know!"

"Don't ya be so foolish, Uncle Am! You're up in age 'nough to have better sense."

Martin had heard Garf talk down to his father several times before, but not since Garf had moved out.

"Sense?" Ambrose questioned with his eyebrows drawn together.

"Yes — sense," Garf replied. "And you got none. Now is ya gonna get on the sled or have we gotta go without ya?"

"Well, that takes the cake," Ambrose said. "I never thought. . . ."

"Well, what's it gonna be?"

Ambrose dug his eyes into Garf as if he had joined Martin in his lunacy. "You're just as bad as he is, ain't ya?" He brushed his overalls as he strode forward and looked at the nail in the drawbar, then reached down and ran his fingers over the tip. He grunted something unintelligible.

Garf turned and smiled into the wind. He would not dare let his father know he was laughing at him.

Reluctantly, the old man stepped onto the sled. "Now Martin, for God's sake — take your time!"

"You got it, Dad!"

Garf sat aboard and the snow machine jumped and moved forward.

Martin turned the skis and picked up the path once more. He looked over his shoulder and caught the dirtiest look his father could throw his way. At the base of the hill he nipped the trigger to the handle and the butterfly went horizontal. Gasoline mist sprayed into the carburettor and the Ski-Doo began the climb, the roar of the engine drowning his wild laughter. He hoped that his father wouldn't be too mad at him today, and that he would forgive him for his poor driving. After all, it was Good Friday.

7

ON THE CRIMSON PATH

Martin found a parking spot, turned off the engine and went stiff on the seat. "That black off there," he exclaimed, "is that seals?"

Garf snatched his gaff off the Ski-Doo, held it by the hook and slid his other hand up and down the shaft, peeling the snow away in quick jerks. "Yes, that's seals," he said gently, as though the furry mammals would hear him. "Perhaps a million!"

"A million?" The boy could not believe his eyes, and thought Garf must have meant ten million. The great herd of harp seals from Baffin Bay now lay no more than half a mile off the land, smothering the ice all the way to Belle Isle in the northeast, and west to Sacred Island. Nearly two hundred square miles of hot-blooded creatures crawled like black maggots on the floating mass of ice.

"Go and get your gaff off the sled," Garf instructed. "And pray to God that the wind don't drop out!"

Ambrose tugged on the frozen rope around the two gaffs on the sled.

Martin yanked the lost gaff from the snowmobile. He had stopped at the top of the hill and walked back for it despite his father's inclination to move on.

"Here, gimme that," Garf said. "Perhaps somebody down by the whistle house owns it. Go and help your father with the other gaffs like I said. I'm goin' on down and have a look around." He slung his hauling rope on his back and ran down the hill in long strides, heels digging into the hard snow.

Ambrose pried the knots open and handed Martin one of the gaffs. Used as a killing instrument, this stick could beat a young harp's skull to pieces with one smack. The hook allowed the sealer an easy way to pull seals together in a pile, and the pointed tip could prevent him from slipping when he jumped from pan to pan. Used as a lifesaver, the gaff could prevent a man from going under the ice if he fell through, and could help him pull himself back to safe ground.

Ambrose slammed into the whistle house to break his run down the hill. "Whaddaya see, my son?" he said to John Parsons, who was looking through his binoculars.

John flashed a toothless smile. "Sees you trying to kill yourself," he said. "Shouldn't run into the wall like that or you could knock the whistle house off its foundation."

"Main patch, I wonder?"

"Here, Ambrose, have a look for yourself." He held the binoculars out.

"Sure that's no good to me, boy; I'm not able to see nothin' outta that!"

"Ya got one good eye, Ambrose," he said. "When it comes to lookin' out of a pair a spyglasses, that's all ya wants." He looked at Martin and winked.

The boy had never seen binoculars before but had heard of them. "Mind if I have a look?" he asked.

"Look away, my son. No trouble to see a seal; that's one thing for sure."

"Careful ya don't drop 'em, Martin," Ambrose warned, taking out his chewing tobacco and stuffing a small pinch into his cheek. He peered around the corner and saw that Garf was waiting for them at the path leading down to the gulch. "I'm havin' a smoke now," he said. "And Garf is just gonna have to wait."

John took a package of Export A cigarettes from inside his sweater and stared curiously at the old man's coat flapping in the wind. "What happened, Ambrose? Looks like ya hooked into somethin'."

No response. The old man was reliving his trip down the hill.

"Put your baccy back in your pocket," John said. "'Tis hard enough to smoke that stuff, let alone eat it." He held out the green pack. "Here, have a tailor-made."

Ambrose's face seemed to glow. He pulled out a perfectly round cigarette, pushed it under his nose and smelled the richness. "How 'bout you?" he asked, sticking it in his mouth. "You havin' one or what?"

"Two days now," he said with a spark of pride. "Tryin' to give 'em up but 'tis hard. Still carries 'em with me though. Don't know why — but I do."

"My God!" The binoculars shook in Martin's hand. "Just look, Dad, 'tis worth your while to have a look! I can see 'em with their mouths open and everything! And the men — everything looks so handy!"

John kicked his feet together. "Alec is gone off there somewhere. See if you can spy 'en."

Martin scanned the ice. "Who'd he go with?"

"No one. I told 'en to buddy up with someone in case he fell in the water, but 'fore the words was outta me mouth he took off like a streak a shit through a tin whistle. His mother was the same way."

Ambrose lit his cigarette. "That Alec, boy," he said with his mouth clouded in smoke, "he sure knows what a gaff is for."

"Gaff — he got n'ar gaff with 'en, my son!" John pointed to the one leaning against the building. "That's his gaff there," he said. "Garf just brought it down over the hill to me."

Ambrose felt disappointed that his older son had not waited. "Bad thing for a man to do," he said, "go off on that ice with n'ar gaff. And 'tis a bad thing when ya don't stick together. Where's Garf?"

"Down below. Said he'd wait for yez there."

The wind roared through the gully that led to the frozen sea. Using their gaffs as walking sticks, Martin and his father dug their chins into their shoulders to protect themselves from the uprooted ice particles. Martin felt his toenails dig back into his toes as the path suddenly lost elevation. "I don't think Garf would leave us, Dad. He's prob'ly down on the ballycaters waitin' for us right now. But that's only what I thinks."

"Think," his father said disgustingly. "You're always thinkin'! That's why you're like you is, my son!"

"I thinks, yes, when I got somethin' to think 'bout."

"Well, why don't ya think 'bout the way you acts sometimes then?"

Martin chewed on his bottom lip and said, with a mouthful of resentment, "You don't understand very good, do ya, Dad?"

"Sure I understands," his father said with mild rudeness. "I understands you're three parts crazy. And that's good 'nough for me."

A sealer appeared at the end of the gulch with two small black seals on his hauling rope.

"How's the swiles?" Ambrose asked.

The sweating sealer, tall and muscular with a silver-grey crewcut, dug his feet into the worn path and strained against the rope. He stopped abreast Ambrose, reached his hand farther down the rope and pulled the seals near his feet. "Aahhh, I got two here, boy," he said. "Would a took more but ol' Tucker's gonna get the money — not me." His breath came in short gasps. "And I'm not gettin' any younger."

"How's the ice?"

"Tight as a billy goat's arse," he replied.

"How's the seals?"

"Thousands! Millions!" He rubbed his forehead and wiped the sweat onto his knee. "First trip this marnin' or what?"

Ambrose's eyes turned on Martin. "We had trouble with the Ski-Doo."

"Well, better late'n never." The sealer wrapped the rope around his hand, flicked it over his shoulder and took up the slack. "Well, gotta keep movin'," he said. "Wish ya the best!" Martin and Ambrose stepped aside and let him pass and he walked on, his logans turned sideways, slipping, searching for the best foothold, leaving moulded prints like uprooted plaster casts. Martin saw the rope sink deeper into his shoulder; saw the stretched necks of the seals rising and falling with his every step.

The path had now become crimson, holding the boy's attention as he continued his journey to the ballycaters. Farther down the numerous rifts and platforms, they met more sealers headed up the cape with their seals in tow.

The path became redder and ran through a pool of gory slush at the edge of the ballycater where Garf stood and leaned on his gaff. As he slid from the last rift to the landing, Martin lost his grip on his gaff and it rolled across the ice, stopping by a knob of hard ice near his brother's feet. "Finally made it," Garf said with some disdain about him. "'Bout time too!"

November gales had whipped the sea into a frenzy, had tossed it high into the air and pounded it against the rocky shoreline, where it had frozen on contact forming a thick layer of ice, a platform from which the sealers could slide directly to the rough Arctic ice below.

"Where was you fellers at?" Garf asked, cocking his head. He tapped his knife handle and looked over the edge. "I thought yez was lost somewhere."

Ambrose did not bother to answer.

A shout from atop the rift, "Wait for me, boys; I'm goin' off with ya!" Paddy Mitchell threw his gaff ahead of him to the platform and slid down, stopping a foot short of the bloody puddle. He picked himself up and smiled at Ambrose. "Don't mind some company, do yez?" He stepped lively onto the ballycaters and drove his gaff spike into the ice.

"No," Garf answered with a reminiscent grin. "Got no moonshine to give ya though."

Paddy pushed his glasses up, looking slightly embarrassed. "Got carried away, boy," he said.

Garf sat on the edge of the ballycater readying for the slide to the sea ice. "Just jokin' with ya, Paddy boy. You can go off with us, yes."

"No need for a man to go off there by hisself," Ambrose

reassured him. "Only askin' for trouble!"

Paddy held Ambrose's arm out and let it drop. "Fell off the sled again, I see."

Ambrose looked away, wishing Paddy hadn't been the one to find him stranded on the open tundra a month ago with a torn jacket and a bleeding nose, after his sled struck a bump and threw him off. Garf hadn't noticed him gone until he reached their woodcutting lot three miles beyond the Karpoon hills, so it had been Paddy who took him there.

Martin snickered, unaware of the incident.

"Glasses with ya, Paddy?" Garf asked.

"Don't take 'em with me on the ice, boy. 'Fraid I might lose 'em." He tapped Martin on the shoulder from behind. "Got your knife sharpened or what?"

Garf disappeared over the ballycaters.

"Oh yes, got it sharpened purpose for today," the boy replied.

Ambrose sat on the ice cliff, ready to make the slide. "He ain't got n'ar knife, Paddy my son — that's a lie for 'en. I told 'en he's not to be trusted with a knife and no more he's not!" The old man stared at the ice below. Twenty feet looked a long way down.

"OK Dad," Martin said. "Jump and get it over with!" Didn't seem to be said in the right context, he thought.

Ambrose slid down the ice wall and came to a stop near Garf's feet.

The boy sat on the edge, tossed his gaff over and skidded to the bottom.

His father picked the stick up and returned it. "Don't ever throw 'way your gaff, my son — what's wrong with you at all! Could save your life sometime!"

Paddy slid onto the dry, rifted slob like an old seal, arms

outstretched and snow packed on his face like a cream pie. To see again he had to remove his glasses and clean them on the lapel of his thick cotton shirt.

Garf sucked air through his teeth. "Now boys," he said, pointing to a big pressure ridge of raftered ice that had looked minuscule from the platform. "Once we gets past there we should be into the fat."

They walked and ran in single file, jumped and fell on the rough ice, following the crimson path that ran all the way up the ridge and over the top. Almost to the wall of crushed ice and three hundred yards from the shore, Martin thought he heard something. "Hark," he said to Paddy loping along behind him. "What's that noise?"

Paddy cupped his ear. "Seals barkin'," he said.

The heads of two sealers dotted the ice above the pressure ridge, shouting — their words lost to the wind. They pulled their dead seals to the summit and pushed them off the other side in a quivering, sloshing stack of bloody hair and warm flesh. Stumbling and hurrying down the side, they all messed their bottoms with the mucky gore and grease but lost no time in shouldering their ropes again for the home stretch to the land.

"Looks like bad walkin'," Garf said as they met, wanting to know the ice conditions beyond the ridge. He motioned for his men to stand out of the path but Ambrose kept forging ahead and climbed to the top of the ridge.

The lead sealer rose his head, his hair a dense twisted growth of white curls. He slackened his rope with three seals at the end. Garf recognized him as Norm Andrews, the first man to leave the island, with his house tied to his motorboat and his ninety-year-old father falling and breaking his hip while climbing aboard. He had been instrumental in getting the others to move, through his daring efforts at putting his old house on long skids and pulling it two hundred feet across the field to the beach when everyone said it couldn't be done. He had hauled it ashore and set it up on the other side of the cove in Karpoon, near John's house, and after that he had helped launch six more.

Martin and Paddy stood admiring the plumpness of the seals and commented on the price they would bring. "Eight or ten a them seals'd put a man on his feet pretty quick," Paddy said. "Wud'n be long 'fore he'd be on the top shelf."

"Yuh," the sealer replied, throwing fidgety glances at Garf.

"How is they?" Paddy asked.

"Everywhere," he said, hesitant to talk.

Garf knew the reason for his silence, for he had once reminded this same man of his hasty departure from the island, and of how he had single-handedly destroyed a whole village with total disregard for his family and everyone else's. Old Mr. Andrews had died soon afterwards at the hospital in St. Anthony and, abiding by his wishes, his son had taken him back to the island for burial.

Paddy turned one of the seals onto its side and stroked the back with his hand. "Fat too, ain't they? Just like a ball a butter."

Garf directed his attention to the other man, a thin, sickly-looking chap with two seals behind him. "How's the path?" he said. "Looks kinda rough."

The sealer took off his tossel-cap and ran it over his face. "Path's not too good," he said hoarsely. He squinted through slitted eyes in a golden brown face, as if he were on the verge of becoming snow-blind. "Takes more'n two or three seals, you'll strain your balls."

Ambrose sat facing the wind atop the ridge, silhouetted

against a grey-blue sky, and sucked cigarette smoke down into his lungs like a diver sucking air just before plunging into the water. The wind crawled inside his torn jacket and puffed his back up like the side of a balloon. Behind him he could see the lighthouse, the whistle house, twenty or more men coming from the gulch and another ten waiting their turn to slide down the platform. On his right the ocean spread endlessly to the east, the northern and western horizons blotted only by Belle Isle and Sacred Island respectively.

Paddy and Martin climbed the ridge and stood straight on top. Garf was the last to crawl in over.

"Well, here they is, boys," Ambrose said, tossing his butt to the wind. "Lotsa gravy there, eh?"

Martin stood in awe, his mouth open and eyes glazed with excitement. Below them more than a hundred seal pups crawled on the ice, their soft whimpers mixed with the barks of old seals nearby, and less than two gunshots in the distance a thousand harps moved among bright trails of greasy blood. Fifty sealers walked through the great herd and prodded the young ones with their gaffs, trying to decide which and how many to kill. Fifty more had already wetted their blades and now knelt on bloodied patches of ice and strung the seals on ropes. Thirty yards to the right a sealer swung his gaff and broke it on the head of a small black seal. He cursed and threw it down, then plunged his knife into the writhing mammal and used what was left of the stick to bash in the heads of two more. Wiped his blade in the snow.

Directly ahead but parallel to the main path, a group of five sealers with taut ropes ingrained in their shoulders made their way over the jagged ice, painting a new path behind them. Their gaffs thumped and clinked on the hard ice clumpers and punched round holes in the snow as they searched for better footing. They talked loudly among themselves, and laughed and sang with the merriment of schoolchildren.

Garf's voice trembled with the confident expectation of recapturing his youth on the sealing ship *Arctic Flyer*. "Geez boy," he said. "'Tis a picture, ain't it? Just look at 'em. That's the same way we used to do it — one behind the other." He jumped off the pressure ridge and the others fell in line. Almost immediately he stopped and told his comrades, "No killin' until I says so, OK?" He told his father to take the lead while he spoke to Martin.

Then Ambrose said, "OK Paddy, you're with me." He might not know how to fix snowmobiles or be a great leader like Garf but he did know his older son. Martin would get a lesson in the sealing code of etiquette and procedures, a lesson that every first-time sealer must be taught or else learn on his own the hard way, and he preferred that Garf teach Martin rather than him learning it from the cruel North Atlantic.

Garf walked a little to the side of and behind Martin, with his head lowered and his eyes dug into the seals that yapped and whined like hungry dogs in a pound. He spoke in a soft voice, as if they could understand him. "Now Martin, we won't do no killin' here in this spot. What we'll do is run off there a little farther and see if we can luck into a couple a young hoods."

The boy tripped and fell on rough knobs of ice the size of two-gallon water buckets and shaped pretty much the same. His gaff slipped from his hand and he swore.

Garf helped him up and handed him the stick. "Take your time now," he said. "We'll slow down here and have a look and I'll show ya how to pick out the best ones." He pointed to a black and white seal near its mother. "See that one there? Anything like that is no good."

Martin shot a fearful look at the old seal snapping and growling, twisting and hunching her way towards them. "Geez Garf, ya mean the big one or the small one?"

"Small one," Garf said. "Big ones is no good." He corrected himself so the boy would understand. "The big ones is good, yes. 'Tis just that right now we're after the young ones 'cause they're easy to get at and brings the most money." He continued, while watching the old one, "That spotty-lookin' seal is not s'posed to be like that, y'know. He should be either black or white — not two colours."

"Sick, is he?" Martin asked.

Garf reached out and held the boy back from stepping onto the mother harp's territory. "No Martin," he said with a chuckle. "He's not sick — he's sheddin' his coat. When they gets like that 'tis better to leave 'em bide 'cause they're not worth much. Ya wants to pick out the ones that's fast-furred."

Paddy ran back through the herd and shouted, "What's we gonna do, boys — start killin' 'em now or what?"

Feeling he was qualified to answer, Martin said, "Not yet, Paddy! Wait till we gets out amongst 'em a little farther. Might be some hoods off there."

Garf grinned at the success of the lesson as they put on a burst of speed to catch Ambrose.

At the edge of the path a whitecoat whined and nudged its mother. The old seal turned on her side and welcomed her pup. It searched wildly for its breakfast in her belly fur, blowing steam from its tiny black nostrils. Then the whimpering stopped.

A young black seal lay wedged in the crevice of a split ice pan that had been forced from the water by the pressure of the ice, and it looked trapped. Martin stepped from the path, fitted his hand around the back flippers and pulled, but its sharp claws dug into the ice. The boy tightened his grip and tossed the harp onto the open pan, the seal rolling like a short log wrapped in a fur coat. It regained its balance and scurried back to the same place.

Garf stopped and watched his brother play with the seal for a moment. "OK, Martin," he said, still in his instructive tone, while watching Paddy gain on their father. "Let the seal bide there. You can haul 'en outta that a dozen times and he'll make back there every time."

Martin went to the path, expecting to hear more wisdom.

"Now," Garf said in a different tone, "we gotta keep movin'! Looks to me like there's nothin' here on this pan, only old ones and raggedy-jackets. We gotta get off where the big lot is." He started running, reached Paddy and passed him, then ran past Ambrose and kept going. The seals began to lose their numbers as he raced along, but a hundred yards off the barking grew louder.

About a rifle shot to westward, Ambrose saw a man standing on a pinnacle and waving his arms over his head. "Whaddaya 'low that feller is lookin' at up there?" he shouted back to Paddy.

The panting sealer ran up alongside and took his sealskin cap off his head. Pushed his glasses up. "Seals, I daresay!"

They both shielded their eyes from the glare of the ice and snow and shouted to Garf, stopping him in his tracks. Garf determined by their pointing arms that they had seen something curious. He had not heard their message, only a garbled, hollow noise like someone shouting with his head in a barrel. His back now to the wind, he stared at the man on the pinnacle, looked towards Cape Bauld and in the direction the man pointed. "Crowd a men runnin' off in there," he shouted back. "Might be hoods off here after all!"

The man on the pinnacle jumped down and disappeared behind the cluster of high clumpers.

"Go on, Garf," Ambrose bellowed, with a mad shooing motion of one arm. "See what's off there 'fore that crowd gets there first!"

Garf never heard his father's command but recognized the arm gesture, and took up the hard running pace again.

Martin joined his father and Paddy in the race. Slipping. Falling. He had planned to kill four or five seals but, tired now, thought how strenuous it would be to haul them ashore with blocks of ice piled everywhere.

The path became greasier and redder now, with small crimson trails leading into it like ragged tributaries into a main stream. Warm blood from the opened chest cavities of infant seals had melted the snow, making it sticky and wet and giving it the lustre of red plastic ribbons.

Martin played with his thoughts. Would Garf kill all the seals for his group? If his movement over the ice had been an indication of his intent, by the time he and Paddy caught him he would have slaughtered every seal he'd seen. If, when they arrived there, he had killed enough for them all, Martin assured himself that he would not muck ashore one seal that Garf had killed. He would kill his own seal, or go ashore with nothing in his hand but a gaff and an empty rope.

He liked to believe that the trouble between him and his father was not really a problem. He looked upon it as more of an inconvenience, in that he had no idea where he stood in relation to what was required of him. He knew there was no way he could please the old man no matter how he tried, so for the last year or so he had given up trying. Ambrose had always told him what to do and what not to do, although the boy did not necessarily understand the nature of it all. Most times he was utterly confused, for his father told him something one day and told him the complete opposite the next.

He had been nine years old when his father had told him that he intended to buy him a new snowmobile, from Mr. Tucker, as a Christmas gift that year, and that he could drive whenever he wanted to. Martin was delighted and waited for the snow to fall, but the cool autumn days on the island seemed longer than ever.

Then one day long after Christmas passed, with little hope left, he tramped home through the deep snow, swinging his bookbag by the strap, and as he approached his house he saw something yellow by the corner of the woodpile. He threw his bag to the side and ran as fast as he could, stood there for a moment and breathed in the bright colour. He had never seen a snowmobile before, but he had seen a picture of one, and of all the colours on the island that day none was as bright as the yellow cab on his Ski-Doo.

He was astonished at his reflection in the windshield, and smiled, licked out his tongue and rolled his eyes. At the front of the snowmobile were two long yellow skis with red tips, and as he sat on the red seat and gripped the handlebars, pretending to steer, he became the best driver in the world. He dug his top teeth into his bottom lip, shouting, "Voom, voom, varoom — va-*room!*" He beamed with excitement as his mind carried him across ponds, over hills and through gulches.

"Get off that Ski-Doo," he heard his father say. His journey into fantasyland ended and he drifted back to his nine-year-old reality. "Get off right now and get in the house!"

He wondered why his father didn't want him on the snow machine. Couldn't understand this at all. "Can I just stay here for a little while, Dad? I won't hurt her."

Ambrose stepped off the bridge without a jacket. His logan strings dragged in the snow as he charged towards him. "No, ya won't hurt her, no — you'll only pick her to pieces!"

"Can I just sit on her till Mom gets supper ready?"

"Come on, get off like I told ya! By'n by the once you'll be gone 'cross the bay on her and have her lost down through the ice!" He grabbed Martin's wrist and pulled. "Now get off her 'fore I gets mad with ya!"

"Please, Dad — please! You said 'twas my Ski-Doo!" He cast off his snowy mitts and held the handlebars tight. His eyes stung and he half swallowed a lump. Swallowed again but it didn't go down. "And you said I could drive her. You said, Dad — you said!"

Ambrose pried the boy's fingers off the rubber grips. "Don't ya be so foolish, my son! I never said no such nonsense. Now get off like I told ya!"

Martin held on with one hand but he was torn from the snowmobile, his bottom smacked all the way to the house. The boy flicked around his father and ran to the Ski-Doo, wiped his eyes on the back of his hand and hacked and spat on the windshield. In his same moment of glory he kicked the cowling, then turned and said, "Take your ugly Ski-Doo! And do whatever ya wants with her!" He ran to the house, jumped on the bridge and looked back at Ambrose wiping the spit off. "And you can shove her up your shitty arse!" He spat on the house. "And if ya don't know how, then I'll go in and get Garf to come out and show ya!"

Now, directly in front of Garf, an old bitch harp lunged to the path and halted. She growled and reared her head, showed a full set of serrated teeth that looked like the cutting edge of a lumberjack's crosscut.

A flock of squawking crows flew overhead.

Martin stopped running and confronted Paddy. "Look, that seal is gonna eat Garf if he goes any closer!"

Paddy almost ran him over, laughed and fixed his glasses. "Garf is not too concerned 'bout that old cow," he said. "He can eat ten like her." He frowned and ended off with a heavy breath as if he had been under water too long. "Boy, ya shouldn't stop in the middle of the path like that! S'posin' I knocked ya down and fell on ya?"

Martin laughed and blew some heavy breaths of his own. "Gotta get rid a that pelt ya got on ya, boy. All that weight's no good for ya!"

Paddy patted his stomach the way a mother would pat her baby. "Took a lot a grub off a Mr. Tucker's shelves to put that there," he said. "Be a sin to lose it all — a real sin."

Garf stopped, moved away from the old seal a bit and waited for his father.

Ambrose rushed up with a thin trace of sticky froth on his lips. "Where's they goin'?" he asked, his hand to his chest and wheezing fiercely as he fought to draw fresh air into his lungs. "Hoods?"

"Can't be," Garf replied. "Unless they're on the other side a the bight. If that's the case then we made a big mistake by comin' off here from Cape Bauld." Looked at the old man.

"You got that pain in your chest again, looks like."

"Where I was runnin'," Ambrose gasped. "Gets me breath, I'll be number one."

"Gonna go off farther or what?" Garf asked. "Don't see the need, but ———"

"This is far enough," his father said, reaching into his pocket. "I gotta have a smoke."

The old bitch rambled off the path on the same side she had entered from, and was soon lost among her twins.

Garf unzipped his coat halfway, and watched the runners loop and mesh among the clumpers until he could no longer see the whole group. He climbed a pinnacle and watched them further.

Ambrose lit his cigarette, sat on a small clumper and took off his cap. He punched with his fist and drove the crown into position.

"That ol' seal," Martin quizzed from fifty yards away. "He wud'n hurt ya, would he?" Added, "How would ya get 'en ashore if ya killed 'en anyway?"

Paddy stooped and petted a small white seal that kept staring at him. "You'd have a job to tow her in round," he said. "Best way's take the pelt and leave the carcass on the ice. The meat is no good anyway — too tough. But one time, though, you wud'n leave nothin' behind. People loved to get a piece a fresh seal meat no matter if 'twas young harp or old harp. Rough times then, boy — not like today." He tickled the seal's chin. "Looks some nice, don't they — almost a sin to kill 'em, ain't it?" His glasses fell down his nose. "Hurt ya?" Seemed he had just heard the boy's question. He stood and brushed the white hair off his palm. "Some a them ol' ones, my son, they'd tear ya limb from limb — that's if ya got 'em cornered. I wud'n trust 'em no further'n I could heave 'em." He looked at Martin and grinned. "And that's not very far."

Thin, dried films of tissue known as whelpin' bags lay everywhere. Big clots of blood and afterbirths like beef liver littered the yellow depressions, showing the places of birth. Old seals wobbled over the ice pans and sniffed their pups, fully aware they were being watched by human intruders. A white pup lay on his back, dreaming. Twitched his nose, shuddered and sighed. Martin knelt on one knee and rubbed his hand over its hairy belly. The white fur was as soft as . . . the only thing he could think of was soft fur.

"How heavy ya think he is, Paddy — a hundred pound?"

"No no! Jumpin' dyin', Martin, ya knows he's not so heavy as that!" He stuck his eyes in Garf on the pinnacle and looked to Ambrose near his feet. "What's Garf gonna do, I wonder?"

Martin took the seal in his arms and studied the pincushion nose. He plucked the needle-like whiskers gently and watched the big black eyes close, thick globules of phlegm squeezing from the eyelids and running down its face. Looked as if it were crying. The eyes opened again and blinked slowly. More tears trickled from the corners. He had heard his father speak about this but had never believed it, until now. He jounced the pup in his arms to mentally weigh it. "Fifty pound, Paddy?"

"Forty or fifty pound, 'long there."

"OK boys," Garf shouted to his men. "You can start the killin'!" He jumped from the pinnacle and threw off his rope. "Over there, Uncle Am!" He pointed his finger. "Pick out four or five a them black ones!"

Ambrose spat his butt out and faced the wind. "Garf, I believe the wind is droppin'."

Garf pulled his knife from its sheath and straddled a sleeping young harp. "That's only 'cause we're off here on the ice," he said. "Down low. Now if we was in there on the cape it'd still be blowin' a starm." He flicked his finger at a small army of men leaving the whistle house and running to the gulch. "See, they're still comin' off."

Martin ran to his father and Paddy followed. "What one ya gonna kill first, Dad?"

"Makes no difference, I s'pose boy, long 'tis not a raggedy-jacket."

The boy looked around. "What ya call a raggedy-jacket?"

His father pointed to a white seal with a black stripe running down its back. "Right there — that's a raggedy-jacket — not worth killin'. See his head? That black hair showing through there is fast fur. Can't pull it off." He reached down to pluck it. The seal barked and snapped at his mitt. He pulled back, picked up his gaff and poked. The young mammal wheeled and snarled at the stick. "He's a saucy one," Ambrose said. He glanced sideways at the boy. "Somethin' like you." He poked again. The seal growled and lay still.

Martin leaned closer to his father, poked with his own gaff and spoke softly. "And my teeth is just so sharp."

The barking seemed louder now. The air felt warmer, perhaps because the sun had climbed higher in the sky and its outline could be seen through the thinning cloud cover.

Ambrose pulled off his coat and walked out of sight between two high pinnacles.

Paddy unshouldered his rope. "I'm gonna kill a couple here, Martin. Watch me and then you can kill a couple."

"How come that young seal barked at Dad?"

"That was a young harp, boy."

Puzzled. "But they're all young harps, ain't they? 'Cept

the old ones — ya know what I mean."

Paddy scratched his head. "Well, I s'pose they're all young harps, yes." Looked at Martin. "You don't know very much 'bout this racket at all, do ya?"

"Don't know nothin' 'bout it," he said. "This is me first time."

Paddy looked around and waved his forefinger. The hand was still. "Hold on now," he said, "I'm just lookin' for one that's all white." He moved among the herd, inspecting. Found a small white seal with its head thrust between two vertical ice pans. "Here ya go! Now, what'd that one look like to you — a young harp, a whitecoat or a raggedy-jacket?"

"That's a whitecoat," the boy answered.

"OK," Paddy said, "let's find out." He pinched the white hair on the seal's back and plucked, then held the tuft between his fingers for Martin to see.

The curious youngster reached down and plucked also and the hair came away in his hand, leaving a black patch behind.

"When the seals is barn," Paddy explained, "they're all whitecoats, OK?"

Martin brushed his hand on his knee and listened.

"When they gets round two weeks old the hair starts to come off 'em — they starts sheddin'. Inside that white hair there's a new coat growin' — a black one. Now that black one's their main coat, understand?"

"Yes, I understand. But they should be called black-coats when that happens."

Paddy shook his head and smiled. "Let's put it this way. Just 'cause a young seal is white don't mean he's a whitecoat. If you can pull the hair off 'en like ya just done, then he's a raggedy-jacket. Another five or six days and this one here'll be all black and then he'll be takin' to the water. When he gets black, and even when he starts to get black, he can tell when someone is out to hurt 'en so he starts to get saucy. You'll never see a little whitecoat try to snap your hand off 'cause they don't know what hurt is, but if he got the hair comin' off 'en or if he's all black, like I just told ya, you'd better watch yourself."

Martin grinned and shook his head. "You sure knows a lot 'bout seals, don't ya, Paddy? Funny how ya can tell one from the other."

"And that's not all," Paddy continued. It seemed he was eager to carry on the lesson. "After them young harps gets in the water, they'll slew around and beat it back down north again. That's why when they gets in the water they're called beaters."

Ambrose stepped from behind the pinnacle and fixed his overall straps on his shoulders. He tugged on his behind and kicked his leg out. "How many ya got killed, Paddy?"

"We ain't got none killed yet," Martin horned in. "We was waitin' for you."

"I'm not talkin' to *you*; I'm talkin' to Paddy! How many ya kill, Paddy?"

"N'ar one, Ambrose boy. We was waitin' for you."

The offended sealer plucked on the seat of his overalls, pulled on his jacket and sauntered off towards Garf.

"Well," Martin said, enchanted by the moment. "Gotta chase 'en, I s'pose."

"Looks like he's half mad," Paddy said, taking his knife from its sheath.

"Aahhh, Dad'll be all right when he gets over his fit. He thinks I tried to kill 'en this marnin' on the Ski-Doo."

"Did ya?"
"You think I'm crazy, Paddy?"
"No, but your father do."

8

KILLING TIME

Ambrose pushed the peaked cap high on his head and ran the back of his hand across his brow. The wind did not cool his forehead the way it had. He targeted a black harp and raised his gaff the way a baseball player might raise his bat, and made a swift blow to the head. A thin jet of blood squirted across the snow and the seal lay motionless. He hit again and turned to Martin. "See how quick that was?" He straddled the young seal and turned it belly up, took his knife from the sheath and drove it deep between the two flippers, a quick gush of blood covering his hand. He withdrew his blade and cut through into the lower jaw, took his rope and pushed the eye splice into the mouth, pulled it out the front and slipped the bight over the nose. He tugged it tight and stood up. "There ya go," he said. "That's how ya kills seals — nothin' to it!"

"Looks pretty simple," the boy said. "When can I kill one?"

Ambrose turned the seal on its side and drained the blood. He drove the knife in the snow, wriggled it, wiped it on his thigh and looked for another one to kill.

To the left Martin saw Paddy raise his gaff. "Can I have a try, Dad? I wants to kill one."

"Think ya l'arned enough from what I just showed ya?" the old man asked.

"Nothin' to it," Martin replied. "All ya gotta do is smack 'en over the head and ram the knife in 'en."

Ambrose sneered. "Funny thing 'bout it — you always thinks 'tis nothin' to everything." He searched among the herd for another black one. "Well, c'mon then," he said. "If ya thinks you're ready for it I'll let ya kill one."

Martin heard a strange sound behind him. The seals barked and whined all around them but there was something different about this sound. Short, gurgling grunts. He turned and saw the young harp, blood pouring from its eyes and nostrils, scratching the ice and swinging its head back and forth in a swimming motion, then crawling six feet on a carpet of steaming gore and stopping.

"Dad!" the boy screeched. "Dad, look over here! My God, Dad, that seal you just killed is still alive!"

Ambrose looked around, clearly unconcerned at his son's medical diagnosis. "'Magination troubles again, Martin?" He blew a long, heavy breath and went back to look. "My son, this is no place for 'maginations!"

The boy stood pointing. "Just look, Dad — that seal is still alive!"

His father grinned. "How can he be still alive if there's n'ar drop a blood left in his body? Tell me that!"

"I don't care, sir! I knows that seal is not dead — you can say what ya like!"

"Martin," Ambrose said, trying to enlighten the young boy floundering in a sea of hysteria and wonderment.

"Listen, you got a lot to l'arn. That seal is dead, yes. Sometimes they does that, y'know. I've seen 'em meself crawl twenty feet or more with n'ar stain a blood left in 'em at all — dry as a bone inside — pumped right out."

"If he was dead, why'd he crawl round on the ice like that?"

Ambrose had been hunting seals for forty-five years but he had never given a commentary on the killing procedure. "If ya hits 'en too far up on the head," he began, "ya won't stun 'en right proper. Ya gotta hit 'en on the nose, and the farther out on the nose the better." He ran his hand over the bloodied face, feeling the crushed bone from the eyes to the nose. "I daresay that's what happened there — I might've hit 'en too far back."

"Geez," Martin said. "Think if ya hit 'en on the head, it'd be easier to knock 'en out that way."

"OK, come over here and I'll show ya what I means." His father spat on the snow. "Certainly," he said, "you're that stun, I s'pose ya won't see what I'm talkin' 'bout!" A black seal scurried along the pan and he stopped it by sticking his gaff in front of its head. "Now, watch this and see if you can l'arn somethin'." He raised the gaff and looked at the boy. "Now watch! Don't go lookin' round at the other seals!" The gaff whistled through the air, and again the familiar squirt of blood. "See that — right on the nose that time!" He turned the seal over and pulled out his knife. "Here ya go, Martin. Stick 'en."

"Me?"

"Yes — you! Who else ya think I'm talkin' to?"

"But I wanted to hit 'en with the gaff," Martin protested. "And I wanted to stick 'en — I wanted to kill 'en meself!"

"Look," his father said, becoming more irritated by the

minute. "When ya slices open his heart, boy, that means ya killed 'en." He held his knife out. "Here, take it!"

Martin took it, dropped to one knee and ran the wet, glistening blade along the short hair between the front flippers, the bloody handle sticking to his hand like molasses to a spoon. He thought about his mother.

"Don't look at the knife, boy; kill the seal with 'en!"

Martin drove the knife into the snow and stood up. "No, I'm not doin' it!"

Ambrose picked his nose and droned, "Well, what's wrong?"

"I wants to bat one meself. I don't wanna stick one you already got knocked out!"

"What in the world's wrong with ya, boy?" Ambrose looked his son over and took the knife. "You're not afraid, is ya?"

Martin took off his cap, rolled the rim and put it back on. "No, I'm not afraid. I just wants to do it all by meself." He decided not to argue the point but to get another lesson instead. "You stick this one and I'll watch."

His father looked astounded as he straddled the seal. "OK, this is where ya puts the knife." He eyed the youngster. "You're sure you're all right, is ya?"

Martin stooped. "Oh yes, nothin' wrong with me, boy."

Ambrose hesitated and found room for a rude remark but said, "Well, somebody gotta kill 'en, I s'pose. He'll come to the once and then I'll have to bat 'en again." He set the tip of the knife between the flippers. "Right here — this is where ya gotta put the knife, OK?" He pushed hard and the steaming hot blood erupted like dark red lava, ran over the belly onto the snow and disappeared into a black hole. He placed the knife at the throat, moved it to the chin and stroked the bristly hair. "When ya goes to put the rope in 'en ya gotta make sure he's cut far 'nough back." He illustrated this. "If ya cuts 'en right here, too close to the chin, you'll bust the jawbone out of 'en when ya hauls on the rope, 'specially if he hooks up in a clumper."

Martin knelt on the snow and lifted the hinder daddles. "I believe he shit hisself, Dad." Added blindly, "Why can't ya tie the rope around his head instead a cuttin' through his chin?" He knew it was a stupid question and wished he hadn't asked it.

Ambrose dropped one corner of his mouth. "Well well well!"

"Forget I asked, Dad."

"Forget?" his father blared. "How can I forget?" He sounded as if he had just fallen off the sled again. "I don't know what's gonna happen to the young race when all the old fellers is dead and gone, I don't know! Listen to me, for God's sake! If ya ties a seal on and ya gotta slip your rope in arder to get ashore you'll either drown or freeze to death, 'cause time ya gets 'en untied the ice could be gone apart or ya might be up to your neck in slob. What's ya gonna do then, eh?"

"But if I gotta slip my seal like you're sayin' — wud'n it be better if I throwed down everything I had and just runned?"

Ambrose straightened up and stared inquisitively at Cape Bauld. "Your rope, boy — you can't forget your rope! S'pose ya comes to a place where ya can't get 'cross, whaddaya gonna do?" He pressed his tongue to his cheek, scraped and spat. Looked towards Garf, then towards the cape again. "You'll never get 'cross if ya ain't got a rope to throw to someone!"

Martin felt sharp. He said, "If there's someone to throw

the rope to, then *they* should have a rope" — he grinned and rubbed his finger along the chest wound — "shouldn't they?"

His father didn't answer, for he seemed distracted by something on Cape Bauld.

"Shouldn't they?" Martin repeated.

Ambrose was lost in thought. "What?" he said, then spoke to himself in a whisper: "How many seals is Garf gonna kill, I wonder."

Martin was eager to carry on the lesson. "The other crowd, Dad — they should have a rope, shouldn't they?"

Ambrose sighed. "Myohmyohmyohmy!"

His son chuckled. "What's wrong, Dad?"

"If they all thought like you," Ambrose said, "nobody'd have a rope, would they?"

Martin felt the blood rush to his face and he realized his father's wisdom.

"If that was the case," the old man continued, "you'd wish you had a rope now, wud'n ya?"

The boy said nothing, but watched his father cut into the thin layer of fat in the lower jaw and then push the tip of his knife into the mouth to widen the slit at the side of the tongue.

Ambrose took his rope and made another bight farther up. "Now, you listen to what I'm sayin' and don't leave your rope behind for nothin' or no one. If ya can't slip your seal fast 'nough, then chop it off with your knife as tight to the seal as you can get." He wiped his hands in his overalls. "I'm goin' over here and kill 'nother couple," he said. "You go over there where Garf is and see if ya can l'arn somethin' else."

Martin climbed a pinnacle and saw Garf kneeling by a

black seal off to the right.

More sealers ran across the ice, coming and going, shouting and singing like voices inside a tin can. And the sun seemed to have gained more power, he thought — or was the wind dropping?

Martin pulled off his mitts near a young harp and cast them to the side. He touched the tip of his gaff to its nose. "Well," he said, stroking the stick up and down the black fur. "Looks like 'tis just me and you now." The seal did not move. "I don't think you're so saucy as Dad said ya was." He looked towards Sacred Island four miles in the distance, and at the seventy or eighty men scattered throughout the great herd. He thought of how empty the island was, how white it looked wedged between the ice and sky, almost invisible to anyone who didn't know it was there.

He raised his gaff, his mind racing. Better get a firm grip on the gaff, he told himself. Had to make sure of what he was doing. He couldn't miss — his father was only fifty yards away. He swung with all his might and the gaff made a sickening thud. He saw the head cave in. Saw the squirt. Held it high and swung again, heard the crack. He raised it and swung again. And again. Blotches of greasy blood spattered his legs and the snow around him.

He heard his father call out, "STOP! STOP! STOP!" And held off on another strike, the gaff suspended above his head.

"NO! NO! NO!" Ambrose ran towards him, slipped and fell, jumped up and charged like a wild boar.

Paddy heard the commotion and looked around.

"Hold on, Martin," his father yelled. "Don't hit that seal no more! Put that gaff down!"

"What's wrong?" Paddy shouted. "You cut yourself, boy,

or what?" He threw down his rope and ran.

The boy lowered his gaff, bewildered by the attention he was getting. "What's the trouble?" he asked anyone who cared to answer.

Ambrose grabbed the gaff from him and tossed it behind a clumper. "You're the trouble," he said in a huff. "You can't go beatin' up the heads a them young harps like that!" His bottom lip trembled. "What's wrong with you at all? I showed ya just now what to do — got it forgot already, have ya? How come ya went and bat that seal anyway? You ain't got n'ar knife to kill 'en with so why'd ya go the work and bat 'en?" He kicked the seal in a fit of anger and waved his finger in the boy's face. "Now don't ya touch n'ar 'nother seal off here no more today!"

Was it the heat from the sun, the boy thought, or was it the blood rushing to his face? Inside he felt something bubbling, ready to burst. "I was only killin' a seal, Dad," he said. "'Nothin' to get tore up 'bout!"

Ambrose squealed like a stuck pig. "Killin' a seal? My God, ya don't call that killin' a seal, do ya, boy? That's not killin' a seal — that's barbarizin' a seal!"

Paddy turned the young harp belly up. "What's wrong, Ambrose? I think Martin done a pretty good job for his first time on the ice. Don't you?"

The old man took off his mitts and forced them into his back pocket. "What's wrong? — my God, Paddy boy, ya knows what's wrong! Martin is gone right clean and clever off his head! He ain't got a clue, boy — ain't got a clue!"

"Why's that, Ambrose? Sure he got his seal killed, ain't he?"

"Killed? Big difference in killed and sacrificed!" He kicked the seal again. "Just look — look how he got his head all beat up!"

Paddy pulled out his knife — just as long as the old man's, but the handle had thin black leather strips wound around it, and a lion's-head butt of yellow brass that he had filed and carved himself. Eyes dotted with red paint.

"I'll stick this one for 'en now, Ambrose, and show 'en how to hook on his rope. Everything's gonna be all right."

"Go ahead, Paddy my son, 'cause I can't do nothin' with 'en!" He reached in his pocket and pulled out his tobacco, rooted his ass and went back to his seals.

Paddy smiled and pushed his glasses up. "I'll stick this one for ya, Martin, and then you can stick one yourself."

Martin stood there and wondered if he should leave and go ashore or simply start walking for Sacred Island. He wanted to kill his own seals and tow them ashore. He wanted to tell his mother he had made the kill himself. He wanted the money the pelts would bring. He didn't want another argument. And he didn't want to go to the island yet.

Blood issued from the wound as Paddy ripped through the short hair and drove his knife home.

"Not the first seal you killed, eh, Paddy?"

"Not the first, Martin, no." He dug his knife into the snow and wiped it on the black hair. "One thing for sure, I'll never kill so many as your father killed — I'll never live long 'nough."

Martin placed his hand on the seal's belly, away from the blood. "Dad is a lot older'n you too. He's been at this kinda stuff since he was a boy."

"That's right," Paddy said. "But he didn't have no choice, did he? That's the way he was reared up and ya can't 'xpect 'en to be any different. He wants to see that everything is done right. Your father never had it so easy as you got it now. Sure, I knows he's a bit rough on ya sometimes and I knows he got his ways but ya gotta overlook that. That's Ambrose for ya."

"I s'pose I shouldn't've hit the seal so hard as I did," the boy said regretfully. "I thought I was doin' OK — like I seen Dad do."

Paddy secured the seal on Martin's rope and wiped his hands in the snow. "Oh, ya done perfect," he said reassuringly. "Just remember next time not to hit 'en so hard, that's all." He took his glasses off, put them to his mouth and blew. "Know why your father got mad with ya just now, Martin?"

"Don't know — ain't got a clue."

"Your mother makes brawn, don't she?" He wiped his glasses with his finger and thumb and put them back on. Looked towards Cape Bauld. "I wonder what that crowd's doin' down there on the ballycaters like that," he said. "Seems to me like they're just standin' round."

"Prob'ly waitin' to help the men up over the cliff with their seals."

"I don't think so," Paddy said, his eyes filled with speculation. He turned to the boy. "What was I sayin'? Oh yes — your father. Not your father, no — your mother! Brawn, boy — brawn! Your mother makes brawn, don't she?"

Brawn was a concoction of boiled seals' brains and flippers with the skin and bones removed, mixed with spices and salt in a fairly large bowl. After it had cooled, it was cut in chunks and eaten like cake.

"OK, get to the point," Martin said.

"Well, ya like it or don't ya?"

"Yes. Good stuff it is too. Why?"

Paddy looked towards Cape Bauld again. "Somethin's

goin' on in there," he said with great concern in his voice. "Don't look right to me somehow!"

"Don't warry 'bout that crowd in there, Paddy! What was ya gonna tell me?"

"Brawn, boy!" He faced the curious youngster. "Any bones in it when ya eats it?" he asked.

Martin lowered his head and pushed his eyes together in their sockets with his thumb and forefinger. "I've never seen no bones in it, no." He wondered why Paddy asked such silly questions.

"Uh-huh."

"Whaddaya mean — uh-huh?"

"And why'd ya think 'twas no bones in it? Now think 'bout it for a spell!"

Martin reached down and picked up a handful of snow, squeezed until it conformed to his hand, making finger grips like those on a knife handle. He squeezed it tighter and watched the water run from between his fingers, smiled and threw it down. "OK," he said. "I can see it now — plain as day! Not only bones but blood too! Right?"

"That's right." Paddy smiled. "Bones and blood! You wud'n eat the brawn if your mother cooked it like that now, would ya? That's why ya gotta be careful when ya hits them young seals." He narrowed his eyebrows and went serious. "No trouble to spoil their heads like that, y'know — drive the blood and bones right through their brains, my son. Them small shards a bone can choke a horse. You ain't gotta hit 'em half so hard as ya did. Not so many times for sure."

Martin slung his rope over his shoulder and pulled the seal a short distance from the other members of his group. He needed to be away from everyone so he could kill on his own. Just batting a seal with his gaff did not make him a seal hunter.

A shaft of blazing sunlight ripped open the sky and shot across the ice in a long strip of brightness that did not stop until it reached Belle Isle. The whining pups and grunting mothers were louder now and the air was warmer, although it was still a bit breezy. The wind must be dropping, Martin thought, yet his father had not mentioned it to Garf a second time. He climbed a low pinnacle and looked around. The number of men had doubled. The seals were blacker. The paths were redder. Snow was whiter. But the wind no longer stung his eyes. Did anyone else notice the difference? It would be pointless for him to run across the ice and tell his father — he'd only laugh and say he was crazy. Martin could hear him: *Somethin' wrong with you, boy. Didn't you hear what Garf just said? Why don't ya listen sometimes instead a buttin' in where 'tis none of your business — no good to tell ya nothin'! Look what I told ya about beatin' up them seals' heads!* Maybe the wind wasn't dropping. Perhaps he had wondered too much about it — about what would happen if it did drop.

He knew he had to find another seal and kill it himself, not just bat it over the head and have someone else ram the knife into it but kill it outright and proper. Twenty feet to the right a raggedy-jacket caught his eye. Behind it a mother suckled another one. To the left and not more than fifty feet away a dozen more basked in the warm sunlight. Martin jumped off the pinnacle and strode over to where they were, and tested the value of their pelts by plucking the soft fur on each one. He went to a black seal near a triangular ice pan stuck on its end, and poked his gaff out. Almost lost his balance when the seal sprang forward and snarled.

"Aahhh," he said with a burst of encouragement. "You're

old enough to know what's goin' on, ain't ya, boy!" He gripped his gaff with two hands and swung hard. The seal's head recoiled into its body with just the nose sticking out, like a gluttonous turtle. Blood spurted from its nostrils. He hit again. The eyeball burst and a thick slime ran down its nose. A small translucent sphere of soft jelly rolled onto the snow. He threw his gaff to the side and looked to see if his father was watching him. Two smacks on the nose had been plenty — not quite on the nose, but if no one was watching then no one could condemn.

He grinned and reached into the warm darkness of his pants pocket, tangling his fingers in a piece of cotton twine as he curled them under his I.X.L. He pulled it out and dug his thumbnail into the silver slot. Opened the knife. He had sharpened it himself a week ago, especially for this day, and had not opened it since. Now, imitating his father's actions, he straddled the young seal, turned it belly up and placed the knife tip between its flippers. He clenched his teeth and pushed the short blade deep into the mass of warm fat, pulled towards him and sliced through to the red muscle underneath.

The fleshy walls fell away from his knife, widening the wound till it was like a cut in moulded gelatin. A quick plunge into the chest cavity and he felt the hot blood erupt onto his hand. "Geez," he said out loud. "'Tis boilin'!" He wondered how the blood could be so hot. How it could be that dark — almost black. The rich, bubbling fountain cascaded up his wrist and down the sides of the belly and spread around his feet as he worked the knife and drove it deeper, severing the vital arteries and puncturing a lung. The seal shuddered and blew a cache of glistening red bubbles from its nostrils. He cut the chin, withdrew the blade and wiped it clean on a flipper, leaving two red marks like rope burns, then placed the knife on a clumper, crushed a knob of snow in his hands and wiped them on the arms of his jacket. The young harp twitched and jerked its head around as if it had been speared, but he grabbed his gaff again and hit it squarely on the nose, driving its head into the ice.

Martin fastened the seal onto his hauling rope, stood up and pulled the two mammals together like trout on a wire. He wiped his hands again, put the knife in his pocket and sat down to wait for further orders.

Paddy saw him and shouted, "How's ya makin' out?"

"Perfect," he said. "Soon be ready to go in or what?"

"I was ready ten minutes ago," Paddy said. "Your father and Garf is ready too, I believe." He looked to a place behind a high pinnacle that Martin could not see. "Yeah, they're comin' there now."

"How many ya get, Paddy?" the boy asked.

"Three!"

Ambrose and Garf had four young harps apiece strung out behind them, and a new tributary began its journey to the crimson path.

"Ya got 'em, Ambrose," Paddy said with a broad grin.

"Took us long 'nough, too," Garf replied.

Ambrose saw the boy's seals and grunted. "Who strung on your seals for ya, Martin?"

"Done it meself," he said with a small chuckle. "But it don't look right somehow, do it?"

Garf laughed and picked up the young sealer's rope. "You can't tie seals on like that, boy. They'll go together in a lump when ya starts draggin' 'em ashore. You'll only beat yourself out for nothin'."

Ambrose smirked and took out his tobacco. "How come

ya tied 'em on like that? I told ya how to put the rope in 'em
— didn't ya see me?" He pinched out a wad and dropped it
onto his paper.

"That's all right, Uncle Am," Garf said. "Only a flick now
and I'll have it all fixed up for 'en." He pulled the boy's
rope back through the two chins and made a bowline three
feet from the spliced end, pushed the bights through each
chin and slipped them on over the noses. "There ya go,
Martin," he said. "Should make it a lot easier for ya."

Ambrose rolled the tobacco, put the paper to his lips and
pulled it across his tongue. "Boy, I'm that thirsty I ain't got
enough spit in me mouth to stick the paper."

"Should a took our nunny-bag with us," Garf said, flicking the rope over his shoulder. "I feels kinda thirsty meself,
and a bit hungry."

"I never took n'ar lunch with me," Paddy said. "Didn't
think the ice was gonna be in."

Ambrose lit his cigarette, sucked in his cheeks and drew
out its smoky guts, held the cloud in for a while then blew it
high above his head. Watched it disappear in the breeze
and turned to his son. "Where ya get the knife?"

Martin picked up his mitts and put them on. Only useless
to avoid him, he thought. "I carries that knife with me wherever I goes," he said strongly. "Now, if ya got somethin' to
say 'bout it, then this is your chance!"

Ambrose raised his eyebrows and shrugged. "Well, at least
ya knows what he's for. Ya killed the seal with 'en so that's
all that counts."

"He done a good job, Ambrose, my son," Paddy said.
"For his first time off on the ice I say he done a excellent
job. Whaddaya think, Garf — think he done a good job or
what?"

Garf moved forward, his seals trailing in a straight line. "Good job?" he said without looking back. "He always tries to do a good job, don't he? Just somethin' always gets in the way and frigs 'en up!"

Ambrose fell in behind Garf, the glow at the tip of his cigarette racing towards his lips.

9

THE BLUE DROP

Scores of jubilant sealers, their hauling ropes sunk into their shoulders and their mouths dried with thirst, struggled under the weight of their kill to keep from falling on the slippery ribbons of blood. Their shouts of victory turned to an old sealing song:

> *Oh, we are the sealers of the old,*
> *not the new Newfoundland*
> *We're the roughest and toughest and*
> *want you to all understand*
> *We can fight with the best, bare knuckles and fists*

— everyone who knew the song raised a clenched fist and shouted, "Yeah." The song continued—

> *We've walked to our knees in the blood*
> *And we stand proud and tall while around us they fall*
> *Vic'ry never tasted so good.*

Martin had never heard the song before but he mulled it

over in his mind, imagined bare-knuckled men fighting real ghosts and afterwards drinking moonshine from earthen jugs with broken handles. He jabbed his gaff into the side of a bluish-looking clumper and chipped off a nugget that he popped into his mouth and sucked like a lollipop. He bit down and heard it crack. The empty coldness of the centre tasted smooth as he flicked the chunks around inside his mouth, bathing them in pools of saliva. His tongue grew numb and he swallowed the water, cool against his burning throat. Blood-engorged veins behind his Adam's apple constricted like a hungry stomach, and something that felt like a knife-edge passed his sinuses and slammed into his forehead. Cold like an icy drill bit pressing against his frontal bone, pushing — pushing. He slapped a palm to his brow and rolled his closed eyes. Waited for the pain to go away. He spat the pieces out and sucked the air through his teeth. He held his breath and pressed his tongue to the roof of his mouth. Gradually the pain melted into euphoria.

Ambrose pulled his four seals from a small fissure, wiped his face with the back of his mitt and pawed at a daub of seal blood on the arm of his unzipped jacket. Three unfastened shirt buttons showed above the bib of his greasy overalls. Bloody knife prints marked his right thigh like tally marks.

Martin and Paddy hauled on their ropes, glancing up only to check the progress of their colleagues.

"Dad," Martin yelled. "Behind ya — look!"

"Stop shoutin', boy, and put your back into it!"

His son pointed. "Someone got a fire lighted on the cape!"

A chill at the nape of Ambrose's neck jerked sharply down his spine. He turned his head and recognized the danger signal that every sealer dreaded the most. A smoky fire on the cape meant that the wind was dropping, and warned sealers on the ice to run for land. "Oh my God!" he cried. "Ice is goin' apart!"

Garf heard the commotion, and one look at the smoke put him in command again. "OK, Uncle Am," he shouted with a show of courage and repose. "Wait for the boys to get 'longside a ya and I'll dodge on till I comes to a big sheet a ice. That's where I'll stop and wait for you fellers!"

Paddy and Martin ran up to Ambrose, their ropes dug into their shoulders and their seals slithering over the ice behind them. Martin knew now why everyone on the cape had stood around and done nothing a short while ago. Knew why Paddy and his father had stared and wondered at the land so much.

Paddy pushed his glasses farther up on his nose and showed his teeth when he squinted. He tugged his rope tight and took an extra turn in his hand. "We're gonna have trouble gettin' ashore," he said, his voice shaky and full of fatigue. "We'll be lucky if we makes it!"

"I figured early this marnin' the wind was droppin'," Ambrose said. "But I didn't think it would drop out blast ca'm." He flicked his rope onto his shoulder and stretched it tight. "We gotta go, boys! C'mon — no time to waste!"

Shouts of pandemonium shot across the ice floes as everyone spotted the smoke. A hundred men ran for the safety of the land with their dead seals jiggling and bouncing behind them. Men on Cape Bauld waved their arms and shouted frantically, "In the bight — go for the bight!"

Ambrose reached the pan where Garf waited, and together they towed the old man's seals to the centre and dropped them.

"Look, Martin!" Paddy said, glancing behind. "She's

openin' up under your feet! Jump to the side and hold onto that clumper there!" Towers of loose ice and snow crumbled into the sea. Paddy let out his rope and jumped to the bigger pan that Garf was on. "Here, Martin, jump on this one with us!"

The boy ran with the ice disintegrating under his heels, let out fifteen feet of rope and jumped, his seals floating behind him in the blue drop. Garf and Paddy grabbed his rope and pulled them onto the pan.

"Gonna have to slip 'em, I 'low," Ambrose said, his breath coming in short gasps. "That's if we wants to make it ashore!"

"No sir," Garf retaliated. "I ain't slippin' mine!" He spoke defiantly. "Not till the very last minute!"

Martin's eyes told him that Cape Bauld was now moving westward. He shook his head and told himself it was impossible. "Look at that, Paddy," he said. "Looks like she's movin' — whaddaya think?"

"Not the cape no," Garf butted in. "We fellers — we're the ones that's movin'! We're goin' round the cape like a shot." He pulled his seals off the pan and stumbled with them to another one. Called to his three comrades and told them to hurry. He continued the rush towards a crowd of men lumped together on a large pan of ice near the land.

Ambrose said, "Go, Martin! Chase Garf and don't stop till ya gets on that pan!"

"No Dad, I'm not leavin' ya!"

Ambrose soured. "Go and get on that pan a ice like I told ya! You only got two seals there so ya got a better chance a gettin' ashore!"

The boy latched onto his father's rope. "Lemme take your seals, Dad, and you take mine! I can haul four seals no problem!"

Ambrose sucked his lips into a squished doughnut shape and tried to spit but he had nothing left in his mouth. "Then why didn't ya *take* four?"

Martin sank his own hauling rope into his back and ran with his seals across the ice. The pressure ridges were all gone, toppled into the sea and consumed like sugar cubes in saucers of hot tea. The pinnacles, solid pans of flat ice that had been spewed up from the floating quagmire by powerful winds and tide, had returned to being common pans of ice. He pulled his seals onto the edge of the big sheet where ten men, including Garf, tested the loose ice with their gaffs for a stepping stone to safety. He threw off his rope, ran back and helped his father.

Groups of panicky sealers ran towards the billowing blue smoke. The men on shore had ripped clapboards off the whistle house to build a fire, and had placed blackberry bushes on top to create smoke.

John Parsons stood by the transmitter tower, binoculars pressed to his eyes. A hundred yards or so outside the last man in the advancing army of sealers, a lake had opened all the way from Sacred Island to Cape Bauld. The sealers ran like madmen, some towing seals and more with empty ropes but all headed for a long sheet of ice on the west side of the cape. Behind them, eddying currents carrying huge chunks of ice and lumpy mush boiled to the surface. A tide rip started at the very place where they had left Cape Bauld for the killing fields, and now the turbulent wall of white water and slob, caught in the backlash, prevented any kind of landing there. Bigger pans banged and crashed against the rocks, splitting on impact.

The old bitches left their whelping pans and went in search of codfish and herring, leaving their young to sniff the water for the first time.

Forty yards from shore, on a good-sized pan of ice, the thirteen stranded sealers discussed their fate without looking at each other. Some said they would be drowned when the pan fell apart under their feet; others said they would be drowned when it melted after taking them to some far southern country. More said they would be drowned from jumping into the water and trying to reach land before the pan could take them offshore. Yet these sealers laughed and talked about how many seals they had killed and how they had managed to survive jumping onto ice pans that had sunk under their weight and, in the same heat of conversation, why they believed they would be rescued.

Sealers on shore ran along the ballycaters and searched for a low platform where the men could land before being swept out to sea. Running towards the bight would delay their catastrophic journey around Cape Bauld. But the tide was the problem now, not the ice.

Someone shouted from the shore that a suitable landing place had been found. A group of men scrambled to the selected spot, calculated the distance to the big pan and uncoiled their ropes. Tied them together and made five or six ropes of over a hundred feet each.

Martin saw his friend. "Alec," he called.

The young boy turned and his eyes livened. He wore a black windbreaker with the zipper badly torn, and the knees of his denim jeans were soaked with seals' blood but he stood in them tall and handsome. Smooth babyface. Straw-coloured hair that hung in a long bang. "Martin," he said, "I didn't know you was off here, 'specially on the same pan as we fellers.

"Where ya been all the time, Alec?"

"Well, y'know. . . . "

Martin saw his father bum a smoke from one of the sealers. "Yeah, I know."

"So, how is ya?"

"Good. You?"

Tide struck the pan and all chatter ceased. The men backed away from the edge and watched as the mushy ice surged and gyrated towards them.

The rescue team leader shouted his orders: "OK, men — if you're gonna get ashore anywhere 'tis gonna have to be right here! We'll throw two ropes and take two men at a time — one on each rope! Have to leave your seals behind though, 'cause they'll only slow ya down!"

One sealer turned his nose up at the idea and spoke out of the corner of his mouth. "I ain't leavin' my so'n'so seals behind for no one and I ain't gonna be hauled through no water like a friggin' dog either! If anyone wants to," he said, "they can follow me!" He pointed to what looked like solid ice farther in the bight, and stepped off the pan onto a ridge of packed slob. "I'm goin' ashore over that way!" He swung his hauling rope onto his shoulder and picked his way across the rubble with his seals. All watched him. Twenty feet. His gaff became his eyes, telling him where to step. Forty feet. He turned. "Comin'?"

A short man, face wrinkled and weather-beaten, eight months pregnant and toothless, pulled his seals across the pan to the edge. "I don't know 'bout you fellers," he said, "but I'm gonna chase 'en." He stepped onto the slush with his rope in his hand. "If I falls in the water I daresay I'll drown but I'm gonna chance it!"

"Ya won't drown, boy, less'n ya goes down head first," someone said. "'Nough fat on that carcass a yours to keep ya 'float for a twelvemonth!'"

He took ten steps forward and plummeted to his throat in the slob. "Helllp! I'm sinkin'!" His eyes were wild with fear as he bobbed up and down in the freezing white muck. "Throw a rope to me, boys, for God's sake! Hurry!"

Someone reached with a gaff and hooked his rope, pulled him back onto the pan, where they booed and ridiculed him: *You can't walk on water, ya silly ol' man! Good shot ya had a thick pelt on ya! Only Peter and the Blessed Master could walk on the water! Too bad ya never drowned! Bet ya won't try that no more! No one wud'n a missed ya anyway! Try it again!*

He shivered and brushed the slob off his clothes. Never said anything except that he had stepped on the wrong pan. Slinked away into the crowd.

The rescue leader coiled a rope and handed the whipped end to one of his team members. "OK boys," he yelled to the castaways. "One man to a rope! Tie yourselves on and jump when I says jump, not before!"

Alec and another sealer were the first to catch the ropes. They grumbled about having to leave their seals but they tied themselves on and waited, gaffs in hand. Five or six rescuers lined up on each rope, like contestants in a tug-of-war.

"Jump!" yelled the leader. "Be smart now!"

Alec held the rope with both hands and floated across the chalky mire like a frog on a lily pad, but the bigger man stumbled and fell on his face as the sealers pulled him through the slob.

Garf caught one of the two ropes thrown back again. "Now, Martin my son," he said. "'Tis your turn." But the boy took the rope and flicked it around his father's waist in a granny knot.

"Jump!" shouted the team leader, and before Ambrose knew what was happening he found himself plucked from the pan and knee-deep in a swampy muck that wanted to devour him. He tried to use his gaff as a crutch, but in a few seconds the water rushed in over his boots and he sank in the soupy slob to his armpits. He gasped as the chill went through his body and he felt the rope tighten around his waist, ready to bisect him. Then the pulling stopped and the other sealer passed him, his gaff pulverizing the ice as he fought to stay up on all fours. Ambrose heard a loud cry from the land — "KNOT SLIPPED!" — and felt himself sliding down into the muck.

"Throw 'nother rope!" cried the leader.

One of his men picked up a coiled rope and slung it fair on top of the old man's head, the half-loops and semicircles unravelling around his face. Ambrose battled with the mess until he found the tautness leading to the land, then wrapped the rope over and over around his arm and held on with both hands as the team pulled him to the surface and up onto the ballycaters. He crawled in over, shaking from the cold and pointing to his cap and gaff near the hole he had made in the slob. "Mecapmecapmegaffmegaff," he squawked, his voice roughened by his numbing ordeal. Turned to one of his rescuers and said, "He's gonna do it one've these days, y'know."

"Do what?" the man asked, as he held out his hand to help another sealer to safety.

"Kill me," Ambrose said while untying himself. "That's what he's tryin' to do, y'know. He tried to get me this marnin' on the way down here, too."

The rope was thrown back to the pan and another hauled in with a freezing, kicking sealer tied to it. The rescuer did not remark on the old man's concerns; instead he pointed to a green packsack and told him to take out the bottle of medicine and pass it around to the wet sealers.

Paddy had been the eleventh man pulled ashore, and now only Garf and Martin remained. The boy had refused to go without his two seals despite Garf's orders, and Garf had refused to leave without his younger brother.

A great tidal bore struck the big sheet and veered it off-shore, creating a wide channel of dissipating mush.

"I can't swim," Martin lamented. "If I jumps in that water I'm gonna be drownded!"

Garf tried to comfort him. "If ya don't jump in you're still gonna be drownded so what's the difference?" He smiled as two rescue ropes landed near their feet and said, "This way we can get your body."

"Perhaps we should a followed that other man when he went," Martin said, too sick in his stomach to recognize the joke. "Maybe he made it without any trouble."

"Don't warry 'bout what someone else does," Garf said, taking one of the ropes and tying it around the boy's waist in a bowline. "For all we knows, he might be sucked down through the slob somewhere and drownded." He tied a bow-line around his own waist. "Take a couple a turns in your hand now" — he wrapped the rope around his hand to show the boy — "like this. And don't let go, no matter what!"

Martin wrapped the rope tight around his hand and clamped it shut. Waited for the team leader to give the signal.

"Jump!"

A second before he saw the rope tighten, Martin hooked his gaff into the loop at the end of his hauling rope. He felt himself being torn from the ice pan and heard himself cry out like a scalded cat, his eyes closed in unthinkable pain as the freezing ocean sucked him down. He drank from a salty wave over his face as the tug-of-war team pulled hand over hand on the rope. Twenty feet from the pan, his hauling rope tightened and the strain of his tow nearly wrenched the gaff from his hand. The rope cut deep into his shoulder blades and armpits as he jerked to a halt. He turned and spat, saw a similar wave spurting over Garf's bobbing head. His brother was gaining on him, his arms thrashing the water in a fruitless effort to speed himself along. "Haul me in!" the boy cried. "Pull — *pull!*"

"He brought up," someone yelled from onshore.

"His gaff," yelled another. "His gaff is hooked!"

Ambrose passed the bottle of moonshine to a wet sealer and looked to see what the shouting was about. He saw Martin's gaff attached to his hauling rope. "Well well," he said, and smiled, wiping the alcohol from his lips. Tapped one of the rescuers on the shoulder. "Haul 'en in, boys — he got his two seals there and he ain't lettin' 'em go."

The sealers regained their foothold and took up the slack. Martin let the rope unwind off his hand, allowed his mitt to be whisked away, then used his nearly dead fingers to help the others already set weakly around his gaff. "Pull," he shouted, the freezing water flopping into his mouth and ears. "Hurry! Hurry!" He began moving again and then twisted until he was belly up. Another hand-over-hand motion by his rescuers, and his seals slipped off the pan and into the water. Less than a minute later he was on his hands and knees, panting for breath near his father's feet.

Ambrose unhooked the rope off his gaff and pulled in the seals.

Garf sat on a bare rock with his naked feet planted on his

boots, wringing the water from his socks and shivering. Someone passed him the bottle of medicine. He took it to his brother, and helped him up. "Here," he said, with a moderately nice smile. "You have the first drink."

Martin looked to his father, not for permission but to hear what he would say.

The old man nodded his approval, told Garf not to stand around on his naked feet, then slung the boy's rope over his shoulder and mucked his seals up the hillside to the top of Cape Bauld.

One of the rescuers pulled off his worsted mitts and handed them to Martin. "Here," he said. "Put those on. Gonna have to get your mother to knit you a new pair."

Martin shook the soggy bag from his hand, put on the warm mittens and accepted the medicine from Garf. He let it pour down his throat like Pepsi, tipped the bottle down and gave it back. Wiped his mouth and tried to speak but couldn't. He whacked a hand to his chest, steadied himself and started coughing.

"Looks like you're ready to go back and kill more seals," laughed the rescue team leader. "But don't choke for God's sake, or else everybody's gonna have to fight over your seals."

The whole group gathered around and remarked on how close he and Garf had come to being drowned, cheering them and slapping their backs, only going silent as they watched their own seals disappear behind Cape Bauld.

10

BREWING FOR TROUBLE

Ambrose sat on his snowmobile seat and peeled the two
stockings off the bottle of tea. He took off his boots and
poured the water from them as though from leather pitch-
ers, rolled off his wet stockings and wiggled the dry pair
on, first the left and then the right. He reached into the
packsack again, pulled out the shirt and extra stockings
and tossed them to Martin sitting on the sled near his seals.
"Haul off your shirt, boy, and put that dry one on," he said,
a bit more politely than at other times. "And if your feet is
wet, shove on them stockin's too."

Martin took off his logans, shook the water out and slipped
them upside down over the sled horns. His jacket he hung
on one of the boots, after he had removed his stockings.
His feet were red and steaming with the warmth of having
walked up the hill, and there was a hotness in his stomach
from the moonshine. The heat from the noonday sun warmed
his neck and he felt it penetrate his windbreaker, tempting
him to lie on the sled and relax. "Gimme a drink a tea,
Dad," he yawned. "Mouth feels right dry."

Ambrose handed him the bottle and watched him drink

nearly half of it.

Paddy sat on the seat of his own snowmobile with Garf and munched a slice of half-frozen bread. His binoculars swung from their strap tied to the handlebars. "Y'know," he said with his glasses in his hand, "funny thing 'bout it — here we got bread almost hard as a rock and the tea is still a bit warm." He looked somewhat unfamiliar like this — eyes too close together and sunk in their sockets like nailheads in soft fir, and two red stripes on the sides of his nose that no one saw when his glasses were in place.

Garf held out his hand for the bottle. "The reason for that," he said — "give it here, Martin." The boy passed it to him. He shook the tea into a froth and unscrewed the cap, downed a good mouthful and wiped his chin. "Ya mightn't know it," he said with a noticeable lisp, "but nothin' freezes when 'tis wrapped in wool."

Paddy leaned to one side and farted. "And why is that, kind sir? Tell us if ya please."

"Well, just look at it this way," Garf began. "Did you ever hear talk of a cold sheep?"

The old man noticed his son's eagerness to talk foolishly and decided that today would be no day to celebrate. "Garf," he said. "How much a that moonshine ya drink?"

His son scratched his head and said very cheerfully, "Aahhh, just had a couple a good glutches, Uncle Am." He shrugged and put on a bright smile. "They opened up 'nother bottle after you left and 'twas a sin — a nawful sin — for us not to stay and help 'em drink it!"

"How 'bout you, Paddy?" Ambrose asked. "How much you drink?"

Paddy fitted his glasses on his eyes and took another slice of bread from the molasses-soaked bag. He tossed the wrapped raisins along to Martin. "Two sips, Ambrose. Just the two."

The old man grinned and pulled another piece of bread from the bag. "Must a been big sips."

Martin dumped the raisins into his mouth and stripped off his windbreaker and wet shirts. He wrung the clothes out and hooked them on the other boot, wiped his body with the dry shirt and put it on.

"Well," Ambrose said, patting his pockets, "long's y'all made it ashore, that's the main thing." His hand stopped on his bib pocket and he made some quick breaths in and out. "Oh my, I daresay me baccy is sogged right to death!" He pulled out the pack, opened it and looked in like a child peeking into a cookie jar, pinched a small wad in his fingers and held it up. "Look," he said, as if he were about to cry. "Sogged right to pieces!"

Paddy put on a sad face and told the old man that he felt really sorry for him.

Garf went on with a full breath of *Idon'tknowIdon'tknow-Idon'tknow*s.

Ambrose overlooked the festive mood of his comrades, opened his mouth and crammed the wad inside. "If I can't smoke it," he said, "I'll chew it!"

"OK," Garf said, as though drunkenness had never overtaken him. "Time to go. I'm starvin' to death!" He pulled the Ski-Doo around with his father still on it and started the engine, nipped the trigger and moved forward. Martin lay between his two seals, twiddled his toes inside the dry stockings and closed his eyes for the ride home. Ambrose hooked his feet in the snowmobile stirrups and watched the path ahead, not once looking back or spitting to the side.

≈

The eastern sky was white near the horizon, reflecting the large icefields, but shaded into dark hues above the big hill, which now looked washed out behind a foggy haze, its slopes like worn galvanized shims. Woodsmoke from tin stovepipes floated fifty feet into the humid air before deciding to turn northwest. Sharp echoes of a hammer pounding on a steel oil barrel resounded in the grey hills under the low cloud cover, and the heavy *chug chug sniff* of John Parsons' sawmill cut through the stillness.

Ida watched a big, orange-stripedy cat smell the seal nearest the bunkhouse and sneeze. It shook its scarred head and pawed gingerly at the matted excrement between the back flippers, then disappeared into a hole under the building when she tapped the window. A pot of salt herring and potatoes boiled on the firebox, the smell strong with fresh blubber, but her nose welcomed the foul odour as she spread her husband's torn jacket on the table and pulled her pincushion off the wall. She withdrew a small sewing needle from among its embedded associates and took the reel of black cotton from the shaving mug. She had cried while wringing the water from Martin's wet clothes, and now every stitch hung behind the stove to dry: his jacket, two shirts and windbreaker on nails; his cap, mittens, stockings, boxer shorts and logans on the warmer and his jeans on the oven door.

Ambrose stamped his feet on the bridge, opened the kitchen door and dumped his armful of wood into the woodbox. "Where's Martin?" he asked. "Still in the bed, I s'pose."

"Sleepin'," Ida said. She knotted the end of the thread

and pushed the needle through the two ragged edges of the arm. "My oh my," she sighed, beginning the second pass through the nylon. "How lucky was you fellers in the name a God? You could've all been drownded out there today. And for what? — nothin' only for the sake of a seal." She wiped her eyes. "S'posin' ya lost Martin out there today, Ambrose — what would you'd a done?"

Her husband pulled off his black and green checkered jackshirt and hung it behind the stove. "Well, not much I could a done," he said. "If we'd a lost 'en, been his own fault. He was told not to jump off the pan with his seals in tow but that's the very thing he went and done. Went right against everything he was told."

"But my God, Ambrose, he's only a boy! Here he is in there on the bed now with a blanket hove over 'en — shiverin' like a dog shittin' razorblades!"

"I knows, Ida — I knows! But what I don't know is what's gonna happen now!" He went to the cupboard and got a new pack of tobacco and papers and sat on the daybed. "'Nother three or four days and the seals is gonna be gone. Then the hunt is over, 'cause we fellers never shoots 'nough in the water to pay for the paint we scrapes off our boats. And if the slob comes in and bars everything off, we won't get a single one." He rolled a cigarette and licked it. "Here's me and Garf now with our spring lost — ain't got a seal to call our own."

Ida listened to him talk as she finished sewing the long seam, then went to the stove and pulled the pot back. "Well m'dear," she said, "try not to dwell on it too much 'cause you'll only make yourself sick again." She forked the headless herring onto a platter and took them to the table.

Ambrose lit his cigarette and looked in the bedroom at

his son asleep with a comic book near his hand. "Martin," he called softly. "Your supper's ready. We're all sittin' down now so get up and have a bit 'long with us."

The boy never moved.

Ida pulled the table off from the wall and checked to make sure she had placed it properly. "Gotta go in and get Mother up from her nap too, I s'pose," she said wearily. "Get ready for 'nother row."

"Call Martin too," Ambrose said. "'Cause Garf is gonna be over the once and show 'en how to pelt his seals." He went to the porch and opened the door, looked out at the gathering dark clouds. Smoked his cigarette down to his fingers and tossed it off the bridge when his wife called for him to sit in.

Martin was up and sitting in his spot under the radio shelf, yawning and rubbing the sleep from his eyes. He slid two steaming herring from the platter onto his plate and filleted the white flesh with his fork, picked out a dozen or so needle-like bones from a small piece and popped the steaming chunk into his mouth. He chopped a potato in two with the fork and stowed half in his cheek. He had been too tired to eat anything after changing his clothes and washing the salt off his body, so, wrapped in one of his mother's finest towels, he had fallen like a log onto his bed. His hands were sore and his back hurt; his eyes burned from the brightness of the sun on the ice, but the moonshine had made him sleep. And now he was hungry.

"My jeans?" he asked his mother. "Is they dry yet or ain't they? And what'd ya do with that bit a money I had in me pocket?"

Ida peeled the bluish-black skin from half a herring and removed some of the bones. "Your dollar bill was sogged to death and almost spoiled, but I dried 'en over the stove and got 'en put in on your room table on top a your comics."

"And what 'bout that bit a change was there?"

"Hope ya don't mind," she said, "but I took that and went over to Mr. Tucker's when you was sleepin' and bought you a can a peaches. They're good for drivin' the chill outta your bones. They're right there in your jam dish, and the rest is there in the cupboard whenever ya wants 'em."

Her mother sat beside her and made little sniffing sounds as she picked and poked at her supper, all the time keeping an eye on Ambrose.

"Any change left over?"

"Got your change in me purse there in the room. After supper I'll get it for ya."

"Nah," he said, cramming half a fillet into his mouth. "I don't want it. Keep it."

Ambrose watched the boy lay a strip of the hot herring in the middle of his bread and make a sandwich. He sipped his tea, slurped hard, his eyes wide in fear of burning his lips.

Martin reached for another potato. "Goin' down the cape again t'marra, Dad? Might get some more seals."

The old man sliced his herring down the back with a fork and opened it on his plate like a book. "'Cardin' to the glass," he said, lifting out the backbone, "the wind's gonna go round southeast t'marra evenin', and if that happens all that ice'll be gone out in the middle of the strait in less'n a hour."

"But what 'bout in the marnin'? The ice'll still be in then, won't it?"

Ambrose picked a dozen stiff, sharp bones from his herring. "Look," he said. "We all knows what happened today — the wind dropped out and all the ice went abroad. No-

body's not gonna be out on the back a the land t'marra unless they're off their head." He slid a piece of herring onto
his fork with his finger and held it to his mouth, the meat
looking like a dirty, flat cotton ball laced with straight pins.
"And that ice is not gonna pack in no more till the wind
comes in round eastern or northeast again — somewhere
'long them points."

"When y'expect the wind to come in round again?"

Ambrose hacked a little, picked a bone off his tongue
and snickered bitterly. "I don't know, boy — I'm not God,
y'know!"

"No, that's true," Aunt Kizzie said with little effort. "You're
the devil!" The old woman laughed and her dentures slipped
halfway out of her mouth. She flicked them back with a
slap of her hand and wiped her nose on her wrist.

Ida slammed her fist on the table. Her plate struck the
milk can and tipped it over. "Start, ol' woman — start now,
if I was you! That's all I wants now — you to start again!"
She shoved the table back in one hard push, and the wooden
legs jumped across the floor like a stick running down a
clapboard wall. Dishes rattled. Two glasses of cold water
tipped over, one into Martin's plate.

He pushed the table out and jumped up, strained the water
onto the herring in the platter. "What's the matter, Mom?
Ya got me supper ruined, maid — just look!" He turned to
his grandmother and said, "You're brewin' for trouble again,
ain't ya, ol' woman!"

"And *you* got two more herrin' spoiled," his mother said.

Martin pushed a finger into the herring on his plate. "Cold
now," he said. "Just so well to heave it in the slop bucket!"

His mother put her elbows on the table and lowered her
head with two thumbs dug into her eyes. "'Tis just like a

madhouse here all the time," she mused. "Been better if we never moved here at all."

"Been better if we all got drownded comin' 'cross the bay," Aunt Kizzie said. "Then me and you and Marty'd be rejoicin' up in heaven and Am and Garf'd be ga'pin' for breath over in hell." She dumped her glass of water into Ambrose's plate. "There," she said callously. "Now *you* eat cold herrin' and see how it tastes!"

Ambrose tipped the water out onto the table. "Boys oh boys oh boys oh boys," he said slowly and rhythmically. "You're all gone right clean and clever off yez heads! You're not right in your mind — n'ar one of yez!"

Ida clinked the mug on her teeth as she drank her tea.

Determined not to touch his grandmother this evening, Martin left the table. "You, Dad," he said maliciously, "you're the one that's not right in their mind!"

"Watch your mouth 'fore I beats 'en off a ya," his father warned. "Y'oughtta be thankful you're here, my son! If Garf never tied that knot in your rope no better'n the one ya tied in mine, you'd be out there face up on the bottom now with the crabs pickin' the eyeballs outta ya!"

"Garf, Garf," the boy imitated with revulsion. "Everything is Garf! Who the hell is Garf any more'n anybody else?"

Aunt Kizzie chuckled and plopped a chunk of herring into her mouth. "Give it to 'en, Marty," she applauded. "Give it to 'en!" She dipped a greasy fork in her coffee and stirred, bouncing it off the sides in annoying clicks. Then, as if the argument were a part of accepted table manners, she said, "Get 'ar bit a gum for me last night, Marty, or didn't ya?"

The boy went to his ski jacket hung on a nail behind the stove, came back and dropped the gum onto her plate. "Here

ya go, ol' woman," he said. "Shove that inside your gob and
don't open 'en no more till ya gets it all chewed!"

Ida began crying and ran to her bedroom.

"Look what ya got done to your mother again," Ambrose
hollered. "Ya won't rest till ya drives her in the grave, I
s'pose. Ya got *me* just 'bout killed so I s'pose you're tryin' to
kill her too!"

Martin went to her, he cupped his hand around her back
where she sat on the bed and hugged her. "Stop bawlin'
now, Mom," he said. "And listen to me. I didn't mean to
hurt ya — honest!"

"You're always hurtin' me, Martin — you and your father
both of yez!"

"I don't know what else I can do to please yez," he said.
"Y'know, Mom, I honestly to God don't know what you and
Dad wants from me. No matter what I does I can never do it
right. Garf over there can do whatever he wants and if he
does it wrong then Dad'll still say he done a perfect job,
s'posin' 'tis the wrongest thing in the world. Perhaps he
wants me to be like Garf; perhaps *you* wants me to be like
Garf. Well, I'm not Garf — I'm me. I'm who I am and no
more. And if you're not satisfied with that, what more can I
do?"

"You can try behavin' yourself sometimes, Martin. You
can eat your meals without startin' a row every time ya sits
to the table, can't ya?"

"You knows that's wrong what you're sayin', don't ya,
Mom?" he said. "I don't always be the one to start the rows
and you knows it." He sat beside her, locked his fingers
between his knees and leaned forward. "What is it 'bout
me that you and Dad don't like anyway? Tell me!"

"Your ways, Martin," she said without thinking, the tears

beginning to slow. "We don't like your ways!"

"Mom, I can't believe what you're sayin'! You're brain-washed, m'dear! The ol' woman and Dad got ya brain-washed!"

"Well, why is ya like ya is then? Tell me that much!"

"I'm like I am 'cause I got no other choice — you fellers got me made this way! Ya gotta show me some respect!"

"'Bout time you showed we fellers some respect, ain't it?"

"I do show ya respect, Mom!"

"No ya don't!"

"I do but ya don't see it 'cause whenever we meets we don't talk — we just fights!"

"You're wrong, Martin."

"Listen, Mom," he said, leaning back and playing with the edge of the bedspread. "Do ya know why Alec don't come here no more?"

"Why?"

"'Cause he got sick'n tired a listenin' to Dad mouth off 'bout how no good I was!"

"You're wrong, Martin — you're wrong! Your father loves ya with all of his heart!"

"Don't try to feed me that nonsense," he said. "I knows the difference!" Just look at Dad there to the table, look at 'en. Y'ever notice anything weird 'bout the way he talks to me? Think everything is perfect, Mom? He don't care 'bout me; he don't care 'bout you, Mom, and he don't care 'bout the ol' woman. All he cares 'bout is Garf. He don't care 'bout nothin' or nobody else long's he got plenty to eat and plenty a baccy. Now, tell me I'm wrong — tell me!"

Garf plucked the knife from his sheath and placed the tip at the cut in the chin, ripped down to the wound between the flippers and then to the tail. Back up at the chin again, he lifted the fatty edge and slipped his knife underneath, working it along the carcass in long strokes. He cut behind the shoulder, slicing it off as part of the pelt. He did the same to the other side and carefully cut the lower lip away, carved around the corners of the mouth to the top lip, moving the knife in slow, easy curves upward into the nose and back over the head until the pelt rolled off the bloody skull. He wrapped his fingers around the cold, slimy neck and lifted it up, sliced underneath through the string of meat and fat that joined the vertebral column to the skin and cut all the way back to the tail, chopped the pelt free and dropped the carcass onto the snow.

Garf pushed the tip of his blade through the thin stomach membrane and cut upwards, like an Arctic tern skimming plankton off the ocean swell. He rammed his hand into the tepid chest cavity and in one yank tore away the windpipe and lungs, and dragged the guts out. He rummaged through what a stranger would call a gruesome mess and cut away the elastic arteries holding the gallbladder, kidneys, liver and heart, then cut the head off and sliced through the soft bones until the carcass lay in eight pieces. He cropped the two shoulders from the pelt and washed his hands in the snow.

"OK, Martin," he said, packing the meat into a white-enamelled pan, "ya seen how 'tis done so go ahead and pelt the other one."

Martin had watched the pelting process with great interest but felt it a little too complicated to try just now, especially with only two pelts in their possession. A tiny slip with the knife could render the skin worthless. "No," he said. "You do it and I'll finish fillin' up the pan."

11

SACRED ISLAND

Ida hooked eight hot eggs from the steaming kettle with a spoon and piled them into a soup bowl. She took the butter dish from the oven, grabbed two slices of smoking bread on the damper and tossed them along to Ambrose, who had been waiting impatiently for his breakfast since six o'clock, after he'd lit a raging fire, filled the woodbox and checked the barometer twice.

Last night, he told his wife he was worried they might have to spend another winter in this house if the ice did not return with more seals, and with no money and no way to get any, Mr. Tucker would surely look unfavourably upon him.

Ida put two more slices of bread on the stove and went to see what was keeping her mother. The old woman was up and dressed but had said she was feeling a bit qualmish and was going back in her room to pray for more wind.

Ambrose rolled a small cigarette, put a match to it and crossed his legs.

"You ready, Mother?" Ida called from outside her door.

She heard something about "Marty" in the prayer as it ended. "Breakfast is on the table so come on out and sit down."

A tower of smoke rose from the sizzling bread on the stove. "Bread's burnin'," Ambrose said, in the same tone as a cardplayer would use to shout, *Gaaame-O.*

Ida ran from the inside part and flicked the two slices onto the table. "My God, Ambrose, what's the trouble with ya — growed on or what?"

He blew tobacco smoke her way. "Now, Ida, don't go gettin' in a huff. A bit a smoke is not gonna hurt nobody." Laughed and patted her bottom. "Gonna call Martin up for a bite or what ya gonna do?"

"Not yet I'm not," she said firmly. "I'm gonna let 'en sleep in today. After all that boy went through yes'day he deserves to rest."

"Yes maid," he said with a nod. "'Tis a wonder he wud'n drownded. I never told no one down the cape what was goin' through me mind but I figured he was a goner. If that rope would a broke or would a slipped he would a been lost, no two ways 'bout it."

"Well, no good to look back and wonder," she said. "We just gotta be thankful he made it." Ida tapped an egg on her plate and broke the shell. "But, Ambrose, s'posin' he didn't make it — what 'bout that?"

Ambrose watched Aunt Kizzie roll an egg from hand to hand, then stick it in her egg cup and saw its head off. He never answered.

The old woman caught his stare, and in a flash she jumped from the table, grabbed the kettle off the stove and swung it wildly towards him. Steaming hot water spilled onto the floor and over the daybed as he dived for cover in Martin's place under the radio shelf. "I had a mind to scald the eyes outta ya, ya dirty frigger," she said as she made little offers at him with the kettle.

Ida pushed her chair back and tried to take the boiling weapon from her. "What's wrong with you at all, Mother?" she cried. "My God, maid, I don't know what to do with ya! Put the bloody kettle back on the stove and sit down and eat your breakfast! Or go the hell in your room somewhere and don't come out no more today!" She grabbed onto the handle and pulled. "Leggo, Mother!"

The old woman's face looked as if someone had walked on it with hobnailed boots. "No, no, no," she raved, the loose skin on her jowls trembling with every word. "Lemme fix 'en for ya — good'n proper!"

Ambrose cowered under the radio shelf, his eyes blank. "What's her trouble now?" he asked. "I never even opened me mouth and she went the work and jumped right down me throat!"

"You," the old woman said with absolute disdain. "You're the trouble! Look what almost happened to young Marty yes'day!" She pushed the kettle at him and sloshed more water from the bib. "I never got n'ar wink at all last night — not one — thinkin' 'bout how he could a been drownded out there on that ice or lost or gone down through or ——"

"Gimme the jeezly kettle, Mother," Ida said as she went after it like a basketball player. "Now you either gives me the kettle or I'm gonna wake up Martin and tell 'en to come out and put you in your place!"

"Call 'en up Ida, do, for God's sake," Ambrose said, afraid of what the old woman might do to him should she follow up on her threat. "Go in and call 'en up and then me and you'll leave the house!" He grinned and looked Aunt Kizzie in the face. "We'll give 'en five minutes with ya 'fore we comes back." He began to feel brave as he let his mind rove through what Martin might do. "Five minutes, ol' woman — that's all he'll want and I betcha you won't grab n'ar 'nother kettle for nobody else!"

Aunt Kizzie backed off and carelessly handed over the kettle to her daughter. "Here," she said, in a declaration of victorious surrender. "You take it! You can scald the eyes outta the ol' son of a — outta the ol' brute yourself as well as I can!"

Ambrose crawled from Martin's chair to his own. "You wud'n call Martin, would ya?" he said to his wife. "I've a good mind right now to call 'en meself so he can get up and wring her bloody neck!" He brushed himself off as if he were covered with snow. "If I had me time back I'd a let 'en strangle the ol' witch the other day. Been better for all of us!"

Aunt Kizzie sat at the table and held out her cup to Ida and said, "Pour me up a little drop a water, will ya m'dear?"

Ambrose was drinking the last of his tea when he heard someone step on the bridge. "Hark," he said. "Someone's comin' in."

"I don't wanna see no one today," Ida said, with tears in her eyes again. Boots stamped on the bridge. "Garf," she said, looking at her husband. "What's Garf doin' over here this early?"

The kitchen door opened and Garf stood there with his eyes flashing as he looked from his mother to his father. "Where's the Ski-Doo?"

"Where ya left her in the garage, I s'pose," Ambrose said. "Where else ya think she is?"

Garf put on a queer smile. "God only knows."

The old man went to the window, noticed that the ice was melting in the corners and looked out at the fog rolling off the hills.

"Where's Martin?" Garf asked.

Ida poked a knuckle in her eye and rubbed. "Martin's still in bed," she said. "Don't tell me you're goin' 'cross the cape again."

Garf went to his brother's bedroom and pushed open the door. "Still in bed, eh?" He nodded towards the empty bed. "And how long've he been invisible?"

From where he sat on the snowmobile, under an overcast sky at the edge of the grasslands, Sacred Island lay more than two miles away, separated from the bay ice by a wide channel of Arctic mush. The line of demarcation extended westward as far as he could see, ran a hundred yards off from the black cliff that marked the eastern boundary of the grasslands and continued in a fairly straight line to Karpoon Island, at a point about half a mile outside the harbour entrance.

The coast of Labrador looked ten miles closer, and Belle Isle, smeared with dull patches of snow, loomed out of the mist like a side of bacon. The well-beaten snowmobile path under him led down the slope and around the beach to other villages farther in the bay, and houses he had only seen like tiny dots on the shore during his fishing trips with his father. He gunned the throttle and followed the track around the beach for five or six hundred yards, hoping to find another that would take him safely onto the smooth, gigantic sheet and back home. He found none, so he turned the skis off the path at the entrance to the bay and a mile later stopped the Ski-Doo at the edge of the Arctic pack.

He took Garf's sealing rope, coiled on the back of the snowmobile seat, and put it on his shoulder, knowing now that, without it, his chance of survival would be lessened if he encountered a situation like yesterday's. He pulled Garf's gaff from the footrest, and listened to the sharp clicks coming from the engine as it cooled. He hoped no one had heard him leave the house before daylight, or heard him drag the Ski-Doo by its skis from the garage and push it down the hill to the harbour. Hoped his father wouldn't miss his mended jacket from behind the stove — his own had not been dry enough to wear.

He thought how Sacred Island looked much bigger to him now than the day he had left it; how he had sat in the stern of his father's fishing boat and watched it get smaller and smaller. He hadn't seen the direction they were headed, just the direction they had headed from. His father had not said a word for the entire trip to Karpoon, had stood there with the tiller-stick in his hand and stared blankly over the heads of his wife and her crying mother sitting on a pile of tied bedclothes in the bow. Martin remembered that the old man never once looked back at the island and seldom dropped his eyes to their only possessions, packed in the midships: table, chairs, bed frames and thick feather mattresses; old suitcases with busted handles, bulging and straining against the grey, pencil-sized trawl line that held them shut; stove, washstand, daybed, slop bucket, water buckets, cooking pots, teapot, kettle and frying pan; dishes wrapped in washcloths and towels and packed with everyone's Sunday clothes in the steamer trunk. The small boat they towed behind them had been filled only with long firewood, the same wood that had been cut behind the hills of Karpoon a year earlier and transported by water to the island. He remembered the rodney twisting and turning in the wake of the motorboat, fighting the waves, trying to break free and almost capsizing twice. Garf had stood in the engine house and dropped his chin onto his folded arms atop the sliding roof cover, saying nothing.

Now the island, its low hills and jagged perimeter buried under a blanket of snow, began to look like his old home. Martin saw the entrance to the cove where his house used to be. He tested the rubble with a prod of his gaff, took one step and clinked the gaff on a hard subsurface that indicated stronger ice. A dozen more uncertain steps forward he stopped and listened, heard nothing except the ice growling like an empty stomach. He prodded some more; then, keeping his gaff clinking on something hard, he began jogging, darting and weaving across the channel, dodging the maze of ice blocks until he jumped ashore onto a small, snowy field of bedraggled saltwater grass.

After searching for the Ski-Doo behind his father's garage, behind the house, the bunkhouse and woodpile, Garf went to the edge of the hill and looked down onto the shoreline at a fresh snowmobile track that entered the main path, from the garage.

"Hard to say where Martin's gone," he said. "Been other Ski-Doos back and forth this path already and got his track covered up."

"He's gone back to Cape Bauld," Ambrose said, his forehead wrinkled and notched. He shot a worried look at the fog scraping the tops of the hills and softly descending on the town. "This wind picks up, ya won't see a hand in front a your face."

Garf told him he would run across the cove and ask John Parsons to take him to Cape Bauld on his snowmobile. Said, "You stay here, Uncle Am, in case Martin's gone for a joyride. If he comes back 'fore we gets home, then you and he — two of yez — jump on the Ski-Doo and come down the cape and let us know."

The old man couldn't believe his ears. "Do what?" he asked, his voice raised to an extraordinarily high pitch. Then back down. "Garf, you don't 'xpect me to do the like a that, do ya?"

Halfway down the hill, Garf shouted back that he did.

Martin sat on a bare rock at the top of the plateau and looked down on the tiny cove that had once been his home and playground. The harbour was shaped like a pear and filled with a mat of loose ice that ran past the reefs to open water at the north end of the island and to the tip of Cape Bauld in the east. Two scaling whitewashed houses — a two-storey box trimmed in leafy green and a perfectly square bungalow trimmed in red with a dark patch where its porch had been — stood a good thirty yards in from the beach. A few old red-ochred twine stores with their heads resting on the landwash and their asses planted firmly on the edge of a wide field, had neither roofs nor windows and all were partly filled with snow. There were fragments of other buildings: caved-in sides, partially dismantled roofs, detached porches, overturned bridges and long ladders with missing rungs. Pulverized furniture: smashed bedroom bureaus and kitchen cabinets, collapsed drawers, upside-down tables with missing legs, rusty bedsteads, rusty bedsprings, torn mattresses leaking clumps of dirty feathers, and broken stoves that still held some shine on the chrome. Empty brown oil drums that had once held gasoline for the motorboats, filthy black cod-oil barrels that had been filled over and over with rotting fish liver, all useless now and scattered throughout the cove. His father's wharf, severed from his fishing stage and frozen under a thick shell of ice, lay on its side on the beach, eight or ten of its sturdy spruce logs littering the shore. The empty floor of the wall-less stage still clung to the scurfy bedrock, the round wooden supports cemented in solid ice and jammed tight into the sills.

The desolate picture of isolation before him did not surprise the boy at all, for he had witnessed the destruction of his village while he lived here, his father and Garf swearing to their Maker that they would never draw a nail they themselves had hammered home. He had heard the boisterous laughs and shouts of nervous, excited villagers tearing armfuls of personal belongings from their houses and mucking them down the grass-lined paths to their stages, across the wharves and to their boats, where they dumped them all aboard like bales of soggy hay. At least, that was how he remembered it.

Only the fishermen returned, and carried to Karpoon what they had had no room for on their first trip: cod traps, salmon nets, herring nets, fishing trawls, ropes, buoys, killicks and graplins, mooring chains for their boats, reliable drums and liver barrels, splitting tables, splitting tubs, pieces of wharves and old fish flakes. They took windows and doors, bundles of strapped lumber, clotheslines, washing tubs, fencings from around their small vegetable gardens and even water barrels half filled with fresh water from the village well. Then the animals: eight or ten yapping crackies, six or seven frightened cats, a dozen or so sheep, fifty or sixty hens, ten cows, and one lone bull who refused to follow his blaring harem over the gangways of two-tiered planks from the beach to the waiting boats. But he made the trip off the island all the same, heralding his unwillingness to do so with one end of a rope around his neck and the other end tied to an iron ringbolt in the sternpost of his owner's motorboat. What remained after the villagers had become sickened by their mistake now lay dead on the dead grass, covered in a cold, ghostly white shroud.

Martin wanted to see his house from the inside again, to look at the cove through the windows and see in his mind the loaded fishing boats come in the harbour and tie onto the stageheads. Wanted to watch the men drive two-pronged pitchforks into their catch and heave it up onto their wetted wharves, to see himself run down the path to his father's stage and cut fish throats under a blazing sun with the old man's hunting knife. To wash his bloody hands in a bucket of cool salt water drawn from the cove and pulled up the side of the wharf on a knotted rope. He wanted to catch connors again, pluck out fish eyes and use the little translucent balls inside for bait. He had done all these things at his father's new fishing premises in Karpoon, but somehow they didn't mean as much to him as did the memory of how he had lived here.

He pulled his rope into his collarbone to keep it from slipping and hiked down the hill, a huge patchwork of rock and snow, to the cemetery leading into the village. Seventeen people were buried here, nine with white marble headstones set in black mud less than four feet deep. The villagers had used wheelbarrows to bring extra mud from other parts of the field, to build the ground up enough to cover the caskets.

Martin leaned across the picket fence and read one of the inscriptions down to where the words disappeared beneath the snow:

IN LOVING MEMORY OF
GEORGE TRIMM
WHO WAS
ACCIDENTALLY DROWNED
AUGUST 8TH 1967
AGED 35 YEARS

IN MY FATHER'S HOUSE
ARE MANY MANSIONS
IF IT WERE NOT. . . .

He read more of the marble-cut names, unknown to the masons who had cut and chiselled the stone, probably checking the spelling against the scrawled handwriting of the fishing merchants who had placed the orders for the bereaved families. His father wished to be buried here and had shown him where — tight to his own father's grave, three stones in from the wooden gate. Everett Bellman had a simple epitaph adorned with three crosses wrapped in a cold, uncoloured vine:

In memory of
Everett Bellman
1871 – 1952

He shall send down from on high
And fetch me out of many waters.

The old man had spent nearly a lifetime of summers away
from home aboard twelve-dory fishing schooners working
the Grand Banks. After surviving four shipwrecks and
twenty-six days adrift in an open dory with nothing to eat
but raw fish, he had lost his stomach for the high seas and
returned to the island. For ten of the last twelve years of his
life he had hauled the cod traps and trawls with Ambrose
and a crew of sharemen, until the paralysing stroke hooked
him and left him stiff as a beam in his bed for two years. He
had died with Ida tending him as though he were a child.
His wife, beside him in her unmarked grave, had died on
Christmas Day from a massive heart attack at thirty-six.
Effie, her retarded sister, resting in the northwestern corner, had helped with young Ambrose's upbringing as best
she could, shoving him off on the charitable villagers whenever she didn't want him, until he turned eleven and went
to live with the Butler family.

Martin left the cemetery, ignorant of his family history,
and trudged through the snow to what remained of Max's
twine store. Inside the roofless box, he saw an old single-
cylinder engine sitting on its mounts in the middle of the
floor and looking ready to start. But autumn frost had severely split the back of the cylinder, due to it leaking rain-
water through the priming cup in the flat head. A hundred
pounds of lightly barked twine, uselessly covered by a piece
of grubby sailcloth, was home to maybe a dozen field mice
whose tracks were scattered about the store like their drop-
pings. Short pieces of broken roof boards and loops of dark,

frazzled rope, worn-out engine parts, a wooden chair with no back, seven or eight dry-cell batteries the size of rum bottles with a slinky black cat on the labels; a wooden box of rusted nuts, bolts, crooked nails, a wooden rasp handle and broken glass. A two-winged brass propeller hung on the wall with a big nail through the keyed hole; its five-foot shaft stood in the corner behind the felled one-hinged door, the cotter pin and the nut still fastened.

From the doorway he looked directly across at the Salvation Army church, the gaunt uprights and double-beamed wall plates the colour of old lead and stripped bare of all clapboards and lumber. A quarter of the roof was still there, tattered with patches of black felt and holding up a four-foot wooden cross. The church had served not only as a place of worship but also as a town hall and a schoolhouse, with hardwood desks and chairs pushed back against the walls during prayer meetings. Now they lay strewn about the flooring and buried in the snow.

The islanders had built the church back in the forties, shaped the pulpit and made the pews from sawlogs cut behind Karpoon and run through old Albert Parsons' sawmill. When the winter northeaster of '55 broke in one side and ripped the roof off, Albert's son, John, sawed more logs with the same saw and even went to the island to help with the rebuild. They had enough boards left over to store on the beams for casket building.

The boy left the twine store and walked above the hardworn path that he knew lay under the snow, dented with long, shallow ruts made by wheelbarrows laden with salt fish on their way to the flakes for drying. He crossed the four-board bridge, not seeing it but remembering its place on the path over the dribble that ran from the village well, now under eight or ten feet of snow. He passed where the henhouse and clothesline used to be and then stood at the door of his father's house. Ambrose and Garf had cut the top storey off when he was two years old, and had taken the door from the west and put it in the south. The door had still opened into the kitchen but they had moved a few partitions around to help compensate for the lost top floor, and had made the stairwell, pantry and half of the living room along the north wall into four small bedrooms. There was never a need for a bridge because the house practically sat on the ground.

Martin noticed that one glass in the four-paned window at the kitchen side of the door was broken and gone, just shards left in the grooves like shark's teeth. He inspected the living-room window on the other side of the door, across from the bare, blackened boards where the porch had been, and found it intact, with a white lace blind and a brick-sized flowerpot holding an inch of fly husks on the dried mud — or three inches of husks, if there was no mud in the pot. There were no windows in the east and there was no damage there, but he walked completely around the house to check its condition, and found the four bedroom windows in perfect order, along with the one in the west wall of the kitchen.

He leaned his gaff against the house and kicked away the snow from the door, untied the two half hitches around the nail in the doorpost and unwound the rest from the brown porcelain knob in a blur of widening circles. Turned the knob and pushed open the door.

A large, flower-patterned linoleum square covered the middle of the red floor. The baseboards were black and the walls were painted a weak blue. A long swath of snow ran from the broken window, across the white Formica counter-top, and ended in little more than a wisp near his parents' bedroom door.

Martin looked out the window at the old twine stores and stages too rotten to be beaten apart for recycling, and the slipway like a big, twisted ladder under a sheen of ice, wrecked on the beach by the seas. Upside-down motorboats, too old to fish, lay on the outermost edge of the field with their backs broken; rodneys, condemned to the black mud, lay on their sides with cracked hulls and broken timbers. Fatal wounds bandaged in a smooth dressing of pure white snow. And beyond all that — the empty harbour.

He opened each of the five drawers in the cupboard and saw a few crooked nails and rusted stove bolts in the top one. In the next one there was an old *Family Herald* maga-zine minus the cover, and a Zippo lighter with no fuel-absorbent cotton or metal case. He flicked the wheel and it sparked. In the bottom drawer there was a bunch of wet score sheets from a card game with *We* and *They* scribbled above two columns of double-digit numbers, one column always ending in a scrawled *120* with *Game* written through it. He pawed them over and saw *Max* and *Me*, *Norm* and *Me*, *Dulcie* and *Me* and *You* and *Me* written on others, even one with *Martin* and *Me*. There were stubs of two pencils, the handle from a ladle or an egg turner — he couldn't tell which — and nothing in the others.

He crossed the white swath and saw through the west window the shambles on vacant lots, between clothesline poles and rotting porches. Looked across the ditch, through the church at nothing but his own tracks leading down the field from the cemetery. At an earlier time the meadow would have been peppered with footprints weaving in and out between the houses, narrow trenches in the snow, the small incline leading to the north end and the hill behind the Trimm house scarred with furrows made by the backsides of sliding children.

Saddened and strangely alone, he looked up through the black hole in the ceiling where the stovepipes had been, saw his congealing breath for the first time since entering and remembered how warm he used to feel here, standing next to the hot, crackling stove, while he waited for his mother to make breakfast. If he had brought matches, he thought, he would have lit a fire — if the stove had still been here and the pipe hole in the roof had not been boarded over. But he had only wanted to see the place, not to stay in a village without houses and people.

He went into each of the two empty bedrooms off the kitchen, found them neat and orderly with shiny clean, canvassed floors, and frilly white lace curtains. It looked as if the family had intended to return and carry on as though they had never left, or as if someone else had been expected to move in and take over, for his mother had washed the whole house from top to bottom immediately after stripping it.

In the second bedroom he admired the platter-sized picture he had drawn on the wallpaper of the German battleship *Bismarck*. Her long guns blazed from round turrets and black smoke rose from her nearby sinking target. Sons of the British Commonwealth in a sea of fire and floating debris, arms reaching for a single lifeboat, were hammered with hefty oars by their frightened comrades inside, who saw them as flies crawling over the top of a molasses jar — that was how he had imagined the scene while he drew it. Behind them on the burning bridge of their ship, the brave captain stood in a farewell salute, shouting, *God Save the King*. Martin had placed the words inside a bubble whose tail snaked along the smokestack and into the captain's mouth. Billowing smoke hid part of the sun in his picture of carnage and confusion, and Adolf Hitler, in an inset below, clutched the throat of a fat little man with a thick cigar in his mouth. The Führer's eyes glowed like coals at the sight of the swastika left in his enemy's forehead by the branding iron he held high in the air. The caption in block letters underneath read: SUCH A GLORIOUS DAY FOR THE FATHERLAND.

There was nothing in the inside part, either on the walls or on the floor, that anyone could hold in his hand except the window blind, the flimsy metal rod that kept it up, a flowerbox and another handful or two of fly husks. Martin tipped the box and saw the mud.

Garf's bedroom at the north end of the living room was nothing more than four bare walls, and in the adjacent room, his grandmother's old rocking chair, painted turquoise like the living room and missing the left rocker and its two legs, lay dead beneath the windowsill. He pulled open the blinds and looked out as if to check his location, and went back to the kitchen.

The curtain covering the broken window fluttered in a small breeze that swept through the house, whisking the steam away from his mouth. He felt hungry. The peaches in the cupboard had been his last bite and he wished he had brought a lunch, but the risk of waking his parents by making molasses sandwiches had been too great.

He decided to check out the Trimm house, see what treasures it might hold, and then he'd walk back across the island and arrive in Karpoon for another fight before dark.

Once outside, he met with a stiff southeasterly wind off

the hill behind the two-storey, backed by a huge, leprous grey cloud that he watched roll into the cove and smother what was not already buried in snow. In less than a minute the whole village was blanketed in fog. The boy's heart raced as he stood there, unable to see any farther than the church. If there ever was a time to leave, he thought, it was now. He tied the door, picked up his gaff and started running in his old footprints back through the village, past the church and past the twine stores until he reached the cemetery. He had stayed too long, been too careless in his observation of the weather, and then he thought — had he really made an observation or had he just not cared?

12

THE SEARCH

When Garf and John Parsons returned from Cape Bauld three hours later, Ida met them on the bridge, Ambrose tight behind her. "Did ya find 'en, boys?" she asked, her eyes wet and puffy from crying the whole morning. She'd made a dozen trips or more to Martin's bedroom since he went missing, sitting on his bed for a minute, looking through his window for two and then going out on the bridge, where she'd stay for another minute, listening for the sound of the snowmobile. Then she'd go back to his bedroom again.

Garf didn't know how to answer her. He put his back to the house and listened to John say how they had searched for her son on every Ski-Doo track that criss-crossed Karpoon Island. How they had given up the search, thinking he had gone someplace else.

"Give up? My God, John," Ida objected angrily, her face showing more strain than it ever had. "You can't give up — you ain't even started yet!"

John realized his blunder. "No no no, Ida m'dear! I didn't mean it like that — didn't mean it like that at all!" He put his hand on her shoulder and she felt the weight of him. "What I meaned to say was, we're gonna have to look somewhere else."

"Yeah," Garf said, finally admitting that they had not found his brother. "We looked all over God's farm for 'en down on the cape and the rest of the island, so what we're gonna have to do now is look for 'en on this side of the harbour."

"This side," Ambrose said, echoing his speed and tone. "Where ya think you're gonna find 'en to on this side of the harbour?" He made a sharp outward sniff to show his displeasure with the idea. "If you're gonna find 'en anywhere," he said, stepping around his wife and going to the end of the bridge, "'tis over there." He pointed to the blank wall of drifting fog that barred Karpoon Island from sight as if it had never been there. "If he's not 'cross there, then he's on the bottom."

John put his cap back on his head and looked at Ida, numbed and completely lost for words. He leaned forward and spat on the ground, buried the wet spot by scraping snow on it with his boot as he listened to Garf say something about choosing words more carefully.

"Well, wherever he's to," Ambrose established, "he's not here. *So* — what's the next step?"

"This cursed fog," Ida said, going back into the house and leaving the door open. She spoke to her mother, and then the old woman got off her chair and went to her bedroom.

"We might a missed 'en too, y'know," John said, directing his voice through the doorway, attempting to lessen the woman's pain. "He might a been on one path while we was on 'nother. Easy to miss each other that way."

"What's we gonna do, boys?"

"Gotta run back home, Ambrose, and full up the tank 'fore we does anything. Best thing I knows is for you to see if ya can get a couple a Ski-Doos on this side of the cove to go in and have a look 'long the edge of the woods. If ya gets anybody, tell 'em to keep goin' till they gets to the grasslands. We'll have a bite to eat, and then me and Garf'll go on down to Cape Bauld again. Only thing I knows what to do."

"And whaddaya think he's doin' in the woods, John? Martin never cut n'ar stick a wood in his life. Wud'n even know what end of the axe to hold onto. All he ever done was frig round and spend money and read comics."

Ida came to the bridge with her mother's flashlight. "Here, Garf," she said. "Take this light and don't wear out the batteries. And for God's sake find 'en!"

"Don't warry, Aunt Ida," he replied. "We'll find 'en. And 'fore dark too. I hope."

"I'll go with yez," Ambrose said.

"Not enough room, Uncle Am. Less'n ya wants us to hook on the sled for ya."

Ambrose backed off and never mentioned joining the search again.

As soon as Garf had finished eating, a group of snowmobiles pulled up near the bridge and waited for instructions. By the time John Parsons arrived towing his stubnosed sled, painted fire-engine red with a huge white diamond on the bars, all orders had been given. Without John shutting off his engine, Garf jumped on the sled and they headed off in the fog for a second search.

❧

Martin reached the end of the island, his heart beating out of his chest and his clothes sticking to his body with sweat. He looked at his tracks where he had landed earlier and saw that there were none on the ice, and right away he knew the pack had shifted — how much, he didn't know. The fog blinded him from seeing more than fifty yards in either direction. With the ice moving through the channel in widening patches of open water, he told himself he couldn't take the chance of crossing.

Tired and frightened, he ran along the low ballycaters through the stiff grass, jumping the narrow crevices, searching for a break in the fog and hoping for a patch of solid, unmoving ice. Why had this thing happened today, he asked himself. If the wind and fog had only waited another hour or so he would have been gone from the island, and would probably now be burning the rest of the gasoline in his father's Ski-Doo. The Ski-Doo — was she still at the edge of the ice, he wondered, or had the ice broken up and taken her with it? Maybe a crack had opened directly underneath her and she lay on the bottom in forty fathoms of water. Maybe his parents had discovered that the snowmobile was missing and had sent someone to find him. Maybe they hadn't checked his bedroom yet. He wished Alec had come to his house this morning, so that his father could have pushed open his bedroom door and again told the boy how useless his son was. That way the old man would have known he was missing. Then Garf struck his mind, and he convinced himself that if his brother were here everything would be all right, for Garf would certainly know what to do.

The loose ice crunched softly against the ballycaters as it passed the island, moving into the Strait of Belle Isle like a lazy river that would, in a million years, empty itself.

Martin stood on the highest rock he could find, cupped his hands around his mouth and called out for help, throwing his long, drawn-out syllables in a slow side-to-side motion. After the third "Helllp" he stopped and listened, hands cupped behind his ears. All he could hear was a more distinctive crunching of the ice, and a slight murmuring of the wind that was now beginning to cool his face in a weightless mask of dripping condensation. He watched the mist, trillions of tiny glistening water droplets, blown along like micro-pollen in the intensifying southeaster.

Ambrose rolled his last bit of tobacco into a cigarette and crunched the pack in his hand before tossing it into the slop bucket. He struck a match and watched it burn, holding the flame close to his face like a jeweller gaping into the works of a pocket watch, touched it to his cigarette and sucked back, then let it burn down to his fingers. His son had never been missing before — been late coming back from the restaurant a few nights but that didn't seem serious now. He had taken more dirty looks and slurs from Aunt Kizzie today than in the last two years, and as always he had ignored them but today he had had to bite his tongue. His wife had been withdrawn the whole evening, speaking only when spoken to, but since a couple of her friends had dropped by expressing their concern she seemed more uplifted, and went about setting her table.

Max Butler's wife, Sadie, had made a pot of mutton soup and a pan of fresh bread rolls and had mucked them through the snow all the way from the other side of town. She sat on the daybed like a dark hunchbacked pygmy, her feet crossed at the ankles, neatly curled raven hair covered with a bright red bandanna and looking over her cat's eyes glasses at Aunt Nel Peyton stamping the snow off her boots inside the kitchen door.

The old woman was nearly crippled with arthritis, and carried her ass on her back and a partridgeberry pie in the crook of her arm, but she let everyone in the house know that despite her disability she had come to offer her support and to pray for Martin's homecoming.

"Come in, Aunt Nel," Ida said, standing at the stove and dipping hot soup into a bowl. "Ya don't know how glad I am to see ya — you and Sadie two of yez."

"Yes, come in," Aunt Kizzie echoed. She stretched her gum out and coiled it around her finger, poked it back into her mouth. "Come in and get your gut full. Lots to talk about this evenin'!"

Ida worried about her mother's behaviour. "I don't know what I'd do if somethin' happened to Martin," she said, "I don't know. I daresay I'd go and jump off the head a the wharf."

Aunt Nel put the pie on the end of the cupboard and wiped the dew from her face, pulled her hem down and her worsted stockings up. "Ah, don't go gettin' on like that, girl. You gotta put that kinda stuff outta your mind. Won't be long now 'fore the boys'll have 'en found."

"Oh my, I don't know," Ida sighed, taking the soup to the table and bringing back another bowl. "This fog is a killer. When Garf showed me Martin's empty bed this marnin' a lump come up in me throat so big as a apple. And it's still there." She put two fingers into her solar plexus and pressed. "Right there, look — just like I'm kinked right off."

Aunt Nel and Sadie nodded at her discomfort.

"Ok, we'll all sit in now and have our supper."

"Never come for nothin' to eat, Ida maid," Sadie said. She untied her bandanna and draped it over her coat, slung on the back of Ambrose's chair. "But seein' ya got it on the table I'll have a drop a soup, yes."

"OK, Ambrose. C'mon."

"How 'bout you, Aunt Kiz?" Aunt Nel asked, going to the washstand and picking up a towel. "How's you holdin' up in all of this?"

"Well," Aunt Kizzie said, headed for her place at the table, "I was sayin' to Ida just now that if Martin don't come back 'fore dark we're gonna have to have a word a prayer for 'en."

Aunt Nel wiped her face in the towel. "Oh yes," she said, positively in control of her religious beliefs. "And that we is. Without prayer he ain't got a chance." She waited for Ida to show her where to sit.

Ida pointed to the chairs under the radio shelf. "Right there, Aunt Nel; you can sit down there and Sadie can sit 'longside a ya."

The only talk around the table was about Martin — the kind of boy he used to be back on the island, how he had always obeyed his parents and how he had been blessed with such a good upbringing.

"Had it too good," Ambrose said, sipping his tea with his elbows on the table. "Perhaps if we'd a never treat 'en with kid gloves on he'd a turned out OK."

Aunt Kizzie wanted to claw her son-in-law's eyes out, and told him so in the look she gave him.

"And only yes'day," Sadie said, "Max told me he had alike to be drownded." She swallowed a chunk of mutton fat and wiped her mouth. "He said 'twas a real miracle he got ashore when he did 'cause another second or two and he'd a been a goner. Max said 'twas lucky anybody made it."

"Only the Blessed Lard to thank for that," Aunt Kizzie said, trying not to show her temper. She dunked half a bread roll into her soup and added, "If He never stepped in when He did, the whole works of 'em would a went to hell in a handbasket."

Aunt Nel gave her old comrade a stern warning just by saying *Kiz* without looking at her.

"What I meaned to say," Aunt Kizzie said graciously, making up for the outburst, "was that 'tis a lucky thing we got a good God up in heaven lookin' down on us. That's what I meaned to say." Slightly embarrassed, she stuck the roll on the edge of her plate, took her handkerchief from her sleeve and wiped her nose.

"Yeah, He's a good God all right," Aunt Nel said, her eyes turning to the old woman. "Good shot He is, too."

Sadie licked the juice off a small bone and chewed its end down to a ragged stump, then pushed it under the rim of her plate. "Can't understand somethin'," she said. "Why a bright young child like that would go the work and get kicked outta school."

❧

For a brief moment Martin had believed he would be rescued. He had heard a snowmobile across the channel and had thought it might be someone out searching for him, had imagined the driver pulling up near the edge of the ice and then racing away for help. He had stayed at the end of the island for three hours and now he was hungry; his jeans were sogged and he could feel the chill on his back through his father's jacket.

Had he made the right decision by returning to the village a second time, or had he given up the chance of hearing another snowmobile? However he thought about it, he had done what he believed Garf would have done in his place.

He had broken the padlock on the door of the Trimm house and had searched every room for matches but had found no more than a few charred stubs in a box. There was nothing left here but dirt in an empty shell, with a rusty stove for a kernel; rusty pipes, and the lifter still in the damper slot.

The lower cupboard held a single empty ketchup bottle with a reddish-black scab at the bottom, and a white-enamelled dipper having two holes, a further hole already repaired with a pot mender. In the top cupboard there were two plates, a cup with its handle gone, some spilled sugar, a small egg-shaped cork bobber, used in fishing for trout, and a left-handed leather-palmed glove.

The drawers held a vast array of useless items including a mousetrap with a broken spring, several tin stoppers from lime juice bottles, two big lobster claws and the lock and trigger section from a Cooey 12-gauge shotgun missing its firing pin; fathoms of homespun wool tangled in a web of clothespins and some radio antenna wire wrapped around a small stick. Two jokers from a pack of playing cards, new lamp wick, four empty Canuck shotgun cartridges and one full one, a woman's Bulova wristwatch without a strap, neatly folded brown shopping paper and the ends from five rolls of wallpaper.

George Trimm and his wife, Dulcie, had lived here for seventeen years with his parents and his retarded brother,

Alfred, but after his drowning, the parents had gone to live with another one of their sons in Karpoon, under the resettlement program. Alfred had gone with his Aunt Nel, and Dulcie had taken Judy and gone back living with her mother until she married Jack. Martin remembered helping the family carry their belongings down to the boat, and the old man giving him two dimes and three pennies, the old wife clutching a white hanky and continuously wiping her eyes.

A clutter of Mason jars, assorted long-necked bottles and old cake tins with pictures of exotic places on the lids lined the shelf above the woodbox in the porch. Three-quarter-length jackets, green khaki trousers with torn zippers, shirts, wool sweaters and caps, hard leather boots and dirty sneakers without laces, short rubber boots and chopped off thigh rubbers, empty fruit cans, milk cans and a thousand catalogue pictures littered the kitchen floor.

Upstairs in the four bedrooms: bottles, ugly piles of clothing, flashlight batteries, worn-out worsted stockings, perfume bottles, broken ornaments, a broken clock, hundreds of torn pages from at least a dozen schoolbooks and a couple of perfectly good-looking handbags. There were numerous envelopes with shabby openings, *Eaton's*, *Economic Trading Co.*, letters from friends and family as far away as Boston, and Christmas cards and Easter cards with holes where pictures had once been.

Another hour and it would be dark. He beat his hands against his legs to warm them in the damp mittens and kicked his feet together. Surely his parents had missed him by now, he thought. They were probably searching for him this very minute, calling his name through the fog. But maybe they thought he was joyriding and had no intentions of searching at all.

Downstairs, he took off his rope and his jacket, pulled on a pair of the big, green trousers over his wet ones, buttoned the waist and hauled on a sweater and a stinky three-quarter. Exchanged his tossel-cap for a bright yellow one with a black band. The dry clothes didn't warm him instantly — if anything they made him colder — but a minute or so later, with a few crazy dance steps around the kitchen and some handclapping through the glove and a wool stocking, he began to feel better. But he was so hungry, and he had never known that feeling before. There had always been plenty to eat at his father's house, both here and back in Karpoon, and now on this wretched island there wasn't a scrap of food he could smell, much less put in his mouth.

He looked past the rain beating on the window to the harbour, saw nothing but the still forms of village remnants in the growing darkness. His legs were tired so he went to the porch, brought back the woodbox and turned it upside down near the stove, then sat on it with his head drawn into his shoulders and his hands wedged between his knees. How pointless, he thought, to sit in front of a cold stove on an empty woodbox when he could have sat on the box in the porch and accomplished the same thing. He kicked the old clothes and heard a boot bounce off the wall. He wished he had taken up smoking, for then he would have matches or a lighter. He wondered about the lighter he'd seen in the drawer at his old house and thought that if he had it, it might give him some comfort.

He opened the door and went outside. Water was dripping from the eave and blowing away in the wind that baffled around the southwest corner. He pulled his too-big coat around him and, with his gloved hand keeping his too-big trousers up, ran through the rain to his father's house, found the lighter and flicked it to make sure he hadn't imagined the spark, and ran back to the Trimm house. He had decided it would be best to stay there, with a stove and good windows, rather than at his own house, with a pile of snow on the floor and the wind blowing through it.

Once inside, he tried lighting a piece of catalogue paper with the spark, flicking the wheel rapidly and throwing bright stars against the dry tinder. But nothing happened. He took the tangled wool from the drawer and pushed a short string of it down around the burnt wick in the shield, buried it in a shower of sparks from the spinning wheel and smelled it scorching but saw no flame. What he needed was something that would burn quickly and create enough heat to make something else catch. But what could he use?

He thought about the shotgun cartridge and pulled it from the drawer. If he could get the gunpowder out he could make an explosion, but could he do it without blowing his fingers off? The idea of bleeding to death in the house seemed worse than freezing to death. Or what if the shell went off and he shot himself accidentally? But, he could not shoot himself once he had taken the lead shot out, and if he was careful in removing the powder he might have a chance at being warm again. If he believed in his comic-book heroes and their survival techniques, then he had to believe in their method of starting a fire with raw gunpowder and a spark from a flint.

He pulled the woodbox to the window and sat down with the cartridge in front of him on the sill, took his pocket knife and hooked out the wadding. He found the two lime juice bottlecaps and dumped the shot into one and the powder into the other, then groped around for handfuls of pictures and stogged the firebox; tossed the old rubber boots and sneakers near the stove and tore long, heavy strips of paper from the wall. He dumped the stubs from the matchbox and poured in half the powder, lightly placed tiny pieces of brown paper inside and sprinkled on the rest of the powder. Took the box to the edge of the damper hole.

He tipped the lighter bottom up and as close to the concoction as he could without touching it, and flicked the wheel, but the sparks would not drop. He flicked harder and faster. A few sparks fell into the matchbox but still nothing happened. He pushed the lighter closer and flicked harder still. The wheel jammed. He examined it at the window. He couldn't tell what was wrong but some hard pressure from his thumb soon had the wheel moving again. It made a coarse grinding noise but no sparks. The flint had worn out.

The house seemed colder without the tiny bright stars, and it was much darker. He listened to the rain on the window and thought about his mother. What were his parents thinking about now, he wondered. Had they been out searching for him? Were they still searching? Had they started searching yet? What kind of a mess had he put himself into, and what kind of a mess had he put them in? There would be no forgiveness for his stupidity this time. This would be the thing to set the old man off and keep him that way. He thought of his grandmother and wished he hadn't been so hard on her, thought that if he were back there right now and she began mouthing off he wouldn't say a word to her. He would freeze to death here tonight and would not be found until next summer when some islanders came to visit the cemetery, if in fact they ever came at all.

He knew he had to stay warm to have any chance of seeing daylight again so he got down on his hands and knees and crawled around the floor, gathering all the clothes he could find. He carried the musty garments to the woodbox and dropped them inside and went upstairs, dreading to do so, for he thought that a cold, withered hand would reach out and grab him on the steps. He picked up an armful of rags and hurried back down.

He got in the box on top of the clothes and fixed a couple of the three-quarter coats around his legs and upper chest, then reached outside and pulled in all the upstairs stuff, fitting everything snugly around him until he had himself completely surrounded and almost buried. After tucking his arms inside, he slid down into his dirty bedclothes and pulled his head under, shutting out the frightening sounds of the wind, and the evil darkness.

The rain seemed louder on the window now, and he heard it lash against the outside wall like someone throwing sand at the clapboards. He imagined wild animals coming up the path and circling the house, Indians in strange, grotesque masks, with war clubs, stopping near the door, waiting for him to fall asleep. But there was no sleep in his eyes. There were only tears.

13

GREAT WHITE MONSTER

This was the first time the Tilley lamp and the stove had been kept lighted all night since Ambrose had taken them off the island. Even back there, if he had seen a single glowing ember in the firebox he had always doused it with water before going to bed, afraid, he'd say, of what might happen if it flared up or went down through the cast-iron grates and rolled onto the floor. And he had never stayed up past midnight with the lamp lighted, even during his card games, but here he was now, pumping up the light among the dirty dishes on the table and listening to the droning chatter of his island friends and a few he had come to know since moving here. He had smoked almost a full pack of tobacco since dark yesterday evening and in two hours it would be daylight again.

Paddy had been the last man to return from yesterday's search, having told Garf he would cut across Karpoon Island once more and look in some of the small coves where hardly anyone had ever gone in more pleasant times. It was long after nine when he stopped his Ski-Doo by the house and made his report to the waiting crowd, saying that he would have kept searching if not for the fog drowning his headlight and smearing his glasses. Ida had wiped the water from his face with a towel, stripped his socks off and sat him down near the stove with his naked feet on a junk of wood in the oven, scolding and praising him at the same time for his determination to find her son. After eating a hearty late supper from the tons of food brought by everyone in town, he had gone home and put on dry clothes and returned later in a show of support for the family. Now he sat at the end of the table near the cupboard, on the chair from Ida's bedroom, scraping the peel of a baked potato with his bottom teeth and looking over his glasses at Garf.

Max Butler sat with his legs crossed on the daybed, smoking a cigarette and tapping the ashes down his boot. He and another man had travelled to the neighbouring villages to spread the word of the missing boy, and had been assured that a search of that area would be carried out without delay. A light-haired youngster about twelve or thirteen sat beside him with his back to the wall and his chin slumped onto his chest, lips pouting with every outward breath. He hadn't been involved in the search but his mother had sent him here long after dark with a steaming pot of salt meat and vegetables, along with two lemon pies and half a pack of sweet biscuits.

Ambrose and the thin, sickly-looking man he had met on the ice earlier conversed quietly on the storage bin and took turns shaking their heads in disbelief at the many troubles that had befallen them over the years. Every so often the thin man would look at Ida while she hurried about the kitchen tending to everyone's needs, and say, "Wunnerful woman ya got there, Am me boy — wunnerful woman. 'Markable. 'Markable!'"

Sometimes someone would go to the window and look out or help wash the dishes and put clean ones back on the table. Others would go on the bridge to drive the sleep from their eyes and to check the weather conditions. It seemed there was always someone eating and always someone making a joke to pass the time, and once someone said that it looked like a wake but apologized immediately, with a kiss on the cheek for Ida and a nod towards Ambrose.

Sadie sat on Aunt Kizzie's chair, listening to the chatter behind and in front of her. Whenever Ambrose mentioned the old days back on the island, she'd twitch her ass and say, "Right boy. You're right, Ambrose. Truest words y'ever spoke, my son."

The old woman had stayed up well past one, but Ida hadn't been able to tolerate her lectures on why she believed Martin had disappeared and how his father should be held responsible if they couldn't find him so she had shuffled her off to bed by the scruff of the neck. Her guests had devoured every word, and went over the script behind her back until Garf put a stop to it by saying the old woman was full of shit just like anyone else who listened to her. For a moment there seemed to be a great uneasiness in the house, but when Aunt Kizzie sneaked out of her room and rammed her fingers into Sadie's mouth and started rooting, the tension broke and the place went up. There was another wild outburst of laughing and coughing after she had gone back to bed, when Sadie told the crowd that she hadn't been chewing gum at all, but the gristle off a piece of salt meat.

Jack Burns had dropped by shortly before midnight with a pot of chicken soup and a couple of loaves of bread but he hadn't stayed long, said that the baby was a bit crooked and he had better get back in case his wife needed him. He had brought a little silk scarf wrapped in nice paper that his mother had sent to Ida as a goodwill token, and a short scribbled note saying that she hoped to see her at the Easter service on Sunday evening seeing as how she'd missed the service on Good Friday.

"Still foggy," came the report from one of the men returning from the bridge. "Still rainin' too."

"Well," Garf said, pulling his jacket from under the thin man's ass on the storage bin, "can rain and be damned. Everybody got their rubber clothes with 'em, so soon ever John pokes his nose 'cross the cove now we're gone. Wherever Martin is, he's not warm and he's not dry so we gotta find 'en 'fore this wind chops from the nar'west, 'cause once she veers she's gonna turn frosty again."

"But where is he?" Ambrose asked. "I don't know where else ya can look, Garf. I don't know. Ya looked everywhere so where in the name a God can ya look different? Tell me!"

"Over the edge of the ice."

There was a live silence in the house and no one took a breath until Ambrose spoke. "What?" He went squealy again and looked from Garf to Ida. "What's he doin' over the edge of the ice?" He rubbed his nose in suspicion of his son's arrogance and was about to say something else but Ida cut him off.

"Martin's not drownded, y'know," she said. "He might be lost but he's not drownded."

"I never said he was drownded, Aunt Ida."

"But Martin's not over the edge of the ice, Garf." She nudged Paddy to get off the chair. "Lemme sit down, Paddy."

"I never said that either," Garf replied with his hand on the doorknob. "But that boy could a went off there in this fog, thinkin' he was goin' somewhere else. Only God knows where."

A low rustling sound came from the crowd as they all looked at each other and nodded in agreement. "Easy done too," said the thin man, pulling his jacket from underneath him. "Can mind one time me and poor ol' Dick went off there back in ——"

"We gotta find out for sure. Then we'll know."

Ambrose put his hand on the back of Aunt Kizzie's chair and helped himself up. He went to the window and looked out, turned around to Garf. "I wouldn't put it past Martin to say somethin' so foolish as that, Garf, but I never 'xpected to hear it from you." He pulled his green and black jacket off the wall behind the stove and put it on in the stillness. "He's out friggin' round somewhere, that's where he's to, not over the ice."

Garf hauled on his coat and zipped it. "This hour in the marnin', Uncle Am?" He looked around at all the eyes stuck in him. "Smarten up."

Ida went to her son and straightened his collar. She spoke kindly and in little more than a whisper. "Your father, Garf — no need to talk to your father that way, is there boy?"

"Aunt Ida," he said, realizing what she was doing. "You're not talkin' to Martin now" — he poked a finger into his chest — "you're talkin' to me, and I says we should go out to the edge of that ice and work our way up so far as the grasslands. We covered everything on the land so now we should try the ice."

"Sounds sensible enough to me," Max said, checking the clock for the time. "Goin' for half past four already. Daylight five."

Ambrose spoke against the idea. "Too big a chance to

take," he said. "This southeast wind got everything pushed off and there's nothin' out there on that edge anyway, only the blue drop. Goes out there in 'this fog ya might drive clean overboard. Only a lunatic would do the like."

Garf smirked. "In that case we got no other choice but go."

"Why's that?"

"Martin's a lunatic, ain't he, Uncle Am? You said so yourself."

The old man realized his son's wisdom and tossed his cigarette butt in the bucket. "You goes," he said, "I'm goin' with ya. Full up the nunny-bag with grub, Ida, and put in a pair stockin's and a pair mitts."

Garf skinned his tossel-cap on over his head and rolled the rim up to his forehead. "You'll have to get on somebody's sled."

"Don't warry," Ambrose snapped. "I don't mind gettin' on the sled, long's they don't beat me brains out and then run away and leave me." He went to the porch and put on his rubber clothes, grumbling with the door open.

"You can get on my Ski-Doo with me," Max said. "Be a hard muck with two hands on her in this wet snow but yes, you can get on with me, boy, if ya wants to — no problem."

"That's OK, Max. Hook on your sled for me."

Max smiled and the light from the lamp glinted off his gold tooth. "Already hooked on, Ambrose. Figured you'd wanna go today so I went the work and took her — just in case."

The old man flashed him one of his mistrusting looks but said nothing.

John Parsons and Alec stopped by the bridge ten minutes later, at first light, and went in the house, where Garf had just finished giving the men their instructions. When he saw the boy he asked John how he expected his Ski-Doo to pull both him and Alec on the same sled.

"Oh," John said, pulling down his son's hood, "Alec is not goin' with we fellers — wanted to he did, yes, but I told 'en he'd better stay here and look after Ida and Aunt Kiz in case they wants somethin' while we're gone."

Sadie got off the chair and came over to the boy, took his coat and cap and tossed them on Martin's bed. "I'll get a cup a tea for ya now," she said, combing his hair with her fingers. "And I'll warm up a drop a soup for ya. What kind ya want — mutton soup or chicken soup?"

"Chicken," he said, looking around the kitchen, a little shamed at how his grandmother fiddled with straightening his clothes and especially the kiss she planted noisily on his forehead.

"But," she said, "the mutton soup is what I made and, oh Alec, you should oughtta taste it — better'n all the chicken in the world."

"OK, the mutton," he said. "And a slice a bread to go 'long with it."

Ambrose slapped the boy on the chest as he went through the door to the sound of more snowmobiles pulling up by the bridge. "Good choice," he declared. "You eat whatever your puddick can hold, and what ya don't see, ask for. All ya gotta do is keep the woodbox full and the water barrel full. Don't warry 'bout the rest."

Alec's grandfather rubbed his head when he passed by and messed his hair. "Try the chicken soup," he whispered. "Better'n all the mutton goin'." Then he followed Ambrose outside.

Eight drivers, all dressed in black rubber clothes, some

with Cape Anns on their heads and others with sealskin caps, and hoods pulled around their ears, listened as Garf told three of them to search Karpoon Island again, and three to trim the edge of the woods as far as the grasslands. The other two would go with him to the edge of the ice.

Martin woke with a dry mouth and a jolt in the darkness under the old clothes and for nearly ten seconds thought he was home in his own bed. Then it came to him that he was home but not in his own bed nor in his own house, but he was warm and he felt alive again. He pulled the collar of a black three-quarter from his face and felt the chill of the daylight strike him, looked around at the untidiness in the house and was glad that he had not awakened more than twice during the night.

He had dreamt that he was fishing with his father at the back of the island on a calm, sunshiny day, drifting lazily with the tide and waiting for the fish to strike. While he was baiting his hook a giant codfish jumped out of the sea and landed in the midships. It lay there, its head with the gaping mouth pushed up one side of the boat to the gunwale and the flat, spiny tail hanging over the other side, shivering and thrashing about until it had thumped every ounce of its life out on the planking. His father then lifted the great fish up in his arms and dropped it overboard, saying nothing. It had been a good dream because of the calm sea and he had not been afraid in it, but losing such a prized fish had seemed so unnecessary. As the sleep escaped from his eyes he could still hear the thumping — much slower now, like the fish in its last stages of death — and he realized the door was banging. He pushed his heavy bedclothes down to his ankles and got out, feeling a little cramped in the neck, but a couple of hard rubs with his hand soon brought back his youthfulness.

The rain had stopped and now only traces of it, what he called spider's piss, ran in small sinuous paths down the window. The wind still raced in through the cove and tore at the house as if it wanted to rip it apart, thrusting its weight against the wall like a battering ram. Everything in the entranceway to the Strait of Belle Isle and for a hundred miles down its throat was still buried under a thousand feet of fog, smothered in a cold grey emptiness that made the outside world seem non-existent.

Martin went to the door and looked out, shivered at the thought of having to walk across the island again, thinking how useless it would be to shout for help with no ice in the channel and no one close enough to hear him. He picked up a handful of wet snow, sucked the water out and ate a bit.

Inside again, he decided to keep wearing the green trousers and the long jacket for today at least, so to make the clothes fit tighter he cut four feet from his hauling rope and tied one of the unravelled strands through the belt loops to keep the pants up. Then he buttoned his jacket to the collar and tied the double strand around his waist. His own clothes would have to stay here because they were too wet for him to wear.

The snowbank by the side of the house that held his gaff was much smaller now, melted down by last night's rain, and some of the ruins that had lain beneath the snowcap yesterday were showing their blackness. He slipped his coiled hauling rope onto his shoulder, took his gaff in his gloved hand — on the other he wore the wool stocking — and wondered if he should go to the end of the island or check out the view from atop Trimm's Point. The fog might not be as thick on that side, and with the bight cleared of ice there could possibly be a boat out searching for him. The thought of a boat encouraged him to climb the hill and, before the vision faded of his rescuers cheering to see him on the shore, he had reached the summit, staring into a fogbank. There was nothing he could do here for he could see only a hundred yards down to the sweeping curvature of the rugged shoreline; the real shape of the cove and the tip of Trimm's Point were fogged in on his left. There was ice here but he couldn't tell where it ended and the sky began. "Ice," he said out loud, his hopes of crossing over to the mainland rejuvenated but immediately quashed by the southeaster beating in his face and flapping his coattails. This wind, any wind from the south, was exactly the kind to clean out the bight, and as long as it blew from that direction he knew he would never cross over.

As he was leaving he thought he heard someone call his name. He turned around and listened with both hands cupped to his ears. No, he told himself after three or four stifled breaths, only the wind could make that kind of sound. Then he heard it again. This was not his imagination and the sounds were not of someone calling his name, but of dogs barking, or seals.

He heard the barking again, fainter now and in a strange way not like barking at all but more like the sound of ice grinding against the shore, yet there was no movement near the ballycaters. Had he only imagined the barking? He convinced himself otherwise with the next bark, which he estimated to be no more than seventy yards offshore. He ran along the slippery, glasslike ballycaters towards the point and halfway there he stepped up onto a platform from where he sighted six black seals without having to turn his eyes.

He tested the ice with the wooden end of his gaff and jumped onto it from a small crevice and began running. Less than thirty yards offshore he felt a bit unsteady on his feet, looked down and saw the ice breathing as if he were on the back of a great white monster. He watched it rise and fall in a perfect reproduction of shallow respiration, almost as though the ice were struggling for air, but there was a reassuring solidity to it that told him to find the seals and not be afraid, to make every second here worthwhile. He saw them huddled together like children lying around the floor on Christmas morning — not six but eight of the oddest-looking seals he had ever seen. They were about twenty pounds heavier than the ones he had killed on Good Friday, with slate-blue backs and silver-grey undersides, untarnished and free of spots like those of the harps. He did not know these seals, for harps and raggedy-jackets were all he had been taught.

From here the land looked faded and washed out, much as if he were looking at it through a sheet of wax paper on a bright day. He was glad he had found the seals without losing sight of the land, for if they had been much farther the risk of searching for them in this fog would have been too high, and he was already lost — sort of. But seeing a full day ahead of him, and telling himself that his father and Garf were out looking for him, he believed a rescue was imminent. Yet the value of these seals was questionable: were they worth killing and towing ashore? Or would all that work be a waste of his time and energy?

As far as he could peer into the wind, the fog seemed a

darker shade of grey than it had from the land, and he could tell that the monster was breathing more heavily just another fifty yards away. Beyond that he knew there was open water, but he also knew that the ice would not go apart unless the wind dropped, and that it could not trap him and carry him out to sea. What was left of the Arctic pack ice had been wedged solidly between Trimm's Point and the east face of the island. Still, he wondered what his father would say should the seals be worthless.

A sure way to test their fast-furredness, he remembered, was to pluck at a tuft of hair. He took the stocking off his hand and reached out to a teary-eyed mammal that seemed more interested in looking the other way than in watching the stranger who was considering killing it. As soon as the boy touched its back the seal whipped its head around and lunged, snarling like a wild dog. The other pups swarmed and lunged in unison, startled by the presence of the intruder. He jumped back. What if they all decided to attack him? He wondered if seals had the intelligence to think of such a thing. If they had, maybe challenging them wasn't such a good idea. But one look at the emptiness between his thumb and forefinger gave him the push he needed.

He dropped the gaff and rammed his hand down inside the green trousers into the front pocket of his jeans. His knife felt warm in his curled fingers and he imagined how hot it would feel after he had driven it past the handle into the boiling blood of these eight unusual looking creatures. For him to reach the heart he would have to do as he had done a few days ago — open the walls of fat wide enough to allow his hand inside, make another similar incision in the red meat of the breast and, when the blade had gone its length, thrust it through into the chest cavity and work it back and forth. He pulled the knife out, opened it and stuck it in the snow near his feet, then raised the gaff above his head. The dull thud and the long squirt of blood were familiar to him now, almost as if he had known it all along. The seal's black face recoiled into its body and it shivered a little before he struck again. Two smacks on the nose would be enough; he didn't want any more complaints about broken skulls and bloody meat, and his mother, today, would have all the heads she could handle.

He welcomed the hotness of the blood as he drove his knife deep between the flippers, bringing forth a massive surge of thick, red gore that drowned his hand and part of his sleeve. Before turning the seal over and emptying it onto the ice he put both hands into the ebbing fountain, watched idyllically as the spurting gore squeezed between his fingers, bringing back their nimbleness, and he felt the heart begin to slow. Then stop.

These seals were harder to tow than the smaller harps, but he still took two at a time, and pulled six, one by one up through the crevice and onto the flat ballycaters above.

His throat was beginning to feel dry and scratchy again, so he scooped a handful of the streaming wet snow from a small catch basin on a ballycater and squeezed the water into his mouth as someone might squeeze juice from half an orange.

His fourth trip out, he thought he felt the ice move a little against the shore. He ran his eyes along the bottom of the smooth upright wall, telling himself he had only imagined it moving. A dozen steps later he felt the breathing under his feet again. By the time he had hooked on his last two seals the monster was wheezing heavily — unquestionably the ocean swell rolling in silently underneath the ice.

As he hurried towards the shore, he heard a thunderous roar behind him. He looked over his shoulder and felt every drop of blood drain from his head as a mammoth black and grey seal broke through to the surface and hauled itself up onto the ice, shedding water and driving chunks of ice everywhere. Dark nostrils flared as the animal lunged towards him with yellow fangs, its bearlike mouth opened wide in a snarl, the portal closing behind it in a whoosh of boiling water and slob. A bizarre-looking sac, as big as a football, inflated with a loud gurgling noise behind the bulging, bloodshot eyes and rolled across the top of its head, covering it all the way to the tip of its nose.

Martin went stiff. As the bulk of quivering fat and muscle neared the hind flippers of the last seal on his rope, the beast reared up on its haunches and rolled its head from side to side with a throaty bellow that could still be heard after it had crashed through the ice and disappeared. As quickly as it had emerged, the brute was gone.

Had he imagined all this? He didn't take the time to answer the questions in his head. He just dropped his rope and ran as fast as he could, thinking that he had come face to face with the devil.

Almost to the shore, he felt he could sense the seal breathing on his neck, and he glanced around to reassure himself. His heart was beating out of his chest, not just pounding as it had in the excitement of the hunt but knocking like an old revved-up engine with badly worn bearings. He tried to swallow, take extra air down into his parched windpipe, but something had stuck there. When he jumped ashore in the crevice of the ballycater his whole body was trembling. He felt as if he would faint, and he had never fainted before. He crawled in from the ledge and hid behind a rock, all the while keeping a sharp eye on the ice. This thing, whatever it was, he asked himself — could it walk on dry land? And if it could, how far could it travel?

14

THE SERMON

Aunt Nel sat behind the pulpit on a long wooden seat with
Aunt Kizzie on her left and old Mrs. Burns on her right,
going over her notes on her sermon for this evening's Easter
service while she waited for more worshippers to arrive.

She had left her dinner dishes on the table nearly two
hours ago to come here and put in a fire and pin some of
Alfred's new paper cut-outs on the wall among the ones
that he and the children had coloured for their little skit on
Good Friday. There were dozens of rabbits, blue, pink, pur-
ple, red — whatever shades could be found in a box of
crayons; lots of brightly coloured eggs bearing mottled bands
studded with squares, diamonds and circles; different-sized
crosses, some looking like a plus sign; and baby chickens,
every one of them coloured sunshine yellow.

Some of the townspeople had requested a replay of the
skit, saying that the children had done a wonderful job in
re-creating the scene where Peter betrayed Jesus, especially
when Alfred, hidden behind the pulpit, had waved his cardboard rooster high in the air and cock-a-doodle-dooed three

times, as loud as he could, whenever his Aunt Nel gave him the nod.

She was pleased that her nephew had adapted well to the changes of living here, and that all the children had accepted him into their games despite their great age differences and his bouts of imagination tantrums, in which he claimed to see ghosts and demons in nearly every shadow. In June he would be forty. He was reasonably handsome, tall and slim with greying temples and on seeing him, a stranger might not think he had the mind of a six-year-old. He sat now with Judy and her mother in the second row, directly behind an old man and old woman who kept turning their heads every time they heard the door open or someone cough.

Aunt Nel looked down at the congregation of mostly women and children, and sighed at having to mention a young boy being lost from their community. Seeing Ida in the front row on the other side of the church, with her hand on Alec's leg, made her task that much harder. She had been chosen by the island people many years ago as the one to lead them in prayer and to comfort them in times of trouble, after the proper clergyman, based at St. Anthony, had had his fill of ice in the channel, rough seas and high winds. As the years passed and the preacher's visits to the island dropped off, the people looked to her for all their spiritual needs, expected her to perform the duties they had bestowed upon her without remuneration, and she had felt obligated to carry them out. In the last thirty-four years she had delivered, christened, married and buried more than half her people. It was only after she buried her father that someone at Salvation Army headquarters sent her a certificate promoting her from ordinary citizen to lieutenant.

With that title came a small salary and a teaching position at the school. When she retired from teaching after twenty-two years, her old-age pension helped pay her bills and, since she had moved to Karpoon, caring for Alfred had brought a small sum from the government as well.

She heard the door creak and smiled curtly at Sadie, who was keeping it open for a couple of youngsters who barged in under her arm. With a quick smile back, Sadie pushed the door closed and brushed her hand down her uniform to straighten it. In her other hand she held a bouquet of plastic flowers packed loosely in a pickle jar with the green and white label still on it: ZEST. She walked up the narrow aisle between the two rows of wooden benches, scuffing her black, fur-topped boots on the bare boards, passed the pot-bellied stove in the middle and placed the flowers on the altar before stepping up onto the platform.

A slender young girl with every strand of hair tucked neatly under her bonnet sat by Mrs. Burns and tapped out a fast beat on her leg with the two drumsticks from the snare drum that lay beside her feet. She stopped and pushed the sticks under her thigh as soon as Sadie sat next to her.

Aunt Nel leaned out in front of the old woman and whispered something to her comrade about her late arrival. Sadie was rustling papers and didn't hear what was said, so she leaned as far as she could across the girl's lap to have the message repeated.

"I was wonderin' what was keepin' ya," Aunt Nel said. "How 'bout the boy — what's the news?"

Sadie felt the girl's thighs shift under the weight of her elbow and looked up into her face. "Sarry, love," she said. "Don't mind me." And to Aunt Nel, "Max and Ambrose just got home from their second trip today already. Gonna gas up the Ski-Doo and go right on back again soon ever they gets somethin' down in 'em."

"Not too loud — sshhh. What 'bout the rest of the men?"

"Some is back and some is not, sshhh."

"Can't find 'en or what?"

"Searched high and low for 'en but not a sign nowhere, sshhh," Sadie replied, checking herself by saying *sshhh* after every sentence. "Some of 'em come back for more gas and gone on again — never had no dinner, sshhh." She looked up and past the pulpit at the twenty or so blank faces and turned back to her news report. "For God's sake don't tell no one I told ya but I heard Max say they thinks he's gone. Sshhh."

Aunt Nel put a finger to her lips. "Gone?" she questioned softly, numbed by the words she had dreaded to hear. Then before anyone else could speak, "Keep this to yourself," she warned. Looked at the young girl and then Mrs. Burns, both of whom had no doubt heard the conversation. "And you two — don't n'ar one of yez breathe one word of what yez just heard — not one word!"

There was an attention-grabbing cough from the other side of the row. Aunt Nel straightened up on the seat and was met by a moody and silent stare from Aunt Kizzie and another old Salvationist whose cloudy eyes were nearly covered with cataracts.

"What's ya doin' all the whisperin' 'bout?" Aunt Kizzie asked. "Not backbitin' me again I hope, is ya?"

"Hush," Aunt Nel said, her mouth barred from public view by a thumb scratching under her cheekbone. "We got better things to talk 'bout than you, Aunt Kiz."

"Well, what was ya talkin' 'bout then? Tell me."

"Nothin' — we wud'n talkin' 'bout nothin'."

Aunt Kizzie made a loud sniff, as if she wanted to be noticed from the pews. "Well, if that's all you was doin', get up and talk 'bout nothin' to the sinners down below."

Aunt Nel put her hand on the Bible in her old friend's lap. "Time for you to give up that talk now, m'dear," she whispered kindly. "Our days is gettin' numbered here in this ol' world so we should start thinkin' 'bout gettin' ready for the next one."

Aunt Kizzie expelled her breath in one burst and said, "Anything like this one, I don't wanna go there."

"Hush," Aunt Nel said again, her eyes jumping around the church to see if anyone had heard the blasphemy. "Shouldn't talk like that, Aunt Kiz. Should ask God for forgiveness, and ya better do it 'fore ya leaves here today."

Aunt Kizzie looked into her old eyes and said, "I'll do it now." With that she jumped off the seat and marched to the pulpit, before Aunt Nel had a chance to stop her. She put on a cheerful smile, rattled the leaves of the opened Bible on the stand and said, "Don't look like we're gonna get any more souls here this evenin' to share in this blessed Easter Christmas so we're gonna have to make do with what we got." She coughed into her fist and pretended to search for something in the Bible while Aunt Nel inconspicuously tugged on the hem of the old woman's dress to get her to sit down.

The gathering sat up straight and produced a short bout of coughing before settling down and listening to their annual Easter sermon. Mothers touched their children to warn them that the service had started.

"On this very, very special day," Aunt Kizzie began, speaking in long, drawn-out syllables, "we're all come together again to celebrate the suffering of our Blessed Lard as they nailed His body to that rugged tree up there on Calv'ry's mountain. If He could only come back and tell us how He suffered, I knows — I knows without a doubt — I knows that everyone of you fellers here today'd be right clean outta yourselves. And I knows if yez got yez hands on that bunch what done it you'd nail 'em to the cross yourselves."

Aunt Nel got up and modestly elbowed the old woman away from the pulpit, and flicked through the pages of the Bible in search of the passage she had picked out as her sermon and forgotten to bookmark.

The ousted Salvationist pulled her handkerchief from her sleeve and waved it above her head before she sat down. "I'm gonna let Nel take over now," she said loudly and in her own tongue. "She's gonna have a spell tellin' yez 'bout the Lard now, and what He done for her in the last four or five year and how He can do the same thing for you fellers. Amen."

Aunt Nel hardly knew where to begin. She watched Ida try to make herself smaller in her seat, and gathered enough strength to glance nearly halfway around, without looking directly at Aunt Kizzie, and say, "Thank you, Aunt Kiz, for that lovely sermon." Then, turning back and addressing the gathering: "We mightn't all say it right sometimes, what we're trying to say, but with God's grace I'm sure we all tries to say it the best way we knows how." She tapped one finger on her lip as she ran another down a column of verses from Matthew, Chapter 27. "I was gonna read this little passage here from God's Word on how Jesus was crucified for our sins and how He rose again from the dead, but with all that's happened here in our little community in the last two or three days I can't tell yez enough how sarry I am that this tragedy had to happen. A young boy, who I helped bring into this world, is lost, and no one don't know where he's to. The Bellman family is more'n thankful, I knows, for all the help they got from the people here, and I knows words can't tell yez how much they 'preciates your husbands and your sons out lookin' for 'en." She stopped when Ida burst out crying and clung to Alec.

Judy heard a woman behind her say — to whom she didn't know, for she didn't turn around to see — that she dared say he was drowned and no amount of searching would ever recover his body. She was sure the old man and old woman heard her too because they both turned around with sour looks, as if they were thinking that she or her mother had said it.

"I knows 'tis hard on the family," Aunt Nel continued. "'Tis hard on all of us. But if we believe on the Lard Jesus Christ and that He died for your sins and mine, then we'll all meet again over yonder on that beautiful golden shore where the streets is made outta gold and where the roses never fades, and where all tears'll be wiped from our eyes and sarrow will be no more."

The more Aunt Nel went on, the harder Ida screeched. Alec looked very uncomfortable as she fell against him and kept saying *Martin, Martin* over and over, digging her fingers into his arm as she held it to keep from falling any farther. He slowly brought his left arm around and laid it gently on her shoulder, whispering, telling her not to worry, that Martin was all right.

Judy looked across at Ida and took a tissue from her pocket. She wiped her eyes and squished it around a little in her nostrils, blowing quietly into the soft folds. She had heard Aunt Nel say the same things about her father while he lay in his casket at the church back on the island, and had heard the same high-pitched screams from her mother.

"They'll find 'en, Judy," Dulcie whispered. "Try to bear up now, for Ida's sake."

The girl leaned against her mother and said weakly, "Martin is gone home."

"Sshhh," Dulcie said. "Don't let anyone hear ya say that."

Aunt Nel had been watching her island friends and had heard Judy's innocent remark. "I can understand," she said, looking around at Aunt Kizzie and back again, "I can understand why we says things sometimes we don't mean, and when we do mean 'em it seems like they just don't come out the way we wants 'em to." She picked up her hymn book and nodded to the skinny girl to strap on the drum. "OK," she said, "we're gonna turn to hymn number 624 and sing God's praises, after which Mrs. Burns'll lead us in prayer."

Aunt Kizzie coughed again and Aunt Nel knew she wanted to be the one to do the praying, but Aunt Nel had been afraid the old woman would go on with too much irreverence and turn the service into a show. There had been a time when Aunt Kizzie could pray as well as any Salvationist, but in the last few years she had been slipping in her religious responsibilities and there were some who feared that she was losing her mind. Aunt Nel was one of them.

The drum sounded with a *rat-a-tat-tat* and, before Aunt Nel could give the signal for everyone to stand, Judy stood up and said in a strong, loud voice, "Martin is not lost; he's gone home."

Aunt Nel looked down with pity in her eyes. "M'dear child," she said, "we don't know that kinda stuff; that's only for the good Lar ——"

"No," Judy said, her mother hushing her and pulling on

her coat. "He's not drownded — he's gone home to the island."

The fire crackled in the stove, deafening in the silence that followed. The wind in the stovepipes drew the smoke out faster than it would have floated out on a calm day, and the church sounded as empty as it did without people. Everyone had heard what she'd said but no one spoke. Ida raised her head from Alec's chest, stood up and wobbled across the floor to the front row on the other side. She stuck her eyes in Judy and put her hand over her mouth. The old man and old woman slid a ways towards the end of their seat and motioned for her to sit down but Ida just kept staring at Judy, her eyes wet and red and ugly-looking.

"'Tis true, Mrs. Bellman," Judy said. "What I'm sayin' is true."

"Sit down, child," her mother advised, aware that everyone was looking at them.

Aunt Kizzie left her seat and came down, put her hand on her daughter's back.

"Martin is gone home," Judy declared. "He told me not to tell no one where he was gone, and I never — until now."

Ida stiffened, reached behind her and held onto her mother's dress. "You sure 'bout this?"

"Yes, that's what he said he was gonna do."

Ida let out a cry of relief and sat down next to the old man.

"Go," Aunt Nel said to Alfred. "Run so fast as your legs can take ya, 'cross the cove and up to Ambrose's, and tell 'en where Martin is! Go!"

Alfred dropped his hymn book and bolted down the aisle and out the door. He was gone in the fog before Aunt Kizzie pointed out that Ambrose might not believe him.

"Judy," Aunt Nel said, "you'll have to go too, m'dear, and for God's sake tell Ambrose what you told us here today! If he don't believe ya, then tell 'en to come and see me!"

Mrs. Burns and the other old Salvationist made their way down off the platform and spoke of their concern for Martin, wondering aloud about his condition after spending the night alone. The young girl leaned across the pulpit and listened to Sadie telling her everything she and Max had talked about since Martin had gone missing. Ida, as well as the rest, couldn't help but overhear.

"If he's on the island, he's all right," said the old man, casting a black look at Sadie. "He's a smart young boy — I knows 'en — and he'll do the right thing in this fog. He'll stay there till someone comes to look for 'en."

Aunt Kizzie had been right: Ambrose did not believe a word Alfred told him, and gave Max the signal to start the snowmobile. Only when Judy ran up the hill screaming for them not to leave, and cried to him on the sled that Alfred was telling the truth, did he push his cap back and consider it.

"Whaddaya think, Max?"

"Don't know what to think."

"Why'n ya tell somebody 'bout this before?" he said, listening to Alfred snivelling and saying, *'Tis true, 'tis true, true's the Bible.*

"'Cause Martin told me not to tell," she said. "If I'd a told he wud'n a spoke to me no more."

"Well," Ambrose said, knocking a loose horn down in its socket with his fist. "We trimmed the edge of the ice up so far as the grasslands and never seen no sign of me Ski-Doo nowhere."

"That's 'cause he's gone off to the island on her. You gotta go off and get 'en!"

"No, he never done that."

"But he told me. He asked me if I liked it here in Karpoon and then he said, 'I'm goin' back,' and he made me promise not to tell nobody, so yez gotta go out there and bring 'en home."

Max knelt on his seat, watching her beg the old man to believe her. "But, my girl," he said, "we was all up around there this marnin' where we used to come back and forth a few year ago and we never seen a track 'cept the ones on the main path. Ambrose can tell ya the same thing hisself."

"Well, he's off there somewhere 'cause he said he was goin' back home. And if ya don't believe me, then Aunt Nel said ya gotta go down and see her!"

Ambrose sighed. "If Martin went off there on that Ski-Doo — like Max just told ya — he had to leave a track." He grinned at Max and shifted his eyes to the girl. "What'd Aunt Nel know any more'n I knows meself anyway? Do she think Martin can fly?"

"He can't fly, Mr. Bellman, no," Judy replied. "And neither can he swim." She turned around and went up close to Max. "You don't believe me either, do ya?"

"Well," he began, finding it hard to call her a liar. "Not that I don't believe ya, Judy — 'tis just that it don't make sense what you're sayin'." He took off his cap and scratched his head. "Ambrose there is right, y'know." He searched for the proper words. "Martin, y'know, well, wherever he went he had to leave some kinda track behind 'en, now didn't he? And that rain we had last night and this marnin' never washed it 'way that fast 'cause there's still tracks eve-rywhere left from yes'day. But there's none goin' off to the island."

"Haul on the cord," Ambrose ordered. "We'll go down the cape again and have 'nother look down there."

Max hauled once and the engine caught. "Stand back, little girl," he said. "And watch out for the sled."

Judy reached out her hand and snatched the key from the ignition. She was twenty feet down the hill before the noise cut off. "Wants this," she shouted from the bottom, "you'll have to come and get it."

Ambrose jumped off the sled and ran to the edge of the hill. He looked around at Max still kneeling on his snow-mobile. "See what that girl just done — you see that, Max? What's we gonna do now?"

"Perhaps she was tellin' the truth."

"Truth!" Ambrose said belligerently. "She don't know what that means. All them youngsters today is alike — every one of 'em. If I told my father a lie like that when I was growin' up I 'low he'd a stripped the skin off me arse and used it for babiche."

"Come back, Judy," Max yelled, running along to the old man. "We're losin' time, Ambrose; gotta get that kay back so don't say 'nother word. Let me do the talkin'."

Ambrose pulled out his tobacco and filled a cigarette paper.

"Me and Ambrose was just sayin'," Max negotiated, "we thinks you're right, Judy. That's the only place Martin can be." He walked down the hill towards her as she took in every word. "The quicker we leaves, the better."

"OK, well, here's the key." She held it up in her naked hand, pulling on her ponytail with the other.

"Big crowd a men out lookin' for 'en too," Max said. "And in this fog they could all go over the edge of the ice and drown theirselves. So give us the kay now so we can go on back and tell 'em the good news."

Judy walked backwards past the two boats, keeping a sharp eye on Max as he broke through the soft snow and went to his knees. "Won't get the key that way, Mr. Butler," she said, laughing ridiculously loud. "Hurry up now 'cause I might drop 'en and lose 'en."

Ambrose had his lungs filled with smoke and was holding it in to savour the taste, but he blew it out before he would have and said, "Y'hear that, Max; hear how that youngster is saucin' ya?" He stuck his cigarette in his mouth, ran around the back of the garage and darted down the hill from another angle, intending to cut her off before she could run away. Judy knew what he was up to and ran as hard as she could past the place where he would have stepped onto the harbour, and stopped a hundred feet beyond that.

Max wriggled his feet from the deep holes and slid all the way to the bottom of the hill, his rubber clothes affording him the mobility of a greased pig. "Ambrose," he called as he saw the girl walking backwards. "No, Ambrose, don't chase her. Aawwww, geez," he said, seeing the girl turn and the old man charge her. "Ya got it done now all right. We're finished!"

Ambrose ran behind her, threatening her, saying he would tell her mother how saucy she was and how she had caused Max to nearly smash off his two legs, and how he would make sure she never set foot in his house again. Halfway up the path to the church on the other side of the cove Judy stopped and waited for him to catch up, saw the other assailant burst through the wall of fog and run after them.

Ambrose's cigarette had gone out but he was gasping for air with it still in his mouth, spitting threats and shouting that she had hurt him badly by not believing him and Max and their good intentions. Then he saw his wife and Alec coming down the path, trailing a bunch of youngsters who made a lot of noise and threw snowballs at each other.

"Ambrose," Ida shouted, sinking to her thighs in the snow. "Martin's off on the island!"

He stopped and rested with his hands on his knees, made a few raspy coughs and watched Judy and Alec help Ida up and hook the snow from the tops of her boots. Asked her how she knew.

"He told Judy, Ambrose — he told her he was goin' back home!"

Ambrose got his breath back enough to speak for a longer time. "Back home, Ida" — the squealing began — "he got no reason to go back home! Not a thing back there — nothin'!"

"Our house is still there, Ambrose," she said. "And so is Jarge's!" She put one foot out and tested the snow, narrowed her eyes and asked with suspicion, "So what's you and Max doin' down here?"

He hacked and spat on the snow, watched her come nearer. "The kay — Judy stole the kay outta Max's Ski-Doo."

"This is what they're after, Mrs. Bellman," Judy said and placed the key in Ida's hand.

Ida moved her head to the right and slyed her eyes at her husband. "You," she said. "You was gonna go on and not listen to her, wud'n ya?"

Max stopped at the shoreline and waited for his heart to slow down while he panted for breath and watched the movements of the crowd.

"No," Ambrose replied sheepishly as she came down to him and clutched his arm. "'Tis just that I can't see how Martin can be back on the island, Ida. We was all up round there everywhere; went right on up so far as the grasslands but we never seen a track — not a single track. We was goin' up for another look but ——"

"Well," she said, waving her arm to Max, "you wud'n up far enough now, was ya? Hey, Max! Come up here I wants ya!" To her husband: "You march right straight off there on that island and you bring my boy back. He's hungry and he's cold."

Max came to within ten feet of her and stopped.

"Max," she said stoutly, "Martin's on the island."

"I knows," he began. "That's what I was ——"

"Shut up, Max! We'll never know if you believed Judy or not but I'm tellin' ya right now — don't go nowhere else to look for Martin! You go right straight to that island and you better bring 'en home!" She held out the key and he took it like a whipped dog taking a biscuit from its master.

He looked to Ambrose and Alec for support. "All clear water in the channel with this wind," he said. "Have to shovel out the rodney and launch her."

Ida put one arm around Alec's neck and the other one around Judy to keep from falling through the snow again. "I don't care if ya gotta shovel out the *Titanic* and launch her," she said. "I wants that youngster home 'fore dark or you and Ambrose'll wish yez was never barn!"

15

THE MAIN EDGE

Ambrose and Max had the boat nearly shovelled out when
two snowmobiles pulled alongside and stopped. At first
Ambrose didn't recognize one of the rubber-clad drivers
because of the dark glasses masking his eyes and the hood
tied tightly under his chin, but when the hood came down
he recognized Lewis Moores. The other man was Norm
Andrews. "Narm," he said, after throwing up a scoopful of
snow and digging the shovel back in. "Martin's gone back
on the island."

"Gone home, ya mean?"

"Knows 'tis a queer thing to say but that's what young
Judy Trimm told us. Said he told her that's what he was
gonna do."

Norm hopped off his snowmobile and took Ambrose's
shovel. "You go and get a quoyle a rope in your stage,
Ambrose, and a couple sets a paddles. And you, Lew, you
run 'cross the cove and grab my compass there on the shelf
in the garage, and that half a quoyle a rope hung up on the
wall. Five gallons a gas there by the door so grab that too,

just in case."

As the men rushed off, Max and Norm shovelled down to the two logs on which the sixteen-foot rodney rested and a moment later lifted it up onto its side, letting it fall over into the upright position. They latched onto the wooden support risings that ran from stem to stern a few inches below the gunwales, and pulled the boat out of the hole and onto the harbour ice.

Ambrose came out of his stage with a cigarette in his mouth, the coil of rope on his shoulder and two paddles under each arm, to see Lewis arrive with his rope slung over the backrest and the gas can nipped between his legs. "Not a full quoyle here, Narm," he said. "But not far from it."

Norm took the things off the snowmobile, lodged them in the boat and directed Max to drive a short distance ahead and stop. "OK, Ambrose," he said. "We gotta get off to the edge of that ice so fast as we can, so whaddaya think we should do with the rodney — lash her fast to the sled or haul her like she is?"

The old man dropped the oars into the boat with a progression of clamorous thuds and resonating clickety-clatter. "Haul her? M'dear man, ya goes the work and does that, there'll be n'ar bit a oakum left in the seams to keep her afloat. And the stem," he said, with the smoking butt stuck in the corner of his mouth. "What 'bout the stem?"

"What 'bout it?"

"Narm," he said, "you knows so well as I do that one hard pluck on that stem is gonna tear 'en right clean out of her. Be the same thing as tearin' the kee-carn out of a rabbit. I say we should lash her on the sled."

Max agreed.

"For the time it takes to do that," Norm said, "we could be halfway off there. This snow is right soft and it'll only make her slide better, so ya don't have to warry 'bout tearin' the oakum or the stem out of her." He shrugged and stuck his hand off to the side as though he were hitching a ride. "Now I don't want to tell you fellers what to do but, for my part, I think 'tis better to haul her."

"No, not gonna do that," Ambrose said. "We'll stick her on the sled."

"OK," Norm said reluctantly. "'Tis your boat." He put one foot on the sled and pulled the four horns from their sockets, untied the packsack and tossed it into the stern of the boat.

Max drove his Ski-Doo alongside and stopped. They all grabbed onto the boat and, grunting and sinking halfway to their knees in the wet snow, hoisted her onto the sled across the two horn junks and lashed her down with a section of uncut rope from the half-coil.

"Gonna be hard goin' with one Ski-Doo," Norm said. "Perhaps we should hook on 'nother one to help ya 'long."

"No need a that, my son," Max said. "Ol' Betsy here never let me down yet." He pulled on the starter cord and shouted above the noise. "Give us a little nudge now to start off."

The three men gathered around the boat and shook it violently as the rubber track began to spin, causing the snowmobile to sink in the snow past its running boards. There were shouts of obscenities and anguish as they gathered around the stern and pushed, driving their legs out behind them, touching their knees to the snow and sometimes falling. Max knelt far back on the seat to give the snowmobile more traction, stretched himself forward and rocked it sidewise, settling it farther into the snow, and amazingly the boat started moving. Not wanting to be left behind, Ambrose spat his butt out and jumped in on the rope.

Norm and Lewis ran to their snowmobiles and escorted the rowboat across the harbour, watching the sled runners bury themselves to the drawbar with every bump. On leaving the harbour entrance, though, the sled dipped into a shallow trough and crushed its right runner like a wrenched ankle. Ambrose felt the shock, took off his cap and sat there in the boat as they all cut their engines and walked back to assess the damage. "Got it done now, boys," he groaned. "Give it 'nother hour and it'll be too late for anything."

They all looked at him. "Why's that?" Norm asked.

"Hark," he said, looking out the bight at the fog. "Hear it?"

Max knelt near the drawbar and sighted his eye along the sled. "Hear what?"

"Sea," Ambrose said. "If Martin's off on that island he's gonna have to stay there another night — perhaps a week — 'cause there's no way in this world we're gonna land with a sea on." He stepped out of the boat. "No harm to say we got ourselves in a fine mess!"

Norm took the bolt from the hitch and put it in the tool compartment of Max's snowmobile. "Untie the rodney, Ambrose," he said. "We'll haul her the rest of the ways — only thing we can do — and if she falls to pieces we'll go back and get 'nother one."

Ambrose opposed the idea again. "Perhaps we should go back and get 'nother sled."

"Yeah," Max said, "tears the stem outta that boat, then we're further behind'n we ever was. If 'twas up to me I'd slew around and go back."

"Look," Norm said, annoyed that no one trusted his opin-
ion. "We can go back and waste 'nother hour or we can haul
the rodney on the dead and gain a hour. So what's it gonna
be?" He waited for an answer. "*So?*"

"If we goes ahead and tears the stem outta that boat,"
Ambrose warned, "you'll be the one to answer for it, not
me."

The wind parted Norm's white hair in the middle as he
turned and faced the old man. "If! And if I had a square
asshole," he said, "I'd be shittin' bricks."

"Take it easy, boys," Lewis said, taking off his glasses to
kneel down and look under the sled. "We all knows the
trouble so there's no need to get on like that." He scraped
away some snow near the broken runner, stood up and put
his glasses on. "I'll go back home and get me sled and while
I'm gone you fellers untie the boat and shove her off to the
one side. And," he added, as he turned and walked towards
his snowmobile, "if ya wants to make headway you can all
get round her and haul her by hand."

The three watched him disappear into the fog. For a moment no one spoke and then Norm said, "Haul her by hand
— if that's what we gotta do, then by God that's what we'll
do."

"No," Ambrose resolved, untying the boat from the sled.
"We'll hook her fast to the Ski-Doo and haul her the way
you said. I just wants to get off on that island and get Martin the best way I can."

Norm helped with the ropes and told Ambrose that Martin would be off the island within the next three hours —
before darkness set in. With the rodney on the snow, he
fastened a rope onto his snowmobile and tossed the end of
the painter to Max.

Half an hour after breaking the sled, they had hauled the boat to the edge of the ice and out of sight of the land, and still Lewis had not returned. They stopped and Ambrose jumped out with his tobacco pack in his hand. "Can't put that boat in the water here, boys," he said, looking around at all the tracks made earlier by the searchers. "Sacred Island is a good ride from here so 'tis better to trim the ice and go on till we runs outta this track."

"Not gonna put her out here, no, Ambrose," Norm replied. "Just stopped to see if we can hear Lew comin'."

Ambrose rolled a cigarette and stuck it in his mouth. "Martin never got on the bay where the ol' path used to be, so he must've went on up to the west'rd and got on up there. Gimme a light, Max."

"Where the hell is Lew?" Max said, handing him his lighter. "Ski-doo must've give out or else he's lost in the fog."

"Not lost," Ambrose said, hands shielding the lighter and cigarette. The wheel made a scraping noise and then there was smoke. He pointed his cigarette to the wide pathway left by the boat's hull. "If he's lost with a track like that," he said, wiping the loose shreds of tobacco from his lips, "he'd get lost goin' from the table to the shithouse."

The sound of a snowmobile to the south cut through the fog.

"That's he now," Max said, looking to the southeast, the absence of land and the wind in his ears making him slightly disoriented.

"No," Ambrose contradicted. "That's a Ski-Doo comin' back from Cape Bauld, my son, and goin' on up 'cross the bay."

They agreed to call out together to attract the snowmobiler's attention. *Helllp — Out here — This way — Over here —* and then as the sound faded Norm called out, *You stupid bugger!*"

They concluded that Lewis was having engine problems and decided to keep moving. Ambrose went to the boat and got in, checked the compass at a few degrees before the WNW mark and kept raking his head around his mates, waiting for the path to end. Ten minutes later the two machines made a sharp turn to the left, leaving the path and nearly throwing him out. Norm turned around and pointed towards several long cracks of open water in the ice, near the edge, before steering back to WNW. Twenty minutes later Ambrose heard him yell something back at him. The engines cut off and the boat came to rest across a well-beaten path made by searchers careering off the bay ice and heading back home.

"This's it," Norm said, rubbing the white, week-old bristles on his face and peering through the fog at the black cliff near the grasslands. "This's so far as they went." He looked to the water, at the big slabs of ice breaking off and drifting away. "'Nother two or three hours there won't be a pan left in the bight."

Ambrose got out of the boat again. "What's we gonna do with the Ski-Doos," he asked, "once we gets the rodney in the water? Leaves 'em here on the ice, we'll lose 'em down through the cracks."

Max turned around, still kneeling on his seat. "Never thought 'bout that," he said.

"Only thing we can do," Norm replied, looking troubled, "is to drive 'em back to the grasslands after we gets the boat in the water, and then walk off and get aboard. But not here."

"My God," Ambrose said. "If that's the case, we won't get to the island till ten o'clock tonight."

"Get back in the rodney," Norm commanded. "And hold on!"

"Whaddaya gonna do?"

The two engines came alive again, the tracks spun a little and the boat started moving. "Get in," Norm yelled over his shoulder. "Get in!" He waited until the old man jumped in and then signalled Max to nip the trigger to the handle-bars.

The boat skidded over the ice, and Ambrose heard the oars rattling against the risings, the snow scraping the hull, saw the drift from the rubber tracks. He hoped that Martin had driven across the channel onto the island instead of doing the proper thing and leaving his Ski-Doo at the edge of the bay ice; for once he wished the boy had done the wrong thing.

A short time later they crossed a lone snowmobile path, followed it to an open lead of water nearly six feet wide and stopped their machines. Ambrose jumped out of the boat and ran up alongside. The path began again on the other side of the water and disappeared over the main edge twenty yards away. For a moment no one spoke; no one could find the right words to say that this was Martin's track, and that he had either taken the snowmobile to the island or accidentally driven it into the sea.

After a quick deliberation, Max said, "Gotta be Martin. Whaddaya think, Ambrose?"

The old man scrunched up his eyes and tried to pierce the fog ahead and behind. "If this is Martin's track he must've went on up to where ya turns and goes in the bay. If that's the case then this track here must've come from the turnoff" — he pointed somewhere close to a northerly direction — "and runs straight off there."

Norm brought the compass up and took a bearing. "Path runs just 'bout north and south," he said.

"Might be a track comin' off from some of the places in the bay," Ambrose declared. "Not Martin's at all."

Norm took the compass back to the boat. "Me and Max gotta put the Ski-Doos in on the beach," he said, "so we'll have a look and see. You stay here with the rodney and wait for us."

Max untied the ropes from the snowmobiles and started his engine. He turned his head away from the wind, blocked one of his nostrils and blew a snot onto the snow. He looked out to sea, shut off his engine and stood on the seat with both hands shading his eyes. "Hold on!" he exclaimed. "I believe I sees somethin'!"

Norm let his pull cord fly back into its housing when he heard Max cry out, and jumped upon his snowmobile as well. "Whaddaya see?"

"Don't know," Max replied. "Thought 'twas a Ski-Doo." He laughed. "Foolish thing for a man to say, I knows, but that's what it looked like first when I seen it — a Ski-Doo."

"Where?" Ambrose said eagerly. "Show me!"

Max pointed northwest. "Can't see it now," he said, "but 'twas right there. If ever I seen a . . . ah, there it is." His voice rose with the excitement. "SKI-DOO," he yelled. "My God, boys, I sees a Ski-Doo drivin' off on a pan a ice!"

"Can't see it," Norm said. He looked to Max. "Show me, Max; show me where you're lookin'!"

"Geez, boy, right there," Max said, still pointing and jabbing his hand into the air. He looked down at Ambrose and back through the fog. "See it now, Ambrose?"

"No," the old man confessed, "I can't see it, no!"

"Where?" Norm repeated. "Show me where ya sees her!"

"Hold on," Max said. "I got her lost again." He searched the blackening fog, took in the long, flat sheets of ice drifting silently throughout his field of vision.

Another crack started behind them. The rate at which bay ice fell apart depended on the magnitude of the sea rolling in underneath, and on how fast the sea was mounting.

Norm reached into the boat and untied the end from the biggest coil of rope. "Here, Max," he said. "We're gonna have 'nother lake a water here pretty soon so take this end and tie onto the arse a my Ski-Doo. You and Ambrose is gonna go off there and tie the other end onto that pan a ice. Whatever ya does don't tie it onto the Ski-Doo 'cause ya might haul her off the pan. When you're ready give the rope a couple a good yanks to lemme know. Then heave the slack overboard and I'll try to tow the works ashore."

Ambrose opposed the plan. He helped launch the boat into the first crack, now eight feet wide. "'Nother hour and it'll be dark," he stated.

"Two hours," Max horned in.

"Still a waste a time."

"If that's a Ski-Doo what Max seen," Norm said, holding onto the painter, "then whose ya think it is?"

The old man blinked and spat on the snow. "Don't think 'tis mine, do ya?"

"'Tis nobody else's only yours."

Max got in the stern and put out a set of oars. "Hurry up, Ambrose," he said as the old man climbed aboard. "If ya wants your Ski-Doo back then put out them paddles and row like hell!"

Ambrose stood on the hawser in the bottom of the boat

and braced himself with the edge of the wooden seat dug under his kneecaps. He took an oar and used it to pole away from the crack and into the open water. Once there, he put his oars over the side and slipped the small circular rope lashings — fishermen called them *wets* — over the wooden thole-pins, and together they picked up the rhythm of rowing, the rope in the midships unwinding from the coil as it fed through under Max's right oar and over the stern.

Norm pulled his snowmobile around by the skis and drove it thirty yards south. He walked back to the edge of the first crack, letting the rope slide through his hand, and watched the four oars dip and glide, saw his friends melt into the backdrop leaving him nothing but the sensation of a small fish tugging at the end of a line.

The wind had carried the ice pan another eighty yards since Max had first seen the snowmobile, but shortly before he lost sight of the main edge he spied the yellow cab.

When the old man saw the snowmobile he lifted his blades from the water. "By God, that's she all right," he confirmed. "'Tis a miracle, 'tis a miracle!" On reaching the pan, twenty-five feet long and six feet wider than the snowmobile, he climbed out and held the boat alongside as Max tossed the waning coil and an oar onto the ice. He ran his hand up and down the cab and looked it all over.

The waves licked the side of the pan and caused the boat to heave up and down. "No time for that, " Max said. "Turn the quoyle over and haul off ten or fifteen fathoms of rope and sink a bight down over the two ends."

Ambrose poked the rope underneath the pan muttering: *Like this, Max? — How's I doin', Max? — Tell me, Max — How's I doin'?"*

"Doin' fine, Ambrose, doin' fine." Max let the rope slide

through his hand as the wind carried them farther out to sea. "Little more to the left there on that one. There ya go — ya got her."

The old man threw the slack overboard and stepped onto the small wooden landing at the front of the boat, driving the head down and splashing water onto the pan. He dropped his oar across the two seats and Max yanked on the rope as hard as he could, shouting to Norm to start pulling. They were surprised to hear him call back. The fog had made them feel a thousand miles apart, and neither had considered keeping contact by voice for the rope had been enough. They heard Norm start his engine and then they turned the boat away, saw the rope begin to sink in a knot of crushed circles as Norm drove his machine towards land to take up the more than sixty fathoms of slack. The rope hissed, and ripped long seams in the water that healed instantly, tiny beads of water jumping from the hawser when it snapped to attention before going limp again. The engine roared and dropped to an idle.

"She's spinnin'," Ambrose cried. "He got no footin'!"

Norm jumped off, cursing at how he had spun all the snow from underneath his track, which was now on shiny, translucent ice. He pulled his snowmobile back six feet onto the snow, jumped on the seat again and gunned the throttle, watched over his shoulder as the rope went tight and snapped the Ski-Doo in line with the pan. Spun out a second time. A third time. Fourth. He was being dragged to the edge of the ice and had only seventy yards to go before plunging into the sea.

The men in the boat realized that Norm would soon run out of rope and ice.

"Gimme the end of that rope under your feet, Ambrose,

so's I can make into the pan! We gotta tow that Ski-Doo ashore with our paddles!"

Ambrose gave him the rope, dipped his oars and pushed the boat backwards to the ice. "What 'bout Martin?" he asked. "Long's we're at this we're not gonna get to the island tonight."

"Martin's safe enough if he's on the island," Max replied. "We can always get 'en later but right now we gotta get your Ski-Doo." He tied the end into a section of rope near the skis while Ambrose kept the boat steady, then fed three or four fathoms over the side and made a clove hitch in the risings.

The hawser came alive again with the roaring of the snowmobile engine but died within two seconds.

"Seems to be pretty cruel, don't it, Max? I mean to say it looks like we thinks more 'bout the bloody ol' Ski-Doo than we do 'bout Martin."

"Ok, pull," Max said, sitting down and digging his blades deep into the water. He'd heard what the old man had said but did not answer him. "Pull, Ambrose, pull!"

Their rope tightened as they dipped their oars in sync and hauled the round handgrips back. Their blades magnetized the water and pulled it behind the flat wood in a swirling pool of bubbles and sucking sounds.

Norm dragged his snowmobile back again and watched three of the six feet of slack rope on the ice behind it slink over the edge like a fleeing snake. He dragged his machine back some more and jumped on, gave it enough throttle to tighten the hawser and jolt him forward when he stopped abruptly, but not enough to spin out. He kept his thumb on the trigger, rocking the snowmobile from side to side until he smelled the drive belt burning. He shut off the engine and shouted to his comrades behind the veil of fog that he was unable to pull the Ski-Doo in, and that they should fasten a rope of their own while he tried digging his feet in and hauling by hand.

"We got her in tow," Max yelled back. "Pull, Ambrose! Pull whatever ya got in ya!"

The weight of the ice pan and the waves pressing against it was too much for the little boat to pull, and with every dip of the oars, it moved, not in a forward direction, but backwards.

"Gonna lose her," Ambrose said, driving his feet into Max's seat to brace himself as he pulled harder, the cords in his neck ready to pop through the skin. "What's we gonna do — let her go or what?"

"Your Ski-Doo, Ambrose — up to yourself what ya does but if 'twas mine I wud'n let her go till the very last minute!" Max positioned one foot against the sternpost and put extra effort into his rowing, heard a sharp crack and a dull thud behind him as Ambrose snapped a thole-pin and fell off his seat onto the forward landing, losing his paddle overboard. He maintained his long, powerful strokes while turning his body slightly to see the old man pick himself up and pluck his paddle from the sea and bang it down on the ends of the seats.

"No spare to'e-pins aboard," he said. "No mistake, we're into it now."

Max shipped one oar, pulled a thole-pin from the gunwale and handed it to Ambrose. "Here," he said. "Pop the ol' piece out and I'll make meself a wet."

Norm stood at the inside edge of a fresh crack and hauled the hawser tight, unable to hold the same section of rope for more than a few seconds. He had another fifteen fathoms he could work with but knew that, when they had passed through his hands, he would have to untie the rope from the tow hitch and call his men back.

Ambrose knocked the broken pin up through its hole and into the water, tapped the new one in with the heel of his hand and pushed the oar out, slipped the wet on over and resumed his steady dip and pull . . . dip and pull. Stopped. "Hark," he said, watching Max tie a loop in the risings and push his oar through. "Somebody's comin'!"

"That's just your mind," Max said, tying another knot in the loop, searching ahead for the main edge. He waited for Ambrose to make the dip and when he saw the oar crest in the air, dripping water, he held his breath and plunged his blades beneath the surface at the same time his partner did, then carried through with the rhythm.

The old man stopped rowing again. "Hark — y'hear it?"

Max held one of his oars with his elbow and cocked his ear to the wind. "Can't hear a thing."

"Ski-Doos," Ambrose said. "They're comin' off to get us!"

Norm could do nothing but sit on the ice with the rope in his hands and watch it pull himself and his snowmobile towards the sea. He heard the engines far off, stopped his heavy breathing and listened. He yelled across the ocean, "They're comin', Ambrose! They're comin' off to get us, Max! Pull on them paddles, you buggers — put your balls into 'em!"

Five snowmobiles roared alongside, with Lewis in the lead and Paddy behind him. Norm screeched out for their help and told them that he was holding onto Martin's Ski-Doo. The drivers scrambled off their seats, and latched onto the six fathoms of rope left on the bay ice, cursed vehemently at their awkwardness in trying to stop the slide. Someone predicted that they would be at the edge in less than a minute, and shouted for Norm to untie his Ski-Doo.

A man in a black rubber jacket covered in white paint blotches said, "No, geez — don't untie her," and shoved himself away from the hawser, snatched his hauling rope from the backrest of his snowmobile and tied it onto one of Norm's skis. "OK, men," he announced, taking a turn around his right hand and driving his left leg out in front of him. "No need to get in the water so all hands come back here!"

They all fought to hold their positions for as long as they could, but when Lewis, nearest the edge, jumped clear leaving only two fathoms of empty rope on the ice, the others jumped clear as well and grabbed onto the rope at the front. They grunted like pigs, some hopping on one foot as the steady pull kept throwing them off balance.

Ambrose and Max dipped their oars deep and made long, strenuous pulls, kept watching the hawser hold its tautness, unable to ascertain whether they were moving forward or backwards. They could see nowhere for they were blinded by the fog, and could only hear the shouts and clamorous voices of the men. *C'mon, boys — Pull — Put your backs into it — Pull — Harder — Harder!*

"Pull, Max — pull!"

John Parsons drove up, dragging a flat-bottomed speedboat with an outboard motor hinged on the stern and Garf standing in the midships, and before he came to a halt Garf jumped out and clamped his hands around the hauling rope. "Where's Uncle Am?" he asked, his boots tearing the snowcap off and sliding on the ice beneath.

"Off there," Paddy said with a nod.

For a moment he was puzzled. "What's on the end of this rope?"

"Martin's Ski-Doo," another replied. "He's gone off on the island."

John forced his way between the man in the painted jacket at the end and a short, red-faced man who farted riotously every time he gained new footing and resumed hauling.

"Gonna lose this Ski-Doo here, boys," Garf declared firmly. "You're gonna have to chop her clear — yez knows that, do yez?" The tow hitch was now two feet outside the main edge and above open water, yet no one spoke. Garf plucked his knife from its sheath and ran to the snowmobile, reached his arm over the backrest and severed the rope. It unravelled a little in the cut, its elasticity snapping it eight feet out to sea, and all the men fell like dominoes as they inadvertently pulled Norm's snowmobile back onto the ice.

Ambrose and Max saw the rope go limp, heard the shouts and loud talking inside the fogbank.

"Runned outta rope," the old man said quietly. "Lost it or bust it — one of the two."

Max set the weight of his arms on his oars and put his blades high off the water. "We're finished," he said. "Just so well to slip the lines and row ashore."

"What'd ya do that for?" came a voice from the crowd.

Garf spotted a small, talkative, rat-faced man in a checkered jacket and cap the same as his father's. Heard him say, "We almost had 'em!"

"No," Garf said. "What yez almost went and done was lost this Ski-Doo!" He turned the key, pulled twice on the cord, drove past the speedboat and stopped. "OK," men," he said with a shakiness in his voice as he untied the painter from John's snowmobile. "Let's give her a push."

When the boat was in the water, John climbed aboard and let the 25 hp. Evinrude down and started it.

"Take 'nother man if he wants to go," Garf said, straddling the gunwale with one foot in the boat and the other on the ice. "Gonna run off and tow the boys ashore."

"I'll go," Norm volunteered.

Garf moved to the midships.

John steered his speedboat alongside the retreating hawser, and Norm leaned over the bow with his knees against the rounded planks and pulled in the trailing end. He continued to pull the rope along the stem, hurriedly coiling it behind him on the seat, where the wet circles fell off in a tangle near Garf's feet.

Garf had wanted someone to go with them in the event that extra help was needed, but he hadn't expected Norm to volunteer. Norm had been such a driving force in the destruction of their village, that Garf's recollection of it kept him awake some nights. And he was bothered immensely by the man's lordly demeanour.

"Take the slack," John said above the whir of the engine. "And haul it back from Narm!"

Norm stuck his arm out straight behind him with the hawser in his hand, saw the displeasure in Garf's eyes. "Here, take it," he said. "And thanks."

"For what?" Garf asked combatively.

Norm turned back and began pulling again, talking with his chin in his shoulder so Garf could hear. "What ya done back there," he said. "Savin' me Ski-Doo."

Garf coiled the hawser neatly in the middle of the boat. "Your Ski-Doo?"

"Oh," Norm said, with one side of his mouth curled into a smile that no one saw. "Ya didn't know 'twas mine, did ya?"

"Didn't care," Garf answered. "'Sides — not me ya should thank anyway. Lew's the one who got the crowd together so thank him."

"There they is," John shouted. After a few hastily exchanged greetings, he tied the rope into the risings, next to the motor. "Take in your paddles now so ya don't lose 'em."

As soon as John took up the slack, Ambrose tied the painter into the hawser with a rolling hitch. The spinning blades of the outboard pushed a long trail of shooting bubbles and twisting eddies back against the bow of the rowboat and it wasn't very long before they saw the men waiting at the main edge.

When Ambrose's snowmobile and the rowboat had been pulled safely onto the bay ice, another crack started under the keel. The men, unalarmed at seeing it widen to six inches and then twelve, casually hung around the speedboat and listened to Garf tell them why he thought his father should go to the island with him and John instead of Norm.

"This ice starts breakin' off any faster," Norm argued, one foot on the ice and the other in the bow, "you'll want a extra man to help ya haul the boat 'cross the pans in arder to get back. Ambrose can still go but I'm goin' too."

"Make us too heavy. Slow us down."

"You don't want me to go."

"That's right. Uncle Am should be the one to go — not you."

Norm stepped out onto the ice with the painter in his hand. "OK, Ambrose," he said. "No hard feelin's. She's all yours."

John started his motor and turned the boat around. Before they went behind the veil of fog he took out his pocket compass and set a course due north. He turned the rubber grip on the steering arm all the way to full throttle, pressed the right side of his rump into the engine cover and scraped the starboard hull along a piece of ice before he saw it. Water seeped in between the seams — nothing to worry about according to Ambrose, but when John veered sharply away from another pan that grazed the same side the old man shouted back, telling him to slow down.

"Yes, keep your eyes open and watch where you're goin'," Garf said. "Strikes one of them pans head on 'tis the same thing as strikin' the side of a cliff. Drive the stem right back through the arse of her!"

John heard him above the engine and said with a spit to the side, "Only a bit a oakum, Garf. Nothin' to get rattled over. Two or three minutes with me carkin' iron when we gets back and she'll be so good as new."

Ten minutes and a lot of dodging ice pans later, they saw the thick white line of foam at the south end of the island.

"Not able to land," Garf said.

The old man flicked a loose wrist towards the shore. "Closer, John — go closer."

John steered to the leeward of a big pan and within sixty yards of the breakers crashing on the rocks, their spray driven onto the ballycaters by the wind. "We'll trim the shore and see how far down we can get."

Ambrose pulled out his tobacco and rolled a cigarette, had barely touched the match to it when they met the Arctic mush that had pressed in on the east shoreline.

John turned his boat around and headed back to the south end. "We'll have a look on the back of the island," he said, twisting the throttle halfway.

"No good," Garf advised. "Might get ashore there, yes, but there's nothin' only a straight cliff up and down. You'd have to be a monkey to get to the top."

"Pull her in here," Ambrose instructed, pointing to the

patch of saltwater grass where, unknown to him, his son had landed yesterday morning.

"Can't do that," Garf declared. "Strikes the boat on them rocks we'll capsize."

"Not if we does it right," his father said. He filled his lungs with smoke and held it.

"Whaddaya want me to do, Ambrose?" John asked, releasing the throttle and letting the boat ride on the waves. "I can go closer if ya wants me to but like Garf said — if we strikes her we'll prob'ly tip over."

The old man let out a long breath of smoke that the wind tore abroad and devoured. "That notch there," he said, pointing to the lowest section of the icy shoreline, then looking back at John. "If ya can fit her in that notch, I can jump ashore."

Garf disagreed. "And if ya slips on the rocks you'll be drownded. What's we gonna do then, eh? Tell me, Uncle Am — tell me! What's we gonna tell Aunt Ida?"

Ambrose chuckled and tossed his butt overboard. "Tell her I'm gone to a better place."

"You're not jumpin' ashore. I won't let ya. S'posing ya gets one of them pains again ——"

"If I do, I do. Just so well to die one way as die the other."

"Time is goin'," John said. "'Nother hour it'll be pitch-black and all them pans is gonna be down on us, so stop that nonsense and make up yez mind what yez gonna do."

Ambrose flicked his wrist and John moved to within ten yards of the notch. The waves crested like the plumage of a rooster's tail and hurled themselves against the island with a crash.

"Steady now John," Ambrose yelled, bringing his legs up and swinging them over the seat. "I'm gonna get in the f'ard standin' room and when I says 'go' you give her the dart and I'll jump ashore."

Garf put his hand on his father's shoulder and wheeled him around. "Get back here, Uncle Am. Lemme get there where you're to and I'll jump ashore instead."

"And if ya slips and falls and gets drownded, what's I gonna tell your mother?"

"I'm not gonna get drownded."

"Ya don't know that."

"Yes I do know it." Garf tugged on his father's jacket. "I'm serious," he said. "I'm not lettin' you jump ashore on that island less'n I goes first."

The old man looked out into the fog at the swells heaving up, followed them in, saw them pass underneath the boat and watched them crash on the shore. "Steady!"

"Hear me talkin' to ya, Uncle Am, or don't ya?"

"Hears ya, yes, but I'm not givin' no heed to ya."

John wrestled with the steering arm, trying to keep the boat in line with the notch as he used his right hand behind him to throw the motor in and out of gear. "Start countin'," he said. "And when ya jumps, make a good one."

Garf was angry. "What's Uncle Am gonna do with gettin' ashore? Tell me! He's just 'bout sixty years of age for God's sake. Slips and falls in that water he'll be a goner!"

"Shut up, Garf!" Ambrose watched for a lull in the waves and then the crash of the swell over the ballycaters. "That's the first one."

John turned his head and counted "two" as another swell rolled in and splattered on the seashore. He threw the motor out of gear and widened his stance.

"Jumps on that island, Uncle Am, ya might be there a month 'fore anyone gets ya."

The old man put his hand on top of the stem, watched another swell roll in under the boat and crumble onto the rocks. The foam cascaded down the sides of the notch and ran in a river of bubbles to the sea. "That's three," he said, climbing up onto the risings and crouching over the front like a cat ready to spring. "Now John, give her a dart!"

John shifted the motor into forward gear. Ambrose cleared the bow, but in the rush he stumbled and fell headlong, losing his cap and banging his knee on the rocks.

Another wave crested and slammed a ton of water into the notch, buried the old man, tossing him like a rag doll across the top of the ballycaters to the edge of the grass. Garf told John that his father had been killed by the impact.

"He's not killed," John replied, fixing his eyes on the old man as he rose slowly to his knees and looked about in a daze. "He's tougher'n we thinks he is."

"Go back! We gotta get 'en off that island so quick as we can!"

John moved the boat away from the danger zone and turned it broadside to the shore, watched an ice pan get caught in the surf and break into four or five chunks when it smashed onto the rocks. "Know what you're sayin'?" he asked. "Or don't ya?"

"We can't let Uncle Am stay on that island like that," Garf reasoned. "He's sogged right to the bone and another few minutes the chill's gonna go through 'en like a dose a salts!"

"We can't go back. He's there and he's gonna have to stay till he gets Martin. We goes back in that notch again we'll only risk beatin' up the boat."

Garf sat weakened on the front seat and watched his father

haul off his rubber jacket, hobble through the grass and disappear in the fog as he began to climb the hill. "So, John — ya thinks your boat is more important'n a man's life, do ya?"

John threw the motor out of gear and the engine purred in its smooth and peaceful idle, driving a ragged stream of warm coolant water and steam from its exhaust every time the boat rose on a wave and lifted the tail. "Yes," he admitted shamelessly, sitting on the rear seat and facing forward. "Right now this boat is more important than anyone or anything. This is the only way to get your father and Martin off that island and without it they're gonna punch in a hard night."

"Sea is makin'," Garf said. "Give it 'nother half-hour and they won't get off anyway. Once it gets dark and that sea is twice's big, ya won't get handy to the land."

"Your father'll be back 'fore it gets dark, don't warry. And Martin's prob'ly on his way 'cross the island right now. He might've heard us comin' so don't say they're not gonna make it. You gotta put them ol' thoughts outta your mind, Garf. I knows 'tis hard for ya to take in that your father had alike to be washed off the rocks but" — he moved his outstretched arm across the water — "look, he made it!"

16

DEVIL IN THE OUTHOUSE

Martin was in the woodbox, not asleep but sitting there with the yellow cap on, the bloody three-quarter buttoned all the way to his chin and the old clothes pulled around him, watching daylight creep from the kitchen and listening to the wind and surf.

All through the day he had tried to elude the thought of hunger by making at least four trips to the south end, the first trip being more of an excuse to get away from the frightening thought of the big seal than an attempt at getting rescued. On returning he had used his gaff to pull his seals one by one from Trimm's Point to the top of the hill, where he pushed them down the other side, and he even laughed a little when they slid all the way to the bottom the way he and his mates had done while playing games in the snow here. He had not been able to retrieve his hauling rope and the last two seals, for the sea had loosened the ice and made it too unstable to walk on. Somehow he felt relief in that blameless perception, liked to think he would have recovered the lot, but he knew the real reason why he hadn't: he had been too frightened to go back on the ice.

Even now as the darkness settled around him, he saw in the shadows the balloon-head, the open mouth and the razor-sharp fangs; could hear the guttural roar of the beast calling his name. He pulled his head down into the musty dampness, tried thinking of happy times to ward off the nightmares he knew would come with sleep, but the images of the morning kept repeating themselves. Again he heard his name, not like before but more the way his father would shout it whenever he, the boy, did something wrong. He pulled the clothes down to his chin and listened but heard nothing aside from the wind and surf, yet he couldn't bring himself to believe he had only imagined someone calling his name. He arranged the dirty garments around his face once more and closed his eyes. He prayed that sleep would overtake him soon and that he would not awaken until morning, that tomorrow night he would sleep in his own bed.

"MARRRTINNNNN!"

If his eyes had not been fastened in their sockets they would have undoubtedly fallen into the woodbox. Martin threw off the clothes and jumped out, the hairs on the back of his neck standing stiff and straight like darning needles, his spine tingling as the cold shivers refused to leave his body. There was no mistaking his father's voice and, through the window, the hurrying silhouette on the path leading from the church to their old house. He ran to the porch and opened the door, left it that way and raced outside, yelling, "Dad, Dad, you found me!"

The silhouette stopped and fell to its knees, panting and gasping for air.

For a moment the boy lost recognition of the figure before him and wondered if it was his father at all, but when he went closer and saw the old man lift his wet head and say his name again he felt more safe than he ever had.

"Dad," he said, taking off his cap and using it to wipe the water from his father's hair. "How'd ya find me?" He put the cap on the old man's head and rolled the rim up, fixed it halfway down over his ears and helped him to his feet.

"Martin! The boat — we gotta get back to the boat!"

"What boat?" the boy asked. "Who's with ya? And why's ya so wet?"

Ambrose took off the cap and ran it over his face. "Speed-boat. Garf and John is waitin' for us!"

"At the end of the island?"

"Yes!"

"And you fell in the water gettin' ashore."

"Never fell in the water, no."

"How'd ya get wet then?"

The old man pulled the cap back on, wrung out the wrist-band of his sleeve and shook the water from his naked hands. "Big sea on," he said. "Quicker we gets back the better."

"What 'bout me seals?"

"Seals?"

"Yeah, killed eight this marnin'. Got six there by Jarge's house."

Ambrose looked at his son. "Eight seals. By Jarge's house."

"Uh-huh."

"Do I look like I was barn yes'day?"

"Come up to the house and I'll show ya," Martin said. "Six seals — every one of 'em bat twice and stuck through the heart."

"Go 'way with ya, Martin." The old man tugged on his son's arm. "And how come you're dressed up in Jarge's clothes?"

"Got wet," he answered.

"How'd ya get wet?"

"Never mind that, Dad. Come back with me to see the seals."

Ambrose pulled harder on the boy's sleeve, nearly shucking the tent-like jacket from his arm like the shell off a shrimp. "No," he said. "You're comin' with me to the boat!"

"But Dad ——"

"No buts, Martin. We didn't come off here to see if you was here and go on home again without ya. We come off to get ya, boy, so come on — let's go!"

"But what 'bout me seals?" the boy insisted. "Lotta money there — we just can't leave 'em!"

"Stop it, Martin!"

"C'mon, Dad boy, ya gotta believe me!"

"I believes ya," he said. "We'll come back and get 'em when the sea pitches back. They won't spoil here and if they're dead they're not gonna crawl 'way. And there's nothin' on the island to eat 'em, so there!"

"Lemme run back and get me coat," Martin said. "Then we'll leave."

"Gotta go now," his father said, turning and hurrying down the path. Looked over his shoulder at the boy walking slowly behind him and begging him to wait. "'Sides, 'tis my coat — not yours."

"Lemme get 'en anyway." He had hoped to persuade his father to go to the house, thinking that once he saw the seals, maybe he would help tow them back to the boat.

"C'mon Martin, or you'll be left behind. Garf and John is not gonna wait all night for you to get aboard, so put them seals outta your mind and come on!"

The boy watched as his father began to fade in the foggy

darkness that had descended on them so quickly during their squabble. Only the blackness of the land and the wet wood of the destruction were visible now.

Would his father actually leave him, he wondered, after just finding him? Or would he hide behind the fog and wait for him to catch up? What was his purpose in coming to the island if not to rescue him, and what would Garf say if the old man returned empty-handed? He's bluffing, Martin thought; he'll wait for me near the graveyard. He called out but the old man didn't answer; called several more times but heard no reply. The wind whipped his collar onto his face, not as strong now and not as damp but just as cold. He listened for any sound that might tell him Garf was still waiting at the end of the island, heard only the wind in his ears and shuddered at the thought of spending another night in the woodbox. The appearance of his father seemed like a dream. He told himself that the seals would have to stay here and, although he knew no one would ever believe he had killed them, he vowed to return once the seas had moderated, load them into a boat — stolen if need be — and take them home. *Home* — he had never before applied that word to Karpoon, and wondered why he did now. He thought of his mother, his grandmother, all the colours and smells inside their house, the rattle of dishes, the platter overflowing with steaming food, the fire crackling, the lamp buzzing and throwing off its oily scent, his comic books and all the stories to be read for the third and fourth time, his father's Ski-Doo and how he would never be allowed to use her again — providing they'd found her. And how had they known where he was?

"Hold on, Dad," he yelled. "Wait for me, and don't say ya can't hear me 'cause I knows ya can!" He took one last look at the open door of the Trimm house, and ran across the field.

He found his father at the cemetery, leaning with one arm propped on a fencepost and the other set off in a crook by a bunch of knuckles wedged into his side.

"Didn't think ya was comin'," he said.

"Didn't think you'd leave me," Martin pointed out.

Ambrose led the way up the hill and down the other side to the south end, with the boy tight behind him, trying to step in his tracks, both of them churning the snow and squishing the black depressions made there in the last two days. At the far edge of the grass the sea drove the surf and small chunks of ice twenty feet into the air. The old man put his hand on Martin's shoulder and told him, in short gasps, to call out through the darkness during the next calm spell for the boat to come and get them.

Martin wasn't sure if a boat could land here or not. "Can't see 'em, Dad," he responded. "And look at all that ice!"

"Sing out to 'em; they'll hear ya!"

Martin cupped his hands around his mouth and emptied his lungs towards where his father said with one long *Helllp*. "Gonna have to move back outta this," he said. "Or else we're gonna be drownded."

"I'm drownded already," his father announced. "And we can't move back no further 'cause they won't see us!"

"Can't see us anyway — 'tis too dark!"

Ambrose tried shouting to the boat but he was too weak and only squawked. A breaker rolled in and exploded in a cavernous boom against the ballycaters, sending up a funnel of seawater that buried them both.

Martin gasped when the coldness struck him. "C'mon Dad," he shouted above the roar. "We gotta move back farther on the bank or else we're gonna be washed off!"

"No," the old man said. "We're stayin' right here till they comes and gets us!"

"They're not comin'," Martin said. "The bight is breakin' up. That's where all the ice is comin' from!"

Ambrose spoke without turning around, his eyes glued to the wind. "I knows the bight is breakin' up but there's not enough ice for Garf to turn his back on us. Sing out to 'en again!"

Martin went to the old man's side and held onto his arm, encouraging him to move away from the sea and out of danger.

"They've gone and left us," Ambrose said quietly, the wind pushing the salt water back along his cheeks like rain pressed against a window. "Garf is gone and left us."

Two hundred yards offshore, Garf was involved in a fierce argument with John over his decision to head back to the main edge. They had been forced to leave the island and lose it in the fog because of the ice bearing down on them and nearly pinning them to shore. The boat was being tossed around more than ever and a new leak had started near the keel.

"Oakum's comin' out of her," John said, standing in six inches of water and using his free hand to bail. "Got no choice — we gotta go back. 'Nother twenty minutes we'll be too soggy to move."

"Should a brought a bigger bucket," Garf said with indignation.

"Shouldn't a runned into them pans of ice."

"Whose fault was that — mine or yours?"

John kept the engine in gear at an idle and threw the water out and up like a dog tossing dirt into the air while digging a hole. "Garf," he said, "I can't believe you're gettin' on like this. What's wrong with ya?"

"Wrong — whaddaya mean wrong?"

"Just listen to how you're gettin' on. You're not the same man. What happened to ya?"

Garf looked towards the land and then across the black ocean dotted with pans of dark grey ice. "Uncle Am is not gonna make it," he said. "Leaves 'en on that island, he won't see daylight."

John turned the throttle and moved the boat away from an ice pan. "Your father's tough, Garf. Just that he depends on you too much for everything. You knows that so well as I do."

"Who else can he depend on? Tell me!"

"Hisself for a change." John dropped the bailer with seven inches of water still in the boat. "We gotta get back to the main edge," he said. "That's if there's one left. We got a bunch a men in there somewhere waitin' for us."

"And we got two more on the island," Garf conveyed, kicking water back at the big man in the stern. "What 'bout them?"

"'Tis out of our hands, Garf. Nothin' we can do no more'n we done. We can't get ashore and we ——"

"That's 'cause 'twas all in your hands to begin with. If I had the wheel we'd a been on the island now — no two ways 'bout it!"

"What would we'd a done with the boat, Garf? Answer me!"

"Let her sink," he said, the whites of his eyes flashing his anger. He drove his left hand into the sea and kept it there while he stared back at where the island should have been. "What's we gonna tell the crowd when we gets in? What's we gonna tell Aunt Ida?"

John took out his compass, jammed it to within ten inches of his eyes to see the luminescent dial and set a course due south. There had never been a bad word spoken between them until now, and he showed the anguish of the quarrel on his face. "Tell 'em the truth," he said. "What else can we tell 'em!"

~~~

Martin led his father into the Trimm house, dumped the clothes from the woodbox and turned it upside down. "We gotta light a fire," he said, sitting the old man down and kneeling in front of him. "Matches — you got any?"

Ambrose reached into his pocket and Martin heard a rattle in the darkness.

Ten matches later, they still hadn't seen a spark. "They're all wet, Dad!"

"Try 'nother one," his father said.

"Only four or five left. What should I do — light 'em or what?"

"Yes, but don't strike 'em so hard," the old man counselled, shifting his weight on the woodbox. "Just take it easy and watch what you're doin'."

Martin scraped another one along the strip and still there was no spark. He scraped another and another — nothing. "They're soakin' wet, boy — they're sogged to death!" He counted the matches in the box by touching them with his finger, *one — two — three*. "Only three left, Dad! What should I do?"

"Not much you can do only try 'em," his father said. "Don't try, you'll never know."

"But what if they don't light?" The boy heard a click in the dark.

"Then you'll have to use this."

A flame the size of an Indian arrowhead illuminated his father's golden brown face, casting flickering shadows over the deep wrinkles in his forehead and the lines from the bridge of his nose to the corners of his lips. The old man smiled, something the boy could never truly remember him doing, and made new shadows with the crow's feet of his squinted eyes.

"A lighter — where'd ya get it?"

"Max's," he replied, holding it out, still lit.

Martin took the lighter, felt the warmth, then the hotness, as he shielded the flame with his hand while he carried it to the stove. He took a piece of catalogue paper from the firebox and touched it to the fire, watched it burn to his fingers before dropping it onto the pieces already in there. In seconds the whole kitchen was shimmering with dancing shadows, the four cold, depressing walls and the unsightly ceiling springing back to life, regaining some of the spirit that resettlement had taken away. He snapped the lid over the flame and tipped the gunpowder into the fire. A blast drove smoke in his face, knocking him back in fright.

"What's that bang?" the old man wanted to know.

"Gunpowder," the boy admitted. "I thought 'twas spoiled." He set some of the heavy wallpaper onto the fire, stowed in two rubber boots and put the damper on. When he told his father how he had tried to ignite the powder, the old man went into his squeal and chastised him for being so careless and stupid.

"What was I s'posed to do?" Martin asked. "Freeze to death or what?"

Ambrose didn't comment either way, but held his hands over the stove and rubbed them together. "How's the pipes — ya look at 'em or didn't ya?"

"Don't know but they're still there anyway."

The old man took the lighter and went upstairs. When he came down he closed the door to the stairwell behind him. "Pipes looks OK," he said. "Bit rusty but nothin' to warry 'bout." He went to the porch, checked the outside door and closed the one to the kitchen.

"Listen Dad, I s'pose ya wud'n have a bit a bread or somethin' on ya, would ya?"

Ambrose remembered, went stiff and said with considerable effort, "Nunny-bag's still in the rodney." To help ease the boy's disappointment, and perhaps make himself more comfortable about forgetting to bring the food, he added, "Wellwellwellwell, 'twas right there in the bottom of the boat and slipped me mind to take it out!" Then he had to explain how they had organized the search for Martin, and how so many people had become involved so quickly when they heard he was missing.

A thick cloud of black smoke rose from the damper hole and sent a smell of burning rubber throughout the house when Martin jammed more wallpaper and a sneaker into the stove. He asked his father how they had known about him being on the island.

"That young Judy," he said. "She's a wunnerful little girl. If she never went the work and told us where you was at, we'd a never found ya. This's where you would a perished."

"Y'know Dad, I told her not to tell. S'posin' she listened to me?"

"'Twas a foolish thing ya done, Martin, but what's done is done. Ya can't undo it so ya gotta make the best of it." Ambrose dug into his bib pocket and hauled out his tobacco, expecting it to be wet, but found it surprisingly dry. His papers were sogged and matted in their pack but in no time he had a crude cigarette made, using a piece of catalogue paper that flared like a lighter when he lit it from another piece dipped into the fire. His tobacco smoke wafted through the kitchen as he pinched the cigarette in the middle to stop it from unrolling, the reddish-orange tip flittering in the dark as he talked eagerly while rubbing a fist in his palm to offset the cold.

"Y'had anything to eat today?" he asked the boy.

"Nothin'."

"What 'bout yes'day?"

"Nothin'," he said, digging his fingernails underneath the wallpaper fitted snugly against the kitchen doorposts.

The old man didn't see what he was up to, but roared at him when he heard the paper tear in a long strip to the floor. "Don't tear up Jarge's house," he grouched. "'Tis not ours so leave it alone!"

Martin tore the heavy paper into strips the size of small cod fillets, then poked them into the fire, which glowed intensely and gave off a heat that tempted him to keep the damper off. He asked if he could leave it that way but the old man told him to put it back on.

"Knows ya can't keep the damper off, Martin — we'll be all gas-ted! What's wrong with ya, boy — gettin' worse, ain't ya?"

"I only thought. . . ."

"You thought wrong." Ambrose stuck his cigarette in the corner of his mouth and kicked off his rubber pants, leaned inward on the stove as far as he could, his knees touching the side. "Y'know," he said, patting the wetness of his trousers into his legs, "we gotta get that fire goin' better'n that. If we don't we're gonna perish like sheep and, time t'marra comes, won't be nothin' left a me and you only two carpses."

"I can tear off more paper," Martin offered, unable to see anything of his father in the dark except for the glow of the cigarette on his face and the occasional streaks of light squeezing through the cracks in the stove and falling on him like long, disfigured leeches.

"Canvas," the old man allowed, dropping to his knees and finding a hole where he could hook his fingers. "We can tear the canvas off a the floor."

"What's the difference in canvas and paper?" the boy asked. "Still Jarge's." He heard a long ripping sound.

"Tar in the canvas, boy," the old man said amiably, tearing it into smaller pieces and dropping them one by one onto the fire. "When that starts to burn, look out." The flame cast its glowing warmth on his face and what was left of his multicoloured cigarette. "And yes, I knows 'tis still Jarge's, but there's no need to make the place look worse'n it is by ramshackin' the walls. Right?"

Martin told himself that answering either way would probably trap him and lead to an argument that he could not tolerate here. He wanted to blast him, though, for not bringing the packsack, for not ever considering him anything more than useless, brazen, saucy, no good, stun, stupid and lazy; for saying these things openly around his friends as if they were true. Just thinking of their many differences caused his stomach to tighten more. He felt he should lash out at his father, if not for the harsh things of the past, then for all the humiliating things the old man would say if and when they were ever rescued. Then he felt his stomach knot, and he doubled down in pain. "Dad boy, you mightn't believe me but I feels some hungry."

"I'm hungry too," he said, putting the damper on. "Ain't had a bite since me dinner today."

The boy untied the rope around his jacket and let it fall behind him on the floor, kicked it back against the cupboards. "Dad," he said, going to the pile of clothes by the woodbox and sifting through it for something dry to wear, "how long can ya go without eatin'?"

"Whaddaya mean?"

"I mean how long can ya live without havin' somethin' to eat?"

The old man sucked the last of the smoke from his cigarette and tossed the butt on the stove. "Don't know." That clothes there," he said. "Anything to fit me, ya think?"

Martin found a sweater and a pair of trousers. "This'll fit ya," he replied, tossing them along. "More stuff upstairs — all kinds a stuff. Little damp but anything's better'n we got on."

When the stove had been stuffed with more canvas and another boot they both went upstairs and, using the lighter to guide them, gathered up more clothes and came back down. The smell of rubber and tar had been strong there, and the boy had mentioned it to his father, but the old man had assured him that the pipes were safe and that he had checked for redness by standing near them and blacking out the lighter.

Ambrose hauled off his overalls, wet except for one side of the bib and, though he could not shed the topmost part of his combinations underwear without taking his trousers off, he let it hang around his ass and tied the arms together.

"Don't mind me legs wet," he said, lodging his tobacco on the end of the cupboard. "Long's the chill don't strike me lungs."

Soon they had removed all their drenched upper clothes and dressed themselves in musty, damp garments from the top loft. Ambrose flicked the lighter to check how he looked in his new outfit. He had put on a plaid blue and white cotton shirt with no buttons, and a pink turtleneck sweater that he told his son could stretch to the end of the island and back if he pulled on it hard enough. On top of that he had a tan three-quarter jacket, lined and with a brown fur collar — but with the buttons stripped. He told his son, "Women saves everything and wastes nothin'."

"Don't feel bad," Martin said, rolling his head and adjusting his neck to the white short-sleeved blouse he wore under two nylon windbreakers — one thin yellow shell with three blue stripes down the side, and the other dark brown or black, lined with synthetic white fur and split at the armpits. "You'll find there's no zippers in this house either."

Ambrose crammed more canvas into the stove and set about hanging the wet clothes around the warmer, at the end of the stove and flat on the oven door.

"We can make a clothesline," Martin said, kicking off his old trousers. "There's a piece a wire in one of the drawers there."

"Well, don't just stand there, boy. Get it!"

Two hours later there was steam coming from the clothes on both the oven door and their antenna wire clothesline — a line they had rigged across the stove from a nail in the wall to a sock dropped over the other side of the door leading to the porch.

Now they sat side by side on the woodbox, basking in the

warmth like cormorants drying their wings, turning their backs to the stove now and then to dry their behinds, their dialogue reduced to short remarks about how well the fire was burning, how dark the night was, how foggy it was and how they wished they had something to eat.

Martin told his father about the seals again — not that he had any desire to eat raw meat — yet the old man still refused to believe the story, even when the boy begged him to go outside and look. But he was glad he wasn't alone. Sometimes he would watch the light from the flames dance on his father's hands while the old man rubbed them continuously on his knees, the thick, bulging, crooked veins in his wrists branching off like limbs from old trees that had their trunks buried underneath the sleeves of the turtle-neck. Although he could not see the crooked finger now, because of the poor light, for the sake of conversation he asked what had caused it.

"That finger," Ambrose said, leaning back and putting his hand close to his face to inspect the nail. "I'll tell ya again what happened to that finger, my son." He coughed and spat towards the bottom of the kitchen door, pushed his finger into the light where they could both see it. "Wonder to God I never lost me hand," he went on. "Me and poor ol' Jarge, we was off pickin' berries one fall and you, oh you was just a young gaffer then, two or three year old, I s'pose — not big enough to see up over the table. Jarge come out for me one marnin', said he was goin' up on the west'rd side of the island to look for a few pa'tridgeberries. I said, I think I'll go 'long with ya. Certainly Jarge had to take his gun — that's somethin' he had to do. Wherever that man went, he had to take his gun. I can mind one time when Alfred said he seen the devil down through the hole in the

outhouse and come back up the path screechin' blue mur-
der. Well my son, 'twas so good as a concert. Jarge took his
gun off the wall and went down, stood back 'bout twenty or
thirty feet and shot up in under — BANG! There was shit
flyin' everywhere."

Martin burst out laughing and the old man sniggered a
little himself.

"True, my son," he said, reclaiming some of his stoicism.
"I was there — I seen it with me own two eyes, and I smelled
it too."

"Jarge kill the devil?" The boy's breath stopped short and
his stomach jiggled with pent-up laughter.

"Never killed 'en, no, but ya should a seen his mother."
Ambrose picked his nose, searching for the right way to
lambaste the old woman. "My son, she had a conniption.
Only way I can 'scribe the look on her face when she come
through the door is, if there's ever a devil up there in hell,
he was down in the shithouse that day wearin' a dress."

Martin felt somewhat awkward in his new role as the old
man's audience, yet something about the humour seemed
real. To keep the excitement alive he said, "Your finger —
you was gonna tell me 'bout your finger."

"Oh, that? Jarge done that after we got back home. He
was so mad 'cause he never seen nothin' to shoot at that he
slammed the door behind 'en 'fore I got a chance to step
foot in the porch, and where should that finger be but right
in the way." Ambrose got up and brought his tobacco back
to the woodbox, pushed the finger in and rooted. "Good rig
for diggin' out me baccy though," he said, and then, with a
touch of panic in his voice, "Oh my Lard, I can touch bottom!"

In the next hour hardly a word was spoken. Ambrose

smoked a single cigarette and Martin filled the stove with canvas three times.

"Good ya had a lighter, eh, Dad?"

"Good I forgot to give 'en back to Max, he said, looking around in the fragmented darkness at two streaks of light that danced wildly on the kitchen door. "What we wants is a bit a wood to go on top a that canvas — somethin' to give off a slow heat."

"We can burn the woodbox," Martin said reluctantly.

"No no," his father replied, patting the end of the box. "Does that, we won't have nothin' to sit on. Might be here two or three days 'fore that sea pitches back." Ambrose went to the window, wiped the moisture off with his bare hand and looked out. "Y'know," he said, "I thought one time when I was a boy that this was all there was." The old man spoke very gently while looking up at the sky. "I can still mind the day when me father told me there was more people like we fellers on the other side a the bay there. Took the good right outta me, 'cause I thought sure we was the only people in the world."

Martin let him speak.

"I was twelve year old the first summer I went fishin' out to Belle Isle, fifteen 'fore I ever sot foot in Karpoon. Ol' Mr. Butler, that's Max's father — and a fine man he was too — fished with him, I did. But he got deaf 'fore he died and I means deaf. But 'twas a funny kind of deaf. He could understand what me and Max used to say, 'specially if Max went on with some swear words, but Sadie — he couldn't understand one word she said. Every time she spoke to 'en or asked 'en somethin' he just shook his head and pointed to his ears. But when she sung out 'Suppertime' — he was always the first one to the table. He used to look after me summertimes out there like I was one of his own, 'cause ya can say that me and Max growed up like brothers almost.

"I can mind one fall me and Max was puttin' new felt on his mother's henhouse; oh, we was 'bout fourteen or fifteen, I s'pose. Anyway, the hammer fell off the roof and I went down the ladder to pick 'en up. Max said he'd catch 'en so I went the work and throwed 'en up to 'en. And where should that hammer take 'en but right in the gob. Smashed off one of his teeth tight to the gums."

"And that's how he got his gold tooth."

"Not right away," Ambrose said. "He got that tooth after his father died. Y'see, the ol' man had that gold tooth in the first place — got 'en when he was overseas in the First World's War. When he come back home he told ol' Mrs. Butler that if anything ever happened to 'en he wanted her to have the tooth. She used to keep it in a little blue dish up in the cupboard and whenever anyone come in to see it, and people seen it more'n once too, youngsters 'specially — whenever they wanted to see it she'd take it down and show it to 'em, no more'n that to it. My son, that was a wunnerful thing to see — that tooth when he was in the dish. I 'low he was a inch long or more, every bit of it."

"Well, how'd Max end up with 'en in his mouth?"

Ambrose came back to the woodbox and sat down. "One time Max took it to St. Anthony with 'en, after the ol' man died, and told the doctor there he wanted the broke-off one took out and the gold one shoved in."

"Yuck," the boy said, letting a long string of spit fall to the floor between his knees. "From one mouth to the other — that's sick!"

"Oh no, Mr. Butler never had the tooth in his mouth at all. He winned it in a poker game over in France one night just 'fore the war ended."

"Poker game?" Martin smiled. "Then it was in someone else's mouth." He waited for his father to reply. When he didn't, the boy carried through. "OK, now what if Max dies — what's gonna happen to the tooth? I mean it should be worth some money, shouldn't it?"

"Told me if he dies 'fore I do, to take 'en out of his head with a pair pliers and give 'en to Sadie. 'Don't use no more hammers,' he said. 'Use the pliers.'"

"Will it fit Sadie then?" Martin asked, hearing his father scratch his head in the darkness.

"My God boy. What's Sadie gonna do with a gold tooth in her mouth? What she should have in her mouth is a bit. Audrey gets the tooth — that's their daughter. She's down the States somewhere. Runned away a few year ago with a Yank what come up here to go teachin'. Left it all and took off."

Martin knew vaguely of a woman from Karpoon who had gone to Boston and he knew she was Alec's mother but that was all. "Why'd we leave, Dad? Why'd we ever leave home?"

"Well, I don't know. Sometimes I thinks we left for the money and more times I thinks we left so's everyone else could get the money."

"Whaddaya mean?"

"Well, Narm Andrews was pretty well up on things when it come to the news on the radio, and readin' letters, writin' letters and stuff like that, y'know, and he was behind this movin' racket in the first place. 'Twas a few families here who wanted to move right or wrong just to get off the island, and 'twas another bunch here who wanted to move for the money. But at that time, in arder for anyone to get one red cent from the gov'ment, everyone in the place had to move.

Every family had to get out — can you 'magine? Every-one!"

"Our house, Dad — how come we never took it?"

"House is old. Garf said he'd prob'ly fall apart 'fore we got 'en halfway 'cross the beach. Narm offered to help us but Garf said no. So I left 'en here. To rot." The old man yawned, making a roar that seemed to go on forever, one arm crooked and flexed at the bicep and the other driven high in the air. When his stretch was over, he said, "Forgot to ask ya but where'd ya sleep last night — or did ya sleep at all?"

The boy knocked the side of the woodbox. "Right here," he said. "But you can have it if ya wants to 'cause I'm not sleepy."

"In the woodbox?" His father didn't squeal but spoke slowly and clearly, as if he believed him and pitied him at the same time. "If ya never stole the Ski-Doo," he stated firmly, "none of this wud'n've happened."

"Would you'd a give her to me if I'd a asked ya?"

"Don't talk so foolish, boy; y'knows I wud'n."

"Then what'd ya 'xpect me to do?"

Ambrose got up and went to the window again. "No mat-ter what I tells ya, Martin, ya never listens. Why is it — is it 'cause ya thinks I'm wrong all the time or is it 'cause ya don't believe a word I says?"

The boy lifted the damper and poked at the burning can-vas, the flames lighting the old man's shape against the window. "How's we gonna get off the island, Dad?"

"Boat," he said. "When Garf comes back in the marnin'."

"How's we gonna get me seals off?"

Ambrose sighed heavily, took his tobacco and returned to the box. "Give it up, Martin." He rolled a cigarette from the catalogue paper, licked it and clamped his finger and thumb around it. "Why's ya keepin' on nig-naggin' 'bout your seals all the time? My God, boy ——"

"And why don't ya believe me when I tells ya somethin'? I told ya I had ——"

"Put the damper back on, do!"

Martin did as he was told, not because his father had ordered him to but because he had poked the canvas enough. "You asked me if I thinks you're wrong all the time — well, you never believes anything I says so you must think *I'm* wrong all the time."

His father grunted and said bitterly, just before he flicked the lighter, "You're wrong most of the time. Ya don't know how to shut up — that's why ya never listens." He lit his cigarette, inhaled deeply and held his breath for nearly ten seconds. Exhaled. "What's ya goin' on 'bout the seals all the time for anyway? Geez, make no wonder your poor ol' mother is just 'bout off her head. Ya got her drove!"

The boy jumped off the box and pulled the kitchen door open, releasing the line and sending the semi-dry clothes onto the stovetop, where he heard them sputter and sizzle before he opened the outside door and dashed around the corner into the night. The coldness gripped him and made his muscles tight. He grabbed his gaff stuck in the snowbank, hooked it into the mouth of a seal and dragged it through the porch into the kitchen.

"There ya go, ol' man," he said despisingly to the shadowy figure holding the smoking garments in his arms. He unhooked the gaff and drove the spike into the floor, leaving the gaff standing by itself. "That's a seal — my seal!" He went to the stove and pulled the damper off to let his father see. "'Fore you calls me a liar again, take a good look and think 'bout what you're sayin'!"

The light fell on the old man's wrinkles, making him seem older than his years as he held onto the hot clothes and stared at the dead seal. His face went blank, expressionless, and the flame bounced off the sides of his eyes.

"What's wrong, ol' man?" Martin sneered, with a gutful of nerve and insolence. "Looks like the cat got your tongue!" Waited for his father to say something. "Well, whaddaya gotta say for yourself?"

The old man tried to speak but floundered in his awe. "Aahhh, myohmy — ohohohohoh."

The cold wind rushing into the kitchen mangled the stream of smoke that poured from the stove, and when the fumes became near unbearable Martin slapped the damper on. He stood in the tormenting smoke, which made his eyes water, and said, "Believe me now, ol' man? Or have I gotta go out and drag the other five in?"

"Thought you had eight," his father said without moving an inch.

"Six I said — I said 'twas eight I killed."

"Where's the rest?"

"Devil took 'em."

Ambrose laid the clothes on the woodbox and heard the boy leave the kitchen. He put out his foot to find the seal, stepped over it and followed him to the outside door, where he found him hacking dryly and spitting into the dark. "Your other seals, Martin," he said, with a touch of clemency in his voice. "Where's they to — on the other side of the house or what?"

"Yeah," the boy replied between dry, raspy throat-clearings. He felt as though he wanted to vomit, not from the smoke, but the smoke had certainly done something to his empty stomach to make it burn that way. He knew he had never hated his father, but for the moment he thought he might. He thought about his mother, and as the old man nudged him aside and ran around to the east wall he wondered, for the first time, if he hated her too.

"My God," Ambrose exclaimed as he came back to the porch door. "Six seals killed! Where'd ya get 'em?"

"Six?" The boy sounded surprised.

"Yes," his father replied, filled with delight and shock at what he had just seen. "I can't believe it — ya got six seals killed!"

"You must be seein' things, Dad," he ridiculed, turning around and going back into the house. "I ain't got six seals killed. You told me I never killed n'ar one, so that means ya must be seein' things. And you — you're never wrong."

Ambrose pulled the gaff from the floor and dragged the seal outside to the north end, peeked around the windy corner and counted the others against the snow again. He came back in and shut the two doors, still talking about the seals. The boy sensed the old man's eagerness to talk and heard him try to apologize.

"How come I never listened to ya, Martin?" he said. "How come ya never told me?"

Martin went about spreading the warm clothes around the stove, feeling the hurt and anger bubble up inside him. "Don't start, Dad," he said. "You knows I told ya — over and over again — so don't say I never told ya. You've blamed me for enough already, and you've made me believe I was stupid and no good for nothin' but I am good. I'm so good as you or Garf and I'm not puttin' up with no more of your shit!" He draped his father's nylon jacket across the warmer, letting the arms dangle over the back. "If ever I gets off this island, I'm gone. And for once in your life you'll be a happy man."

"Where ya gonna go?"

"Never you mind, but wherever I goes it'll be far enough away from the likes a you."

Ambrose pulled the box back from the stove and sat with one side of his ass on the clothes. "I should a listened to ya," he said. "Perhaps I was a bit too hard on ya sometimes."

"Sometimes," Martin said unsparingly. "You was always like it, Dad — ever since we moved to Karpoon. Perhaps ya was like it back here too and I was just too stun to see it when I was smaller, I don't know!"

"No, Martin," he said. "'Tis not like that at all. Ya don't understand."

"Don't understand — what is it I don't understand?"

"I'm not sayin' ya don't understand, no. I'm sayin' perhaps ya never seen what I was tryin' to do."

"Oh yes," the boy said with a nervous shiver in his voice. "I seen what ya was tryin' to do and everybody else seen it too. You was tryin' to make me into 'nother Garf but it won't work 'cause I won't let ya!"

"I knows that, Martin, and that's not what I was tryin' to do. Ya gotta believe me. I was just tryin' to bring you up the best way I knowed how."

"Well, ya done a poor job."

The old man didn't speak for a while.

Martin wondered if he had run out of words or was just too ashamed to say anything. Whatever the reason for his silence, the boy didn't care. They had come to the final stage of their relationship and he hoped with all his heart that he had made that clear. He truly did hate his father.

He hated everything about him. Then he heard him speak.

"If I told ya I was wrong, would ya believe me?"

"Don't have to tell me. I knows you're wrong."

"What if I told ya I was sarry for how I got on?"

The boy hadn't expected that line. "Sarry?"

"Yeah," Ambrose said, reaching out in the darkness and grazing Martin's leg, feeling him pull away. "I knows I said some things I oughtta be 'shamed of, yes, but you was never what ya might call a angel yourself, was ya?"

Martin tugged on the clothes under his father, felt him roll to the side and release them. He rearranged them all on the warmer but said nothing.

The old man got up, found the clothesline on the wall and strung it back across the stove, opened the kitchen door and dropped the sock over the top. Shut the door.

"That tongue is your downfall, Martin. Till ya l'arns how to control 'en you'll never be nothin'."

Martin hung his father's jacket and pants on the line.

"Heard ya got kicked outta school."

The darkness was like a wedge and, blinded as they already were by it, it gave them more space than they needed, for there were only the sounds of the fire, the wind and the surf between them.

"I quit," Martin proclaimed.

It took a while before the old man spoke again. "Ya done the right thing," he said. "Now I'll have someone to help me cut me firewood. We can keep two houses goin'. Me and you'll do the cuttin' and Garf'll do the haulin'."

"Eh?"

"And ya can go fishin' with us too next summer ———"

"Lemme explain somethin' here," Martin interrupted. "I'm not goin' fishin'. I might be leavin' home, like I said —

perhaps go somewhere and look for a job. Or go fishin' with someone else."

"Sharemen gets half a share."

"Half a share?"

"Yeah, means every hundred dollars the skipper makes, you gets five."

"Five dollars?"

"Yep, that's good money. Starts mendin' the twine and gettin' the gear ready round the middle of April, then round the latter part of May month, soon ever the ice clears outta the harbour, everybody spends two or three weeks luggin' ballast and fixin' up the wharf."

"But that's not fishin'."

"Gotta get the gear ready, Martin, y'knows that."

That sounded reasonable. "Well, OK," he said.

"Oh yes," his father added, "whoever ya goes fishin' with, you're gonna have a week scrapin' and paintin' the boats 'fore the gear goes in the water. Should be ready for fishin' I'd say round the middle of June — that's if the gardens is dug. But that's only four or five days' work anyway, week at the most."

"I won't have to go at the gardens though, will I?"

His father laughed. "Now what's the sharemen all gonna say if ya don't help out?"

"What?"

"Gonna call ya a sissy."

There was a long silence and then, "I gotta think 'bout this first," Martin said. "'Fore I makes up me mind. Perhaps I might go back to school again — don't know yet."

"Gimme your knife, boy."

"What for?"

"Might haul the jacket off one of them seals comin' 'wards

marnin', and roast a bit a meat on top a the stove."

"Geez, that'd be the same as eatin' it raw," the boy said, reaching into his pocket and pulling out his knife. "You'll be poisoned."

His father found his hand and took the knife. "Oh, I'm not gonna eat it," he said. "I'm gonna roast it for *you*."

When Ambrose suggested that he'd watch the fire, Martin uprighted the box where it was, tossed in the rubbish that he had come to know as bedclothes and jumped in, surprisingly tired and desperately wanting to sleep. The sleep he longed for was not the kind tendered by a warm feather bed with heavy blankets and patchwork quilts, drool-stained pillow, small, stinky farts that couldn't escape except by passing his nostrils, but the kind that allowed him the comfort of vivid, colourful dreams with no awareness of the emptiness in his stomach.

The old man scraped together some of the smaller clothes and tucked them gently around his son, making sure not to poke too hard near the sides lest it lead to another argument. "I'm gonna sit here awhile and have a smoke," he said. "You done a hard day's work so go to sleep now and don't warry 'bout nothin'. And when daylight breaks Garf'll be here to bring us home."

17

FALLEN STATUE

Just before the last of the darkness evaporated from her bedroom, Ida turned on her left side and brought her arm up under the covers, straightened it and let it fall on the spot where her husband had slept beside her every night for thirty-seven years. She awoke, startled into sudden alarmed absence, and felt the coldness, the emptiness, realized the truth but refused to accept it as she told herself she was dreaming. The rattle of dishes and the low, indistinct voices from the kitchen brought with them some of the reality she had hoped to avoid, the long shaft of golden light at the top of her closed door and the squeaking floorboards reminding her that she was not dreaming nor alone in the house. She hadn't slept properly the whole night, merely dozing and jumping nervously whenever she heard a cup strike the table or the outside door open.

Garf and the searchers had arrived home at something after ten, none of them saying a word as they piled into her kitchen and stood around as if in a daze. She'd known by the look on their faces that Martin was dead and, seeing

Garf come towards her with his eyes all bloodshot and watery, she hadn't waited for him to explain about anything; she had just run to the boy's bedroom and flung herself face down on his bed. Not even when he told her that his brother was safe and that his father was now on the island with him did she lift her head and ask for details, but only screeched louder, with the pillow driven into her mouth. She heard him say how he had made arrangements with everyone for the morning, to go in their boats to Sacred Island and to make another rescue attempt, but he didn't say they would be successful. For one single moment she thought she might die.

Now she rolled onto her back, lifted her head off the pillow and listened with her hands clamped around the edges of the four quilts, two blankets and flannelette sheet, like a drowning woman clutching a pan of ice. There was a sweet smell in her room that she recognized as that of frying seal meat and onions. She threw back the covers and sat on the edge of the bed, listened while breathing slowly through her mouth, nailed down one of the voices as Norm Andrews asking someone when breakfast would be served, but who answered him was beyond her. At first it sounded like Paddy, a soft, gentle flow of words that seemed to stretch on forever as he explained the process of cooking to his giggling patrons. She heard the lid come off the pan and then a loud hissing noise as he poured in a little water from the kettle. Heard Dulcie say very clearly — she knew her as soon as she spoke — that he had better not burn up the meat. When the cook spoke again, she put Jack's face to the voice and pulled her dress from the back of the chair. She hadn't been eating well for the last few days, and the thought of fresh seal meat, onions and hot juices over a thick slice of white bread drew her from her bedroom and into the midst of a houseful of sleepy men and women.

≫

Daylight crept into George Trimm's kitchen as slowly and silently as a cat stalking a mouse. Ambrose had seen the inside of the house only once since he had left the island, during a trip for a load of lumber from the walls of his stage, when he strolled reminiscently through the village and looked in the window. In the darkness of last night he had imagined it somewhat as it had been when he'd come here, probably four nights a week, to pass the time with George and old Mr. Trimm. These two never attended many card games but their wives went whenever there was a game in the cove. It was the quiet times that the three enjoyed the most: the old man telling stories from his boyhood years and George talking about his hunting trips and the new shotguns that showed up in the Eaton's catalogue twice a year. The time George intended to buy one with a five-shell magazine with room for another shell in the breech and Dulcie said it would be best if he got it as a Christmas present from her and Judy, saying that maybe Santa Claus would bring it to him — but Santa Claus didn't visit the island that year because by December the island was empty.

About two hours ago Ambrose had smoked the last of his tobacco and burned the pack. He had no way of telling the time but around what felt like midnight the wind had nearly blown itself out, and outside, while he scraped snow into a Mason jar to melt on the stove for drinking water, he discovered that it had veered to a light breeze from the southwest.

In the kitchen there was only the sound of the fire and Martin's occasional snores. The old man hadn't closed his eyes for the night. He had once or twice caught himself nodding but blamed his carelessness on the surf, for it had always allowed him the comfort of a deep sleep. He looked at the boy in the box, with the old clothes over his legs and packed against his chest as though they were his favourite toys. Another half an hour and he would wake him, but he let him sleep now while he went outside again to prepare breakfast.

The fog had lifted some, allowing him to see the whole hill behind the cemetery and the point of land on the other side of the cove, but there was still ice in the harbour and a thick haze in the bay. He listened for engines, imagined the dipping of oars and men calling their names, but there was nothing.

He hadn't seen Martin's seals in the daylight yet but when he rounded the corner and saw the one he had dragged from the kitchen his jaw dropped. He went swiftly to the east side and gazed upon the other five. "Hoods," he said. "My God, Martin got six hoods killed."

He looked at the bloody path leading from the top of the hill to the house, and for nearly a minute stood there and petted the fur, rubbing his hand along the slate-blue backs. After he had given some sober thought to the boy's hunting prowess, he went to the north end, took out Martin's knife and ripped the seal from chin to tail. Using the blade skilfully, and astonished at how sharp it was, he made a few long slices on one side of the mammal, cutting between the meat and the fat until that edge of the pelt fell away, revealing the thick red meat along the spine. He cut the flesh in a wedge from well below the base of the neck to the small of the backbone, a strip of about fourteen inches.

Next he cut through the soft stomach membrane, drove his hand in and pulled out the gut. He chopped free the cold heart, as big as a flattened baseball, and wiped it clean in the snow, then took it and the meat into the house. On the counter he cut the meat into six pieces and sliced the heart into six pieces as well, the way a chef would slice an onion.

Martin had not awakened with the opening and closing of the door but a minute later, when the smell of the roasting meat struck his nose, he woke with a great hunger. He pulled the clothes down from around him, yawned and stretched his arms over his head. His back had stiffened in the night but with some quick hunching of his shoulders he drove the tightness away.

"Seal for breakfast," his father said. "How'd it smell?"

The boy got out of his box and leaned his head over the sizzling meat. "Not bad," he replied, driving the smoke off with his hand. "Careful ya don't burn it up."

"Think ya might eat a bit?"

"Don't know, but I knows I gotta eat somethin' or else I'm gonna die." Martin poked at one of the pieces with his finger and licked the tip. He smacked his lips together rapidly to get the taste and spat across the floor. "God, ol' man," he said in horror. "Just like blubber. Eats that I'll die for sure!"

Ambrose pushed the knife blade under the part the boy had tasted, prised it off the damper and turned it over. "Wait till it cooks and then taste it," he chuckled. "Might be a bit fresh but once ya gets it down in ya you'll feel ten times better."

After another minute with smoke and steam pouring from

the twice-turned meat, the old man scraped the shrivelled pieces off the stove and with the tip of his knife lifted them onto a plate from the cupboard. There was a nauseating smell of burnt blubber in the kitchen, and when he held the curly, wrinkled food out to his son, Martin's jaw dropped.

"Sure it's fit to eat?" he asked. "Smells awful bad."

"Try it," his father recommended. "Once ya gets the taste you'll want more."

Martin grinned, feeling a bit uncertain. "Sure it won't hurt me?"

The old man took an oval piece of the meat and pushed the plate at his son. "Smells like angel's food," he said.

"And what do angel's food smell like?"

"Like the heart of this young seal," Ambrose replied, biting off the end. He flicked the meat around in his mouth to cool it, chewed it fast, like a rabbit chewing cabbage leaves, and swallowed. "There," he said, and made two more swallows before speaking again. "Went down honey-sweet. Could use a bit a salt but beggars can't be choosers."

Martin took a piece and rolled it from hand to hand — not that it was too hot to hold, but he needed the extra time to see the meat up close, and to touch it, before committing himself to the task of eating it. "Why'd ya cook the heart," he asked, "instead of the pieces ya got on the counter there?"

"We'll save that bit for by'n by," his father said. "If we went the work and eat 'em now like this, with no salt and not cooked right proper, we'd be runnin' off our legs — be too sick to move."

"Why's that?"

"The runs, boy," he said, with an uneasy sniff and a little embarrassment. "We'd get the runs."

"Di'rrhea, ya mean?" Martin put the meat to his nose.

"And the heart won't give us that problem?"

"Not the heart," the old man replied. "Only thing in a seal won't 'fect ya that way. Can eat so much as ya like and it won't hurt ya. Gives ya somethin' to go on when ya starts at the carcass."

But for the smell, the boy thought, maybe he could eat a little without wanting to vomit, yet the smell drew him in, and before he realized what had happened he had bitten through the thinly burnt crust into the soft, tender nourishment underneath. He was surprised at how easily the muscle tore away, and the flavour it had. Even the unpleasant smell disappeared and one that matched the taste took over: gamey and sweet, a bit smoky and sour at the same time but very tangy, with a bitterness that caused the juices in his mouth to flow unrestricted.

"How is it?" his father asked, sucking on his second piece.

Between slow and careful chews, suspiciously, the boy said one word — "Good."

"Well, once ya gets a couple more pieces in your puddick you'll be a new man."

Martin stopped chewing. He was about to confront his father on the "man" part but decided on keeping his tongue still, remembering what he had been told constituted a man. Then he swallowed.

Ambrose saw his Adam's apple jump. Nodded. "Now the rest of it's all downhill," he said with approval on his face. "First startin' off is the worst." He closed the knife and put it on the counter, wiped his fingers on the sleeve of his turtleneck and patted his pockets for tobacco, but there was none.

Martin ate two more pieces and felt good about doing it; the last piece he gave to his father. "Not bad," he remarked.

"Bit fresh like ya said, but all in all 'twas a pretty good breakfast." He took his knife, drank two inches of water from the jar and went outside and urinated by the northwest corner. His warm flow stopped at the sound of a double shotgun blast from outside the harbour. He whipped his penis back into his pants, shouted to his father and ran to the south side, where the old man stood gazing through the window and pointing.

"Garf is back," he said. "I told ya he was comin', didn't I!"

The boy hushed him. "Listen!" He turned his head with his ear cocked to the narrows, eyes widened and face screwed up. Two more shots rang out, no more than three seconds apart.

Ambrose ran out the door and stopped near the corner. "That's Garf! I can tell by the sound of his gun."

Martin turned and waited for his father to smile or laugh or do something to let him know he was being funny, but the old man's face was empty of all playful expressions. He looked as though he really believed he could tell one gunshot from another.

"Sshh," he said with his hands cupped behind his ears. "Listen." There was a single shot but much louder. "Two boats," he said. "Perhaps more."

"Two boats — how'd ya know there's two boats?"

"Sshh, listen," the old man said again, but there were no more gunshots so he explained: "Y'hear them two shots side be side — bang bang?"

"Uh-huh."

"Well, that was from Garf's double-barrel." Before his son could confront him on how he could tell one double-barrelled shotgun from another, he said, "That's not the only double-barrel in Karpoon, y'know, but she's the only one with that kinda bang. She come from off here — was ol' Mr. Trimm's. Jarge took her one fall duck huntin' a few year ago and somethin' happened to her. He blowed six inches off one of her barrels — wonder to God he wud'n killed — and when he sawed off another two tryin' to fix her up she had a different ring to her ever since. If you'd a listened to her you'd a noticed it."

"I did," the boy replied. "One bang was louder than the other."

"That was a rifle you heard, boy, not a shotgun. Rifles got a different sound altogether, more of a crack than a bang. More sharper."

"Rifle — who got the rifle?

The old man hacked and spat to the side. "You ask some silly questions."

"Well," Martin said, hunching his shoulders. "Just thought . . . and don't say I thought wrong again 'cause I knows what you're gonna say."

"No, wud'n gonna say no such thing. That rifle shot come from 'nother boat. Nobody in their right mind would shoot off two guns from the same boat, less they was out huntin', and nobody's out huntin' this marnin' — only huntin' for us. Garf shot off them two double shots to let us know he was here to get us, and then somebody else shot off the rifle to let us know he wud'n alone. So now that we knows what's goin' on, we'll go 'cross the island and have a look."

They went back in the house and pulled on their jackets — Ambrose the checkered one and Martin his father's black nylon — and then the old man took the damper off the stove and doused the fire with the drinking water.

"What'd ya do that for?" Martin asked boldly, taking his

black tossel-cap from the warmer. "We're not gettin' off the island with this sea so why'd ya put out the fire?"

The old man lodged the bottle on the end of the stove and ushered his son out the door. "Can't be too careful with fire, my son," he said. "Keeps it goin' we mightn't have n'ar place to come back to. If we don't get off, like you're sayin', where's we gonna crawl into for the night, eh?" Outside, he looked at his own house and continued, "No good to depend on my ol' shack there 'cause that's just so useless as tits on a billy goat."

"So," the boy said, wondering what was next. "What's we gonna do with the seals?"

"Leave 'em here," Ambrose replied, but with the look that appeared on Martin's face he quickly added, "until we knows what Garf is gonna do. Perhaps he'll try to get us off on the south end — that's where we're goin' now — or perhaps he'll go round to Trimm's Point. Whatever he does, 'tis no good for us to muck our seals all the way 'cross the island and then he tells us he's gonna go round to the point. That'd be a waste a time."

Martin pulled his gaff from the snowbank and ran behind his father down the path past the church and up to the cemetery. From the farthest fence post they both stopped and looked back at the thin wisp of white smoke from the stovepipe. The wind had all but gone and the air was not as damp now. When he told the old man that he could see water beyond the harbour but no ice or boats, Ambrose explained that the new wind of the early morning had driven the ice off and that all the boats had gone to the south end to wait for them.

"But how'd ya know that kinda stuff, Dad? I mean to say, what makes ya think you're right? You're half blind so ya can't see nothin'; ya can't see what's goin' on so how'd ya know where they're gone?"

Continuing up the hill, the old man said with a familiar harshness, "Shut up, boy, for God's sake, do!"

"We shouldn't't've left the seals," Martin snapped. "Only bit a money we're gonna see for the spring and you're gonna leave it on the island. I can't believe you're doin' this, Dad, I can't believe it!"

"You can't believe nothin' that's good for ya," the old man barked. "All you minds is gallivantin' round and makin' trouble for someone else."

"What?" The boy squealed like his father. "Makin' trouble — who's I makin' trouble for — you?"

At the top of the hill Ambrose met with a small west-southwesterly breeze, stopped and waited for his son. When the boy came near him he looked him in the face and said with a sweeping motion of his hand, "All this, Martin — who's to blame for all this?"

For a moment the boy was stunned, but he swept his own hand over the top of the island and brought it to a standstill with an outstretched arm that pointed squarely at the village below. He answered with the first piece of repugnance that came to his mind. "Who'd ya think, Dad? Just look down there and tell me who's to blame for all that. Who'd ya think should take the blame for destroyin' our lives?" He burped and the taste of roasted seal meat floated up to his mouth.

The old man looked away, past the huge, moustached waves that rolled in and crashed with thunderous booms on the shore to the edge of the fog at the south end, where he saw three rowboats and a speedboat on a grey ocean that was growing bigger by the minute. He waved one arm high above his head and everyone waved back. "See there," he said with a single nod and a jab of his finger. "They're all here 'cause a you. Every man ya sees off there is here for one thing — to get you off this island."

"And what 'bout you, Dad — they're here to get you too, ain't they?"

Ambrose slapped a hand to his bib pocket and rubbed his chest. "Myohmyohmy, Martin my son, I don't know where we got ya, I don't know I don't know. And I don't know who ya turns after." He left and walked down the hill.

The boy looked at his village for what he believed to be his last time, thinking that if the boats could make a landing his father would not return for the seals.

John's speedboat lurched and rolled. Fifty yards away the white-hulled rowboats bobbed lazily atop washboard waves and fell into the briny troughs as buoyantly as seagulls, their two-man crews leaning on cocked oars and watching.

Ambrose tried shouting *Can you hear me?* — from the inside edge of the saltwater grass, but the roar of the surf and the exploding breakers drowned his voice. He saw Garf cup his hands around his mouth but heard only a yawning sound. "Sing out to 'em, boy," he shouted back at Martin. "See if they can hear ya!"

"HELLLOOOO," the boy yelled, with all the force he could summon. "CAN YOOUU HEEAARRR MEEEEE?"

Garf picked up a coil of rope and fixed it in his hands to throw, but John turned the boat away and headed back out to sea.

Ambrose said with a sombre calmness, "Well, that's our answer. We're not gettin' off today."

"Not with that sea runnin'," Martin said.

"Not that, boy. Garf's not in charge no more."

"Whaddaya mean?"

"Means just what I said," he snapped with enraged disappointment. "John got everything took over, and so long as he's runnin' things we'll be here till June month."

The men in the rowboats dipped their oars and sluggishly moved their boats about as if they had no place to go, sometimes one or two of them making a feeble attempt at waving, but Ambrose and Martin sensed their uneasiness about doing so. They were only standbys, there in case the speedboat needed them.

John waved and pointed towards Trimm's Point, indicating that he would attempt a rescue there, and with that he hooked onto one of the rowboats, the two occupants immediately shipping their oars for the ride down the shore. When the speedboat roared away the remaining rowers appeared dazed as they spun their rodneys about and conversed with each other, but shortly afterwards they broke away and, without waving again, followed in the wake of their leader.

The sky was clearing in the west and already the boy and the old man saw a long patch of blue that looked like a huge pencil with one of its sides chewed away. Cape Bauld was not visible yet and they could see only water and fog. "OK," Ambrose said. "We knows what they're on for so c'mon; they're gonna pick us up at the point."

Fifteen minutes later they passed through the village and began climbing the hillside in Martin's footprints on the north side of the once-crimson path. At the top they looked down and saw the speedboat and the rowboat waiting fifty yards off, close to the place where Martin had killed his seals. The other boats were just entering the inlet, foam wrapped around their stems like white stoles around the necks of rich whores, and they pushed through the sea as hard as the men could drive them.

"That's where I seen the devil," Martin said, pointing to the speedboat. "Right there. First I thought he was gonna eat me, but when he started chasin' me he was that heavy he went down through the ice like a junk a lead. I thought I was a goner."

Ambrose wiped the sweat off his brow and started down the hill with the boy tight behind him. Without much interest, he said, "What was it?"

"'Twas the devil — only thing I can put it to. Never had no harns on his head but he had this big ball — and he was nothin' only the one screech!"

The old man laughed and kept chuckling all the way to the bottom. At the edge of the blackberry bushes he said, "That was he all right. Big ugly brute."

"You believes me?"

"No one can make up a lie like that, my son, not even you."

The boy was surprised that his father had accepted his story so quickly and so easily. "He was the biggest thing I ever seen alive," he said, rambling now. "All 'cept a whale."

"Sure," Ambrose said, nodding as if his neck were fastened to his body with a heavy coil spring. "And he's the biggest thing you'll ever see alive. Or dead. 'Cept a whale."

"He was a monster, great big teeth and great big claws; his eyes was like they was gonna burn a hole right through me."

"That's right," the old man said, watching the speedboat as John steered along the shoreline looking for a suitable place to get them off. Although the rocky cove was sheltered from the ocean by Trimm's Point on one side and the island on the other, the swells were still rolling in and crashing on the rocks, making a landing appear impossible. "We're gonna wait here for a spell now and see what John's gonna do. I daresay he'll try to get a line to us. If he don't we'll have to wait." After another few pats on his bib pocket, he said, "OK, finish tellin' me 'bout the devil."

"He was all black," Martin continued, "and he had one a them big bladders on his head that hung down over his nose ——"

"And every time he blowed 'en up he made one hell of a racket. Right, boy? Just like heaven and earth was comin' together."

"So ya seen 'en then — and ya believes me?"

"More'n once. And yes, I believes every word you're sayin'. First time I seen the devil I was nine year old with me father and a bunch a men off the north end — he got away that time, but four or five springs after that me and Max and his poor ol' father killed one halfway in the bay — shot 'en we did. Took two bullets through the head to kill 'en and then we hauled the jacket off 'en right there and then. I've heard people say you can kill them ol' dog hoods right dead, haul the jacket off 'em and pull the gut out, and the carcass'll still crawl away and worm its way down through the ice, but that's a bunch a nonsense. The carcass on the one we killed never made a move after we shot 'en, but I can mind when we was towing the pelt 'cross the ice that lotsa times the rope was right slack behind us, and once, if we never jumped outta the way when we did, the pelt would a run right over us. Took us right to the land he did — 'twas all we could do to hold 'en back."

Martin laughed because he liked the story, the way his father used words to bring the image to life, and he felt a strong inclination to believe him although he knew it was just a story. He sat on some blackberry bushes and stared at the speedboat, the pelted devil more vivid in his mind than the picture before him. "You said he took yez in to the land — how come he never took yez out farther on the ice?"

"Couldn't see where he was goin'," the old man said gravely. "His eyes was still back in the carcass."

John waved his arm and pointed to the crevice where Martin had pulled his seals ashore, and Ambrose gave the order to move down.

The swells rolled in and smacked against the rim of ice that surrounded the inner limits of the cove. Great gushes and spouts of frothy water heaved up from the ocean floor and slammed into the frozen face, driving high into the air a fine salty spray that Ambrose and the boy tasted on their lips as they cautiously crept along the ridge of rocks that would take them to the low platform of the notch.

Twenty yards out, with his father leading the way, Martin saw a loop of rope around the smooth, eroded vertical of a small boulder cocooned in a glossy shell of ice below him. He stepped down onto the ledge, amid the rubble that had been tossed there by the seas, and grabbed it, suddenly realizing that the rope was his.

The old man hadn't noticed him gone until he heard him call out. "Dad," the boy yelled above the roar of the sea, "look what I found — me rope and two seals!"

Ambrose turned and went back, jumped onto the ledge and helped haul the weight from the platform up the side of the rugged shelf.

There was only one seal at the end of the rope — the other bight was empty — but the boy smiled and drove his fist into the air, overjoyed at reclaiming his property. "Other one come unhooked," he said, pulling the head up to his

chest to show the boats. There was a wave of acknowledge-
ment from every man there. He dropped the seal and petted its wet belly, commenting on how clean the hair looked
and how the sea had washed away all trace of its blood.
"Whaddaya think we should do, Dad — leave 'en here or
haul 'en back 'wards the hill farther?"

"Leave 'en here on the ballycaters for now," the old man
said. "We'll try to get so close to the boat as we can and see
what they wants us to do. If they're gonna take us off here
we'll have to go back for the others and rig up a line."

"You can rig up all the lines ya wants," the boy said em-
phatically. "But them seals is goin' 'board first 'fore I steps
foot off this island."

Garf held up the packsack and instructed John, with a
throwing motion of his free hand, to move the speedboat
closer to land. No words were exchanged as the big man
gently twisted the throttle handle and steered nearer.

"Just look at that," Ambrose said, overwhelmingly re-
lieved at the thought of having something other than seal
meat for their next lunch, but then he heard Garf holler
that they were unable to make a rescue at this time and
would try again before noon.

Ambrose looked at his younger son and jutted his lower
jaw forward. "Did Garf say what I thinks he said?" he asked.
"Did he say we was gonna have to stay here all day or did I
'magine it?"

"Said we're gonna get off in a few hours," the boy answered.

Then Garf threw the pack. It sailed through the air, spinning only once before striking the ice wall and falling into
the sea.

"OhmyGodohmyGod!" Ambrose cried. "He missed he

missed he missed!"

Garf watched a carpet of thick white bubbles converge on the green bag, put his hands on top of his head and sat down.

The speedboat backed away. John lit a cigarette.

The old man's eyes went wide. He drove one hand into his side, rested it there on his hip and squinted to see better. "Is that John I sees smokin'?" he asked his son.

"Yes," the boy replied.

"But he got it give up. Told me hisself. How come he's at it again?" Ambrose went to the outside of the ledge, waved his two arms frantically over his head and yelled for the boat to come back, but it turned and headed out the inlet. ·

By late afternoon the wind had backed into the north, a sure sign, Ambrose told Martin, that a northeaster was brewing. "Whenever it strikes," he said, standing at the edge of the blackberry bushes next to his son and looking at the sky, "whenever it strikes we'll be long gone."

They had dragged the seals across the hill from the village two at a time, with Martin's hauling rope, to rendezvous with the speedboat at Trimm's Point, but an hour ago the rescue attempt had failed again because of the high seas. Garf had then wanted to take them off the island the same way he and the boy had been taken off the ice pan a few days before, but Martin rejected that idea, saying he would rather starve to death than drown, and the old man would not leave without him.

John had, however, twice allowed Garf to lob ashore a one-pound jigger on a small fishing line tied to the end of a rope, and when Ambrose had made bights and slipped them over the noses, he then pulled the seven seals off the island.

Now, to conserve fuel, the mother ship lay a hundred yards offshore, with her anchor down and her standbys strung out behind her like duck decoys with small human heads fore and aft. According to Garf the low tides of late evening would calm the seas a little. Until then they would wait.

"Gotta go 'nother day without baccy," Ambrose moaned, "I'll be fit for the loony bin. Have to bring off a straitjacket to put me in."

"One more day and they'll have to bring off two straitjackets," Martin said. "This sea, ol' man, when's this sea gonna pitch back? Or is it gonna pitch back at all? Geez, I'm gettin' fed up with it — 'nough is 'nough. If I had me time back I'd a stayed in bed for all of me Easter holidays, wud'n've poked me friggin' nose outside the room door till they was over."

"Give it 'nother hour, boy, and we'll be off. If Garf was to the engine we'd a been off long 'go but *nnoooo*" — Ambrose, in an amusing drama, twisted his face into a funny shape — "we gotta wait and see what Johnny Come Lately's gonna do. All right for him, he can sit down out there with his tailor-mades and puff her off right to his heart's content, and here I am with not so much as a bit a dust in me pocket. 'Tis shockin' what a man gotta go through — 'tis shockin'!" He pulled his face back in shape and let it droop in his agony and torment.

"I was just thinkin'," the boy said, sliding his thumb and finger up the small wooded stem of a blackberry bush and peeling off its tiny brown needles. "You told me you was _____"

"Here he goes again," the old man wailed, his eyes closed

to hold back the horror of listening to his son's aggravating ideas. "Gonna do some more of your fancy thinkin', is ya? Well, I don't wanna hear it so you can shut your mouth 'fore ya starts. I'm gettin' sick'n tired of you with your mouth up all the time and I'm gettin' sick'n tired of this island. 'Tis drivin' me foolish!" Ambrose paced back and forth behind the boy's back, grumbling and sputtering about how he should never have jumped ashore to end up in a bigger mess than he had thought possible. If not for his wife forcing him to go, he said, he would have waited until the bay froze over again sometime in late November, and then the boy could have walked ashore.

"Well, to hell with you too," Martin said, turning and grabbing his father by the throat. "All you've done since ya got here was bitch. One more word outta you and —"

The old man grabbed his arm and tore it away. "Better watch yourself, boy!" he said with a nasty look about him. "You're not grabbin' your grandmother now, y'know. You don't be careful, I'll pop you off them ballycaters with the wind knocked outta ya."

"You wud'n knock the wind outta my shit," Martin said with both wrists clamped tightly in his father's hands. "Beejaysuss, all you're any good for is talk!" He stuck out his chest and tipped his head a little to one side. "Here, ol' man," he taunted. "Have a smack!"

Ambrose drew back his hand but there was a shotgun blast from one of the boats. He put his hand down and released the boy's arms. "Good thing Garf fired that shot," he said, without looking out the inlet. "Or you'd a been one sarry little boy here today. You put your hand up against me once more and I'll chop 'en off tight to your arse, remember me!"

Martin saw that Garf was the only man standing in either
of the boats, the gun still raised to his shoulder as though
he were ready to shoot flying ducks. His legs felt weak,
almost betraying him as he ran up the hill away from his
father, his heart jumping around inside his body at the
thought that the old man would have hit him. "Go home, ol'
man," he yelled from the top. "Go home and stay there. I'm
finished with ya!"

"Come back here, you you, you. . . ," Ambrose shouted
brutishly. "I gets my hands on ya, I'll" — he ran after his
son — "geez, I 'low I'll brain ya!"

"Go 'way, Dad!"

"Come back here you!"

"No!"

"Come back I say!"

There was another gunshot but Ambrose kept up the pur-
suit.

"Go 'way, I don't need ya any more," the boy cried,
unworried that the old man might see his tears or that Garf's
new warning had gone unheeded. "Just go 'way and leave
me alone. Make yourself happy."

"Only time I'll be happy," his father roared, "is when I
gets you by the scruff a the neck. Now come back here like
I tells ya!"

When the old man neared the top Martin turned and fled
down the other side, somersaulted onto the seal path at its
steepest grade and slid to the bottom on his back like a
young harp. From there he saw his father sink to his knees
and fall headlong down the hill, twisting and rolling on the
snow as if he were made of rubber.

Ambrose went into a flip that landed him on his face, and
like that he skidded to a stop halfway down where the grade

levelled out. For a moment he didn't budge and the boy thought he had been killed, but then he saw an arm move, yet the old man made no effort to get up. He just lay there board-stiff and fairly straight, as if he were resting.

"C'mon ol' man, get up," Martin whispered while pushing himself to his knees, a strange feeling in his stomach. "Get up get up."

Still there was no movement. Was he dead, the boy thought, or was he playing games, trying to trick him into going alongside. If that was the case, he decided, then his father would most certainly freeze to death in the snow while he waited. A minute passed and then two. "You dead ol' man or what?" The boy was talking out loud now, but not strongly enough for the fallen man to hear. "Come on, ol' man, get up. What's ya waitin' for? C'mon c'mon." Could it be that he was knocked unconscious, or perhaps really dead? Maybe if he went closer and let the old man hear him walking in the snow. . . . Maybe if he called out louder. . . .

A small wind came down the field from the north, bringing a few pecks of fine snow under the darkening cloud cover.

"Y'all right, Dad?" the boy shouted, a bit low at first, but when the old man didn't answer he called again. "Hey Dad, you gonna stay there all day or what? Garf is gonna shoot off his gun now the once again, and if ya don't haul your head outta the snowbank ya won't hear 'en!"

Ambrose still didn't move.

Martin called to his father again. "I'm comin' up where you're at now and ya better not touch me either." He ran the first twenty yards and walked the rest, fearful that the old man was lying in wait for him, yet something about the silence seemed louder than the sea. Ten feet from his father's head the boy stopped and watched for signs of breathing, but there were none. He held his own breath, thinking that if he stilled himself he would see through the amazing show being put on to capture him. A dozen heartbeats later he realized that there was a problem, and rushed to pull his father's head from the snow.

"Dad," he said, as fast and short as the blink of an eyelid. "Dad!" He turned the old man over, brushed and picked the snow from his face, accepting his strange-looking half-closed eyes but afraid of the ashen skin and blue lips. "Dad," he said louder and more drawn out, as if about to ask him another question. "Dad?"

The old man was dead and the boy knew it. He cuddled his father's head on his lap and wept bitterly, rocking back and forth on his knees, saying, "No, Dad, you can't die, Dad. You can't leave me — you can't!" A minute later he pulled the lids down over the glassy black pupils to hide the accusing stare.

Enough time had passed for the boy to get cold when a muffled gunshot behind the hill brought him back from his grief. For a moment he visualized it as another warning shot from Garf, but then there were two more blasts, the last being that of the rifle. Somehow he was glad that he could see the men in the boat and know what they were doing without actually facing them. "You're a smart ol' man," he said to his father. "But now we gotta go home. Garf is waitin' for us and ya knows what Garf is like. If you're not there when he's ready to leave you'll be left behind, 'cause I'm tellin' ya right now — Garf is not gonna wait for ya." He laid his father's arms next to the still body and wriggled his legs from underneath the cold head. They had been curled under him for so long that when he tried to get up he found them cramped and wet, but the cramps went away. Standing above the old man and looking down at him as though he were asleep, the boy couldn't help but feel sorry for saying what he had, and at that very moment, when he admitted to himself that he had done wrong, he felt an overwhelming sense of guilt and great shame.

He was not afraid and left to go up the hill, for he knew he had to do that. At the top a rising north wind blew in off the darkening water, and in the northeast over Belle Isle a wide band of heavy cumulus seemed to have pushed itself up from the sea.

Eight men stood up but only the rowboaters waved when Martin signalled them with both hands over his head. Every man stayed that way until the boy reached the ledge above the platform, and when John slipped the towline from his risings they all sat down and slipped their lines from each other.

How would he tell Garf, he wondered. Should he say that their father was dead or should he lead into it by saying he had some very important bad news to tell him? What if Garf jumped out and was drowned trying to get ashore? What if he sank and John couldn't hook him? On hearing of her two losses, their mother would surely die from the strain of it all. Yet Garf deserved to know.

John steered the speedboat as close to the island as he could and shut off the motor. Garf, in the bow with his hands on the gunwales, bawled out and asked the boy right off where the old man was and why they had not returned together.

Martin climbed down onto the ledge to be nearer and stepped into a thick paste of white froth left at the edge of the shelf by the falling tide. "He's dead," he said, unable to bring his voice up to shouting capacity.

"Where's Uncle Am?" Garf yelled again. "Where is he?"

The boy went closer to the edge. "Been a accident," he shouted with his hands around his mouth. "He's dead!"

"He's where?"

The sea beat relentlessly against the wall. The roar of the surf pounding the island became a tiresome noise to the boy. Finally he convinced himself that there would be no rescue today, and that Garf had only said such a thing to ease the tension of waiting. "He's cookin' up some seal," Martin shouted back. "For supper."

Garf made a few slow, lengthy nods to indicate that he understood. Said with the throwing of his right arm, "Go! I'll shoot off the gun when we're ready for ya!"

The boy nodded the same way, heard the outboard start and saw the smoke from its tail.

The speedboat went ten yards and John cut the engine again. He called out in a voice loud and clear, "You'll hear two shots," he announced. "Two means to come on right away. Three shots means we can't get ya. Then we gotta go home. If that happens we'll be back in the marnin' so don't warry. And don't be 'fraid. You'll be all right. Now go get some supper!"

Martin nodded again and held up his hand, for he felt irritation in his throat from the shouting and did not want it to worsen. He climbed the ridge and made his way to the blackberry bushes, kicked at the blood on the snow to reassure himself of its realness and headed back up the hill to the village. From the top, in the breezy north wind and the dying sunlight, he looked back with great sadness at the boats and the black, unmoving figures they carried, and on the other side he looked down at his father lying like a fallen statue.

The sun was low in the sky now and the village lay under the shadow of the west hill, the rim of dusk slowly creeping up the grade like a black shroud being pulled over the whole island. To return to the house and start a fire he would have to salvage the lighter from his father's pocket, and he hadn't noticed which pocket the old man kept it in. He felt scared to walk down and pass him, thinking he might still reach out and grab him. If that were to happen, he thought, he would probably die from the fright of it all.

He walked lightly in his father's footsteps to where the tumbling began, then made his own tracks as far as the body and patted every pocket until he felt the hard lump in the right front of the old man's trousers. With some fear and trepidation he pushed his hand inside and gently removed the lighter, as if not to awaken him.

Twenty minutes later, having looked through the porch window more than a dozen times, he had a fire in the stove again. The house was as cold as when he had first come here. He leaned over the countertop, smelled the raw meat, and wanted to eat it like that but knew his stomach would throw it back, for it had been all he could do to keep a piece of the cooked heart inside him.

When the stove had heated enough to make spit sizzle at the tip of his finger, he scraped away the old burnt patches of the roasted heart and laid on three chunks of the strip loin. He watched the moisture evaporate from them and the meat begin to smoke, then pushed his knife under and flipped each one and waited until they began smoking again. After a minute or so of doing this he picked a piece off and bit into it, careful at first because it was hot, but when he got the taste, before he realized what he'd done, he had eaten them all.

The jar was empty and he needed water, not to wash away the flavour as before, but to ease his thirst and to help with the soreness in his throat. He took it outside and filled it with snow, looking at the east hill and thinking that his father could pass for a log that had rolled down, the tracks of his fatal tumbling imprinted in the snow like the finger-prints of a young thief along the sides of a well-frosted cake.

Inside the house Martin put the jar on the stove, then drank the snow water while standing at the porch window again. There were no tears in his eyes now but there was an unfamiliar sickness in his stomach, a feeling something like the awful hunger he had come to know since being stranded here, but not entirely like that. It was more as though he had swallowed a huge rock, but he had no sharp pains as he had had before and he was thankful for that. He told himself that the freshness of the meat was to blame, and set about ripping canvas off the bedrooms, and boards off the porch walls for the fire tonight. Another hour would bring the dark, and with it the terror of listening for the footsteps of a dead man.

18

HOMECOMING

Aunt Kizzie chewed fiercely on a piece of gum, eyes sparkling with the thought of an upcoming fight when Ida lashed out at the eight men standing around in her kitchen for not bringing her husband and son home.

"And you, Max," she said. "And you, Paddy," pointing them out in their hiding place behind Garf and the thin, sickly-looking man. "I told you fellers last words not to dare show your face back here without Ambrose and Martin, and here ya goes off again this marnin' — never got 'em last night — OH NO — and here 'tis goin' for ten o'clock on a Monday night and they're still not home!"

"Never told me, m'dear," Paddy said, fixing the ear of his glasses and pushing them up. "I never seen you yes'day. I was out ——"

"'Tis no one's fault, Aunt Ida, and you shouldn't get on like that. Everyone is tryin' to do their best."

"Don't you" — she jammed her finger so close to Garf's face that he had to pull back to see the top with any clarity — "don't you tell me this is no one's fault!" she said, bordering on a scream. "You've had three days to get that boy off that island and you're tellin' me 'tis no one's fault he's still there?" She gave a short, mindless laugh and stirred the pot of soup that one of the women had brought her shortly before suppertime. There was another pot at the end of the stove with soup that someone else had brought, and on the oven door a broiler filled with seal meat and gravy that she'd cooked herself. "If I'd a went the work and used me own common sense," she said, "Martin would a been home now and not stuck off on that bloomination island like he had nobody 'long to 'en. Nothin' to eat, nothin' to drink, n'ar place to put his head and — oh geez, I 'low if I give way to me feelin' I'd stamp the whole lotta yez down through the friggin' floor!"

The old woman sniggered and pulled her head into her sweater. "Give it to 'em, Ida," she said in her glee. "Not much odds 'bout that ol' Ambrose anyway, but Marty" — she took her handkerchief from her sleeve and wiped her dry eyes — "poor little boy's gonna be froze to death and starved to death 'fore anyone gets to 'en. You just watch."

Two young sisters with their bangs cut too high and smelling of too much cheap perfume sat shoulder to shoulder on the daybed and giggled timidly, casting fleeting glances across the stove at Alec on the storage bin with his head in a comic book. Their short, fleshy mother, occupying Ida's chair at the table, hushed them and wriggled her fat ass to alleviate the discomfort of sitting too long.

Sadie and another woman had been playing with a deck of crazy eights on the corner of the table near the cupboard but hadn't really started a game because of the clutter of dishes and pastries they'd laid out at suppertime. Alec had stayed with the women the whole day and had eaten his supper when they had theirs, from bowls cradled on crotches

or barely set on the edge of the table without pushing anything back, without crinkling the tablecloth or soiling it.

"How 'bout you, John?" Ida asked. "Whadda you make
of all this?"

For a moment he didn't speak, but when Norm Andrews
opened his mouth to give his thoughts on the whole thing
John said, "What can I say, maid, any more'n Garf said?
We was talkin' to 'em on the ballycaters out there; they said
they was all right so I s'pose that's all I can say 'bout it." He
unbuttoned his fleece-lined overcoat and took off his cap.
"We'll go off again in the marnin' if 'tis suitable and have
'nother go at it. I don't know what else we can do."

Norm stepped from the shadows of the other men and
tapped the weather glass with two solid jabs of his middle
finger. "Glass is gone back some," he announced. "We're
in for some snow and northeast wind." He tapped it again
and scrutinized the position of the arrow. "Hmm, this one's
sot a little higher'n mine." *Tap tap.*

"Careful ya don't break the face," Garf warned. "No need
to tap it that hard."

"You won't break that face, my son."

"No, but if ya keeps poundin' it like that I'll break yours.
Now give it up!"

"My my. Touchy touchy," Norm said, still studying the
arrow's movements.

"I'll 'touchy touchy' you if ya puts that finger on Uncle
Am's glass any more, and I promise you you'll know it, too."

Max called for Norm to sit down and not strike the glass
again.

"I was only sayin' Ambrose's glass was sot a little
different'n mine, that's all. There's a screw on the back there
— a set screw." Norm took the glass from the wall and held

it upside down in his hand. "Right there," he said, pushing the tip of his thumbnail against the slot. "I'll just ——"

A strong left hook to the nose splattered blood all over his face and he fell lifelessly to the floor, striking his head on the oven door and losing the glass from his hand. His weight shook the house as the barometer rolled towards the water barrel and stopped near Lewis Moores' feet.

Garf opened and closed his fist, shook his hand to drive away the pain that had practically paralysed his little finger. "Take that, you rotten bastard," he said with a torturous smile. "No one picks at Uncle Am's glass — no one!"

For a moment there was only the sound of the fire crackling in the stove. Lewis reached down and picked up the glass, gave it a quick glance and placed it in Garf's outstretched hand. "Not broke," he said. "Good job out of a bad one." There was a loud chattering as everyone rushed to help Norm.

"Ya got 'en killed," Ida said, being the first to kneel on the floor and diagnose the man's condition. "Look at the blood!"

"He'll be all right when he comes to," Garf said, checking the glass for damage. "He's thick-headed."

Ida took the dishtowel from the oven door handle and pressed it to Norm's nose, held it there, then carefully wiped his face. She turned his head to the side and there was blood on the canvas. "Oh my," she said with fear in her voice. "Ya got his head split abroad. Gimme a washcloth on the stand there fast!"

Garf hung the glass back on its nail while Sadie gave his mother the cloth. He knelt beside her. "Lemme see, Aunt Ida — see what you're talkin' 'bout." He rubbed his hand over the back of Norm's head and worked his fingers through the mat of bloody hair. His jawbone was jumping wildly as he concentrated on his doctoring. "Bad news, I'm 'fraid," he announced to the shadowy faces standing over him. "I made a big mistake."

"Ya mean he's gone?" John asked.

"No," Garf replied. "I never hit 'en hard enough." He went to the washpan and washed his hands. "Got a little cut on the back part of his head so long as a two-inch finishing nail — just a scratch. But he'll be number one when he comes to — so long's he keeps his hands off that glass."

There were many nods of agreement from the crowd, and when Norm made a low groaning noise the women rushed back to their chairs as if they thought the men would sit there.

In less than a minute Norm was on his feet, with Ida holding the dishtowel to his nose and the washcloth to his head. She guided him to the washstand where he looked at himself in the mirror with the cloths taken away. "I wud'n a very pretty-lookin' man all 'long," he said groggily while petting his nose with a single finger. "But now I'm gonna look worse."

"Be God," Aunt Kizzie assured, wiping her spectacles in her apron and holding them up to the light, "I don't think that's possible."

Everyone laughed and Sadie called for the men to sit in and have their supper.

For Garf this was not a piece of comedy, and he refused to sit with his adversary. "I'm not hungry," he said. "'Tis gettin' late and I gotta clave up splits for t'marra marnin'."

"That's already took care of," Sadie said, pulling out the table. "Alec there got everything done." She motioned with her hand for Garf to sit inside. "Now boys," she called to the men. "We got room for six so come on and put it down in yez. 'Cardin' ya gets finished, get clear and let someone else sit in."

"Go ahead boys," John said. "Sit in and have your supper. You deserves it." He blocked Max's path as he went to sit down. Said over his shoulder to Ida and Sadie, "Me and Max'll wait for the soup to cold off — that way we can eat more."

"Mightn't be none left," said Sadie with a grin. "But I s'pose we can always find somethin' for yez. Perhaps we'll save yez the bones."

"Perfect." And to Max he said, "Let's go outside and check the weather."

The wind was from the north-northeast, about twenty knots and laced with snow. "Wind veered," Max said, shutting the door behind him. "And dark as the grave too. Wud'n wanna be in their boots tonight."

"We got a problem," John said. "A big problem."

"Yep, and the sixty-four-dollar question is: how's we gonna fix it?"

"Today there in the rodneys — did you or any of the men hear what Martin was sayin' on the ballycaters?"

Max didn't hesitate to answer. "Gotta be jokin'," he said, with a smile that blackened his gold tooth against his open mouth. "We was too far off. Never heard a word. Why — what's ya drivin' at?"

"Martin said his father had a accident. Said he was dead."
"What?"

"Sshhh. Careful now. Watch how ya handles yourself."

Max stuck a finger in his ear and rooted. Wiped the wax off on his trousers. "Martin told ya that?"

"No," John replied. "He told Garf, but Garf never heard

'en and the boy only said it once. He told Garf afterwards that his father was over in the cove cooking up their supper."

"Why'd he say that?" Max laughed and poked John with his finger. "Go on, John, you're tryin' to pull a cod on me."

"No, 'tis true," John insisted.

Max looked up at the black sky. "Who else knows 'bout Ambrose?"

"No one."

"So, where'd that leave us now?"

"We'll keep it to ourselves for the time bein', but 'fore we leaves for the island t'marra we'll have to come up with a reason to take a piece a sailcloth."

"Leave it to me," Max said, going back in the house. "I'll handle it."

The wind beat against the north wall and whistled down the pipe, driving puffs of smoke up around the damper and out the draft hole. Martin could see them in the light from the cracks, the only light he had now. For the first two or three hours of darkness he had been flicking the lighter at every sound he heard, and shortly before the wind picked up it had run out of fuel; ten minutes ago the flint had worn out. What would he do if the men didn't return at dawn, he wondered. Somehow he had felt a closeness to them, but the three gunshots long after the sun had gone down had taken all that away.

His stomach cramps had worsened during the night, and once he felt like moving his bowels, but the urge soon passed with a loud fart that lasted nearly as long as one of his father's smoke inhalations.

He hadn't removed any of his clothes, still wore his tossel-cap and kept his mitts on the warmer, for he had been afraid to sleep or take a rest in the woodbox, thinking that he might doze off and that the house would burn. The thought of burning the two houses intentionally had occurred to him however, and had seemed at the time a grand idea. If there were no houses on the island to come back to then no one would come, for what use would a village be without houses? If he could prevent someone else from dying here, burning the houses was an excellent idea, one that his father would most certainly approve of. He told himself that the island was playing with his mind, making him think foolish thoughts. Was it nine or ten o'clock now, or was it nearing daylight? He didn't know but he knew that many hours had passed, because the pile of broken boards had been reduced to just a few pieces, the last of the canvas was in the stove, and a blizzard was raging outside. Four times he had thought he heard someone on the bridge and at least a dozen times, perhaps more, he'd heard his father call his name, but at the first tap on the porch window a good two hours ago he had nailed a long piece of board across the kitchen door.

There was a loud noise from the upstairs, and the clinking of something falling across the loft and down the staircase. The boy had never heard that sound before but he knew the stovepipes had fallen, for there was an immediate silence in the firebox, and a diminishing of the flames as the stove refused to draw. He pushed open the door to the stairwell and heard it strike something metallic, reached his hand out in the dark along the floor to confirm his suspicions and found the warmth of two pipes. He could do nothing but peer into the darkness at the glowing ash flakes, the flankers, as they rose from the rotten-edged pipe now two inches below the loft floor.

The stove was smoking badly now, making breathing difficult as he rushed to tear the board from the door. He dreaded having to go outside in the dark, thinking that his father or a spirit from the netherworld would grab him as soon as he stepped on the bridge. While that thought was still visible in his mind he tripped on the woodbox and fell hard against the doorpost.

An agonizing pain tore through his left elbow and numbed his hand so he couldn't move his fingers. He lay there on his side and tried rubbing it back to life. The smoke had thickened now and he couldn't stop coughing. A fire started in the ceiling around the leaning stovepipe and began eating the wallpaper behind the stove. The pain abated and soon he had enough strength to get up and tear the board off the door. He took in the cold air of the porch and found the doorknob, the thick, eye-watering fumes chasing him like a wild beast into the darkness of the storm, without his mitts or any extra clothing.

On the sheltered side of his father's bungalow he stood to his knees in fresh snow with his bare hands in his pockets, felt the chill set in his legs and watched helplessly as the windows in George Trimm's house flared pumpkin-orange behind the black wooden crosses of the frames. Flames roared through the roof and jumped ten feet into the air. Within minutes the walls had collapsed. The boy went to the hot ashes and tried to absorb as much heat as he could.

When the blizzard became too much for him he ran back to his father's house, untied the door and went inside. As he paced back and forth from the kitchen to the inside part, breathing warm air into his hands and listening to the wind and the sea, he thought about the many things he wanted to do: go to school again and get his grade eleven, tell Howard he was sorry for hurting him, bring his grandmother more gum, go to the restaurant and dance with Louise, maybe even dance with Hazel if Louise allowed him. He wanted to buy his mother something special with the money his seals would bring, maybe buy her a gold brooch to wear on her Sunday dress, or a gold watch. He wanted a new knife for himself, not another I.X.L. but a Green River with a sheath. He wanted to leave the island.

He felt dizzy, and took the broken rocking chair from his grandmother's bedroom to the living-room window, went to the cupboard and pulled out two drawers, propped them under the left side of the seat and sat down. In the darkness he saw white spots falling gently and soundlessly from the ceiling, knew right off they were in his eyes and saw them just as clearly from behind his closed lids. A minute of resting made the spots go away but made his legs much colder through his wet jeans, so to keep from freezing he took up pacing again.

He felt his stomach knot and rumble. There was no mistaking the pain this time. He had nowhere to pull down his pants except outside in the blizzard so he thought about dropping them in one of the bedrooms, then covering the feces in snow to cut down on the smell. The boy knew from previous bouts of the sickness that diarrhea had a smell of its own, one that didn't cover up easily. And this was his father's house. How could you shit on the floor in your father's house and feel comfortable about doing it?

At first light he was still pacing the floor, kicking his feet together, for the cold had claimed them now and he remembered his mother's words on how easy it was for a person's feet to freeze without them knowing it. He beat his arms wildly across his body, slapping his hands onto his shoulders to drive the cold off, but there was a new numbness in him. Twice he had gone outside the kitchen window to empty his bowels, with nothing to clean himself with but snowballs. Each time he had urinated on his hands to warm them, straining the piss through his fingers. Twice he had let loose into the snowbank on the kitchen floor, extracting every drop of warmth he could from his bursting bladder.

He had longed for this hour and desperately hoped to hear gunshots outside the harbour again, but the storm had not lifted and he could see no farther than the old boats at the edge of the field. His legs hurt and his arms nagged him; he was tired and hungry and wished he had something to eat, anything other than seal meat, but there was nothing. Was God punishing him for being so wrong with his father, he wondered, or did God really have it in for him? With his father dead maybe God would pity him and bring the speedboat; or maybe God would kill him and stop his suffering.

He continued his pacing well into the afternoon, until the weather cleared enough for him to see the harbour entrance, but the winds were still strong and whipped about the house shooting tiny whirlwinds across the top of the waist-high snowbank that blocked the doorway. To get outside he had to push and kick the snow down, and much of it fell back into the kitchen and prevented him from closing the door behind him. If he spent another night here, he thought, he would have to close the door, because this house was his only refuge now and without it he would end up dead like his father. A minute later he had scraped away the fallen snow with his hands and feet and tied the door, the wind tearing at his jacket and driving the chill deeper into his bones. His eyes and stomach hurt from hunger and fatigue so he ate a little snow to help himself.

One look at the hillside and the boy's heart fell. The old man was gone. His first thought was that he had come to life and walked off, probably in a daze and unaware of where he was going, but then he realized that the storm might have buried him. In a minute he would go and dig down in the snow.

There was nothing left of the Trimm house except the wire-framed headboard leaning against the capsized stove and the smell of charred rubble that Martin drew into his lungs as he reached down and pulled the black stub of his gaff from the snowbank. He had been careless, he thought, in leaving it so close to the house, but — his hauling rope was safe, for Garf had pulled it into the speedboat.

With the stub in his hand, Martin ran up the white hillside to where he believed the old man was buried, and he used it to dig away the hard snow, but with four or five holes a couple of feet deep he still hadn't found him. "Maybe he's gone to Trimm's Point to wait for the boats," he said out loud. "Or perhaps he's back in the house." But there were no tracks. "No! You're talkin' crazy talk. Dad is dead and buried. He wanted it this way — to be buried on the island."

The boy put his cold fingertips to his forehead and his thumb in his temple. He felt the pulse beat at the side of his eye and worried about his confusion, told himself that he shouldn't be talking to himself, that he should go to the top of the hill to see if the boats were back.

At the summit the wind tried to knock him off his feet but

he fought to hold the white ocean in his sight. "My God!" he exclaimed, loud enough to be heard twenty yards upwind. "The ice is back — the ice is back and the sea is gone!"

From here he could see more than halfway to Cape Bauld, across a tight field of Arctic ice that the Labrador Current had diverted into the strait on the west side of Karpoon Island. His first thought was to run down the hill and head for home but he began to scan the ice floes for seals. He saw nothing that resembled a living creature.

Rather than go back through the village to the south end, he reasoned, why not get on the ice inside Trimm's Point and walk to the grasslands from there? The ice looked as though it might be good for travelling on, and he estimated that he could run the two miles in less than half an hour. He would tell everyone the truth about his father being dead and they would come and dig him up — if they could find him. If they believed him.

He jabbed at the ice near the crevice with the burnt stub of his gaff in his cramped hands, driving the spike into the snow until he felt the hardness underneath. The winds were still blowing near hurricane force but the snow was letting up, and sometimes he thought he could make out Cape Bauld through the white spots that had begun falling through his vision again. He dropped the gaff and tried to rub more life into his hands, blowing on them and putting his bunched fingertips into his mouth to warm them. He pulled off his cap, pushed his right hand inside and took the gaff; the other hand he kept in his pocket. Another two hours would bring the darkness again, and the bitter cold that came with it. He sprang onto the ice like a child jumping the last two blocks of hopscotch.

A hundred yards south of Trimm's Point the ice was covered in a thick layer of snow, making running impossible. There were deep snow-covered rifts between the pans where sometimes his foot would break through and cause him to stumble. Once he heard the sucking sound of water underneath as he pulled his boot free of the slob, and another time he had to roll onto his side so he wouldn't be trapped in the crevice when he fell. All the time he kept the wind at his back, for he still could not see the mainland, due to the low drifting. Only the tops of the pinnacles were visible above the white blanket that swept over the icefields like smoke. He would have felt completely lost had it not been for the island behind him.

Walking more slowly now and breathing much harder as his footprints filled in behind him, he concentrated on staying upright and away from the danger zones, knowing that if he fell through he would undoubtedly perish. Even a good gaff and rope would be useless now. There was hardly enough strength in his chilled body to climb the pinnacles any more in order to check his direction. He encountered some tiny, shallow depressions in the snow, thinking at first they were half-buried footprints, but then dismissing the possibility that they were anything other than sinkholes.

Then he saw the black cliff of the grasslands. Soon, he was on the beach following the tiny holes through the field, past three rodneys and John's speedboat, to a cluster of shrubbed evergreens where seven Ski-Doos lay parked in the drifting snow like a herd of sleeping cows. Martin recognized his father's snow machine and others that he had seen on Cape Bauld earlier. There was no doubt in his mind as to why they were here; the tiny holes were none other than human tracks headed across the ice towards Sacred Island.

How long ago the men had started their latest search he didn't know, for the engines were cold and dusted with snow. Had it been half an hour ago, a full hour ago or longer? He couldn't guess at the time but soon night would be upon him again, and he must hurry to save his hands. He searched the tool compartments of all the snowmobiles for a scrap of food but found nothing except a flask of moonshine. He took one sip from the bottle and put it back. The liquor did nothing for his empty stomach.

To get home, he knew, he would have to steal his father's Ski-Doo again, but in his weakened state, with his hands no longer obeying him, he couldn't grip the pull cord hard enough to start the engine. He tried repeatedly to hold onto the plastic T-handle but lost it each time the cord tightened. He eased the dirty braided rope from its lair, wrapped the end twice around his right hand and tucked the handle under the loops in his palm. He flicked on the choke and pulled. The engine chugged with no indication that it wanted to catch, but on the third haul it came alive. He slipped the cord from his wrist and jammed both hands under the warming exhaust pipe. The island, he thought, had tried to kill him. He would never go back — never.

Alec had just lit the Tilley lamp and put it in its bracket on the wall. Now he pressed his thumb to the window and melted the thin frost pattern in time to see the headlight of a snowmobile crossing the cove. "Ski-Doo comin'," he announced. "One man!"

"Thang God someone's back," Ida said. She wiped her hands in the dishtowel and pushed Alec away from the window. "Lemme see. Where's he to?"

"Gone 'long under the hill, down on the harbour," the boy replied.

"Well, go in the inside part, my son, and have a look," she ordered, steadying herself against the excitement with one hand on the table as she turned to face the nodding heads and the din of heightened chatter. "And you," she said to her mother, knitting contentedly in her chair by the stove, "you move outta the way now so he can get through."

The old woman knitted off her needle and ran her finger over the stitches, "One, two, three, Jesus. One, two, three, Jesus. One, two. . . ."

Ida motioned for the same two girls as yesterday to move away from the storage bin. "C'mon girls, no need to block everything off now. Let the man get through, let the man get through. Pick up your feet. That's the girls, that's the girls!"

Before Alec could clear the thumbprint in the living-room window he heard the snowmobile roar past the house and stop near the bridge. He came back to the doorway and waited to see who the messenger was.

The porch door opened and then the kitchen door. The house filled with a gust of cold air as a figure broke through the mist and fell to his knees on the floor. For a second or two everyone was speechless, shocked to see the man before them. Only when he raised his snowy head and looked at his mother with rolling eyes did Ida burst into tears and a sobbing scream.

"Martin," she cried, rushing towards him. She kneeled and hugged him tightly. "My God, Martin, you're home, you're home!"

Sadie ran forward and helped her put him on his feet, signalling for another woman to shut the two doors.

"Myohmyohmyohmy," Ida went on. She kissed her son, picked the ice from his eyebrows and wiped the snow from his face with her hand. "OhMartinohMartinohMartin, I can't believe you're all right! I can't believe it I can't believe it!"

Aunt Kizzie got up and dragged a chair to the stove. She pulled down the oven door and removed the rack. "Here," she said, holding the backrest with both hands. "Sit 'en down here and strip the clothes off 'en. And you, Alec, cram the stove with dry splits and be smart 'bout it."

Martin wanted to speak but his lips were too cold to form words, and he only mumbled as his mother and Sadie led him to the chair and sat him down. To prevent further frostbite during his ride home, he had kept his hands alive by pushing them one at a time against the cooling fins of the engine, and now they were strong enough to latch onto his mother's arm as she kept his body upright for Sadie to unlace his logans and wrench the frozen boots from his feet. She took his legs and swung them onto the oven door. They took off his cap, his jacket and the two foreign-looking windbreakers.

"That's my brown windbreaker," said Alfred from the head of the daybed, pointing and looking to the others for agreement. "And look, that's Judy's yellow one." He crossed his legs and sniffed, closed the outdated *Eaton's Spring and Summer Catalogue* he had been looking through and opened a smaller but still outdated *Spring Sale*. "Aahhh," he said, dismissing his enchantment with the old clothes. "No good to me now anyway. 'Tis all tore to pieces."

Ida removed the white blouse Martin was wearing, fitted him with a long-sleeved shirt and a wool sweater, then covered his legs in one of her patchwork quilts. She clamped both her hands to the sides of his head. "Your ears, Martin

— they're like two knobs a ice. You're froze to death for God's sake, ain't ya boy? You're froze to death! Wonder to God ya didn't perish!" To her mother she said, "Go in my room, Mother, and get that bottle a shine under the foots end a the bed. We gotta put some colour back in 'en."

The old woman hurried off and brought back a full 26-ouncer, poured an inch into a tumbler and mixed in a teaspoon of sugar and an inch of boiling water. "Here ya go, Marty, my love," she said, tipping the glass towards his mouth. "Down this now and in no time at all you'll be up dancin' a jig. Put lead in your pencil, boy — put lead in your pencil."

Martin sipped at the hot toddy. Little by little the moonshine disappeared from the tumbler, and when the glass was emptied his mother cradled his head in her arms and rocked back and forth with him, saying his name over and over. Then she asked him about his father.

The boy blinked and turned his head towards the table. When he saw all the food he tried to stand up, but he lost the quilt and nearly fell off his chair. His mother and Sadie helped him to his grandmother's place and sat him down, both telling him that a drop of soup would make him feel better. His feet were so numbed that he barely felt the stubbing of his toes on the leg of the table when they pushed him in.

His mother asked about his father again, and again the boy never answered.

"Perhaps he can't hear ya," Sadie said. "I read 'bout somethin' like this one time in the *War Cry*, where this man was lost in a snowstarm way up north somewhere and when they found 'en he didn't know if he was in the world or out. What it was — they found out after — was that little thing that makes your ears itch inside, y'know when ya can't reach it with your finger and ya gotta hack and spit and just 'bout tear your throat to bits on one side to scratch it? Well, that little thing was froze so hard as a rock inside his head and it took just 'bout a full hour for it to thaw out, but when it did, hold your tongue! Said right there in black'n white — read it meself I did — that when she bust loose he could hear better'n he ever could. Said hisself after that that every time the wind veered northeast he could hear the angels singin' in heaven, and in arder to hear that kinda stuff, buddy, you gotta have some set a ears on ya." She pulled nervously on her collar tabs, which pointed inward like dried squid tails, and said, "Perhaps Martin got the same thing wrong with 'en."

Ida raised her voice, as if Sadie's story had some relevance to her son's condition, and asked him another time. "Your father, Martin — where's your father?"

Everyone waited for his answer.

The boy's lips were swelled and beginning to crack but he slowly spoonfed himself from the bowl of vegetable soup that Sadie had poured for him, and didn't speak.

"See," Sadie declared, proud of her medical knowledge and the fact that she was up on this type of behaviour. "Just like I told ya, ain't it? He's just so deaf as poor ol' Mr. Butler was 'fore he died, perhaps deafer, and God knows he was deaf. If ever there was anybody deaf, he was deaf. Couldn't hear a word, m'dear, not a word."

Martin finished his soup and looked up at her. He shook his head and pointed to his two ears. Tapped the side of his bowl with the spoon.

"What'd I tell ya?" Sadie proclaimed. "Just like Mr. Butler for all the world." She seemed almost proud that the boy had gone deaf, turning around to the crowd and saying, "What'd I tell yez, eh — what'd I tell yez? Just look at 'en. Mr. Butler on the spot!"

Martin tapped his bowl again.

"More soup?" Sadie asked.

"Sure," the boy said, handing her his dish. "And this time don't spare the salt meat."

19

CROSSING PATHS

It was early in the morning, before daylight, when the snowmobilers started their engines and roared past the house on their way to the grasslands for the long walk back to the island.

Martin had been asleep in his bed when the men had returned last night, breaking the news to his mother that they hadn't been able to find him or his father anywhere. When she told them that he was home, and that he had informed her of the old man's death, Garf wanted to wake the boy and ask him exactly what had caused it. Ida wouldn't allow Garf into the bedroom and relayed the story to him as she had heard it from Martin.

Ambrose was buried in the cemetery at Karpoon on Friday evening, in a plain wooden casket that John Parsons had built with seasoned boards from his sawmill. To give it decorative appeal Ida had taken credit at the general store for silver-plated carrying handles and enough white and grey satin to finish the box inside and out. As Mr. Tucker clearly pointed out, he would not allow her, a widow — any widow — onto his books except in times such as this, and he would put the bill against Martin's nine pelts, which Garf had delivered to his holding shed on Tuesday morning.

Aunt Nel had given her sermon to a packed church and enough people standing outside under a cloudless sky to half fill another one. After two hymns and a five-minute prayer, she read from her Bible:

> *The LARD is merciful and gracious, slow to anger, and plenteous in mercy. He will not always chide: neither will he keep his anger for ever. He hath not dealt with us after our sins; nor rewarded us 'cardin' to our iniquities. For as the heaven is high above the earth, so great is his mercy toward them that fear him. As far as the east is from the west, so far hath he removed our transgressions from us. Like as a father pitieth his children, so the LARD pitieth them that fear him. For he knoweth our frame; he remembereth that we are dust. As for man, his days are as grass: as a flower of the field, so he flourisheth. For the wind passeth over it, and it is gone; and the place thereof shall know it no more.*

Six of the final rescue team were the pallbearers: John Parsons and Max Butler led the procession, helping to haul the casket to the cemetery on the water-barrel komatik, and Paddy Mitchell and Lewis Moores walked behind them, holding onto the rope and trying not to look around every time Ida screeched. Against Garf's stern warning not to have

Norm Andrews involved in the funeral, his mother said she wanted him there because he had been part of the team from the beginning and deserved recognition for his work. With his bush of white hair as tangled as a clump of steel wool, and his two raccoon eyes, Norm caught more stares from the crowd than did the casket. The pallbearer who walked beside him was the fire-keeper whom Ambrose had met on Cape Bauld without ever knowing his name.

The old man's wish to be laid to rest on Sacred Island was not honoured.

Azariah Tucker had a horseshoe of grey hair around the sides of his head, and a bald crown that rippled every time he pushed up his eyebrows to check the figures he was totalling in his ledger. His eyes were not centred in the oval of his face but were set noticeably higher than those of most men, which made him look something like a fish, for he was always nibbling his Charlie Chaplin moustache and releasing it from his tobacco-stained teeth with little kissing sounds. He sat in an antique swivel chair, his immensity pushing against the creaking arms each time he looked up to see Martin and Garf pick at things on his shelves and put them back.

"What can I help you men with this marnin'?" he said, laying his gold-tipped fountain pen in the crease of his book. "Anything or nothin'?"

"Come to get straightened up on the boy's pelts, sir," Garf replied without looking at him. He was reading the directions on a box of Warfarin rat poison, and was about to ask about the twelve-cent increase in price when Mr. Tucker cut him off.

"*Boy?*" He opened the drawer above his knees and took out a crinkled pack of Vogue tobacco. "There's a big difference 'tween a boy and a man," he said while dipping into the pouch. "You know what that is, Garf?"

"Well sir," Garf stammered. "Knows the difference sir, yes, but I can't put it to words just like that."

Mr. Tucker pinched out enough tobacco for a thin cigarette and rolled it in a paper from the pack in the plastic sleeve. "Come here and have a look," he said before licking the glued side. "I'll show ya."

Martin took one of the Green River knives from its carton on a shelf near the oil-fired heater at the back of the store, and saw his face in one of the picture-frame mirrors stacked vertically alongside. His lips were scabbed, softened a little by some bad-tasting ointment, his cheeks, his chin, the tip of his nose and the lobes of his ears, as well as the backs of his hands were covered with tender pink blotches surrounded by ragged edges of dead skin. When he saw the merchant turn his ledger towards Garf and light his cigarette, Martin shied from the mirror and eased himself closer to the counter to eavesdrop.

"What'd that say there?" Mr. Tucker asked, pointing to the top of the new page.

"Martin Bellman, sir."

"Now, flick through the book and see if ya can see any boys' names there."

"No need a that, sir," Garf said. "I don't need to know your business."

"Go ahead. Have a look."

Garf turned the big pages carefully, as though he might rip them. When he had turned the pages ten or twelve times, sometimes four and five leaves at once, he seemed ashamed at having gone through the ledger, for he had seen the debts of some of his friends. He said, twisting the book around on the counter, "None there, sir — not one."

Mr. Tucker puffed lightly on his cigarette and tapped the ashes in a glass clamshell. "That's right," he said, turning back to Martin's page. "There *is* no boys' names. Only the names of men — good men."

Garf stepped back and watched Martin put the knife on the counter.

"Sheaths right there in the middle of the shop, son, on that post if ya wants one."

Martin looked around but Garf said, "That's all right, sir; I can make 'en one out of a piece a leather just like mine."

"Well, he got just 'bout five hundred dollars' worth a pelts here. Let's see" — he pushed up his eyebrows and looked at the figures — "ninety-six dollars for the three young harps and three hundred and ninety for the six hoods. Comes to ____"

"Hold on," Garf said abruptly. "I put in *two* young harps — not three. And I put in seven young hoods. Not six."

"You sure?" the old man asked, scrolling his capped pen down through the line of black figures. "Nine pelts altogether, right?"

"Yessir, and you was there when I put 'em in."

"Says here you put in three young harps and six ——"

"Beggin' your pardon, sir, but that's wrong."

Mr. Tucker rippled the skin on his head without moving his eyebrows. "You're sayin' I'm wrong?"

"No sir." Garf leaned over the counter and tapped his hard fingers on the row of figures. "But them figures is wrong."

"I'll add 'em up again if ya like."

"No need," Garf said, picking up the knife and running his thumb along the cutting edge. "Ain't got much l'arnin' meself, sir, but with them figures wrong like that you're gonna come up with the same answer." He scraped the blade along the top of his thumbnail and hooked around the cuticle. "Ya gotta change the figures."

The old man thought for a brief moment, looked from Garf to the boy and back again. "Well," he drawled, "I could run down through" — and then he appeared to have a brilliant idea. "No, tell ya what," he said with his finger digging into the back of his scalp. "I'll check me purchase book back there in the office and see what it says. Whatever it says in that one is what I'll credit yez for, OK?"

Garf nodded his approval and put down the knife.

"What's ya tryin' to do?" Martin whispered angrily as he placed two tins of bully beef on the counter. "You can't talk to Mr. Tucker that way. Keeps it up we won't get n'ar cent at all! What's we gonna do then, eh? Tell me!"

"Settle down."

"Settle down? S'posin' he takes me name out of his book?"

"He's not gonna do that."

"How'd ya know?"

Garf looked at his nail and rubbed it in the zipper of his jacket. "Your name is there to stay, Martin; from now till eternity."

Mr. Tucker came back with his head down, flicking through a small wad of invoices and mumbling incoherent mathematical equations. "You're right," he said to Garf, reaching down and scratching the side of his foot. "Oohhh boy, my foot is some itchy. Gets like that every year round this time; I marks it!" He straightened up, put the chits in the drawer and closed it. Then he changed some numbers in the ledger, recalculated the figures and said, "anyway, boys, your pelts comes to five hundred and twenty dollars. Sarry for the mistake."

"Thank you, sir," Garf said, returning to the poison and taking the box in his hand again. He studied the picture of the rat on the front and put the poison back on the shelf.

Martin stood underneath a bunch of red-soled knee rubbers swinging from two teepees of lines. "I was gonna buy Mom a brooch for her dress," he said to the merchant. "But I don't see any. Thought I seen 'em right here in a little box when I was here with Dad one time, but they're all gone."

"They went in Christmas," the old man said. "Never stood no time." He pulled out his drawer and made a scraping noise with the tips of his fingernails. "Been a while since you was here, wud'n it — sometime last fall I believe."

Martin was about to look for a different gift when Mr. Tucker told him to browse through the remains of his Christmas jewellery on the stand by the ladies' underwear. "Some nice rings there, if she like rings," he said. "And all women do of course; that's one thing a woman'll never say no to is somethin' to shove on her finger." He chuckled and began picking his teeth with the end of a match. "How's your frostburns now? Heard ya had a hard time."

"Toes was the worst," Martin replied, staring at the junk jewellery in a shoebox near the folded rayon drawers and slips. It all looked expensive to him, and he felt good about being able to pick and choose, proud that he had more money coming to him than he knew what to do with.

"We thought they was froze right solid first," Garf said, inching his way along the wall to the ladies' section. "But thang God 'twas just the outside skin. 'Twas a miracle, sir

— miracle he come out of it like he did."

"Tough cookie," the old man said, wiping the scum off the match onto his shirt and sticking the match back in his mouth for another go. His cigarette was burning in its slot at the side of the ashtray. "Some youngsters would a died in all that," he said, pushing the match into the cavities of his rotten molars. "What, four or five days off on that island by theirselves? Me, I would a died on the thoughts of it."

Martin had considered buying a gold-plated chain and pendant he held in his hand, but with the premature decline in his status he dropped them back in the box and touched a pair of white panties.

"Your mother needs things worse'n a ring or a brooch anyway," Garf said as he watched the boy's hand return to paw through the rest of the trinkets.

"Like what?"

"Don't waste your money, boy, on things ya can do without. That's the secret of havin' money." He beckoned Martin to go with him to a shelf with three Tilley lamps and replacement parts. "Your mother's lamp is leakin' pretty bad," he said quietly. "I think ya should spend a few dollars and get a few things back in shape again. Her stovepipes is just 'bout gone too and, tell ya the truth, I can't see what's keepin' 'em up."

"Them Tilley lamps here," Martin asked brazenly across the store. "What's the price on one a them?"

Garf nudged the boy with the back of his hand. "Don't buy the full lamp," he cautioned. "Only the generator that's gone. All ya gotta do is buy a generator for 'en, and a mantle."

"Mantle — why's that?"

"Well, for one thing 'tis a hard job to get ol' mantles off

over the shaft without breakin' 'em. And 'nother thing, 'tis more'n hard to get one *on* — over a new shaft — 'cause they're so cripsy, but mantles is only cheap anyway." He saw Mr. Tucker pull down his eyebrows and squish his cigarette butt in the shell.

Two or three minutes later, Garf said that Martin was ready to pay for his things and that the boy would also like to square their mother's bill.

Four lengths of stovepipe lay opened and fitted inside each other on the counter. The generator, mantle, bully beef and a few other goods that Martin wanted — Brylcreem, a white comb and two packs of chewing gum — were all touched individually by the merchant as he wrote each item carefully in his small bill book. After summing it all up, he checked his arithmetic by running the wet end of the match down the line of figures and marked the total under more figures in his ledger. "All told," he said, after more mental addition using the nib, "comes to six hundred and seventeen dollars and eight cents."

Garf looked puzzled. "Six hundred dollars?"

"Six hundred" — Mr. Tucker ran his pen under the total again — "and seventeen dollars. And eight cents. Yes."

"Thought ya said five hundred just now."

"For the pelts, yes. That's what the pelts comes to — five hundred and twenty — don't forget the twenty."

"Then where'd the six hundred come in?"

"That's what his bill comes to."

Garf looked to his brother, then laid his hand on the pipes. "His bill — for them few things he got here and for what Aunt Ida had for Uncle Am's box — comes to over six hundred dollars, you're sayin'?"

Mr. Tucker took the slab of chits from inside his drawer

and dropped them onto the counter. "That's includin' Ambrose's bill too," he said. "Your Uncle Am's."

"What?" Garf almost squealed the way his father used to do. "You must be jokin'!"

"Let's go," Martin said quietly.

"Don't talk like that, Garf. You knows Ambrose got a bill here so well as everybody else. Everybody got a bill here."

Garf began to get restless and walked about, scuffing his boots on the bare boards. "And what you're sayin' is, Martin gotta square up his father's bill too."

There was a short chuckle. "And who'd ya think was gonna pay it, Garf? Ambrose can't do it. Ida got no way to make a dollar, so how's I gonna get me money if Martin don't look after it? Eh? Tell me that."

"Wellwellwell, I never thought — I never thought."

"So let's see." Mr. Tucker checked the debit and credit figures. "He won't owe me that much, of course," he said placidly. "Take off for his seals and — ought from eight is eight, ought from ought is ought, ought from seven, seven, two from 'leven. . . . There ya go — brings his bill down to ninety-seven dollars and eight cents. Sound better or what?"

Garf spoke with a noticeable rattle in his throat. "I can see if he owes. . . ." He coughed to clear the phlegm. "I can see if Martin owes you any money, sure, like anybody you'd wanna be paid but, my God, Mr. Tucker, that's the first cent ever he seen in his life and now he gotta turn it all over the one time 'wards Uncle Am's bill. That's shockin'!"

"He ain't gotta warry 'bout payin' it off right away, Garf. Summer's comin' and a smart young feller like that got no trouble to find a good berth as a shareman. And next spring, please God, he might hook a berth 'long with one of the sealin' captains and make a name for hisself at the ice. If that scrawny young Lewis boy can get on, I'm sure Martin can get on too." He told the boy, "I'll keep your name here, son, and see how ya makes out."

"Howard, Howard Lewis?" Martin asked.

"Yessir. His father was in here last Sad'day and bought a few things for 'en. Said he was sailin' from St. Anthony on Easter Monday. Boy was no good to l'arn anyway — his father's words."

"So he's not goin' back to school then?"

"Don't know 'bout that, but he won't be goin' back this year." Mr. Tucker shook his pen. "Will there be anything else?"

"Perhaps I should put everything back," Martin said while looking from Garf to the merchant. "I don't wanna owe too much money. What'd ya think I should do, Garf — keep it or give it back?"

His brother let out a big sigh and walked twice around the post in the centre of the store. "Give it back? You can't give it back, Martin. Gives back them pipes or that generator, t'marra or next day the house could burn down. And for what?" He answered his own question: "For the sake of a few lousy dollars!"

"Keep it," Mr. Tucker said. "Don't let it bother ya. And if y'ever wants anything else, just lemme know."

Garf went to the counter and leaned in over, this time almost whispering, begging the merchant to tack Ambrose's bill onto his account and to give Martin his pelt money.

The old man opened the drawer again and pinched more tobacco from the pack. "Y'know," he said, sprinkling it into the notch of his paper, "I'd go so far to say that's what killed Ambrose." He wriggled his ass on the chair and made the wheels creak. "Baccy can do that to a man, y'know. Drive 'en crazy." He hauled his thick, ugly tongue from one end of the paper to the other. "And then just like that" — he snapped his fingers in the air — "bang-O, he's gone."

"Pains done it, sir," Garf said. "Chest pains. Been havin' 'em all winter."

"Don't know 'bout that," the old merchant replied. "Makes ya wonder sometimes." He looked at the boy. "Well, he's gone now. Smoke no more baccy, Ambrose won't."

"Can you do that, sir, what I just asked ya?"

"'Fraid I can't, Garf. No."

"Why's that, sir?"

Mr. Tucker put Martin's things into a small carton and tied his stovepipes with two loops of white string from the cone of twine suspended from the ceiling. "This is a small town, Garf, and small towns got big ears and big mouths. And you're talkin' big money. No, Garf, does it for you I'll have to do it for everyone else." He pulled in a tiny whiff of smoke and blew it out. "Lemme ask ya this: how many seals ya land this spring? Five, six, ten — how many?"

Garf took the stovepipes under his arm and stood there like a scolded child. Martin took the box. "N'ar one, sir, but 'tis not 'cause I never tried. You heard what happened out there so well as everybody else. We had our seals but we lost 'em."

"And why'd ya have the rat poison in your hands twice and put it back twice? Can y'answer me that?"

Garf turned and walked towards the door. When he turned the handle to go out he heard the old man tell him why.

"Ya can't afford it, can ya, Garf? That's the reason ya put it back on the shelf again, ain't it? Ya can't afford it." The chair creaked under his weight as Mr. Tucker leaned forward and closed the ledger. "How'd ya 'xpect to pay a five-

or six-hundred-dollar bill when ya can't afford a box a rat poison?"

Martin followed Garf outside into the chill of the morning air, both zipping their jackets on the bridge, still hearing the denigrating voice in their heads. Mr. Tucker was right, and the boy knew that the old man had been wise not to allow his brother the burden of an enormously increased debt. What he could not understand, however, was why Garf had been so mousey in all of this.

"All them names in Mr. Tucker's book," Garf said, "is people he owns, and they got no say 'bout nothin'. He tells 'em what they can eat and he tells 'em *when* they can eat. And me — my name's been there since I was fourteen. Just like you."

It was suppertime, and Ida poured hot tea into three mother-of-pearl cups and hot water into another. As she so mildly put it, while taking the teapot and kettle back to the stove, the house had been overrun by the town since last Sunday and for six solid days she hadn't known if she'd been coming or going. Today had been her only break to absorb the shock of all that had happened.

"Ambrose is gone," she said, pouring a ladleful of cod chowder from a big dipper into the bowl at the end of the table. "I knows he's gone but seems like 'tis not real or somethin'." She shrugged her shoulders and poured out another bit. "He loved fish — fried, baked, stewed, roasted, burned up, half cooked — didn't care so long's 'twas fish. I never seen a man like 'en. Loved fish more'n he loved his God."

Martin was reading a comic book on his bed and saw the opportunity to make another belittling comment on his father's love of tobacco, but this morning at breakfast his mother had confronted him about school and he didn't want to pick up where they had left off. He hadn't given her a proper answer about going back — had said he might and he might not — but she'd taken it as a no and started crying again.

"If I knowed this was gonna happen," she said, filling another bowl with chowder, "I'd a never left the island — never. Ambrose didn't wanna go, neither did Max and Sadie, but they left for the money and ya couldn't blame 'em. Then 'twas only we fellers left, and what could one family a done off on that rock by theirselves?"

Aunt Kizzie listened from her chair and chewed happily on a big wad of gum, sometimes stretching it out to arm's length and coiling it around her finger like yarn. Martin had given her two packs this morning and already she was on her fifth stick. When her daughter moved to the next setting and spoke again, telling of how Ambrose had resettled so Martin could get an education, she put her knitting down and stood up. "Nothin' wrong with a bit a l'arnin'," she said, pulling down the hem of her dress, "but when ya takes a tatie and tries to make a cabbage out of 'en, all the l'arnin' in the world's not gonna make 'en taste like a cabbage."

Ida tipped the dipper up and drained the rest of the chowder into the bowl at the place setting under the radio shelf. She lodged the empty pot on the cupboard and told everyone to sit in.

Garf had been there the whole day, and together he and his brother had installed the new stovepipes, fixed the lamp, filled the water barrel and chopped enough wood to keep the stove heated for four or five days. Now, at four o'clock, he awakened from his twenty-minute snooze on the daybed, and took his place under the radio shelf. "How come we're havin' supper so early?" he asked.

"I wants to get the place cleared away," his mother said, pulling out the chair that her husband used to sit on. "Be a crowd here again the once and I still won't get nothin' done."

Garf rubbed the sleep from his eyes. "Well, that's what this kinda stuff is all 'bout. I'm glad Uncle Am had so many friends — more'n I thought he had."

Ida looked at Garf and lost what she was about to say when the tears came back. She stood with both hands on the backrest, her chest heaving with the soundless sobs that rose up inside her.

Garf picked up his spoon and touched his face with the cold metal roundness. He had chosen his place at the table willingly, and now, without malice or ill will, he knew what he must do. He clinked the spoon twice on the side of his bowl and called to Martin. "Suppertime," he bawled. "Wants your supper ya better come and get it!"

The boy yawned and came to the centre of the kitchen. He looked at his mother and saw her lips quivering. Then he knew. "No, Mom," he said. "That's not my place. My place's inside." He went and stood by the cupboard with his arms folded. "Go ahead, Garf, you sit there."

Garf pushed his spoon into his bowl and played with his chowder, digging deep holes in it and watching the walls cave in. "I got a place, Martin. Now that place is yours. And the chair goes with it."

"Well, I don't want it."

"Well, 'tis yours whether ya wants it or not."

"Not mine, my son," the boy said, with a passion his family had never seen in him. "My place is behind that table and you're sittin' in it. So move clear!"

"Ya don't understand, Marty," his grandmother said as she pulled out her chair and sat down. "That chair don't mean you gotta take the 'sponsibility that goes with it. Sittin' there only means ya won't have to be bangin' your head up in under the radio shelf all the time." She dipped her spoon into the coffee jar and dumped it in her hot water, the brown granules losing their slope and sinking beneath the surface. "Garf can't sit there 'cause he's out on his own now — like he said."

"Well, no reason he can't move back, is there? Then that chair can be his." Martin took a glass of cold water from Garf's setting and drank it all at once. Wiped his mouth carefully, leaned over the table and took his brother's bowl of chowder and spoon.

"No, Martin," his mother said, "ya can't eat Garf's supper. I got yours for ya right here!"

He put the bowl on the cabinet and slumped down to eat. "If that's my chair, then I can do what I like," he said, and grinned, skimming the spoon along the edge of the white paste. "If I don't wanna sit there I don't have to. Dad's not here no more, so tell Garf to get outta that rathole he's livin' in and come back."

Ida sighed and sat down in her chair. "You still got no respect for your father, Martin, none whatsoever. You never even shed a tear when he died. What's people gonna say?"

There was the sound of boots stamping on the bridge.

Martin swallowed his second spoonful and skimmed the edge again. He decided not to argue with his mother, and went to let the visitor in.

"I'm gettin' sick a this racket," Aunt Kizzie said. "I ain't had a chance to piss since poor Am died — just a squirt here and a squirt there."

Ida's face drew up on one side into a wall of wrinkles. She hit the table and tipped over her glass of water. "Well, you little jeezler!" she said with her teeth set together. "Don't you never — NEVER — say that again!" She wrung her knuckles in her mother's face. "If I ever — EVER — catches you sayin' that again, I'll put y'under me foot and tramp the bloody shit outta ya! When Ambrose was alive, he was this and he was that — and now that he's gone — he's poor Am!"

Norm Andrews, Max Butler and Jack Burns followed Martin into the house. When Norm saw Garf, he said, "I don't want no trouble — I never come for that. Me and the boys here come to see Martin."

"And you wants to know 'bout your house, do ya, Jack?"

Jack slipped off his black earmuffs, cleared his throat and spoke softly as he pulled off his tight black leather gloves, finger by finger. "First of all it wasn't my house, Garf. It was Dulcie's and yes, we've talked about the ol' house on several occasions, but Dulcie — well, Dulcie and I — we never intended to use the place anyway. And like Dulcie said, what was the good of it off on the island?"

Martin put his mouth close to his bowl and shovelled in a spoonful of the cooled chowder. "That ol' house saved my life," he said. "If he wud'n there I'd a froze to death, simple as that."

"Well, we're just thankful," Jack said, "as I'm sure everyone is, that you made it home OK."

"And you, Narm," Garf growled. "What's you doin' back here?"

"I asked 'en to come," Martin said. "Me and he and Mr. Butler and John had a little talk."

Garf slid across the two chairs and stood up in the small space between the table and the cupboard. "Well, I don't want 'en here!"

Martin took his bowl in his hand and went to his father's chair and sat down. "Well, I do and you got nothin' to say 'bout it." He spoke calmly and looked to his mother for support but she said nothing.

"Dad told me he would a took our house off the island, but Garf here got up against 'en and said no." He looked into his brother's nervous eyes. "Is that right or wrong?"

"That ol' house would a been too hard to move," Garf said. "First pluck on the tackle and he'd a went to bits. The house is rotten."

"So rotten as this one," Norm asked.

Garf thought for a moment and said, "Aahhh, well, I don't know. But I knows this one'll soon be gone too, and if Aunt Ida don't have somethin' else to shove her nose in by next winter what she got here's gonna fall down round her head."

"This house is cold," Max said. "And 'tis no shame for 'en either."

"That's right," Norm added. "He's close to eighty years old, perhaps more. And look at where he's to, for God's sake — perched right on top a this hill. Every draft ya gotta find it."

"You knows yourself, Garf — he gotta be cold."

"Yeah, yeah, I knows he's cold, Max. I knows he's cold, boy, but when ya got no money what can ya do?"

"Well, ya got a house back on the island," Max said with his hands in his pocket. "He's old too, I knows that. But he's warm. Only a few year ago sure yez done 'en up — got a new house made out of 'en."

"And you fellers wants to tow 'en 'cross the bay," Garf said. "That's what this is all 'bout, ain't it!"

Martin cleaned his bowl with a crust and stowed the bread in his mouth. "Yes," he said. "I asked 'em if they'd help us. That's by'n by the summer I mean, but they said they'd have to see you first."

"What'd John say 'bout all this?" Garf asked the men. "And how come he never come with yez?"

"Didn't wanna be hung," Max replied mischievously.

"Didn't wanna be hung? Whaddaya mean?"

"Well," Max began. "He said he didn't wanna come over with us. Told me and Narm when we went 'cross the cove to get 'en — said that if you and Narm got into 'nother scuffle he'd have to go the work and kill the two of yez."

Garf zipped his jacket and did not comment on the possibility of his demise. "Like I said, Max, the house is rotten, but if yez wants me to help yez, yes, I'll do what I can."

Norm turned his bruised face and bloodshot eyes towards the barometer. "I don't know why ya thinks that house is rotten," he said, looking back at Garf and twirling his chest hair around his finger. "Ambrose come and got me one day when you was bailin' water outta your rodney and we had a good look up in under. I thought he was in pretty good shape. The sills was a bit rotten — that's only what you'd 'xpect — and the shores, but other'n that he looked pretty good. Looked to me like he was so solid as the church."

Garf smiled wryly. "And what church might that be? Not our church for damn sure, 'cause you and the rest of the scavengers cleaned up on that one pretty fast."

"Ya gotta get over this foolishness, my son," Max said. "I took my share a that lumber so well as everybody else, and you should a took your share too. And for your info'mation I don't consider meself a scavenger."

"Times was changin', Garf," Norm explained. "And we had to change with 'em. Ya knows yourself we couldn't live on that island forever. What 'bout the young race growin' up and what 'bout what they wanted? Off on that island by ourselves was no place for no one. And no, if ya thinks I'm 'shamed of what I done when I got off — no I'm not — not the tiniest little bit! I got a family to look after and they comes first, and if I sees a chance where I can make it a bit easier for 'em and get a few dollars to help 'em out then I'm gonna do it. And you, if ya wud'n so friggin' headstrong you'd a done the same for yours. So ya can whine all ya like 'bout what Narm Andrews done and ya can say what ya like 'bout me, run me name down to the dirt, I don't care. BUT I'm tellin' ya right now, buddy" — Norm pointed his finger in Garf's face and jabbed it back and forth — "if ever you crosses my path once more 'bout this resettlement racket, you'll find out fast enough what 'tis like to taste shit on the back a your tongue!"

The bone in Garf's jaw began jumping again and he lunged at Norm. "You lousy rotten son of a ——"

"Now, boys!" Ida yelled, jumping from the table and putting herself between them. "That's enough a this non-sense so if yez can't talk sensible then shut your mouths, the two of yez! I got no time for this fightin' and scratchin' all the time so give it up right now like I'm tellin' yez! Two grown men — I'm 'shamed a yez for God's sake, I am so! If I was like you two, I'd go and hide away somewhere where no one wud'n see me! Now give it up 'fore I beats the two of yez into one!"

When his temper had cooled, Garf told Martin he would

help take the house off the island and salvage what they could from the one here to add a big porch, but not to expect anything else if Norm was involved.

"Fair enough," the boy said. "And when we shifts in you'll sit to one end of the table and I'll sit to the other end. Deal?"

Garf took Aunt Kizzie's glass of cold water and drank it right down, wiped his mouth on his sleeve and gave Norm the hardest look he could muster. "Nine chances outta ten you'll be wantin' some other stuff done round here too. And ya can't be callin' on strangers to come over every time ya gets a fart jammed so yes, ya got a deal!"

"And you better full up my glass again," the old woman said. "Next thing you're gonna think ya owns the place."

Norm nodded once at Jack and Max and then smiled carefully at Ida and Martin. "Well, with that outta the way we'll be leavin' yez to your supper."

"'Fore ya goes, Max," the boy said, "I got somethin' for ya."

"And what's that, my son?"

Martin pulled the lighter from his pocket. "This is yours," he said, holding it out in his open hand. "Dad forgot to give it back to ya."

Max took the lighter and flipped the lid back. "Still work or what?" he asked.

"No fluid and no flint."

Max tipped the lighter upside down and pulled the metal case off. "Right here," he said. "On top a that waddin' is where you'll find a spare flint. And I see ya didn't look 'cause 'tis still here." He unscrewed the magazine rod and pulled out the long, wiggly spring with the screw, shook the lighter to rid the tube of any cuttings and dropped in the new flint. Next he put the spring back in and tightened the screw at its end, wrapped his lips around the open fuel reservoir and blew one long, hard breath. Slipped the case on and thumbed the wheel. Another flick and there was a bright dancing flame that grew higher and then Max snapped the lid on.

Martin couldn't find the words to fit his surprise. He kept his eyes on the lighter until it disappeared into Max's pocket.

"Well," Jack declared, putting his gloves and mitts on. *"Au revoir."*

"Did you come for somethin' in pa'tic'lar, Jack? Ida asked. "'Cause 'tis awful strange for you to be in with a bunch like that. Or did ya just drop by to say hello?"

"Well, you can say I dropped by to say hello, yes — yes, I guess you can say that. I was on my way over to Mr. Tucker's to get a bottle of friar's balsam for Judy when I seen Norm and Max on their way 'cross the cove there, so they wanted me to come up over the hill with 'em. I said, 'Sure, I'll go up with yez, why not?'"

"And what's the trouble with Judy?" Martin asked. "Is she sick?"

"Must have the flu I guess, 'cause her throat is gone right together in a lump and she can't even get down so much as a soda cracker. Anyway, she said to say hello to ya."

"Say hello back to her for me."

To everyone, Jack said, *"OK, au revoir, mes amis."* To Martin: *"Lundi, monsieur* — right after dinner?"

The boy pushed his plate back. *"Oui, monsieur."*

"Oh yes," Jack said. "I almost forgot." He pulled out a neatly folded dollar bill and laid it on the table. "Judy told me to give you this."

ACKNOWLEDGEMENTS

Thank you, Annie Proulx, for coming into my life and showing me the way. A special thank you to Angel Guerra for believing in my work, never once giving up on his promise to help to find a publisher for this novel. Such determination can only be found in true angels. Thanks to Scott and Gwen Patey for the use of their computer in the drafting stage of my manuscript. Thanks also to The Canada Council for the Arts who saw me through one of Newfoundland's harshest winters, allowing me the comfort of writing without my mitts.

Wayne Bartlett